Courtesy of American Museum of Natural History (After Catlin

Crow Village Scene

THE INDIAN HOW BOOK

By

ARTHUR C. PARKER

(GAWASO WANNEH)

Author of "SKUNNY WUNDY"

DOVER PUBLICATIONS, INC.

New York

Published in Canada by General Publishing Company, Ltd., 30 Lesmill Road, Don Mills, Toronto, Ontario.
Published in the United Kingdom by Constable and Company, Ltd.

This Dover edition, first published in 1975, is an unabridged republication of the 1931 edition of the work as published by Doubleday, Doran & Company, Inc., Garden City (first edition: George H. Doran Company, 1927).

International Standard Book Number: 0-486-21767-1
Library of Congress Catalog Card Number: 74-18592

Manufactured in the United States of America
Dover Publications, Inc.
180 Varick Street
New York, N.Y. 10014

TO

MY FATHER,

Whose loving hand first gave me guidance to the wonders of the woodland, glen and glade, and whose knowledge of the red race through ancestral inheritance gave me a sympathetic understanding of its history and culture, this book is affectionately dedicated

CONTENTS

I: THE HOW OF INDIAN THINGS

II: THE INDIAN HIMSELF

I: THE HOW OF INDIAN THINGS

I

THE HOW OF INDIAN THINGS

I. THE ART OF MAKING THINGS

How is a questioning and answering word. It asks and answers "by what process, means or magic,"—all this and more.

Think if you will of all the strange things in Indian lore you have read and heard about, and then say if you have not often exclaimed, "How I wish I knew how!"

Thousands of people have asked me the how of Indian things. Thousands of them have written letters asking the how of Indian ceremonies, dress, customs, dances, songs, warfare, hunting and home life. As many have asked how canoes, snowshoes, tipis, traps, bark lodges, and war bonnets were made. Nearly every one who inquired about the *how* of Indian things wanted to know how arrowheads were made, how the Indians happened to get to America and how to talk *the* Indian language.

Sometimes queer questions were asked, such as, "How could the Indians live before there were grocery stores in America? How could Indians live before they had salt? How was it that all were not exterminated when Indians all kill each other? How does it come that Indians no longer grow feathers in their hair? How did they happen to lose them?"

The native red man, as a product of the soil, worked out his own way of doing things. They were things that he needed and which fitted his way of life. Now that we, too, are beginning to love the forest and the streams, the mountains and the crystal lakes of the hills, we are learning how to camp, how to find food in the forest and how to find healing leaves and herbs. The way of the red man is becoming our way, because we are going back to nature and trying to live in its sweet embrace, just as the red man did. This is one of the great reasons why we should know how the first American lived and how he made himself master of his surroundings.

The how of many Indian things is simple and quite reasonable. The *how* of making fire without matches is a thing that has attracted much attention among youthful groups, especially Boy Scouts, yet matches came into general use so rapidly that few Indians even in remote places know how to make fire as their fathers did a century ago. There are other Indian things that are not quite so simple. To tell how they organized their tribal hunts, how they venerated the sun, how they organized their tribes and how they held their secret society sessions, requires much explanation.

In this book of *how* will be found many subjects, and most of them are those about which there has been much inquiry. To tell the how of everything, however, would require a very large volume. The reader who masters the knowledge of all the *hows* that are here given will become acquainted with many of the little-known things of Indian lore. This knowledge will be sufficient as an introduction. The Why, Who, When, Where and What of Indian life will be described and answered at some other time. In a practical age we wish to know how to do things; the reason why other people did them is sought when there is more time for reflection.

With the red people of America the word "How" or *haoh,* as they pronounce it, means, "All right," it means, "Let's go!" and it means, "Come on, let's do it."

The pathway to the world of doers in every age starts

with the question "How?" Very well, let us say with the Indians, "Haoh, let us learn how!"

II. HOW INDIANS MADE FIRE

Fire is a mysterious thing. To native people it was still more mysterious, and some of them thought that it was the breath of an unseen spirit. Still, they did not bother much about the spirit side of fire; they had practical uses for it.

In ancient America fire was produced in two ways, and it was gained from nature in two ways, with a possible third way. So far as we know the oldest Indian method was to twirl a stick in a small cavity. Another method was to strike two stones together. It must have seemed an odd thing to find that fire came out of wood and also stone. If fire came out of wood why did it not burn it up in the first place, and if it came out of stone why did not stone burn? These questions puzzled the red men of the forest and plains, but they had no means of answering them.

The art of producing fire by means of friction is very old and was known throughout the world. Most of the Indian tribes used the rod drill, twirled by hand or by means of a bow, the string of which was twisted once around the rod. The upper end of the rod fitted into a socket, and the lower end was placed upon the "hearth." This was a piece of wood or small board of proper material, having a slight indentation near the edge and a groove or slot that led to the tow or tinder that was placed beneath it.

In working the apparatus the thong of the bow was twisted once about the rod, and the bow held across the rod at right angles. The working end of the spindle was now placed in the spot where drilling was to be done and the socket held by one hand at the top. Thus the spindle had two points of support and this was necessary when the bow began its work of whirling the rod or spindle. The bow was grasped firmly in the right hand and shoved ahead to its limit, and then it was quickly drawn back, the process being repeated again and again in rapid succession, care being taken to keep the bow at perfect right angles to the rod. If the bow was slanted the bowstring "walked" up or down the rod as the slant directed. This made the spindle wobble and retarded the friction. Sometimes it threw the spindle out of the socket.

The purpose of this rapid motion was twofold; first to create heat by friction, and second to pulverize small particles of the wood, receiving it in the hearth, at the point where it met the spindle. When, by rapid twirling, the heat reached the point of ignition, the super-heated wood powder began to glow. Fire had then been created, but to be effective a flame had to be produced. When the brown powder in the drilling pit, through the hot wisps of smoke that came forth, gave evidence of fire, this dust either fell through the side slot or was dumped out upon fine and dry tinder, rapidly enclosed in it by grasping the tinder in the two hands, and then blown upon with the breath.

If the glowing spark were large enough and live enough the oxygen and air blown into the tinder brought forth a living flame; the tinder burst into flame. This done, it was thrown down and quickly covered with finely split or shaved kindling. The fire was now ready for its work.

It is one thing to describe the method, but another to get the right wood for spindle and hearth. Not every wood will serve the purpose, and some of the best woods are not found everywhere.

In general it may be stated that the woods used in the fire apparatus must be dry and not too hard. Hard wood will grow hot with friction but its fibers do not pulverize in sufficient quantities to provide substance for the necessary spark. Neither must the wood have resin in it, though resinous wood makes excellent kindling. Generally speaking, the spindle and the hearth ought to be of similar woods and of about equal hardness. This prevents the spindle from drilling into a softer base, or the harder base from resisting the softer spindle.

My own greatest success has been with cedar, the material being taken from old fence rails. Wood from a well-seasoned cedar log or stump will do. The weathered roots of the cotton wood were used in the desert region, the Apache used the stems of the yucca, and California tribes the roots of the willow.

The selection of tinder is most important, for the spark is of no use if a flame cannot be started. Wet or damp tinder is a most discouraging thing to have. Finely shredded red cedar bark is recommended by those who know most about fire-making. This is stripped from the trees and rubbed in the hands until the dust falls out, leaving the long fuzzy shreds. This material must now be thoroughly dried or even baked. A good handful of it, once ignited, will start a fire. Some varieties of grass are used, and the Plains tribe found it of high value.

Fire made by striking stones together was one of the arts of the northern Indians of the caribou country. The Eskimo, Micmac and other north and eastern Algonkian people knew the secret. This art is one of the oldest in Europe, and the two fire stones are found in the most ancient graves. Possibly the secret came over with bold explorers from the lands of the Northmen at a very early time.

Two things are essential for this two-stone process: a good type of flint or chert and a lump or crystal of high grade iron pyrites. If the two are used a good spark results. It is simply necessary to strike the flint against the pyrites to cause sparks to fly off. A few deft strokes brings a shower upon the tinder placed below and ignition soon takes place. It is essential to fan or blow upon this to produce a flame. A little experimentation brings skill in this method.

All races found natural fires and perhaps made use of them. One fire came from heaven above, the other from the earth beneath. A third form appeared on the surface of the earth.

Fire from the clouds came in the form of lightning which ignited trees or dead wood; fire from the earth beneath came from volcanoes. Brands and torches could be thrust in such fires and the flames borne away. The third possible source was from spontaneous combustion. Damp oily bark when piled up starts to oxodize rapidly, causing heat. This heat increases until the dry portion of the heap takes fire and begins to smolder. A little wind fans it into a flame.

Indians had a way of carrying smoldering punk for a great distance. The Iroquois used sheets of dried fungus rolled into tight cylinders and placed within a hollow corncob. There are traditions that fire was carried in tubes of stone. Certain types of stone tubes found in Indian graves contain a black charred matter resembling charred fungus.

Fire was a wonderful thing and the old Iroquois taught their young how to use it for many purposes. "Remember," said their wise men, "fire will burn a warrior's cabin as well as cook his meat."

III. HOW INDIANS MADE THEIR TIPIS

The feathered war bonnet and the conical tipi are perhaps the two things most closely associated with the living

Indian. The tipi sheltered the Indian and his family but the war bonnet only sheltered his head on state occasions. Just as the feathered head-dress is the most spectacular and striking of all head-gear, so for its great practical utility the tipi is the most noteworthy of simple shelters.

Many persons spell the word teepee, pronouncing the *ee*s as sounded in the alphabet, but scientists spell the word tipi, because the *i* is pronounced like the *i* in ma-ch*i*ne, and gives the same value without so many letters. Besides this the Sioux word for dwelling is *ti,* and with *pi* added (meaning *used for*), we have a word meaning *"it is used for a dwelling."*

There are several words that may be used for an Indian dwelling, among them, wigwam, wikiup, and hogan. The tipi, however, is distinctive. It is the conical tent of the Plains people, and is held up by a circular framework of poles brought together at the top in such a manner that the poles cross and hold each other up, or are braced against the four primary poles that are first set up and lashed together.

Originally the covering was of buffalo skins cut out and sewed together in such a manner as to form a semicircle with an extention along the diameter line, as shown in Fig. 2. Frequently tipis required from twelve to twenty buffalo hides, these being soft-tanned and without hair, except in special cases.

The first requirement for a tipi is a set of poles. From sixteen to twenty-four are necessary. The material is straight, slender cedar, pine or spruce. The saplings are selected with great care, cut on the mountain side or foothills, and then hauled to the camp, where they are peeled, freed from projecting branch stubs and then shaved down to the wood beneath the last growth ring. The poles are then trimmed to a length of about twenty-five feet (for a tall tipi) and set up in form to season out. A set of good tipi poles is worth considerable and is frequently sold for a good price. The poles do not grow on the prairies and have to be carried a great distance, whence their value.

Other wooden articles required are wooden pins, from eight to sixteen in number, for "pinning up" the front of the tipi and holding it secure. These are pushed through the holes provided for them. For holding the bottom of the tipi upon the ground forty or fifty pegs are required. These pass through bottom loops.

In erecting the tipi, to follow the Blackfoot plan, four poles are first erected, the tops being tied as shown in Fig. 1. These poles are placed by twos in a parallel position and then crossed at the top, or within a foot or so, at nearly right angles. A stout thong is then looped around the intersection and tied securely. The long end of this thong is about fifteen feet in length, and is allowed to hang down. When in place, the four poles rest on the points of a quadrangle, forming a square. The remaining poles are now placed in position, their tops resting in the forks of the four. The proper manner is to place them in equal numbers on the north and south sides of the tipi, and then the poles on the west side are put in place with the exception of the central pole of the back. *The west side is always the back of the tipi.*

The final touch in erecting the frame is to place the poles on the east side. *The front of a tipi is always to the east.* The east poles are called the door poles. Their tops rest in the forward intersection of the primary poles, and they lean back to the west.

Only three poles now remain to be placed. All is ready for the unrolling of the tipi cover. When opened and stretched out flat, the back, middle pole is laid upon the center of the cover in such a way that the bottom of the

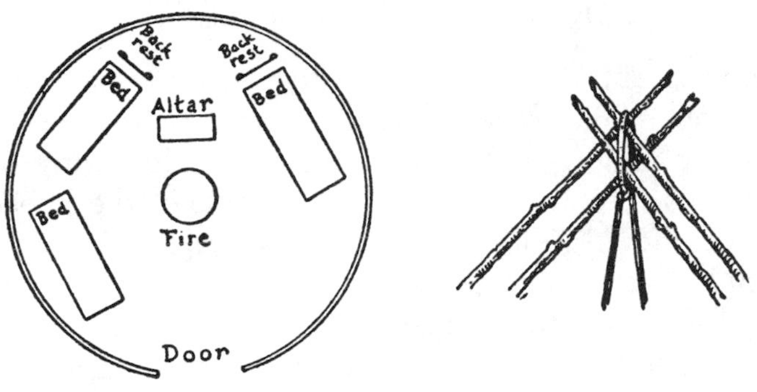

FIGURE I

Diagram of Outside and Inside Arrangement of a Plains Tipi

pole projects only a couple of inches below the bottom of the cover. The place where the pole touches the tip of the cover is now tied to it by means of the string or strings attached to the little flap in the middle of the smoke hole. (See Fig. 1.) The pole is now raised up, lifting with it the tipi cover. The pole is put in position and the cover pulled around the conical framework of poles. This last, or erecting pole, rests in the crotch formed by the two door poles, thus forming a sort of secondary tripod.

Once on, the tipi cover is drawn together at the door and pinned above and below the opening. The pinning all the way up now begins, and to do this the older women of the plains stood upon the bars of a travois frame, using it like a ladder.

The first work has now been done, but the tipi looks loose and irregular. The poles and cover must now be adjusted, and this is done by entering and crawling around to each pole and giving it a proper place to give the tipi a good circle and tighten the cover. When finished, the structure has a conical form, though the back may be a trifle steeper than the front.

The work is still unfinished, for the ears of the tipi, that is, its smoke flaps, hang down in a dejected manner. The two light, slender poles are now placed in the reversed pockets or loops at the corners of the smoke flaps and carried around in such a way that they shelter the hole from the wind. If there is no wind they are pulled around to the rear, displaying the ears "wide open."

All that now remains is to stake down the bottom to secure it to the ground. This is done by driving the pegs through the loops or holes. Of course the oval door is still wide open and will remain so until the shield-shaped cover is hung in place.

The tipi door is from a foot to eighteen inches from the ground and is sometimes as high as four feet, though as a rule it is much smaller, being frequently less than three feet. The door cover is tied at the top by two thongs that act as hinges. It can be tied inside. In warm weather the cover is twisted to one side and thrown against the tipi cover, as in Fig. 1. Covers are made by covering hoops or frames of flexible withes or small poles with skin or cloth and stiffening top, middle and bottom with a rod. At one time the door covers were made of rawhide painted in geometrical patterns. Many tipis, however, still have designs painted upon these shield-like covers.

When entering a tipi one raises the curtain and steps through the opening with one foot, stoops over and thrusts head and shoulders through, draws in the other foot, and, now being inside, drops the curtain to its normal position. The covers were often provided with rattles made of gourds or the hoofs of animals.

To thicken the walls of the tipi, and obscure the poles, a half-way lining was often provided. This was made from softly tanned skins hung from the poles and forming a lower lining that reached to the ground.

Now that the buffalos have gone from their wide ranges, tipis are no longer made of their hides. Instead, canvas has been used. The canvas of the trading store is much lighter than hide and, if properly cared for, almost as durable. It does not become water-soaked and stiff like skin and its seams are tighter. Indians have used canvas tipis for about three-quarters of a century, and they have become so common in the Indian country as to be typical of its scenery. During the past dozen years, however, they have been growing less and less in number as the Indians gave them up for houses built on the white man's model.

The smoke flaps of the tipi are moveable, and at night, or during a storm, may be tightly closed by bringing the poles around to the front and folding the flaps against the forward smoke opening. In some cases where the poles are trimmed evenly at the tip, a cap is provided so that the storm may not even send a trickle of moisture down the poles.

When a tipi was completed, or renewed after a year or two, there was a ceremony of dedication, at which songs were sung, prayers offered to the Wakanda, and a feast provided for the friends and clansfolk who gathered to celebrate.

We left a fifteen-foot thong dangling from the first four poles. It has a use. It could be tucked back of the rear poles in calm weather, but should a wind storm begin to be severe, this thong was brought out, wrapped about a knob or passed through an eye in a stake driven into the ground in the center of the tipi. Drawn tightly and tied, this thong became the anchor rope and held the tipi as rigid as a rock. The storm might rage, it might scatter tumble weeds and lay the grass flat, but the tipi stood erect upon its wooden feet.

IV. HOW INDIANS LIVED IN THEIR TIPIS

The tipi was the home of the prairie Indian, and it was more than a home; it was the personal shrine of the family. Through its upper vent went not only the smoke of the lodge fire but the incense of sacrifice bearing with it the prayers of the father of the family. There were sacred times when the warrior meditated and no one might enter. The tipi was a home, to be sure, but it was also a temple in which lived a man to whom the gods had spoken.

The interior of a tipi resembles a hollow cone. The lodge poles are covered with lining leather sometimes painted with picture writing. Just forward of the center

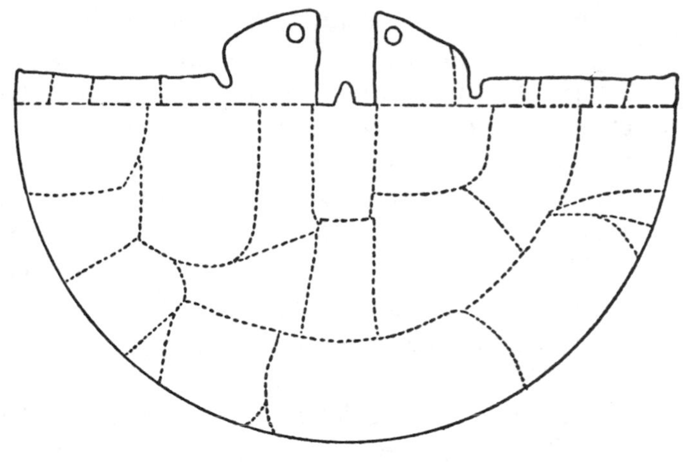

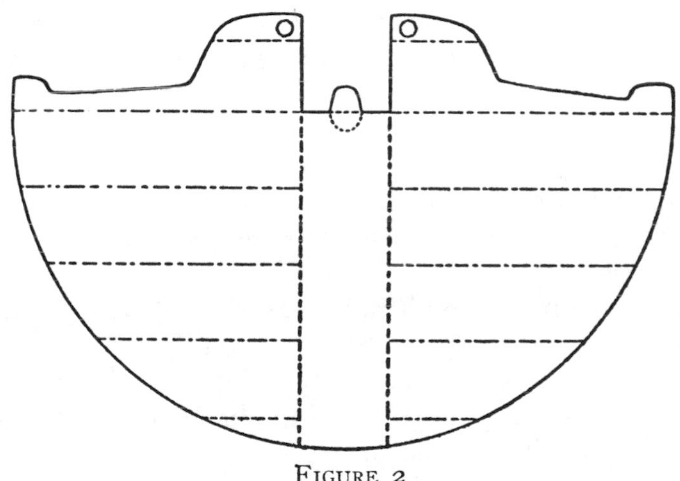

FIGURE 2

Method of Sewing Buffalo Hide Tipi
Method of Sewing Canvas Tipi

is the lodge fire, set in a little depression. This is because the smoke hole above is at the front of the apex—where the poles cross. The fireplace is outlined with cobblestones and is ordinarily a circle, but for ceremonial purposes may be given a different shape.

Back from the center and about a third of the distance from the rear is the family altar upon which is burned the incense believed to be pleasing to the dream totems, the sun, the great Wakanda and the guardian spirits. The smoke from the altar rises when these mysteries are spoken to.

On the north and south sides of the lodge are the beds or couches. These may be raised from the floor, or they may be upon the ground itself. In most cases each bed has a headpiece made from willow rods laid parallel and woven together by means of strong warp. This is held up by a tripod of stout rods. The bottom of this rest is pegged down, so that the whole makes a convenient object against which to lean. The bed itself is padded beneath with dry grass or pelts, and upon these rests a thick pad of old blankets. Over this better blankets are placed, and also the pillows. These are stuffed with hair or feathers, though poor and careless persons sometimes used grass.

The bed on the south side was that of the parents. Children slept at the foot of this bed on their own couch. Guests and others slept on the opposite side. During the day each person kept his place in the lodge, unless moving about in pursuit of some duty.

Clothing and personal articles were tucked behind the beds and under the sloping base of the tipi. Nothing was left scattered about. Cooking dishes and similar utensils were stowed on the south side of the doorway, while the warrior's riding gear was placed to the north. The rear of the tipi was kept for trophies and sacred articles.

(After Catlin)

FIGURE 3

Tipi Life

Here will be found the tripods holding his mystery or charm bundles, his cases of ceremonial regalia and his war bonnet case. Beneath, upon the ground, will be found his pipe bag, his pipe, his tobacco board, his pipe stoker and his stick for picking up glowing coals. The back of the tipi when hung with cases, trophies, medicine bundles and sacred pipe bags, indicates a family of wealth and power, for no one is allowed to have such things except through expensive ceremonies or strenuous experiences.

Among the Cheyenne Indians, according to Grinnell, who knows them so well, a lodge visitor turned to the right when entering. Here he paused for a moment and then sat down. Among the Crows of Montana a visitor in coming to a tipi says "Kahe!" by way of greeting. If the master happened to be outside, he exclaimed, "Bireri!", meaning enter. The seat of honor for a visitor is at the rear of the lodge near the master's bed. The Crows call this place the *acoria.*

Lodge etiquette required that visitors and others never pass between the master and the fire, or indeed, in front of any one. It was the polite thing always to pass behind others, and those others to show good breeding must always make way by bending or shifting forward.

Among the Omaha, who serve as a good example of plains people, two meals were cooked,—breakfast and supper. The house mother cooked this food over the lodge fire unless, perchance, she had a fireplace outside. The tipi, however, was the proper place for cooking. When the food was done it was ladeled out in the individual dishes of the family, but if there were guests dishes were provided. The dishes were set on skins spread around the lodge fire, about which the diners gathered. Before any one touched the food the father or honored guest took a small portion of the food and cast it into the fire in recognition of the belief that all food came through the goodness of Wakanda, the great unseen power.

The mother served the guests and, if there were many, an elder daughter or kinswoman assisted. Children were taught how to eat properly, and were corrected with great patience again and again. Ordinary persons might make a noise with their lips when eating soup, but a great chief never should. He above all others was careful.

At the close of the meal each one thanked the hostess, calling her by her kinship title, as mother, wife, aunt, sister or clanswoman of such a clan. If a stranger were confused, the host suggested the proper term and ended the embarrassment.

Life within a tipi was subject to stated rules of conduct. Its space was carefully allotted to each inmate, and it was required that this space, and the place for all utensils and clothing be respected. An Indian tipi was a place of order and etiquette, and it belonged to the mother of the family and the wife. The man knew this, and as he desired respect he gave it, for his wife was the householder and, like a good husband, he knew his place.

V. HOW INDIANS MADE BARK HOUSES

Most of the Indians east of the Mississippi lived in strong houses of bark and poles. Except on rare occasions, as when they were traveling rapidly or camping out, these Indians of the forest region did not use conical tipis. When they did these tent shelters were generally covered with bark. The tipi with its buffalo hide covering was the dwelling of the open plains; the bark lodge was the abode of the village Indians of the East.

Nearly every book about Indian life shows Indians living in tipis, regardless of how they really did live. This is just as much of a mistake as to show *all* Indians wearing war bonnets. Only the buffalo-chasing Indians of the plains used the tipi, and only a few of these wore the war bonnet. All these facts go to show that many of our ideas of how Indians lived are wrong.

Great houses of poles and bark were used by the Iroquois and by many Algonkin tribes. They were long and narrow,—some more than a hundred feet long. Their width varied from fifteen to twenty feet, or even more. At intervals there were holes in the roof to let the smoke escape from the fireplaces below.

Many persons think that our Iroquois Indians have forgotten how to build bark lodges because they build them no more, but I have helped these Indians build three of their bark houses, have slept in them, dreamed in them, and talked with the old chiefs about them. Some day I expect to find a secluded spot in a beautiful forest clearing where I may rebuild a complete Iroquois town and plant an Indian garden of maize, squashes, beans and tobacco. Here the faithful to the old ways of the red man may observe their ancient rites, and here will be a tiny glimpse of the "happy hunting grounds" on earth.

It was So-son-do-wa who first instructed me in the art of building a bark lodge. Back among the hills of the reservation we talked about the method. Later other chiefs told me, and then we actually set to work.

Let us first determine the size of a small cabin, for the larger ones are but small ones made longer and stronger. Twenty-one feet is a good length, and sixteen feet a comfortable width, and width is quite important. With this decision made we must get our poles, posts, saplings, bark twine and bark.

In the old days it was necessary to burn down the small trees that were wanted, but another age having dawned, we may take an ax and fell our timber within a few hours.

FIGURE 4
Diagram of Interior of Bark House

For the corner posts four stout, crotched pieces are needed. These should be uniform in diameter and about six inches through. Next come four roof uprights. The former are eleven feet long and the latter fifteen. Each is to be driven into the ground one foot. For gable supports, two crotched pieces six feet three inches long are needed. For connecting the corner posts all around some stout, straight poles, five to six inches in diameter, are needed. Those that go across the front are the width of the lodge, sixteen feet, those that connect the front and rear posts are twenty-one feet.

Twenty roof rafters are now required, each twelve feet long. For stiffening the sides sixty small poles, about three inches in diameter are needed. Then there are eight roof "stringers" needed to hold down the bark. These are about four inches in diameter and a little longer than the lodge itself, so that they project front and rear.

Eight poles four inches in diameter are needed for the upper and lower bunks, and for their support twelve more posts are required. Above the storage platform, resting on the fore and aft "plates," will be other long poles for holding strings of corn and dried foods. The modern American who builds one of these lodges will observe that the framework is a compactly arranged cribbing of poles.

Over the frame is put the bark. This bark is usually of elm, peeled in the springtime, and up to mid-July. It is taken off in great sheets, four feet wide and six or eight feet long. To straighten it, weights are applied to hold it flat on the ground. It may even be put in the water to season, for elm bark has an unhappy way of curling up.

The bark is applied lengthwise, and not up and down as it grew. This makes it easier to hold it between the

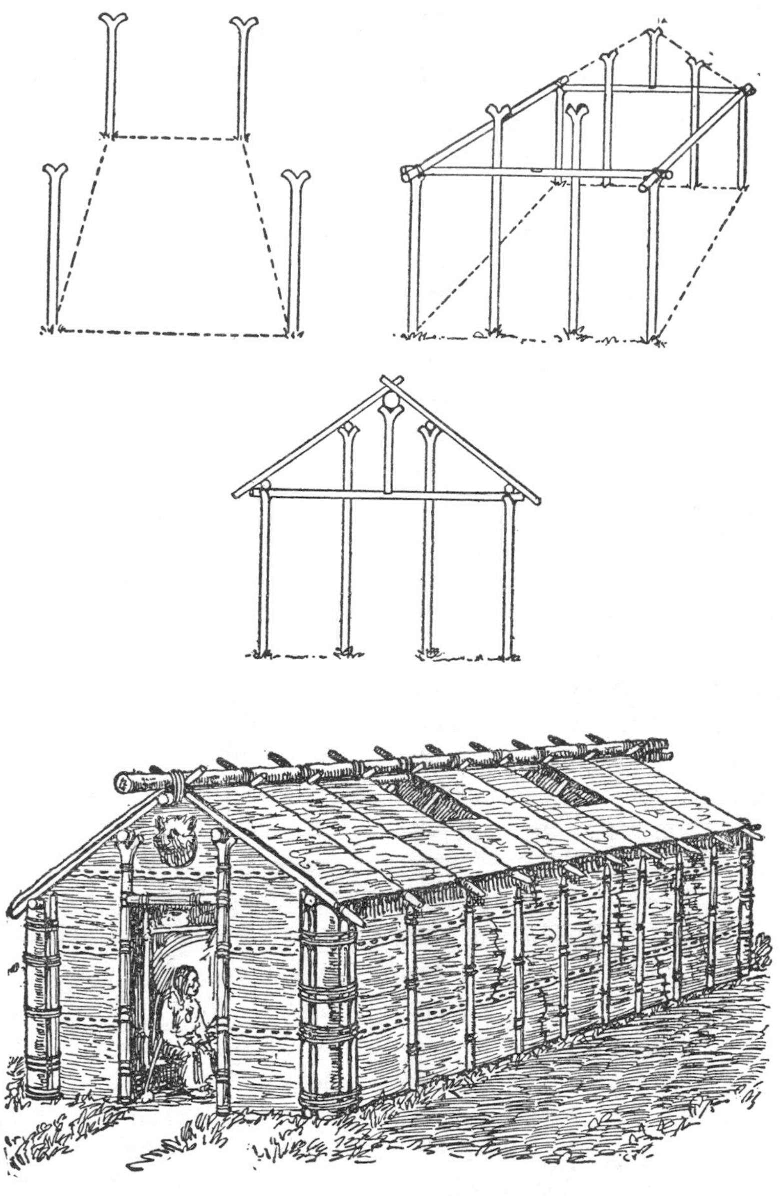

FIGURE 5
Construction of a Bark House

inner and outer clamp poles that pinch it together, and to which it is sewed by means of a bone punch and tough strips of inner bark.

The bunks are about three and a half feet wide and are put along the sides of the room, being divided in this case into three seven-foot sections. The bunks are made by driving crotched sticks about two feet long into the ground to form the corners of the bunks. Poles are now laid in the crotches and crossbars connect the width. A goodly number of long poles are now laid across these, until the bunk is covered. Over the poles are placed several layers of bark, and upon this the soft hairy pelts are put.

Over the bunks are storage platforms or "upper berths." These are supported by posts about seven feet long. In front of the upper platform are long poles upon which the dried corn hangs.

The doorway is high and wide. The door itself is a bearskin pelt, neatly tanned and having thongs by which it may be tied to the jamb-posts. A glimpse at the picture of the lodge interior will give a good idea of its structure. The drawing is from an actual lodge within which I have spent many pleasant hours.

In the center of the lodge is the long hallway where the grown folk lounged on ornamented mats of reeds and husk, and where the children played. In the very center of the hall is the fireplace where food was cooked and where the lodge fire burned to give light at night. The lodge fire is always a small one, never reaching the stage of a roaring bonfire. The Indian says, "Little fire, get close, cook easy; big fire, keep away, burn everything, cook nothing,—no good."

The smoke ascends through a hole in the roof which has bark slides to keep out the rain during stormy weather. In such cases when the chimney hole was closed there were no fires. At best a bark house is an airy place. If one wished to keep warm he retired behind a buffalo skin curtain and rolled up in a big fur; but then, fresh air, plenty of exercise and good blood keep one warm in full accord with the plan of nature.

Those who wish to make Indian houses in the east or middle south will do well to copy the Indian bark lodge. It makes a fine clubhouse for Boy Scouts and hunters. It is a real ornament; besides, it is the only correct wigwam for the forest regions.

Eastern Indian towns were composed of scores of these bark cabins, and many times the towns were stockaded. The stockade was made of fifteen-foot logs set in the earth with an embankment thrown up at the base.

Indians hid many of their treasures in pits under their beds. When they went away never to return these treasures remained. When the houses decayed and rotted down and years passed the hidden things remained in the ground. Farmers often plow them up and find pipes, arrow points, bone carvings and hatchet heads.

VI. HOW INDIANS MADE CANOES

Indian canoes are of three general types,—the wood dugout, the skin boat or kaiak of the Eskimo, and the bark canoe of the forest Indians. In Nevada some of the Indians made balsas of tule grass, and along the Missouri a tub-shaped craft, often nearly round, was constructed of willow forms over which was stretched a buffalo hide.

The shapes of canoes differed considerably, according to tribe, and sometimes the kind of bark used had much to do with the shape. In general, however, the Indian canoe of old days did not differ greatly from their modern canoes, or from commercially made canoes of canvas.

The most beautiful canoe, by far, is that made from birch bark. Indeed, canoe birch was a tree greatly prized by the eastern forest Indians, and it grew in great profusion around the Great Lakes.

An experienced canoe-maker selected a tall, straight tree, free from knots and having a firm, tough bark. Once chosen, the tree was felled with great care, precautions being taken not to bruise the trunk when it fell. The trunk was then examined for defects and, if none were found, marks were made at either end of the log, three times the length of the tallest man, or about eighteen feet, though four or five spans were often added, "for good measure." The trunk was now circled at the marks, and then an incision made lengthwise of the trunk, cutting through the bark.

Caution required that the trunk be lifted from the ground and supported by another log or a good-sized boulder. With wedges the bark was now peeled back from the "cut" and carefully pushed free of the log. It was then pushed downward and off, great care being taken not to buckle it, bruise it or start a tear.

The next process is to flatten it so that it may be carried away to the "shop." Here comes the trick of toasting by means of a torch applied to the inner surface of the bark. The most usual torch for this process was a roll of the waste bark, that is, the outer dry bark. Sometimes wisps of this bark were inserted into a split stick. This was then lighted and, as birch bark is resinous, it burns with a hot, smoky flame. This flame is applied to the moist, inner side of the canoe strip and if evenly applied the bark flattened out like a blanket. The strip was now reversed on the flat ground, outer side up, and rolled with great care into a convenient bundle, which might be packed out of the woods to a place where the canoe frame might be built, or may be ready and waiting.

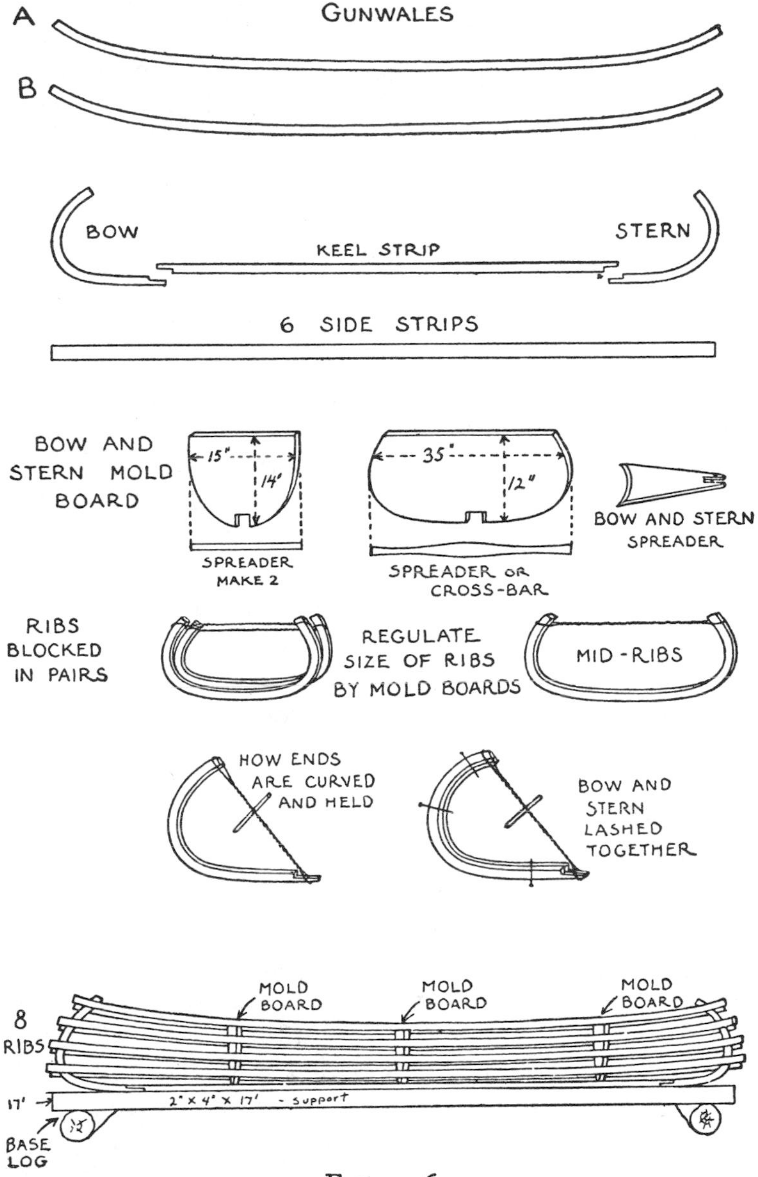

FIGURE 6

How a Bark Canoe May Be Made

It is well here to note that if the tree selected is not large enough that two trees may be used, and the sides of the canoe supplemented by strips from the second tree. Bark can be easily sewn and pitched. It is also well to know that birch bark peels best in spring or early summer. Winter bark is apt to stick and when peeled off brings with it patches of the inner bark, which must be scraped off, for it is only the laminated bark which can be used.

The framework must now be prepared. It must have a proper shape and so formed that it may be readily covered by the bark. To prepare the framework requires a certain measure of skill, and the more practiced the hand the better the canoe. However, even boys who are handy with tools can make a fairly good canoe, as I recall through my own experience, when Jiskogo and myself fashioned a canoe many years ago back on the reservation.

The framework was usually made of cedar, but if this could not be found other straight-grained green wood was used. The long pieces were split out, which made the straight grain necessary. From this the gunwales, ribs and sheathing were made. The interior sheathing was thin and three or four fingers broad. The Menomini called them *anakianuk* or mats.

In splitting out the ribs, of which some four dozen were needed, the bending observed the law that "the heart side is the inside." That rule referred to the fact that the bending must leave the part of the wood that is naturally outer on the outside of the bend. This prevents cracking and splitting. Ribs were as thick as a man's two fingers, that is, about an inch and a half. In width they were from three to four inches broad, the wider being in the center.

Bending into shape was accomplished by boiling the wood in a large steaming box. This was either an old sap kettle or a depression in a bed of clay which was filled with water and heated by means of hot stones. When the wood was steamed and bent into shape it had to be tied. Ribs were paired and tied so as to have them uniform.

FIGURE 7

Setting Up of Bark Canoe

The gunwales were the long strips that gave the canoe its shape at the top. These were carefully made and had an upward bend at either end. The ribs fitted against these, and the form was held in place by three crossbars of tough wood, as maple or hickory. One crossbar was placed in the center and one at the beginning of the sharper curve at either end. They divided the canoe into about four equal parts.

In constructing the canoe the Indians built a form of stakes which they drove into the ground around the framework. At the bottom all stones and rubbish were cleared away so as to leave a smooth, even spot. The bark was placed within the false framework, the gunwales and end pieces being put in place. It may be wondered just how the stakes that outlined the canoe were placed so as to make a correct form. There were two ways, first, an old canoe was placed on the ground and the stakes driven around it; second, the gunwales were put into position and with false spreaders given the shape of the top of the canoe. The stakes were then driven around this.

Once the bark was within the framing stakes (see Fig. 7), the work of fastening the gunwales began. The Menomini Indians called the gunwales *minak.* False thwarts, or spreaders, were put into the required places, giving way later to the well-formed thwarts, which were pierced at the ends and sewed through the bark, the cords passing over the gunwales. Bow and stern shapers were now put into place, if they were to be used.

Before the thwarts were finally attached the center rib and one or two of the wider ones were pushed into place. About this time the rear and bow boards, v-shaped spreaders were wedged in so as to fit into the angle of the gunwales. When these were in place the shape of the canoe was assured. The ribs should then fit snugly and their extremities lie inside the gunwales. In making a specially fine canoe the bark was lined with long strips of basket splints, placed edge to edge in such a way as to fit exactly. This lining lay under the ribs and protected the bark from abrasion. Only an expert could lay the sheathing, which was difficult to fasten at bow and stern and frequently split at the ends.

In ancient times the wood and bark were pierced with awls, and the canoe sewed together with tough roots and the inner bark of elm or butternut.

When the ribs and thwarts had been finally secured, the canoe was taken from the frame and inverted. Then began the process of gumming the seams in the bark with pitch. This was resin mixed with tallow, the whole being heated and mixed into a pasty mass. When applied, the wood was thoroughly dry. Pure resin was apt to crack. For ornamental purposes the pitch was frequently colored black with soot or finely powdered charcoal.

If the canoe-maker wished to have his product unique he painted eyes or other figures at each end, and over the body. In this way a canoe was easily recognized.

VII. HOW INDIANS MADE WAR BONNETS

Among the tribes of the plains the war bonnet had a double meaning. First it was the emblem of a warrior's achievements on the field of battle, every feather representing a major exploit; and, second, when worn, it was regarded as a mighty charm, protecting its wearer and sending up his prayers to the Great Manitou. Not every Indian was permitted to own or wear a war bonnet, and no Indian might make one for himself.

The making of this treasured feather crest was a right that belonged to a man's friends, and the officers of his association or war society. Still, when a bonnet became worn out and shabby, a warrior might have one presented to him by his admirers, or he might purchase one, in which case there was an elaborate ceremony of transfer.

Without attempting at this time to describe the ceremonies of making the bonnet, let us consider the actual work done. In ancient days a broad band of buckskin of a size to fit the head was formed, but in modern times a skin cap or the crown of an old felt hat is used. Around the bottom of this is placed an ornamented band, reaching from one ear ornament to the other, that is, half-way around. If there is to be a tail-piece, a broad band of blanket cloth lined on the underside with red is sewed to the back. This strip is the width of two hands and is bound with a tape of skin or cloth. Sometimes there is a skin inside to give body and stiffness. In length this tail is the height of the wearer from the back of his head to the ground.

When the cap and tail have been constructed the feathers are made ready. Each feather is carefully selected for form and beauty, as well as for its fitness as an exploit symbol. The quill ends are now cut so that a nib like a long pen is formed. This is done by cutting into the quill and taking off a full half for about two and a half inches. This is done so that the tip may be looped up, as shown in Fig. 8. A piece of dyed skin or red cloth is now wrapped about the upper part of the loop and tied on by winding around it a shred of sinew or colored yarn.

When all the feathers have been thus prepared they are sewed upon the bonnet just above the ornamental band. Strong sinew thread is used and the sewing is done with a needle through holes that have been punched in the crown with an awl or knife tip. This is to secure correct spacing. The tail feathers are now sewed on in such a manner that they will stand upright when strung in the middle.

To hold the feathers erect, a small hole is drilled through the quill below its middle point. Through this a strong piece of sized sinew is drawn, as shown in Fig. 8. The pith inside the feather expands and holds the thread in such a way that the quill does not slide around.

The side ornaments are now sewed on, and these may be either a conventional disk or shell, or some article of disk shape that the wearer has dreamed about. With these as a point of attachment, ermine skins stretched out

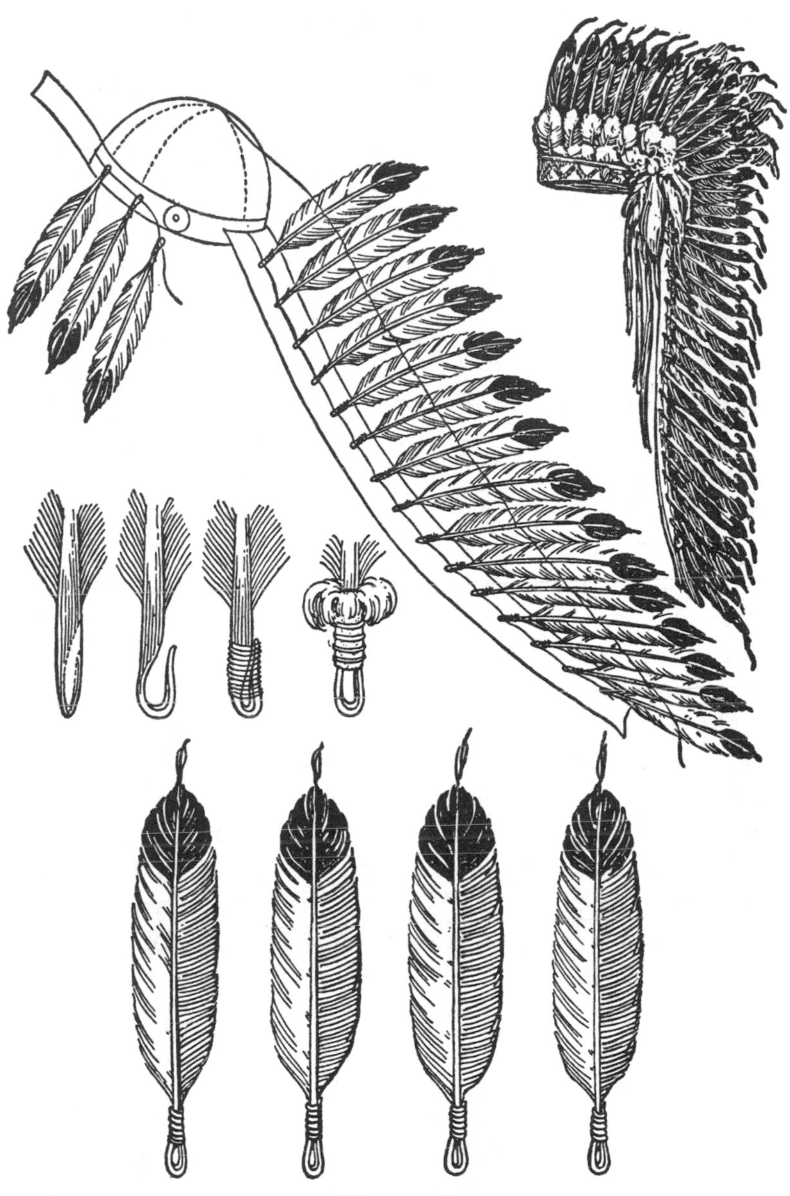

FIGURE 8
Construction of a War Bonnet

to their greatest length were fastened. Sometimes a fringe of hair was placed here also.

The crown of the head sometimes had a spindle fastened to it in which some war feather of the highest grade was placed. As often the skin of a magical bird, believed to be a great charm, was put inside the chaplet of feathers. At any rate, the crown of the cap was covered with down feathers, and to a point just back of the center the draw-string of the tail (the string that supports the middle of the feathers) was fastened.

There is a second type of war bonnet called the horn bonnet. This has no feathers but consists of a tight fur cap having a band around it, and a buffalo horn on either side. Like the feather, the horns signify *power.* In a bonnet of this type the horns are shaved down as thinly as possible, possibly to make them lighter, and possibly for some reason connected with a belief in the mysteries of the Wakanda.

The plains Indians took care of their war bonnets. When not worn it is placed in a rawhide case and hung on a tripod in the rear of the tipi, where it is carefully guarded. Three times each day a smudge of sweet grass is made for it, that the powers above and the sun may know that its owner is faithful to his vows. To prove that its possession is no idle matter, songs about it are sung each day.

VIII. HOW INDIANS MADE THEIR TRAPS

The hut of an old Indian was threatened with wolves. His trembling wife hugged her baby to her bosom for the wolves were lean and hungry and the walls of the hut were thin. It was bad enough that her husband had very few arrows, but to make matters worse, his eyes had been injured by the cold of his last hunt. What could be done?

FIGURE 9

Common Indian Traps

The question was urgent, for the beasts were scratching at the door. The old hunter searched in his medicine bags, while his wife shook her head. This was no time for magic; a good aim and plenty of arrows were needed, not charms. Nevertheless the hunter fumbled in his pouch and drew forth several objects which he wrapped in chunks of fat. With a cry he flung the chunks out of the window toward the wolves.

Scenting food, the pack dashed forward and began to lick up the fat. One pack leader grabbed the chunk in its mouth and began to chew. Suddenly blood began to spurt from the mouths of the wolves that had touched the fat. The smell of this drove the whole pack into a fury of madness. They pounced upon the bleeding wolves and tore them to pieces, while others pounced upon those who were sinking their fangs in the first victims. The yelping was terrifying but soon the entire pack had exterminated itself. Magic had been performed, and the hunter smiled at his wife as he tied up his medicine pouch.

What had he done? Simply taken thin, sharp blades of flint, enclosed them in fat and lured the wolves into cutting their mouths. Blood excites wolves, and they have no love for their wounded comrades. Once blood flows the whole pack goes mad.

Indians had twelve types of traps set in four different ways. Their traps were ingenious but simple. To the red men, traps were necessary because it was difficult to shoot some animals with arrows. As with us, many of the fur-bearing animals were caught in traps, and thus the Indian trapper made his rounds as the modern trapper does. Otis T. Mason, who made a study of Indian traps, said that there were three principal kinds of traps, the inclosing, the arresting and the killing.

Inclosing Traps

(a) *Pen,*—dam, pound, fyke,
(b) *Cage,*—coop, pocket, cone, fish trap,
(c) *Pit,*—pitfalls,
(d) *Door,*—with trigger, fall, cage or fall door;

Arresting Traps

(e) *Mesh,*—gill, toils, ratchet,
(f) *Set hook,*—set line, gorge, trawl,
(g) *Noose,*—snare, spring, fall snare, trawl snare,
(h) *Clutch,*—bird lime, mechanical jaws;

Killing Traps

(i) *Weight,*—fall, dead fall,
(j) *Missile,*—projected point,
(k) *Point,*—impaling stick, stomach piercer,
(l) *Edge,*—wolf knife, braining knife.

It would be an interesting thing to describe all these traps, but two or three will suffice as examples of how the Indians caught their game.

Pits were perhaps as effective as anything in catching game alive, and there were two kinds of pits. The first was a bottle-shaped hole in the ground, deep enough to hold the victim desired. All traces of earth were carried away to remove suspicion. The pit was then covered with light branches or coarse grass. Upon this the bait was placed. When the quarry came along it reached for the bait and fell into the hole. As the sides were steep, and the bottom larger than the top, there could be no escape.

The second type of pit was arranged in such a manner that small game and even eagles might alight upon the bait and, as their hunger drove them to eat it, diverting their attention, the trapper, who was concealed within the pit, reached up and grasped the victim by the legs and drew it in, crushing it between his knees. This was not always done in the case of eagles or bobcats. The eagle was choked before it could resist (though some were saved alive), and the bobcat was skillfully speared from beneath. No mere Indian wanted to hobnob with a wild-cat at short range. An eagle is not without fight even when thus trapped; its beak and its sharp talons are quite likely to severely wound the trapper.

The noose was a common form of arresting trap. It was placed in such a position that the animal either put its head or feet within it. Some nooses were so arranged that they held the animal because it tried to walk forward after the noose was on its neck, others were attached to spring-poles which "horsed" up when the noose pulled the trigger; still others were pulled by the trapper when he saw the creature noose itself. Nooses were placed in animal runways, baited nooses were placed on the ground while the trapper awaited the time when his victim placed its feet within the fatal circle. He then drew the noose tight and caught the unwary beast or bird.

The spring snare was fastened at the end of a pole which in turn was placed under the end of another pole or notch in a tree. As the animal thrust its head in the noose and pushed forward it shoved the spring pole out from under the other pole, and thereby released the bent pole, which flew up, hanging the animal.

An Iroquois snare was so arranged that it was held down by a baited string. The noose hung independently in such a way that the animal that had thrust its head in the loop reached for the baited string and chewed it, releasing the spring pole and hanging itself. This type was good for gnawing animals, especially those that liked fat or salt.

Deadfalls were common in country where big fur-bearing animals like the bear were trapped. Large weighted logs were held up by small sticks that were supported by the bait stick. When the bait stick was moved, it upset the supports and brought down the logs, killing the game. The release of the deadfall is its important part, for if this does not work the trap will not spring. Indians, therefore, placed their releasing stick upon an unstable point which, when moved, brought down the logs or stones. The trigger with the bait was placed against the stick which held up the deadfall.

As animals fear the smell of man, it was necessary to wash anything the hands had touched or to smoke it thoroughly. The beast knows its master and is as anxious to escape him as he is to kill it if he can.

IX. HOW INDIANS MADE THEIR FISHHOOKS

Fishing to the Indian was not a sport but a serious employment. Fish formed one of the principal foods of the forest, but to catch fish in early days before the advent of the European was not so easy, though fish were abundant. There were many ways of catching the finny swimmers of the native waters, but then, as now, the favorite way was to bait a hook and fish for them.

Remember, in those days there was no iron wire out of which to make hooks, and there were no stores where hooks might be purchased. There being no metal in common use, the ingenious Indian made his hooks out of bone. Remember, too, that he had to do this without a "jack knife."

The process of manufacture required that a large bone with a thin wall be used. This, most generally, was a leg or wing bone from a large bird. There was some advantage to this because bird bones are hollow.

The bone was marked off in as many hook lengths as

could be made and then cut off at the extremities. Then the long tube of bone was cut, or rather sawed lengthwise on both sides, so as to divide it in halves. The incisions of division were then sawed into and the "hook-length blanks" separated. This provided four to six blanks out of which hooks could be made.

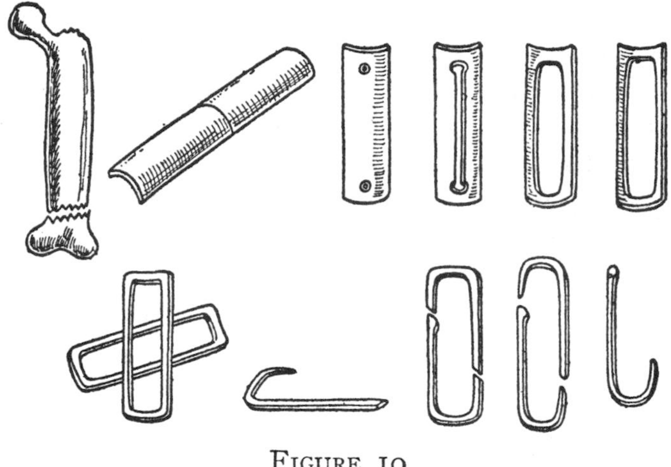

FIGURE 10

Method of Making Bone Fishhooks

One of the blanks was now bored at either end (see Fig. 10), and then an incision, made by scratching with a pointed flint, connected the two holes. The cut was then widened by further sawing until an oval had been formed from the blank. The corners of the "link" were now removed so as to provide well-rounded ends. (Fig. 10.) It now remained to cut an incision at the upper top and left side, making the exact length desired for the hook, or "business end," of the implement. The same was indicated on the lower or right side. (See Fig. 10.) These incisions were then completed and then two hooks fell apart. (Fig. 10.) It now only remained to finish the points by grinding them to the proper size and sharpness. The top of the shank was then roughened a bit so that the line might be attached.

In my excavations in ancient Indian village sites I have often found every part of the process described, and once even found the flint that had been used in doing the cutting. It was a small petal-like knife, thin and with very sharp edges.

The earliest of these fishhooks have no barbs, and it is still a mooted question whether or not the really prehistoric Indians barbed their hooks. Some found in the refuse heaps of more recent Indians have excellent barbs and would easily hold a large fish. The older hooks, however, have smooth hooks and it must have required genuine dexterity to land a fish even when he had the hook in his mouth. There could be no slackening, only a steady pull, until the fish flopped ashore.

There seems to be all the evidence in the world that the early Indians with their bone fishhooks frequently came home with tales of how they had hooked monster grandfather fish of enormous length,—that, after all, got away. The hard-luck fisherman's story is ages old, nor was the grief less sincere then than now.

X. HOW INDIANS MADE THEIR ARROWHEADS

Every really normal person has some interest in arrowheads. There is a charm about them that few can resist, especially if one has discovered an arrow point in a field or in the potato patch. These bits of flint mean a great deal in the history of humanity.

Arrowheads? We know something about them, but how were they made? This question has puzzled both farmer boys and great scientists. I know several men connected with a great research laboratory who delight in hunting arrowheads along the creeks and in plowed fields. Until I told them, they did not have the remotest idea how they were made. So great had been their interest that these men had gone to the far-away corners of the land to pick up arrowheads of rare colors and

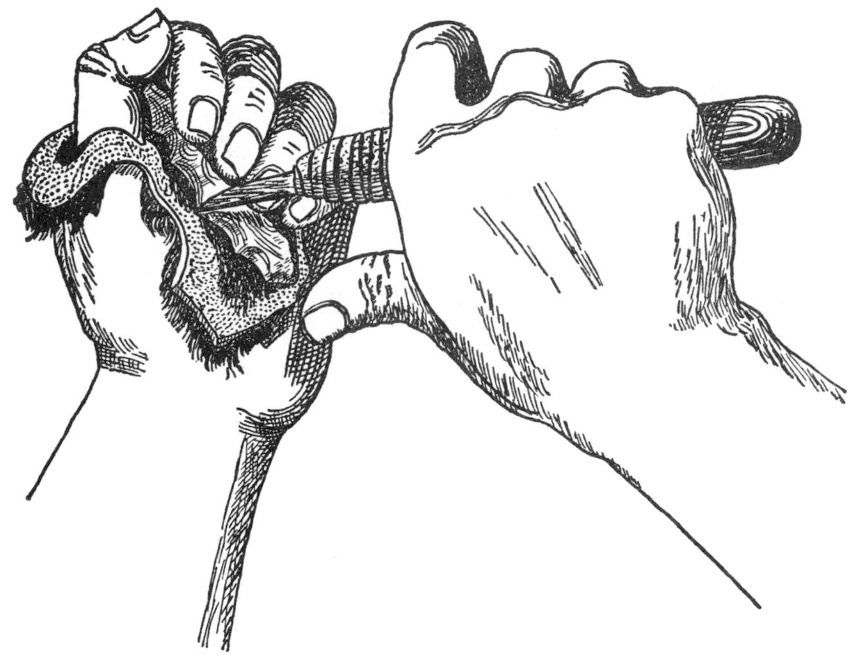

FIGURE II

Chipping Flint with Bone Tool

beautiful form. They had speculated upon the great cleverness of the Indians in making them, but could not guess how.

In the first place, the material out of which arrows and spears are made is very hard; in fact, the harder the stone the better the point or blade generally is. Since the Indians had no steel and no hard metal with which to gouge out this hard stone, most persons seem to believe that some strange process was used. What was it? Was it *fire?*

Some ingenious guessers have written that the Indians heated their flint in a fire and then dropped water upon it, causing flakes to fly off and form an arrow tip. We wonder if any one has ever tried to make a dozen points this way. Of course the method won't work because when flint is heated it develops an abrupt fracture and becomes granulated. In this condition very few good chips can be made to fly off.

Material for points is secured either from natural pebbles found along the creeks or it is broken from rocky ledges of flint, novaculite, jasper, chalcedony, chert, obsidian, or other hard, brittle stone. And now comes the process.

A suitable piece is grasped in the left hand and struck a curving blow with a hammer-stone. (See Fig. 11.) The hammer-stone trims off the chips on one side at a time, or both, as the nature of the stone and its shape dictates. The trick of chipping is soon acquired, and consists of directing the blow in the right direction and with the proper force.

The impact causes a shell-shaped or *conchoidal* chip to fly off. From this fact students of archeology call stones that may be chipped "material with a conchoidal fracture."

The chipping process is continued until the arrowpoint or spearhead takes its general shape. This should be somewhat leaf-shaped or triangular. Oftentimes these partly finished blades are laid aside for trade purposes, and a brisk commerce was kept up among the Indians in what is known as *cache* blades, or unfinished forms.

The roughed-out blade was further finished by use of a bone or antler chipping tool. It is only necessary to press the bone against the thin edge of the blade and give it a twisting or curving motion to *press off* a small flake. Sometimes these pressure flakes are large and carry right across the form.

When the blade has been neatly shaped, a thin piece of bone or antler is pressed against the edge where the barbs are to be eaten in. This takes real skill, and is done by snapping out a small chip, reversing the blade and pressing in on the other side. The process is kept up by alternating the direction of the chipping, from side to side, until the notch is worn deeply enough.

It is not difficult to make an arrowhead once the right material is secured, and if flint is not easy to find a piece of thick glass will do. I have made points in three to ten minutes, in demonstrations before Boy Scouts and classes of school children. A cripple whom I know makes beautiful little points with his left hand, and a museum orderly spends much of his time in developing his skill.

It might be thought that such specimens could be confused with genuine articles, but this is not so because the point has no signs of weathering or age, and its surface under a magnifying glass shows tiny granules and sharp crystals, that prove it fresh and newly made.

The art of chipping flint was never lost, and many Indians in the Rocky Mountain region made them until quite recently. Because flint and allied substances break so easily, and because so many arrowheads are spoiled before being finished, many Indians tried to invent "charm medicines," and when white explorers saw these efforts to secure good luck they confused them with the actual physical process of working out the point. For example, some Indians boiled their flint in charmed water or in deer grease, and others packed it in boxes with sacred roots and leaves. These superstitions were merely expressions of a hope that the point could be successfully manufactured and not break during the process.

Oftentimes arrowpoints and unfinished blades were buried in bags and baskets in moist ground, with the idea that fresh flint chips better than when dry. These *cache* blades were often lost and lucky people sometimes dig them up in modern times, finding as many as ten sometimes, and at others 8,000 to 200,000.

XI. HOW INDIANS CUT DOWN TREES

Instead of saying that the American Indians were living in the "stone age" when European invaders first saw them, it would be better to say that the American natives were living in the "wood age."

To the native of the forest wood was the great necessity. With wood he made the poles for his dwellings. From it he made dugout canoes, dishes, bows, buildings and even stockades. In every Indian settlement wood was the predominant thing.

Now wood comes from the patient bodies of trees, and it is upon legs of wood that mankind has walked out of primitive darkness. The question before us, therefore, is "how did the Indians cut down trees." They had no steel hatchets, no axes of iron, no knives of bronze; how then did they fell trees, and out of them obtain their poles and planks?

Every farmer's boy along the great waterways of America has found Indian relics, and many have found stone hatchets, whose dull edges are marvels of obtuseness. Can it be that Indians used these to chop trees? Yes, these are the Indians' axes.

Let us picture their use, and then shall we know, not only how the red men felled their timber, but exactly how white men in the dim, long ago brought their trees crashing to earth.

The Indian gathered his hatchets; the Algonkin his grooved axes with short handles and the Iroquois his ungrooved hatchets called "celts," in his own tongue, "ah-do-ga." He went to the forest and selected the trees that he wanted and made sure that they would fall free of entanglement. Then he gathered great heaps of faggots and began to build fires at the bases of the trees that he desired. The fires were built all around the trees so that the flames ate their way into the wood and charred it. Rings of clay were stuck around the trunks to keep the flames from going too far.

Of course, as every woodsman knows, flames do not cut very deeply into green timber with a charred surface. It was here that the stone hatchet came into play. With it the charred wood was hacked off, leaving a fresh surface for the flames to attack. Again and again the charred masses were hacked off with the dull-edged stone. If, perchance, the wood were soft and the stone blade actually as keen as a stone can be, some small chips were hacked out, making a bruised and splintery surface, which the fire eagerly devoured.

By having several trees in process the work progressed without much delay, for the fire kept up its work on one tree when the man was hacking at the charcoal on another. After a time a tree would fall, and then another and another. Soon all were down.

Now came the process of trimming off the limbs. This usually was done when the leaves had dried,—that is, some time after the tree had been felled. Then all the branches were burned off, and the log dragged or rolled to the place where it could be used.

Thus, fire was the tool that man used as a cutting implement long before the days of metal. To primitive man the world over, fire was a mighty weapon, and one that the beasts feared more than darts or spears. It seemed to betoken some mysterious power that in man's hands spelled the doom of beast domination.

But fire had to be controlled and directed. It was by felling his trees with fire and axes of stone that early mankind learned how to control, how to direct, and how to *combine*. It was in combining forces that man learned how to invent other useful things for the race.

XII. HOW INDIANS MADE WAMPUM

Almost every one knows that wampum is Indian money, and that it was also used as beads. Indeed, we often hear it spoken of as "wampum beads," but not many know just what wampum is made from or how it is made.

There are many traditions concerning wampum, which because of its value was regarded in the light of a sacred thing. Some legends say that the first wampum was made from the quills of feathers cut off in standard lengths and strung on cords or thongs. Other traditions say that wampum was first made from the quills of the porcupine cut into bead-lengths and strung on fine sinew. It is quite possible that quills did form a part of the substances out of which wampum was made. Certainly a number of American archeologists have dug both porcupine and bird quill beads from ancient graves. More often, however, the wampum they found was made from shell.

The fact is that it is quite probable that any suitable bead, whether of quill, shell, wood, stone or bone, was used for wampum when the occasion demanded.

Soft quills could be easily cut and colored, red slate could be easily rubbed into shape and drilled, but shell was another matter. Shell is brittle and breaks when drilled, unless great care is employed. The beauty of shell, however, with its pearly surface and its luster, made it an attractive substance for making beads. The early Indians did make many fine beads of shell, some large and some very small. Some were so small that it is still a mystery as to how they were drilled.

The Indians had an ingenious way of making their small beads and many of their wampum beads betray the process. In the first place it was necessary to find the right kind of shell. This was one of the species of the Pyrula, or whelk. Within the shells of these species is the central core or columella, around which the shell grows. It may be described as a long tube from which grew in spirals the inner structure of the shell. When the shell is broken this core is revealed. The thin partitions may be broken from it and a fairly good shell cylinder or rod formed. This was carefully reduced by grinding and rubbing to the desired size and then cut into lengths that varied but little from the standard of one-eighth inch. The problem was now to perforate the little cylinder. This was done by holding the bead in a stick of hard wood with one end split as a vise. The *soft spot* in the center of the free side was now attacked with a fine splinter of flint stuck in the end of a fine wooden drill, sometimes of a hawthorn spike. When the hole was worn half-way through, the bead was reversed and drilling started at the other end.

With the coming of the pioneers and settlers came steel drills and then wampum was manufactured in great quantities. With steel cutting implements it was possible to saw out bars of heavy shell, rub off the corners, smooth the blank into a perfect rod and then drill it with long steel rods rotated by a pump drill, great care being taken to remove the shell dust and to avoid overheating.

With steel tools it was also possible to make the valued purple wampum from the purple spot in the clam shell.

These dark-colored shells were regarded as of the highest value and one of them was worth four of the white beads. White men made wampum as late as 1875, and some of the men who made it for the Hudson Bay Company were living in northern New Jersey in 1925.

XIII. HOW INDIANS USED WAMPUM

To the red man the word wampum was a sacred word. It meant many things to him, ranging from beads to belts, and from treaties to the ransom of a life.

Not all Indians called it by the name "wampum" in the beginning. The word as we have it to-day is part of a New England Indian word the whole of which is *wampumpeag.* It comes from the Algonkin words *wamp,* white; *umpi,* string of shell beads, and *ag,* the plural terminal. The New England settlers did not know exactly what the word meant and so they shortened it so that it sounded well to their ears.

In the olden days, when only red men roamed the forests and sped their light canoes over the waterways, wampum was a very valuable thing. The great sachems had wampum beads sewed on their buckskin shirts, moccasins and leggings. Wrist bands and collars were woven from it as decorations. Its chief use, however, was as something to exchange for other valuables, and to string into strands that helped the chiefs and priests remember important rules and events.

Strings as long as a span of the hand were strung, and then clustered in bundles of ten. These had a certain value if used in trade. Other strings were of mixed beads,—white and purple, and were used to record names. So many white beads and so many dark ones meant a certain name,—as Chief Crinkled Horn, and another string with alternate white and dark beads and then a finger's length of dark beads at either end might mean Chief Corn Planter, and so on. The name strings were kept by the eldest matron in the clan, among such tribes as the Hurons and the Iroquois, and when a man died his name string was returned to the "Holder." When a new chief was elected, or another name bestowed by the "Holder," the string of name-beads was given again. In the symbolic language of the Iroquois the giving of a name was said to be "the casting of a necklace upon one's neck."

When one Indian village wished to send a message to another, the keepers of the wampum strung a strand of wampum and sent it by a messenger. Such strings were often tied to little sticks which were notched in such a way as to indicate the number of days which might elapse before an answer was expected.

The most august and solemn use of wampum was in the form of belts woven with symbolic patterns. There were many patterns, ranging from squares, diamonds, parallel lines, human figures, trees, links, bars, animals, hatchets, peace-pipes and even houses. Each figure had a meaning, well known to the Indians.

When a great treaty was to be made, the wampum keepers of the tribe ordered their skilled women to weave special belts which might commemorate the event. Oftentimes these treaty belts showed two men clasping each other by the right hand. When a Council speaker rose to make a solemn statement that the treaty embraced, he handed the other party to the treaty a belt, with the exclamation, "This belt preserves my words!"

When one Indian had killed another a feud was at once started, and many relatives, as well as the culprit, might be killed. Thus the relatives sought to give belts of peace,—oftentimes as many as twenty,—to "wipe away all grief and establish the path of peace." Thus wampum played an important part in the ransom of life. Captives were ransomed with wampum when all else failed.

In general purple wampum symbolized the darker side of life, its heavier and more solemn side; while white wampum represented the lighter and more peaceful side. Purple wampum was used upon the council benches when death occurred; white wampum was used to betoken peace. A belt of white wampum exchanged by two tribes meant that peace had been declared. An alliance was symbolized when there was a white chain on a purple background.

When war was to be declared between tribes that had exchanged white belts, the aggressor painted the white belt with red iron-oxide, or perhaps even soaked it in blood, and then returned it by a war runner. The tribe receiving it might send back peaceful belts, or it might send back its own belt stained red.

Sometimes when a great compliment was intended for a chief, a wampum collar was given him, that he might wear it around his neck and draped down his shoulders.

Indians used wampum in many of their ceremonies, and some tribes, as the Iroquois, still regard it as necessary in their sacred rites. It is still used by them when they "raise up" their chiefs.

The Iroquois word for wampum (in the Mohawk dialect) is *otgora;* their word for wampum belt is ga-swĕ'da'. The great belt of the Iroquois had upon it the symbol of "an ever-growing tree."

XIV. HOW INDIANS MADE MASKS

One cold autumn night many years ago Jisgogo and myself lay upon our bunks in our tent on an Indian reservation. We were weary after a hard day's effort to locate some ancient pit deposits in which we hoped to find numerous Indian relics, such as pipes, pots, implements of bone and knives of flint. Our feet were tired from having shoved the spade with too much enthusiasm. Without knowing what the other was doing, we both began to move our feet as if dancing. This was simply to relax the tired muscles. Then one of us began in a low tone to sing an old Indian dance tune.

Outside the door sat our friend Tahadondeh, or Wood's Edge. He looked in at us and thoughtfully watched our feet. Presently he came in and sat down, while we snoozed off, still moving our feet.

When we awoke for supper it was dark, but the campfire blazed merrily. Wood's Edge was still there and apparently troubled. "You boys have dreamed about the false faces," he stated. "Now you've got to join the False Face Company. You needn't look so dumb; I saw your feet dancing. Now I've got to make a mask for you both."

Upon inquiry we learned that when one dreams of the mysterious masks and dances in his sleep, the power of the faces is upon him. A feast must be given and the way paved for initiation into the strange company of masked faces. We had our feast and our dance. We were anointed with ashes and filled with most excellent false-face pudding. Thereafter we were regaled with the traditions of the order and later paid homage at the shrine of the gathered companies in the long lodge of the Seneca people. It was a dramatic event, and introduced us to the cult of masked medicine men.

There are three principal centers of the mask or false face: the North-West coast, the South-West region of the Pueblo people and the eastern forest region of the Iroquois and Lenape. All these tribes still keep up their societies of maskers.

The most elaborate masks are those of the western part

of the continent. It is not easy to say whether the North-West or the South-West have the more astonishing masks, for both are different in form. The Kwakiutl have compound masks, for example, and faces within faces. A string pulls open the first face and another of different

FIGURE 12

Mask of Pueblo Indian

expression is revealed. There are even masks representing animals and whales.

If the masks of the north Pacific culture are strange, those of the desert are equally so. The Pueblo masks are called *kachinas* and are supposed to represent the spirits of mythical beings or long-departed ancestors. They cover the head completely and have towering ornaments above them. Kachinas are a riot of color, but generally the combination of form and color is pleasing to the eye. One of the dances of these companies is a spectacular sight, never to be forgotten.

It is a common belief among Indians who use masks that the wearer takes upon himself the nature of the mask. His own personality becomes merged in the character that he represents, and the spirit of the mask enters him. Spectators must so regard the masked figure and give it respect.

The Iroquois have two kinds of masks,—those carved of wood and those woven of corn husk. During one of my reservation sojourns I had the opportunity of seeing a medicine mask carved by my host, Big Kettle. Back in the woods, with a priest of the cult, Big Kettle outlined the face upon the trunk of a living basswood, while the priest of the rite cast incense tobacco upon a small fire and prayed.

The face grew upon the tree and finally assumed a form which ended the first part of the ceremony. Big Kettle now talked to the tree and then another worker cut it down, trimmed off the short log upon which was the face, and carried it to his house.

Big Kettle now told us the reason for his actions. A mask to receive the spirit it represents must be carved upon a living basswood tree. The spirit, lured by the chant of the priest, enters the tree and finds its face. The tree now is killed and its life enters the face, which now has life as well as spirit. The face is then taken to the workshop of a mask carver and completed.

The tools used are small adzes and crook-knives. With these tools the face may be hollowed out, and the features formed. When both sides are finished it is painted the right color, this depending upon the face. It is usually

FIGURE 13
Seneca False Face Dancer

red, or red and black. It then remains to put long wisps of hair upon it, drill holes for the thongs by which it is fastened to the head, and to tie medicine tobacco in the part of its hair. The mask is now ready for consecration. A feast is given and false-face pudding eaten by members of the company. The mask, behind a skin covering, peers out and becomes friendly and potent. The feasters look at it, so that they may say, "I know him." When the mask is used in the first dance or healing ceremony, it is thought to be "real." Thereafter it is cared for, protected from anything that may harm it and given tobacco incense regularly. The great Hadui masks of the Iroquois represent the mythical being who promises to defend mankind from harm, but being the Whirlwind, brings much woe at times.

The False Face Company of the Iroquois still lives but its best masks are in the great museums, where they may be seen by visitors.

All masked companies use rattles of one form or another. The North-West coast people have elaborate rattles of wood, the desert people have rattles of gourds, but the Iroquois use rattles made from snapping turtles, the legs of which have been cut off, the shell emptied and the neck drawn out long and filled with a round stick, this being braced above and below by stout, flat pieces of wood. The Iroquois, of which the Seneca people form a part, also use rattles of hickory bark, but gourd rattles are never used by the False Face Company.

XV. HOW INDIANS MADE COLORS

It is quite natural that the various colors should be admired and desired. Nature is full of color, and from the fact that flowers, butterflies, birds and fishes have color in profusion, mankind has the suggestion of gaining color for himself.

The soft shades of the sky at morning, when the sun worshiper looked toward the east, cast a spell upon the heart of the red man and woman, and made them long to secure colors that they might be used in decoration.

Contrary to the general notion, Indians untouched by civilization did not have glaring colors. Their colors were soft and combined with an artist's skill. It was when the civilized trader came with European goods and dyes that "gaudy" colors were given to the red man. His natural love for color now ran riot, and if the wiser white man had such things to trade the Indian took them as specimens of foreign skill, and yet combined them with taste. Look at an example of Indian beadwork and note the evidence of artistic feeling, look at examples of cloth work, quill work, painting, weaving and basketry. There is nothing gaudy about these things, though those who originated this tradition (being men of dark and somber clothes, as well as thoughts) said so and would have had us believe it.

The range of dyes and pigments among Indians was not great. Their colors were few and obtained from colored earths and from plant roots and stems.

Yellow. Yellow dye was obtained from the roots of golden seal, from dock, from osage orange, from hemlock bark and sumac roots. The Navaho used the flowering tops of a native plant known as *Bigelovia graveolens.* These were boiled for six hours until a decoction of deep yellow was produced. The color concentrates being right, the dyer heated a pan of almogen (impure alum) over the fire until it assumed the form of paste. This is gradually added to the yellow fluid until enough has been put in. The dye is now ready for wool, and the tint produced is lemon yellow.

The function of the alum of course is that of a mordant, or substance that *fixes* the color. It may be used with a number of colors.

The Menomini and other eastern tribes used yellow dock, *Rumex crispus.* The Cheyenne Indians call it Maheskoe. The leaves and stems are boiled together, and when the infusion has cooled the dyer puts in porcupine quills and leaves them for twelve hours or more. They come out a pleasing yellow. Tests should be made from time to time to see that the color does not run too deep.

The Cheyenne people also use another dock called *Rumex venosus.* The roots and dried leaves are used, as above. When a deeper color is needed more of the root is put in.

Red. The *venosus* dock mentioned above may be employed to give a reddish color by taking the liquor and mixing it with ashes. The solution is again boiled and allowed to cool. The Menomini used bloodroot and powdered hematite. As red was a hard color to make, the process of combining the substances was kept more or less secret. The Iroquois used the sumac, *Rhus hirta,* employing both fruit and root, and mixing it with plant juices, probably those of berries and bloodroot.

Brown. Brown of various shades was obtained from the roots of the native hemlock, *Tsuga Canadensis.* The bark was also used.

Black. An enduring black required much skill to make. It was so effective, however, that the black buckskin of the Lenape, though exposed to the elements for more than a hundred years, remains good. A visit to any large museum will prove this.

The Navahos, who made their colors with care, used the leaves and twigs of the aromatic sumac, *Rhus aromatica,* which they boiled in a sufficient quantity of water for five or six hours. A good grade of yellow ochre is now pulverized and roasted over the fire until it becomes a light brown. An equal amount of the gum from the piñon, *Pinus edulis,* is finely powdered and mixed with the brown ocher. The roasting process is then continued, the mass being stirred until it assumes the appearance of a tough paste. This is allowed to roast until the mass is dry and hard. More roasting reduces it to a fine black powder. This is then removed, cooled, and later thrown into the sumac decoction, stirred and taken out of the pot and strained. The result is a rich black fluid, which is little less than ink. The Mohawks say that iron ore from along the St. Lawrence river was powdered and boiled with oak galls. This would also produce an inky dye.

Green. Shades of green were made by soaking copper in organic acids or urine until enough of the dye concentrate had been produced. It was then diluted. A careful manipulation of copper green is said to have resulted in a near-blue. Green was a highly desired color and paint pigments of it were obtained from green clay found in the Oklahoma region. It was often used in coloring the skins of birds kept in war bundles.

Blue. The flowers of larkspur (*Delphinium scaposum*) were used as the source of the light blue dye of the Moqui coiled basket plaques. A darker blue came from the seeds of the common sunflowers (*Helianthus petiolaris*). It takes a real experiment to obtain and set these dyes, and perhaps this is still the secret of the desert Indians.

Paint pigments. From naturally colored earths and clays, found in favored regions, the following pigments were obtained: brown, red, green, blue, yellow, orange, purple, black and white.

The reds and yellows came mostly from ocher, but red also came from powdered iron oxide, found plentifully in many regions. White came from kaolin clay and also from gypsum. Black was made from charcoal and graphite.

Earthen colors were mixed with oils and used as

paint, but probably none made a good dye. Sunflower and nut oil was used for diluting earthen paint, and occasionally glue was mixed with it.

Powdered colors were carefully kept in skin bags, especially if intended as body or facial decorations. Frequently paint pouches were beautifully decorated and then consecrated by an invocation to the sun or some unseen spirit.

A source of natural colors to be used in decoration was afforded by the birds. Bird feathers were used for many things. Indians used the following bird feathers: *Red,* woodpecker, *green,* mallard, *orange,* oriole, *yellow,* meadow lark, *black,* quail, *brown,* thrush, *green,* parrot, *iridescent,* turkey, *white,* heron, and so on. Other bird feathers were used for many purposes, but those named were commonly chosen for their colors.

Color had a certain symbolism, and some referred to the cardinal directions. Among the Pomo basket-makers of the South-West colors were given values as follows:

Red, bravery, pride, (Symbol: woodpecker),
Yellow, love, success, gayety, fidelity; (lark),
Blue, cruel cunning, perfidy; (jay),
Green, astuteness, discretion, vigilance; (duck),
Black, family love, beauty, (quail),
White, riches, generosity; (wampum, shells).

Thus a man who was yellow was gay and successful, and a man who was blue was a rogue. Other tribes gave other values to colors.

XVI. HOW INDIANS TANNED BUCKSKIN

Buckskin was tanned in several ways and by using different substances, *according to the tribe.* It is always well to keep in mind that Indian tribes were different

FIGURE 14

Tanning Hides

and that many of them had their own style of doing things.

My information comes from Indians whom I have known, and if followed, a well-tanned buckskin will result. It may be in order to state right at the beginning that Indian *buckskin is not tanned* at all; it is just worked soft.

A fresh skin is soaked in water for several days, usually from three to six. Sometimes the hair is cut off, or at least as much as possible, and then the hide is soaked. A lye made of wood ashes is used for removing the hair from the pelts of elk and moose. In some cases the ashes are sprinkled on the hair, rubbed in, and then the moist hide is rolled up to await the loosening effect of the lye.

The next step, and this is often a woman's step,—is to take the skin from the water and put it over a graining log. This is a log from which the bark has been removed. It is stuck obliquely into the ground so that its upper end is waist high. Once draped over this beam the particles of flesh, fat and sinew are scraped off. An implement specially devised for this purpose is used. In olden days it was a heavy handle of elk horn with an end like a small hoe. To this a flint scraper was tied, but in later times a steel blade was substituted. When this work had been done the skin was reversed and the hair removed with a beaming tool. This was once made from the cannon bone of a deer, and it had two sharp edges. When the stone and bone age vanished, as the settlers came in, this tool was made of wood and had a long iron blade. With it the hair was scraped off, and also the surface skin. When the hair stuck, it was wet with moist ashes which loosened it so that in a short time it could be removed with ease.

Most skin workers took the hair off first and then turned the hide for the fleshing process, but whichever way was used, great care was taken not to work a thin spot in the skin. A good skin is of uniform thickness, though perhaps we should say thinness, for thin soft skins were considered among the best.

When the skin is thoroughly scraped, dehaired and clean, it is washed in clear water, wrung out and then stretched on a wooden frame, being laced to it by leather thongs or bark cords. The skin should be almost as tight as a drum head.

Now comes the trick of mixing brains with this tanning business,—and the old Indian actually thought that it took brains to do it right. A batter of deer's brains is now rubbed into the skin until it is thoroughly saturated. If the skin has been worked and twisted before being "framed" the process does not take long.

Brain paste is prepared by splitting the skull, removing its contents and then dissolving them in warm water. Sometimes the water is quite hot, but at all events the mass is crushed in the fingers and worked into a fluid paste. If brains are lacking, liver paste is added; the two go well together. When there is too much of this solution the brains are mixed with moss and dried near a slow fire. The moss is then squeezed into a cake and kept for future use. To make ready for use the moss was wet and rubbed on the skin in the ordinary way.

Once the brains were in the skin the hide was removed from the frame, soaked again and then wrung out. The wringing process is important, and it consists of twisting the skin lengthwise and then looping it about a tree only to twist it again by means of a stick thrust through the loop. When dry it is stretched out, pulled in all directions, thrown back into water, wrung again, twisted again, pulled again, only to be thrown in more water and to have the process repeated.

The work applied to the skin is necessary for removing

the cellular filling, and to produce a clean sheet of pelt fiber. When this is achieved, and the skin is soft, pliable and white, it is sewed up in the form of an irregular bag with crossed sticks thrust in the mouth to keep it open.

A smoke pit is now dug and in it a fire is built. Rotten wood, punk, cobs, chips of oak, beech or even corn cobs are thrown in upon the coals and a smudge started. The bag is now inverted over this and pegged down at the base. A cord holds the bottom of the bag to a limb or pole. Care must now be taken that the fire beneath does not blaze, and that the smoke fills the bag evenly. To guard against an uneven flow of smoke, all shot and other holes are sewed up. Inspection must be constant, and when the pelt is of the right color,—yellow, tan or brown, it is taken from the smudge and laid away, the smoked surface being folded upon itself. A few days of this sets the color and finishes the hide or *osawi'ksua,* as the Menomini called it. This is the so-called "Indian tan," though more properly it is simply "Indian worked," no tanning solution such as is used in leather making having been employed.

Buckskin is warm and pleasant to wear, and it outlasts any cloth ever made. It is the ideal material for wear in the wilderness for it does not tear or allow thorns to puncture it. Its one drawback is that it wets through easily, but even so it is soon dried and with a little rubbing is restored completely.

Buckskin was not always left with its "buckskin" color. Many Indian tribes dyed the skin various hues from yellow to black. The Delaware or Lenape Indians were very fond of black buckskin. The Seminole people usually tanned their skins brown, and other tribes tinged theirs with green or orange. Even red was not unknown.

With those who loved white, there were processes of bringing about a white tan. The Cree of the north made

(Courtesy American Museum of Natural History)

FIGURE 15

Parflesche Designs

beautiful white caribou skins that were as soft and as pliable as velvet.

For the purpose of both cleaning and coloring buckskin various colored clays and earths were used. Yellow ocher was rubbed into the dry skin until it was thoroughly covered, then the skin was shaken out and brushed. White earth was also used to good advantage.

When skins were made for trade purposes, the tanner was very careful to save the deer's tail. This was kept with the skin and the hair was not removed. Men liked to have deer tails hanging down as decorations when the skin was made up into shirts.

XVII. HOW INDIANS MADE RAWHIDE

The Indians found many uses for stiff, thin hides, and for this need made rawhide. The method was quite simple and consisted of soaking the green hide, removing the fleshy parts and fat, taking off the hair and scraping the whole to the desired thickness.

The skin was then stretched very tightly upon a wooden frame, being laced to it by means of stout thongs. When wet the hide will stretch out considerably, but the thongs must be drawn tighter and tighter until there is no more stretch. The skin now resembles a great drum head. In this condition it is slowly dried in a cool, shady spot.

Some hides as those of the buffalo, elk and moose require ashes in removing the hair, but deer skins do not. The lye of ashes weakens the texture of the skin.

Rawhides were used for *parflesche* trunks. These were made from shaped skins, that is skins that had been trimmed into long rectangles. These were folded at the sides so that there was an overlapping and then each end was turned toward the center, making a package container exactly like a druggist's pill paper.

The outer side of this parflesche was painted in diamond-shaped figures in various combinations and in various colors, many being excellent patterns. The parflesche was the Indian's suit case. In it he kept his spare clothing, valuables and sometimes his charms. The word parflesche comes from the French-Canadian patois and means *shield* or arrow fender, because shields were made of buffalo bull rawhide.

With the prairie tribes moccasin soles were made of rawhide, and some south-western tribes made bags and quivers of it.

XVIII. HOW INDIANS MADE BASKETS

It is said that birds gave mankind the first suggestion of making baskets, but the nests of birds can scarcely be said to exhibit true weaving. Nevertheless the selection of strong material for nests, such as roots and grasses, fibers and sticks, gave a hint as to the wide variety of natural substances that might be used. If a bird can do it why not man,—and this from baskets to flying.

Baskets were needed by Indians because they furnish receptacles or containers for other valuable things. In baskets, large and small, things may be kept, stored and carried. The problems of basket making were then, to find material for them, to weave or coil them properly, to fit them to the purposes intended and to decorate them in a fitting manner. Basket making thus brought about a whole system of correlated industries that, while causing much work and worry, afforded great pleasure and satisfaction.

In a brief article, such as this is, only a few bits of information about baskets can be given. Many large books have been written upon the subject without exhausting it, for Indian baskets are so amazingly beautiful and occur in so many varieties of form, technique and ornamentation, that only a large book could even begin to describe them or the processes by which they are made. Among the best are Mary White's "How to Make Baskets," George Wharton James' "Indian Basketry," and Otis Tuft Mason's "Aboriginal American Basketry," published by the National Museum in 1902.

As an illustration of the types of basketry the analysis given below is adduced to show how ingenious and complicated the art was, and still is:

General Types[1]

1. *Hand woven*, made by a warp and weft process;
2. *Coiled* basketry, sometimes called *sewed*, made by sewing by various stitches, coiled rods, splints, withes or grasses together.

Woven Basketry

a. Checkerwork: the warp and weft having the same width, thickness and pliability;

b. Diagonal or twilled basketry; made by weaving two or more weft strands over two or more warp strands;

c. Wickerwork; made by weaving a slender flexible weft over a rather rigid warp;

d. Wrapped weft, sometimes called single weft wrapped; made by wrapping the weft strand about the warp, or by making a "bite" as it crosses the warp;

e. Twined or wattled; made with weft of two or more elements.

Coiled Basketry

a. Coiled work without foundation;

b. Simple interlocking coils;

c. Single-rod foundation;

d. Two-rod foundation;

e. Rod and welt foundation;

[1] Adapted from Otis T. Mason, National Museum Rep't., 1902.

OPEN CHECKERWORK.

FINE CHECKERWORK.

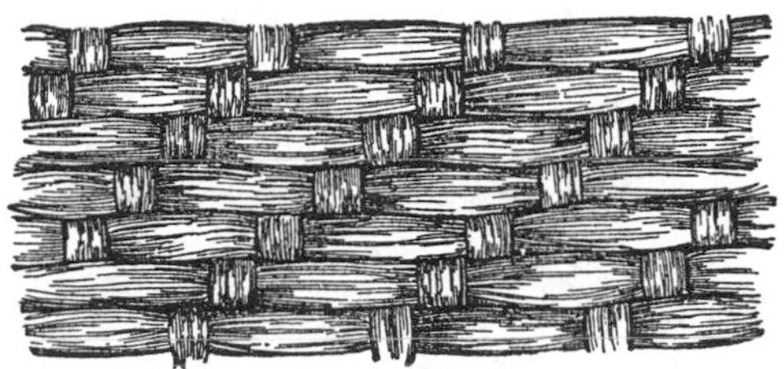
ANCIENT TWILLED WORK

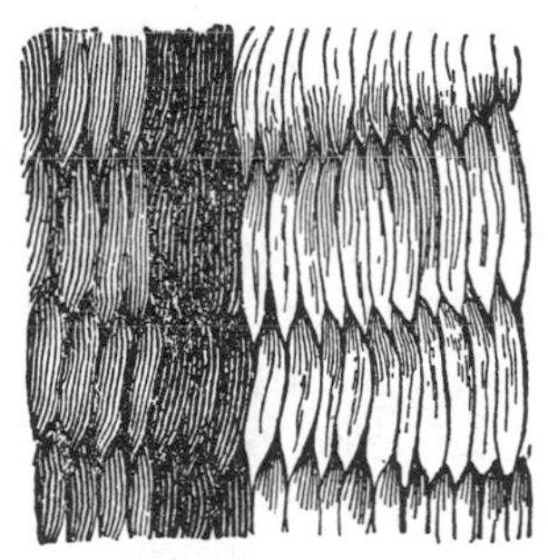
CLOSE WICKERWORK.
Hopi Indians, Arizona.

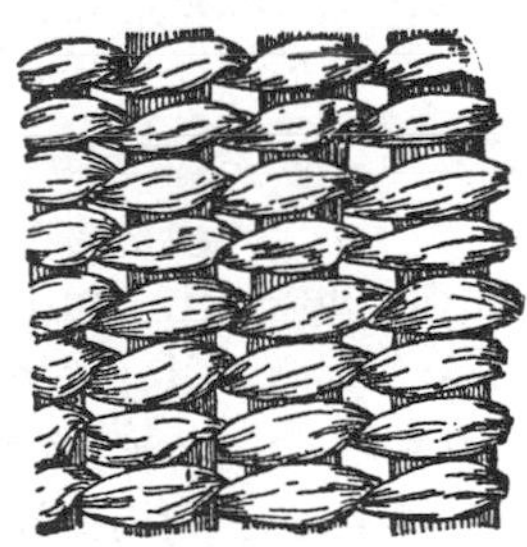
PLAIN TWINED WEAVING.

FIGURE 16
Methods of Weaving Baskets

f. Two-rod and splint foundation;
g. Three-rod foundation;
h. Splint foundation;
i. Grass coil foundation;
j. Fuegian coiled types.

Before a basket is made the worker must spend many hours in collecting and preparing the substances to be used in basket manufacture. The getting of raw material is an occupation in itself.

Tough grasses that may be rendered flexible, reeds, inner barks, and wood fiber are hunted out and prepared. Cane or splints may be used, in which case a large amount of mechanical work must be done.

The common basket splint requires a search for a good black ash log, which must be reduced to proper length, skinned of its bark and then pounded over its entire surface to loosen the annular rings and the lamina that lie between. By pounding black ash the length of the log a strip may be peeled off. This can then be split and smoothed, then cut into long flexible strips for weaving. The common basket of the Iroquois, and many other eastern tribes, is made from such splints.

a. *Checkerwork.* The simplest form of basketry is that in which the warp and weft pass over and under one another singly, the rows of warp being placed side by side and the weft splints woven in and out for the width of the warp. The next weft splint alternates with the first and goes under and over, out and in, in such a manner that the first is held in place by the rise of the warp. Fig. 16 shows this simple form of weaving, which may be fine or coarse, open or close.

b. *Twilledwork.* In twilled basketry, the weft splint passes over one warp strand and then under two, repeating until the desired end is reached. The next splint takes

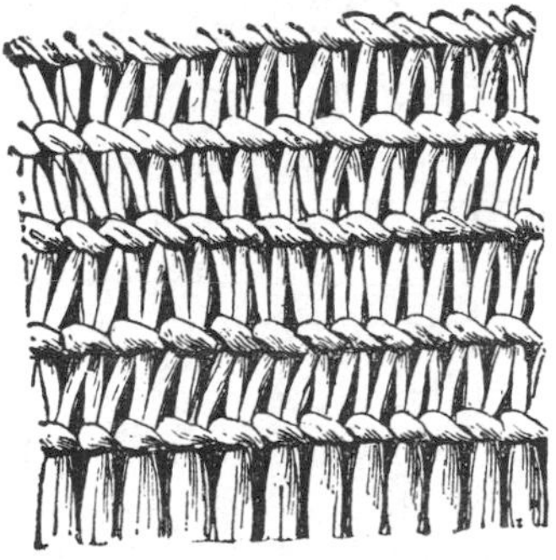

TWINED OPENWORK.
Aleutian Islands.
Enlarged.

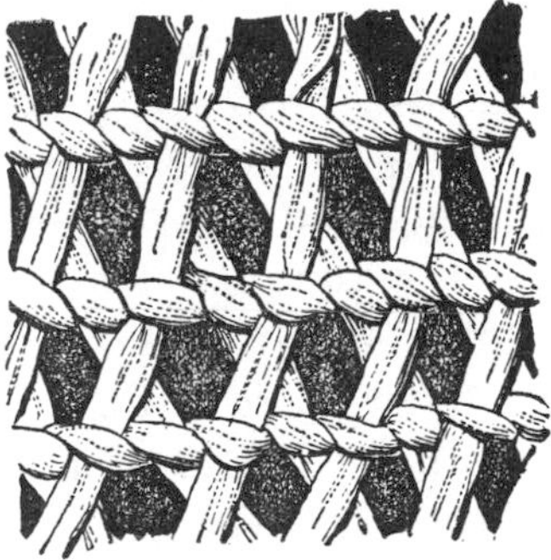

CROSSED WARP, TWINED WEAVE.
Makah Indians, Washington.

DIAGONAL TWINED WEAVING.
Ute Indians, Utah.

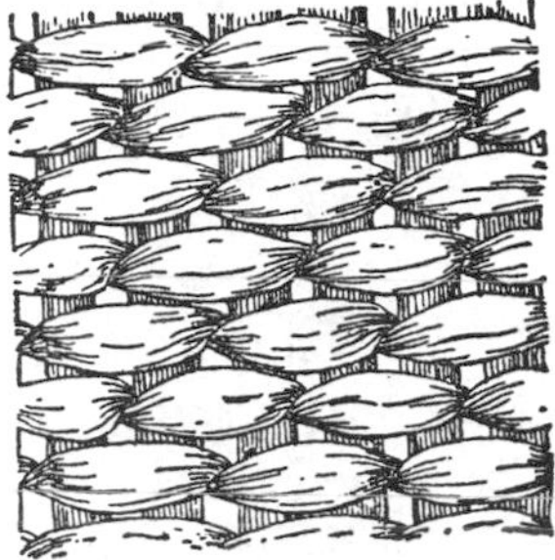

DIAGONAL TWINED BASKETRY.
Pomo Indians, California.
Collection of C. P. Wilcomb.

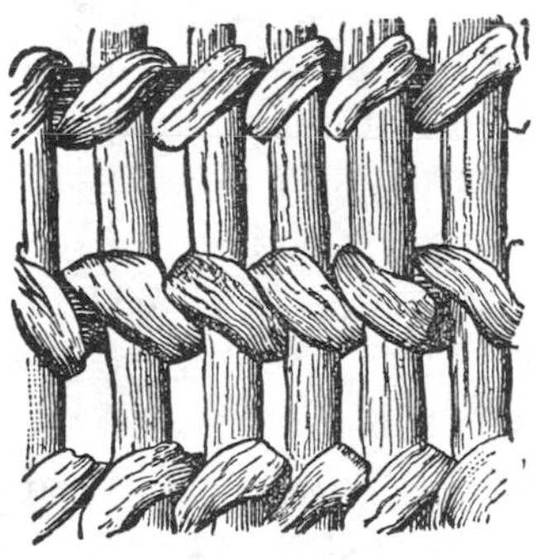

WRAPPED TWINED WEAVING.

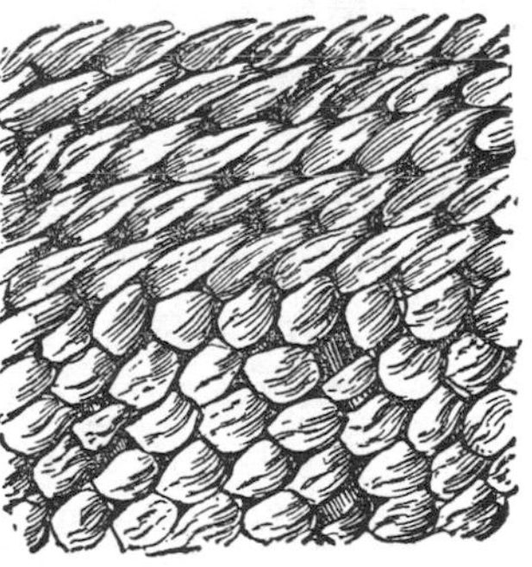

THREE-STRAND AND PLAIN TWINED WEAVING.

FIGURE 17
Types of Twined Weaving

the set oblique to the first, throwing up one of the two deposed by the preceding. It is simply a case of remembering one and two and starting next time one splint in advance and doing the same thing. This is a common weaving stitch in making some modern fabrics. Fig. 16 shows the detailed structure of twilled work.

c. *Wickerwork.* The technique of wickerwork differs very little from checkerwork. The difference is that the warp is made from long rods or thick splints that do not bend as easily as the soft, pliable warp. Whenever there is a difference between the warp and weft in the matter of rigidity, wickerwork appears. It may have the primary form of weaving or it may have the diagonal weave of twilling.

d. *Wrapped work.* Whenever there are rigid rods or splints widely spaced and a weft of light, flexible material that is wound around, half-hitched or knotted about the warp, wrapped work basketry appears. It is commonly used in the South-West for carrying frames. The ancient mound builders used it, as may be proven by impressions taken from fabric-marked pottery.

e. *Twinedwork.* Twinedwork is perhaps the most beautiful form of weaving found in basketry. Many of the finest woven baskets of the desert region are twined. The warp used is somewhat more rigid than the weft strand. The weft is usually handled in pairs, these being alternately twisted from side to side over each warp element. The formula "over one under two" may also be employed to give a diagonal effect. There are several forms of this weave, varying from openwork to wrapped twining. The latter is a form of checker work reënforced by an over-and-over winding of some flexible material at the intersections. Fig. 17 shows the forms of twinedwork. Some forms are very complicated.

Coiled basketry is produced by weaving the weft around

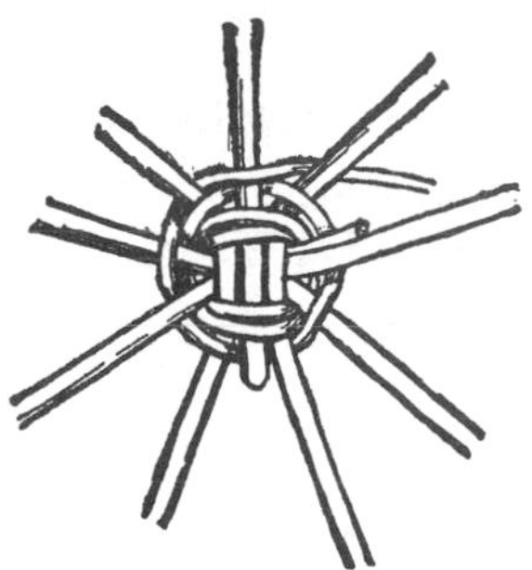

WARP STEMS CROSSED IN PAIRS.
After Mary White.

WARP STEMS CROSSED IN FOURS.
After Mary White.

SIXTEEN STEMS WOVEN IN FOURS.
After Mary White.

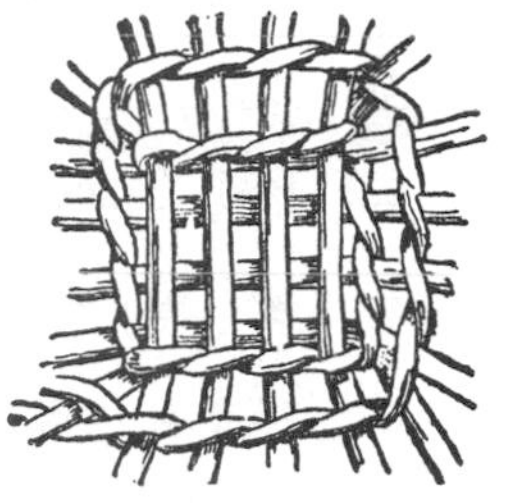

WARP STEMS CROSSED IN FOURS AND TWINED.
After Mary White.

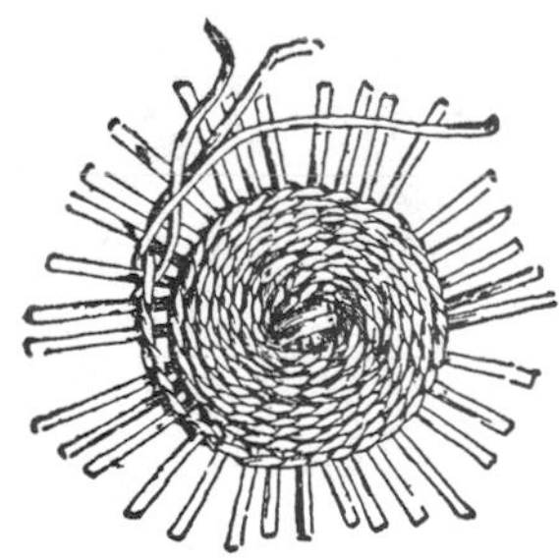

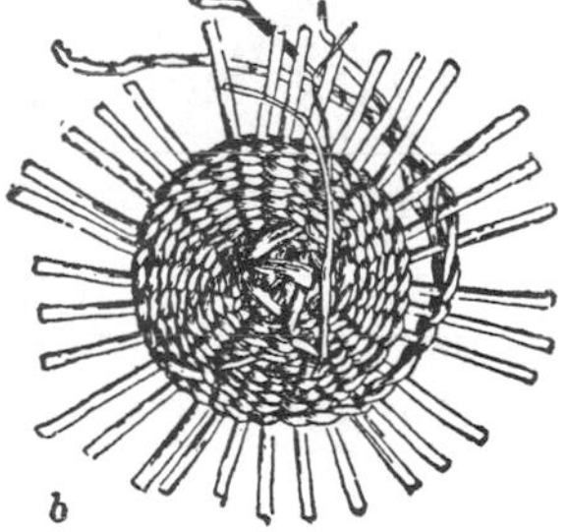

THREE-STRAND BRAID.
a, outside; *b*, inside.

FIGURE 18

Types of Coiled Weaving

a warp that has been crossed in radiations from the center. The rod-warp may be single or in twos or threes. In this type of work the weft element is woven in and out and around and around in ever-widening circles. See Fig. 18.

Basketry Borders

Perhaps the most puzzling thing in basketry is how to finish the rim or border. This is quite essential in order to prevent fraying when the basket is handled. In the case of checkerwork it is done by placing a tough splint on either side and fastening it by the twilled stitch. In twilled work the rim-binding is done by the coiled stitch.

Basketry was a real art and it required a feeling for number and proportion. It seems strange that many of the tribes regarded as very low in the scale of civilization could produce such really beautiful and intricate baskets. Some of these would exhaust the ingenuity and patience of many modern craftsmen. Basketry was an art of the Indian woman.

XIX. HOW INDIANS MADE POTTERY

Four elements were necessary in the production of pottery,—earth, water, air and fire. By a combination of these basic things in nature, the red man of America produced dishes, pots, vessels, vases, bottles, bowls and smoking pipes.

Not all Indian tribes, by any means, produced pottery. Some of the most advanced made none. In general, however, most of the tribes of the east, including those of the Mississippi drainage basin, the Great Lakes area and the gulf region were skilled in the art. In the South-West the Pueblo people made a great industry of pottery, manu-

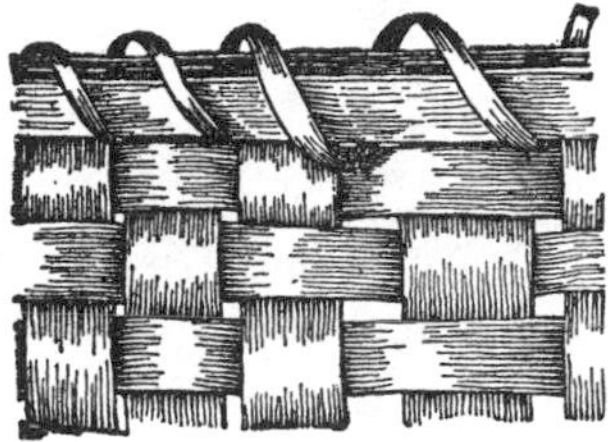

COILED BORDER ON CHECKER WEAVING.

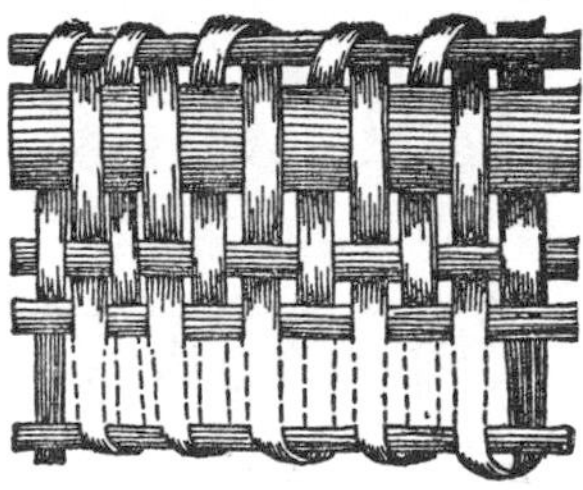

SINGLE-STRAND COILED BORDER.
Moravian Settlement, North Carolina.
Cat. No. 214558, U.S.N.M. Collected by Carolyn G Benjamin.

BORDER MADE BY WEAVING WARP RODS IN PAIRS.
Collected by G. Wharton James.

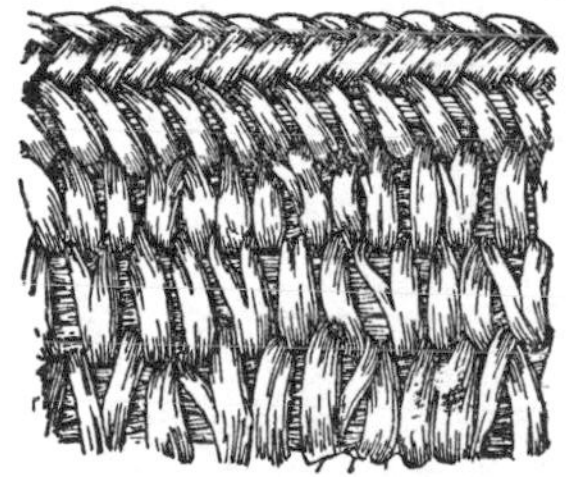

DETAIL OF COILED BASKET.
Tinné Indians.
Collected by Lucien Turner.

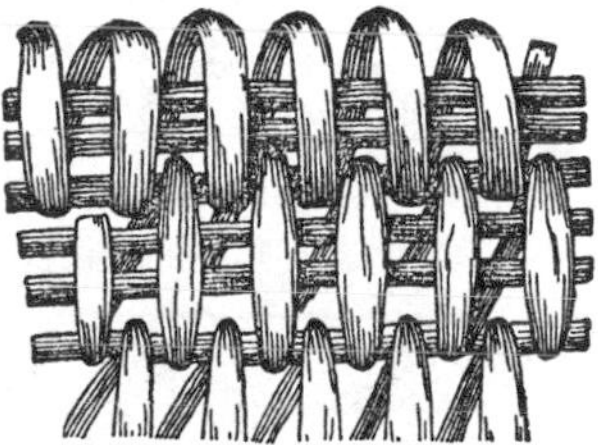

SIMPLE COIL BORDER.
Paiute Indians, Utah.
Cat. No. 14688, U.S.N.M. Collected by J. W. Powell.

THREE-STRAND WARP BORDER IN WICKER WORK.

FIGURE 19
Methods of Finishing Rims

facturing vessels, bowls and dishes by the thousands, and decorating them with artistic skill. So extensive was the pottery working of the tribes mentioned that this art, together with basketry, pelt tanning and stone working, must be classed among the major industries of ancient America.

The first requisite of this art is a good grade of clay, and for this reason clay beds were prospected and when found were examined with care, many experiments being made to test the quality of the deposit. A clean clay was necessary, and when found it was dug, placed in baskets, taken to the work-shop and washed. Here it was worked into batches, kneaded, moistened, kneaded again, rolled, puddled, and then worked into a mass for basket storage. The kneading process consisted largely of lifting the batch and throwing it with force upon a flat rock.

Next came the important business of tempering the clay. This process must have been regarded as a great discovery, because no matter how excellent clay may be, when modeled into vessels, it cracks when the water that lies between the tiny particles evaporates. A crack, once started, takes its course whither it will, like a crack in a piece of glass. By adding "temper" this cracking is prevented; it does not happen.

Temper consists of pulverized granite, quartz and other crystalline rock, coarse round sand and shell. In North Carolina and Virginia the clay was often tempered with pounded soapstone. Mica schist, pure mica, and iron pyrites were also used. In mixing the tempering material some workers spread out the clay in flat sheets, sprinkled it thoroughly with temper, folded the clay, repeated the process, and then kneaded it with stone pounders or wooden billets. As much of the temper was worked in as the clay would hold, in many cases the amount being from 60 to 80 percent. An examination of almost any clay vessel shows that it was composed largely of cracked stone held together with clay as a "binder."

The tempering material was sifted so as to have it fairly uniform though an occasional lump fell in and seems to have done no harm. Mussel shells were employed by some of the eastern tribes, and seem to have served well.

Modeling

When the clay had been prepared it was either flattened and cut into rectangular strips, or was rolled out into long ropes. These were kept moist. A base made of a saucer-like basket or of a gourd was now used in which to build the bottom of the pot. As a saucer of clay appeared, made of the coils or strips, these were smoothed together by means of the fingers and by the application of a smoothing stone dipped in water and rubbed around and around until the form of the coils had disappeared, making the mass one united piece. The coiling continued when the lower part was sufficiently hard to support more weight. In no case was the clay allowed to become dry.

Some of the southern tribes, as the Cherokee, paddled the surface of the pot, while yet plastic, with notched paddles having designs cut into them. As a rule the Algonkian people used paddles around which cord had been wrapped, and the impressions of these may be seen in fragments found in Indian village sites all along the Atlantic coast. The Algonkian people, too, seem to have suspended their pots in bags woven of coarse cords. As the clay was wet and smoothed, these cords pressed into the surface of the vessel and left their impressions. To carry out the use of cord marks as decoration, the rims of the pots were deliberately marked with cords wound around small paddles and rods.

The Iroquois people, including the Huron, were skillful potters, but the bodies of their pots as a rule were kept smooth. They wanted no cord marks to show. Neither did they decorate by stamping in patterns. They preferred to incise or draw into the clay triangular plats of parallel lines, the direction of which was changed in each adjoining plat. For this reason it is not difficult to tell the tribe that made pottery, once it is found.

In the great South-West the Pueblo people made clay dishes of many forms, using several kinds of clay of varied colors. The pot itself was usually of a light clay and decorated by drawings and applications of darker clays or colored earths, such as ocher. The Pueblos made beautiful dishes and vessels, no two of which were ever exactly alike in ornamentation.

Baking

It is one thing to build up the pot form, and another to bake it. Before baking the moisture should be evaporated; the modeled pot should be dry. The potter's fire is now prepared. It was built in a sheltered place and its fuel was of a kind that gave much heat and little smoke. An even heat was necessary. Some tribes filled the pot with chipped bark, buffalo chips or dry flakes of wood. The pot was now inverted over a bed of coals and the fuel piled up around the vessel, care being taken to shelter it from wind. Baking was continued until the pot began to glow a dull red. Ashes were now heaped over it until it gradually cooled.

There were many tricks and secrets of pot making. The Iroquois are said to have mixed their clay with the blood of pigeons and even other animals. In smoothing the interior of their pots they used *unio* shells as scrapers. Small pots were modeled about a gourd, this serving, when turned around to give a smooth inside and to insure a symmetrical vessel. Of course the gourd could not be removed, for the neck of the pot was constricted. The gourd was left in and burned away in the firing process.

Smoking pipes were modeled by the men, and among the Iroquois there were many varied forms, especially in the matter of effigies. Faces of beasts, birds, monsters and men were formed, usually being toward the smoker. Stem holes were punched in sometimes when the clay was still wet, but as this was a dangerous process, spreading and cracking the clay, the stem hole was rolled around a core of twisted grass or a bark cord. Flexible plant stems were also used.

Digging into mounds and ancient graves for ancient Indian pottery has been a favorite pursuit of archeologists, who have made notes and photographs, so that no information might be lost. Many amateurs have forgotten to make records and so have destroyed the very means by which science may gain an understanding of the artifacts and processes of the past.

XX. HOW INDIANS DREW THEIR DESIGNS

An examination of the collections in any American Indian museum quickly reveals the great wealth of design which these people had. Many of these designs are found to be graceful and ingenious. It is possible that American design may become distinctive through a study of Indian art motifs and an application of them to modern decorative purposes.

Indians loved to ornament vacant spaces with drawings of one sort or another. Their weaving, their mats, basketry, and even their pottery bore the impress of their craving for graceful line and harmonizing colors.

It must not be thought that all Indians used the same

patterns for this is far from the case. In North America there were six distinctive decorative design areas. While to some extent they slightly overlapped, it may be said as a general thing that each area presented a distinctive art.

The first area was along the north-west coast of Canada and Alaska, beginning at the mountains along the northern boundary of Canada and the United States. In this area designs were produced that could be found nowhere else. The second area took in the Pacific coast of the United States, and it adjoined the third area which embraced the Pueblo region of the deserts, and extended far into Mexico but excluding Yucatan. The fourth area was that of the Great Plains and took in the region of the western plains from the upper reaches of the tributaries of the Mississippi and extending to the Rocky mountains. The fifth area took in nearly all of Canada, save the west coast and the northern extension of the Plains area. This area, with some modification of its art forms, included the eastern and northern part of the United States, the Mississippi valley and the Great Lakes. The sixth area was that of the Southern States beginning at the Chesapeake and taking in the coast and the Gulf regions, extending westward to the heart of Texas. It is well to keep these districts in mind, for when pictures are drawn or designs applied, there should be no mixture. To decorate a drawing of a Sioux tipi, for example, with Pueblo designs and then to show a north-west coast blanket or canoe in the picture would be a travesty. It would be like drawing an English country house and covering it with Balkan designs, putting a Chinese tapestry on the door step and a Viking ship in the near-by stream.

To a large extent the application and even construction of Indian geometrical designs depended upon the material used. Basketry and cloth lent itself to geometrical de-

Figure 20

Box Designs from the Northwest Coast

signs. Likewise the use of porcupine quills and beads led to linear designs, angles, triangles and other geometrical forms. It is even thought that American Indian designs began with geometrical forms rather than realistic forms. Conventional figures came first.

Many of the most attractive patterns are to be found on baskets, and upon pottery vessels. Elaborate designs are made on sand by "dry painting" with colored earths.

The broad-lined figures of the north-west coast, in which the eye predominates, are distinctive. There is nothing in the Pueblo-Mexican area to compare with them.

On the Great Plains where solid patterns of colored quills and beads are used, the motifs are simple but applied and combined in such a manner as to be striking indeed. Parallel lines, the cross, the triangle, the lozenge, the stepped pyramid, and truncated pyramid are used in combinations of contrasted colors.

Among the eastern Indians there were designs in circles, half circles, opposed curves, parallel lines, dots and dashes. The floral pattern was used to some extent also.

The application of patterns, of course, depended upon the material decorated and the decorative agent. Pottery was painted, skins were decorated with moose hair, porcupine quills, and occasionally by painting or staining, as with the Apache. Baskets had patterns woven in, as did other textiles.

The paint brush as modern artists know it was not used by the Indians. Their "brush" was a stick wound with wool or a tanned and absorbent thong. It was a dauber rather than a brush. For drawing lines a flat bone with a porous edge was frequently used. It held the color and gave it off in the right quantity.

It is interesting to note that the Indians had specific names for their elemental designs, even when they appeared

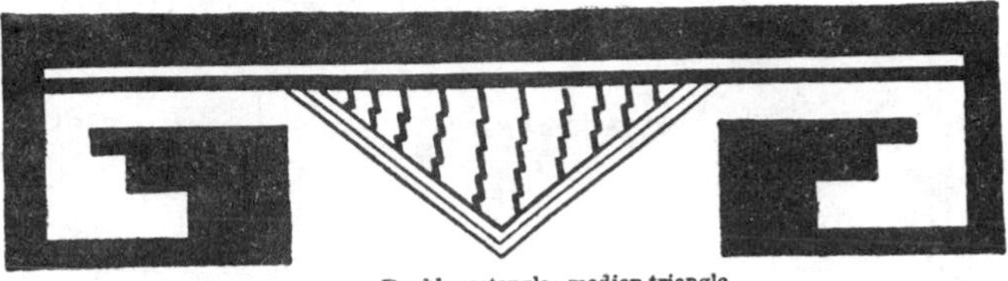

Double rectangle; median triangle

Rectangular S-form with crooks

S-form with interdigitating spurs

Simple rectangular design

Infolded triangles

FIGURE 21

Pottery Decorations from the Southwest

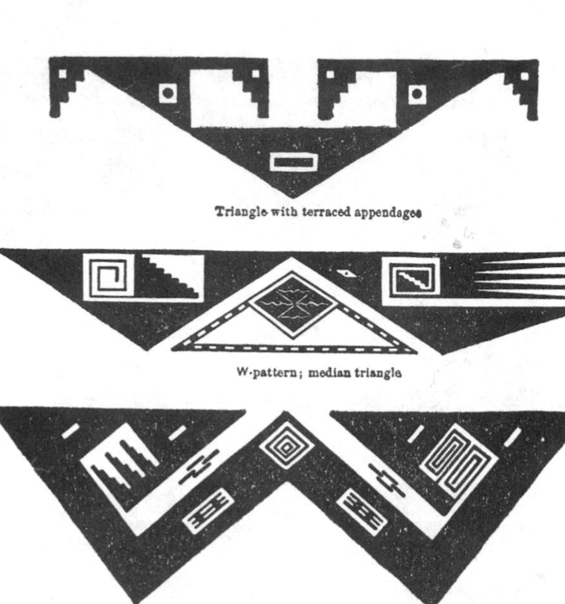

Triangle with terraced appendages

W-pattern; median triangle

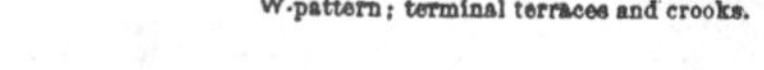

W-pattern; terminal terraces and crooks.

W-pattern; bird form

FIGURE 22

Pottery Decorations from the Southwest

somewhat complex. Among the Sioux, for example, rectangles placed in a stepped position, that is with the upper corner of one touching the lower corner of the other, was called *twisted.* A cross with two bars was called *dragon fly;* two opposite rows of right-angle triangles, points down, were called vertebræ; parallel lines were called *trails;* a line with an inverted equilateral triangle was called *leaf;* long triangles standing upon others of equal size were *feathers;* a single triangular, or rather lozenge-shaped figure with the lower part of a different color was *whirlwind;* a rectangle was bag; an inverted equilateral triangle was *point;* a stepped triangle or pyramid was *cut out;* a rectangle divided into nine rectangles of contrasting colors like a checkerboard was *tripe,* and parallel lines with small squares spaced between were called *filled.* The Navaho called the swastika *whirling logs.* Two semicircles side by side with a third above and in the center all resting on a base with lines below like a coarse comb was cloud *terrace.* This was a common Pueblo design.

II: THE INDIAN HIMSELF

II

THE INDIAN HIMSELF

XXI. HOW INDIANS COURTED

There were two kinds of courtship among the Indians; the supervised and the in-spite-of-everything kind. When girls had been given the ceremony of maidenhood, they were more closely guarded by their parents or relatives. They became less playful about the camp and clung more closely to the fireside and its duties.

At this time, too, they became more beautiful. The young man would walk through the camp or village and look at the girls and try to find one that he liked. He would not show by a movement of his eyes or face that he was "mooning" around, or that he was doing anything but simply walking about for the mere joy of living.

Sometimes the young man would associate with the father or brother and try to find an excuse for talking to the sister just in a casual way. Among the Plains people the young man was an active agent in picking his bride. Among some of the Forest area people the girl herself did the picking, though in many cases it was mutual love. The maiden was not insensible to a good youth's attention.

Among the Iroquois when a young woman had selected her mate she told her mother. The mother then tried to be especially friendly with the young man's mother. If the friendship was agreeable the girl's mother told of her daughter's desire. If all was well the young woman then cooked twenty-four double loaves of "ball biscuit" which she carried in a basket and hung at the door of the young man.

"That's a queer custom," I told my friend Cornplanter. "What happened then?"

"Oh," said he, "if the young fellow took the biscuits and ate one,—*and lived,* he was compelled to marry the girl."

Brides' biscuits, it seems, were sometimes fatal even in Indian days. Among the Crow people the young men sought a chance to go on the village berry-picking picnic, and in this way the couple had a pleasant day together. There was a custom in the spring of having a tribal herald call the young to this gathering of fruit. All the youths would then put on their best clothing, take their berry bags and stand near their tipis. The young man would then go to the girl he loved and ask if he might carry her berry bag and go on the excursion with her. If she consented, all was well, but if she refused he felt hurt and ashamed. If she handed him her bag he placed a horse at her disposal, and if he had none, they walked together to the place of the start, then at the signal they ran to the berry patch and tried to get the best branches. These were broken off, taken to a spot near-by and the two picked the fruit off together. This gave opportunity for knowing each other better.

In returning to camp when the Crow people had horses, the girl sat behind him and sang with him in the parade around the camp as the merry-makers shouted their thanksgiving for the fruit. Then the lover returned the maid to her own tipi.

Once acquainted the youth might ask the maid for permission to go with her when the family went to the foot-hills for tipi poles, and if permission were granted he would help her fell the saplings and peel them.

When the time came for marriage the youth would make his proposal, paving the way by gifts and many evenings playing upon the flute. It might be from one to five years before he gained courage and property enough to make his marriage possible. He might not have courage even then, but send some older friend or relative to make the agreement. The Indian lover was sensitive and was hurt deeply when refused.

In the old days there were *arranged* marriages. These were brought about by rich warriors with many horses or wampum who wished to marry a beautiful maiden. He would talk over the matter with her parents and promise them great riches if they would consent. Sometimes the old people would try to induce their daughter to take the elderly beau, telling her that her life would be easier and their own old age more comfortable. She might refuse, which in some tribes ended the matter, in which case the rich old fellow would have to depart. Sometimes the girl felt compelled to give her consent. In that case if she had a lover, even one who had not declared himself, she might send word to him, or he might find out in some way.

When this happened the young man would tell his near relatives and sworn friends that he intended to steal the girl and run away. They would reason with him and then gather up their wealth against his success.

Cautiously the youth would watch the maid. She might go to a spring or out after wood. She might be guarded in her tipi so that he had to pull up the pegs and draw her out, but in some way he drew her to his arms, threw her upon his swiftest pony, and then raced madly off to a distant village or to some safe retreat. The next day or a few days later he returned with his bride.

Side by side the two would ride into the town, their horses gay with bridal trappings. The groom would dash into the camp circle and cry out his marriage and defy any man to dare to say him nay. It might be that a fight would ensue, but if the friends and relatives had done their duty, word of the presents had been passed and the girl's parents were ready to receive them. If they were angry the young couple rode away and prepared for the family feud. In general, however, youth had its victory, and all ended well.

XXII. HOW INDIANS MARRIED

The idea of marriage among the Indians of America in general was that of all natural races. A man and a woman agreed that they should mate and have a home together. Both the man and the woman wanted a home and family life apart from their parents, though in many instances the young couple stayed with the parents of the one or the other.

During the courtship, the young man brought valuable presents to the family of the maiden and declared his desire to have the girl as his wife. If the father and mother or other relatives agreed, their consent, given in the usual manner, consummated the marriage.

Of course there were elopements in which the young man swooped down upon the home of the girl and carried her away like some gay young Lochinvar. A successful elopement was a marriage. A man who could declare before all men, "This is my wife!" made his marriage real in the eyes of his tribe. Like all bridegrooms he sometimes had trouble in convincing the girl's parents.

Cornplanter, the high priest of the Seneca Indians, once told me that there was a ceremony often performed in the days of the Prophet, and which the Prophet ordered as the custom that should be followed.

When the young man had accepted the girl's proposal,—it was necessary that she propose,—the time for the marriage was set. A marriage council was called in which the youth sat on one side of the fire and the maid on the other. Standing at the side of each was the sponsor. Her duty was to describe the character of the one she stood for, and charge the other to understand and help her ward through life.

It must be understood that no person could marry into his or her own clan. Marriage was always outside the clan. A Bear could not marry a Bear, but a Wolf, Turtle or some other clansperson. Thus when the marriage council was kindled the clansmen of each party assembled on opposite sides.

"Drooping Flower of the Wolves is our daughter," the matron would say. "She is fair to look upon and good. She has learned to make fine garments, she is an accomplished cook, she is faithful to the ceremonies of our Prophet, Handsome Lake. We love her. She may show temper at times, she may not think as the son of the Turtles does, she may desire things that he is unwilling to get, but if he takes her as his wife he must be kind and patient.

"And now you, O our fair daughter, you are about to take upon yourself the duties of a wife. You are to know the cares of a home. You must be faithful to the son of the Turtles, you must give him of your talents. You may find him angry at times, you may find him ill and tired from the hunt, but you must be patient. Good wives are kind and patient. I have spoken."

Then the sponsor of the youth would begin speaking. "Axe Carrier of the Turtles is our son. He is strong and brave. He has learned how to hunt and is skilled with the bow. He knows how to defend his nation as his comrades will tell. He has come back from the war trail with honors to his credit. He, too, follows the teachings of the Prophet. He takes part in the songs and dances that are pleasing to the Maker of All. We love him. He is a man.

"And now you, O Axe Carrier, you are to be a husband. Be true, be faithful, be kind, be patient. There are many occasions which will make you wish to speak harsh words. Withhold them. Depart and hunt for a day before you speak. Then return and speak pleasantly and your wife will be glad to see you. A good husband does not speak unkindly but by his industry and thougtfulness proves himself capable of being a husband and a father. I have spoken."

The two are now brought to the center near the fire and placed side by side. The bride throws her two braids over the groom's head and he gives her a bouquet.

"These two are one," intones the priest. "Let them depart with our good wishes."

The young couple among some tribes goes away on a bridal hunt and does not return for a year. In other tribes the youth goes to the home of the bride's parents and labors there for a full year, supplying the food and doing a man's share of the work. He is then at liberty to go where he will. One rule he must strictly observe, and that is never to joke with his mother-in-law! In certain tribes the two must not speak.

Heckewelder, the missionary who lived with the Lenape, says, "An Indian loves to see his wife well clothed, which is proof that he is fond of her, at least, it is so considered. The more a man does for his wife the more he is esteemed, particularly by the women, who will say, 'This man surely loves his wife.' "

The Cheyennes had elaborate courtships, some of which extended for a period of five years. By this time each family was well acquainted with the prospective mate. The young man was particularly attentive to the girl's father and brother, and did his best to prove his valor, his industry and his fitness as a husband.

In some tribes the married woman wore her hair differently after marriage than before. The Hopi girl, for instance, gave up her high disks of hair that she wound about her ears. The Iroquois woman no longer braided her hair in two plaits, but in one looped up and tied with a string or ribbon. Sometimes a small wooden tablet covered with embroidered deer hair was worn instead of the colored ribbon.

XXIII. HOW INDIANS TREATED WOMEN

There is a tradition that Indian women were misused and regarded as of little account. Travelers who have lived with Indians and who understood their ways never said this, but those who just looked into an Indian camp and saw the women busy with the tanning of their hides. The tradition has come from casual observers.

One of my friends, Jisgogo the Robin, was visiting a Yankee family back east. "You Indians should be ashamed of yourselves," said the Yankee farmer. It was Sunday and the farmer, dressed in his best, sat in the parlor with his boots on the center table. He went on, "I say you Indians should be ashamed to make your women work so hard; only savages would do that."

Outside there was the sound of wood being chopped, some one drove away a strange colt and closed the gate, there was the sound of the pump, a creaky pump. Then there was a fumbling at the kitchen door and a woman, rough shod, kicked it open and entered with an armful of wood in one arm and a pail of water in the other. Jisgogo looked at his civilized friend and gave his part of the conversation. It was the usual laconic Indian "Ugh!"

At one time I asked my old friend Chief Cornplanter what he thought about the idea that the pale faces had that Indian women were worked to death. Cornplanter smiled and replied, "I have been around a good deal,—been all over America, been in England, Germany and France. I been in homes everywhere. All the time I see women working, not men. Women sweep, wash, cook, chop wood, milk cows, work farms, clean up, work all times and it's dark and work isn't done. Then I go to big houses where men I see. What they doing? Jus' sit round at desk, smoke big black cigar, make black scratch on paper, talk, all times talk, make more scratch. Funny, those men look tired doing nothing all times. I feel sorry for those poor women working all times. Then man comes home most dead. Says, 'Where's my supper; I'm hungry. Hurry up I got go to my lodges to-night; where's my shirt?' Yes, I feel sorry white woman do all work all time. Too bad such kin' civilization."

Cornplanter did not understand that "making scratches on paper" was indeed hard work, and the stay-a-day traveler did not understand that even among Indians there is a division of labor, and that the men worked the hardest.

Indian women did their share of the work and no more; the men did their share of the work and often more. Women were treated with courtesy and given all the rights that their clan customs accorded. The work of the hunter and food-getter and of the warrior and defender of the tribe was a difficult one. His duties were heavy, his strength was taxed to the limit and his life was in constant danger.

In many tribes the women owned all the dwellings,—the tipis and wigwams. The soil was their property and might not be sold or given away without their consent. Among the Iroquois, descent was in the mother line and all children belonged to the mother. The women owned the great long houses and could order out any man who was quarrelsome, lazy or offensive. Iroquois women had the right of nominating all the civil chiefs, and the men had to elect the chiefs that the women wanted to rule over them. The men could make laws in the council, but the women could over-rule them. They could unseat the chiefs and even have them killed for not doing right. The chiefs knew this, it was in the law, and they behaved themselves or took a long trip and never came back.

So highly was an Iroquois woman regarded that when captured by the enemy it required twice the ransom to redeem her as for even the greatest chief. The women were the mothers of the race, the mothers of the future, and they were the assurance of its life. The Iroquois believed that their race could not be better than its girls and women, and for that reason they cared for them and gave them great respect.

Women worked, but it was only to do their share of the common labor required of all. Indians were not lazy for the needs of native life made it necessary for all to do a share. The women took over the household duties, the gathering of plant food and the making of clothing. The men brought in the animal food, the meat, and they did the heavy work of securing bark and poles for houses. They dug the trenches, reared the wall of the towns and then fought back the wolves, the panthers and wild men who came against them.

There are cruel men and cross women everywhere, sad to say. There were such people among the Indians too, and some men were cruel to their wives. Some women were quarrelsome and mean. They were rare because it did not pay. When a man was cruel his wife told her brothers and they gave the wicked husband a good drubbing. If he didn't do right then he was driven away and had to shift for himself without a welcome anywhere. Cross women were punished in about the same way. A scolding woman found it difficult to find a mate. It is possible that careless travelers have taken their ideas of the hard lot of the Indian woman from seeing unusual cases, or where the warrior was on his dignity. Indians had one code of behaviour in the presence of strangers, and another when among friends.

Indians, as a rule, treated their women well, and not only were polite and thoughtful toward them, but sought their advice and followed it. Only broken tribes confused by civilization acted otherwise.

XXIV. HOW INDIAN BOYS AND GIRLS WENT TO SCHOOL

Schools were not always in buildings with four walls and a roof. The first schools of all races were out of doors. The schools of the American Indians were much different than schools are to-day. Indian boys and girls did not say, "I am going to school," but they said, "I am learning to play hunting with Strong Buffalo," or they said, "I am learning to play keep house with my aunt."

Play was the Indian way. They learned real things by playing with make believe things. Education was a game, but even a game has its set rules.

In the first place the old Indians explained to their children that they must learn how to live. If a person did not learn that he would have bad luck all his life. Who wanted bad luck? Not any little red boy or girl. To live and have good fortune meant that each child must know how to live according to the rules of the game of life.

"Fire will hurt you; keep away from fire, for there is a demon in it," said the mother.

"Don't believe it," answered the naughty child, and straightway went to the fireplace to pick up an ember or hot stone.

The mother would see her child do this, but she would

not cry, "Don't do that!" She let the child pick up the stone and get burned.

"Ug-yaw!" screamed the little one, dropping the hot stone. "The demon bit me!"

Learning came by experience. If the danger was too great the mother snatched her child from it and then showed what would happen. No mother was too busy to help a child understand life's problems.

Children were taught not to yell for things. Crying was never rewarded. Just as soon as a child could talk it was shown that a polite request secured more than a wailing demand. Parents, too, knew that a child's desires were not foolish things to be laughed at. Indian parents granted every request possible, even some that did not seem reasonable. The child's own experience proved whether the thing were wise or not. Of course both child and parent had to abide by the rules of the game of life, and there were indeed things that must not be asked for or granted. The *taboos* must not be violated. Taboos are things that one must not do for fear of offending the manitos or unseen powers.

As a boy or girl grew and was able to run about the Indian village, some uncle or aunt assumed the rôle of principal teacher. In most cases, however, the mother and her clan sisters taught the girl right in the wigwam.

Girls were given toys, such as dolls, tiny dishes, little outfits for making baskets, and lumps of clay for making toy pots and cups. Playing with these things in the wigwam or tipi taught the lesson of order, neatness and system. Each child had a place in which to play and a place in which to put its playthings. A disorderly boy or girl had its toys swept out into the garbage hole. It was a long time before any similar toys were made for it.

Boys went with their uncles and learned from their

stories how hunting was done. To go on a hunt was one of the great desires of every boy, but before he was allowed to go he had to prove that he could shoot straight. Thus every boy was willing to take lessons in all the things that related to hunting. Among the Iroquois the first lessons were with a tiny bow, and only boys who would not shoot at other people were allowed to have bows and arrows. At first they shot at marks. The first was a bear's paw hanging by a thong. When living creatures were hunted the boy first killed a chickadee. When he was clever enough to hit one of these little birds he was allowed to hunt a squirrel or a rabbit. This done, he hunted grouse or turkey. After that he could be taken on a trial hunt for deer or beaver. Thus there were five grades in hunting; the bear paw kindergarten, the first shot chickadee, the second running rabbit, the third flying partridge and the fourth bounding deer. It was like a big game and the boys all liked it.

A great many other lessons were learned in these "grades." Each had its portion of the crafts to learn. There was hunting for bow-wood, arrow-wood, thongs, the art of making cords, fire-making, arrow-point making, wood carving, skinning animals, making pelts, tanning, tracking, stalking, canoe making, wood chopping, camp making, cooking, food getting, and all the rest.

Boys were taught politeness. One of the first things a boy or girl learned was how to behave. An ill-bred person was considered unfit to associate with. Once shunned by his playmates the offender felt the sting. When he would approach them they would say in Indian, as I have recently heard them say in reservation English, "What kind boy you? Don't you know anything?" The rebuke of playmates is a sharper sting than that of elders.

Indian boys were taught how to talk. They learned little speeches, and spoke them. They went with their parents to the councils and heard the great tribal orators and then sought to imitate them.

Some tribes had boy societies, something like the Boy Scouts. They were organized into companies and became friendly rivals. They tried to outmatch each other. In due time they would have a battle with cornstalk spears and soft-nosed arrows. Indeed, the battle of the boys' bands was something like a graduation exercise, only a bit more exciting. In this manner, boys showed what kind of warriors they would make.

In this school of nature play was the important thing. The young played the game of life, and gradually moved from play to reality. This was done by the problem method. The teachers of the youths would outline a problem. For instance, old Uncle Hemlock would say to his company of boys, "To-day we gather at the council rock down by the river. There you are to take off all your clothes and run to the first trail house near the ford. You are to stay there, make a fire, gather material for clothing, kill a deer or beaver, make some moccasins, and bring back fishes enough for the house of the Clan of the Wolf. If you do not do it I will send the Black Bear band after you and they will have weapons and make war upon you. We are ready; come on, go!"

Off the boys would go, running until they reached the trail house. This was an open camp provided for travelers. Here they would remove their clothing, scour the woods for bark from which to make fringed skirts, they would make crude bows and arrows, hunt animals until they had pelts enough for moccasins, and then having made a fire by the bow and spindle method, they would make fishhooks and proceed to catch a mess of fish. Back they would march, and proudly too, and as they entered the town they would be cheered by their friends, but the boy troop of Black Bears would just grunt, "Aw, it took you longer than it took us." The response would come, "Go try it again!"

The natural education of the Indian boys and girls was a simple method of teaching the young how to live life successfully and well, just as their fathers and mothers had done it. The entire training was done without the use of the whip, the rod or striking by hand. The only physical punishment was by throwing water on the child, or by plunging him into it. Indians did not whip their children.

Indian boys and girls went to the school of life and in it learned from the taskmaster of Experience how to live.

XXV. HOW INDIANS WALKED

A natural people who depended upon nimble feet knew how to walk. The stiff-soled shoe and the styles of the generation have altered our way of walking. We come down with a jar upon our heels, then rock our feet to our toes, thrust the other foot forward and come down upon the heel again. We also turn our feet outward in such a manner that the direction of our movement passes through the middle of our foot, instead of from toe to heel. We toe out. Stiff soles, heel thumping and toeing out injure many feet, and fallen arches result.

Indians directed their feet straight ahead. The body followed the direction of the foot,—straight ahead. Moccasins were worn, which allowed the foot to keep its natural shape. Indians had no corns or injured toe joints. Contrary to the idea that the foot in a loose covering grows large, the Indian's foot was small. The moccasin did not cause it to flatten out. On the other hand, the moccasin favored good blood circulation and strong, hard foot muscles. There were no fallen arches.

In walking with the foot straight ahead there was less fatigue. In walking up a steep hill Indians turned their toes in. This permitted them to grip the ground with the forward and outside of the foot, and prevented slipping.

Moccasins kept the Indian "on his toes" a good deal of the time. He kept a springy feeling. In ordinary walking the heel was not thumped down first, but the ball of the foot, or, occasionally the whole foot, planked flat upon the ground.

Our present day military step is a fatiguing one and in the long run injures the bones of the feet. A good many hikers are trying the Indian way with great success.

During the Civil War, General Grant had on his staff a Seneca Indian who was a Colonel in charge of military engineering. Later he was made Grant's military secretary, but during this Indian's career as engineer there were many forced marches through the Wilderness. The men in one of the brigades became foot weary and were falling out rapidly. The Indian went to Grant and said that he could carry the men through without further fatigue. "Take command," said Grant. The Indian in taking command ordered every man to toe in and march ahead. When they were rested he had them walk with the feet straight ahead instead of at an angle of forty-five degrees or thereabouts. Completely restored, the men went forward and joined the reënforcements.

XXVI. HOW INDIANS BATHED

Most of the Indian tribes who lived in the great forest areas believed in taking frequent baths. Early travelers even tell of instances in which certain ones bathed themselves to death,—but that, of course, was an unusual thing. Bathing never exterminated Indians any more than modern boys.

In many tribes a baby was given a bath as soon as

born, and if the babe were a boy he had a bath every day, rain or shine, summer or winter. The Iroquois were great believers in bathing as a means of securing a strong body.

The most natural bath with almost any people is the "rain bath," and it does not require a tub or a pond. The Indian boy simply stripped and danced around in the rain. Sometimes the boys ran races together, especially when the rain was cold, so as to keep warm. If the rain happened to be warm, as it is in summer, they just sat around in it until they were satisfied, and then went inside their lodges and dried themselves.

The "tall-grass-and-branch" bath was another form of the plain rain bath. It was taken by running through the tall, wet grass during a storm. When there were two or more boys, they took turns switching each other with leafy branches. It was a sort of "tag" game in which one tagged the other by switching him with a wet branch.

Of course, a regular bath consisted of a swim in a creek or convenient lake. Here the boys sported as long as they liked in summer. In winter they merely jumped through a hole in the ice, and then chattered out, exclaiming, "Ah-tcoo, o-to-weh!" The boys who were hardened never even shivered, nor did they chatter, as some of the little fellows did. I have seen some of these older boys playing almost naked in the snow in winter, even when the thermometer was dangerously low.

Another favorite bath was "the mud-smear and wallow." Boys would find a good mud-hole where they would proceed to cover themselves and each other with mud or clay. They would lie in the sun until the mud baked on, making them perspire. Then they would pull off the mud or clay in cakes and jump in a cooling brook, after which they would rub themselves with oil.

A real oil bath, however, was quite another thing. It was given warriors and runners by the medicine man, who smeared them with oil so hot that it almost burned. It was rubbed on and all the muscles were kneaded and slapped. Then the oil was mopped off with moss and the victim given a sweat.

When a hunter prepared for a real hunt, in which by his wits he had to stalk game, he took a sweat, drank purges and emetics and then bathed in water into which certain boiled leaves had been mixed. Oftentimes hunters used a solution of sweet fern. All this precaution was taken to make the body clean, and to remove any human odor. The sweet fern gave a woodsy perfume which was supposed to deceive the animals, who are quick to detect a hunter even at a distance. Thus, you see, even the Indians had their "toilet waters."

Contrasted to the snow rub, which every Indian boy of the northlands was expected to take during winter, was the sweat bath. This was an operation requiring time and skill. A dome-shaped tent, about four feet high, was erected by bending over small poles until a frame about six feet in diameter was formed. Over this were flung mats, blankets, thatch grass, and in fact anything that would cover the structure. Some permanent "sweat houses" were built of bark.

In the center of the sweat house was a little pit about three spans wide and a span deep. There was also a bark bucket of water and a bark dipper.

Outside a roaring fire was built and into it some ten to twenty round stones were placed. These stones were cautiously selected with an eye to the kind that would not chip and splinter with the heat. As the stones were heated they were hooked inside the lodge by means of a crooked stick and then deposited in the central pit. This done, the door was closed.

Then began the ordeal; I know because I have taken these sweat baths many times in my youth. The air in the lodge was hot and stifling from the stones, some of which glowed red in an evil way. The naked bather edged as far away as possible, and I always stuck my nose on the ground.

Still this was not the bath, though sweat rolled down. The next process was to take a dipper of water and pour it upon the stones.

Instantly there was a hissing cloud of steam that quite filled the sweat lodge and condensed on the bather's body. Then came the second splash of water on the stones, then more and more. The air became saturated with steam and breathing became difficult. The most tiny crack in the lodge was sought for as a possible source of refreshing air,—but meanwhile the whole body streamed with perspiration.

Outside the medicine man sang his songs of incantation, inviting evil spirits and disease, fatigue and poison, to leave the body. (As if the body were not giving up all it could!) When the bather could no longer endure the heat and the sweating process, he burst forth from the house of torment and dashed for the creek or pond, a few feet away. In he plunged, and came out immediately, to roll up in a warm blanket and sleep for a couple of hours. Sometimes the water was too cold, and unhealthful complications set in.

Two sweat baths in a season are enough even for Indians, but sometimes they took so many that they weakened and died. The over-indulgence was not for cleanliness so much as to drive out demons.

Often, after the sweat bath, hot teas made from sassafras or wintergreen were taken. Sometimes a drink made from hemlock tips was used, for the sudden closing of the pores required something to open them again.

In regions where water was scarce Indian tribes seldom knew what a bath was. Perhaps to them bathing was not so necessary. They exposed their bodies to the elements, perspired freely and rubbed away any dirt with sand. Indeed, to a large extent everywhere, sand and ashes formed the Indians' "soap."

XXVII. HOW INDIANS SMELLED

Every race has its own peculiar scent.* Each person has his own odor, and any trained bloodhound can quickly trace him by getting a clew from a shoe or a garment. But beyond this there is also a racial odor.

The Chinese say they can detect a white man when he comes into the house, and the white man says he can tell the smell of the Oriental. Neither professes to like the smell of the other. It may be that racial smells have a great deal to do with racial likes and dislikes for one another. It may be also that we are scarcely aware that it is the smell that affects us.

The smell of the American Indians, like the racial odor of other races as the African, the Hindu, the Berber and the English, has sometimes been remarked upon. What is this smell and is it disagreeable?

Before answering, let it be said that in certain areas the racial odors may be modified somewhat by the food eaten and by the manner of living, but that even these modifications do not destroy the inherent body scent. The fish-eating Indian of the North-West coast had his oily smell, the Mexican native had his, but when each is "deodorized" of externals the racial smell again crops out.

Travelers and explorers do not find it disagreeable for it seems to resemble the faint odor of cooking hominy, especially if made from lye-hulled corn. It is not the heavy animal, or musky smell that some other races have.

*This is no longer scientifically accepted as true.—Publisher, 1975.

This may be due to the fact that the scent glands are but feebly developed and that there is little hair about them, as under the arms. The Indian therefore is as scentless and hairless so far as the body is concerned as any race of which we know. This is so far true that some Indians say that they can tell a half-blood by his different smell.

During the World War an officer wrote of his experience in the front line trenches, wherein he dodged into a dark dugout just before a violent bombardment. He sniffed and then decided that there were Indians in the retreat. When the lights were turned on he saw a squad of Indians which verified his surmise. From this story there grew a belief in many quarters that his reference to "smell" meant an unpleasant odor. Some persons going to the Indian country were warned to take along perfumes to cover up the Indian smells. Some actually did this but found no use for them for no especial odor was ever evident.

XXVIII. HOW INDIANS CUT THEIR HAIR

Nearly every Indian tribe, especially those that were well organized, paid particular attention to having the hair neatly trimmed. There were three general reasons why the hair was cut. First there was the reason of convenience and cleanliness. Long hair became tangled and dirty; it was not easy to care for. Second, it became a custom for tribes to adopt special types of hair dressing, whereby they might be known and distinguished. Third, in special instances the manner in which the hair was cut became a symbol of some belief or superstition in magical power.

As a rule the northern Indians, except those, perhaps, on the Pacific coast, had little hair on the face and almost none on the body. Some did raise sparse beards and mustaches, but as a rule the hair of the face, sometimes even to the eyebrows, was removed.

There were three general methods of removing hair. In ordinary practice any one might be used, but because of certain religious beliefs one way was sometimes used to the exclusion of others.

The first, and perhaps most natural way to remove hair, was to pull it out. It was a severe test of a warrior's courage to have his excess hair pulled out one hair at a time, but it was not half as bad as to have it yanked out by the fistful. Just how it did feel was told me by my Wichita interpreter. He had been courting two sisters and could not decide which he liked the best, as both were tall, powerful women who could work in the fields and cook in the lodge with great excellence. For many moons he had tested their cooking, until at last they grew weary with suspense. Finally they decided that the young man had wanted food more than he had wanted a wife. This was wrong; the man was not a natural warrior. It must be his hair that was to blame; it was not cut in proper style.

With this belief, when the youth had called one evening and proposed to each maiden with equal ardor, both girls rushed upon him and knocked him down. Then they literally sat upon him. One cushioned herself upon his thighs where she could pummel his stomach and the other sat upon his chest, from which vantage point she began to pluck out his hairs one by one, calling upon him to be brave like his ancestors and not wince at having his hair cut in ancient style. When all was finished he looked like a warrior indeed, and he had blood in his eye. All ardor had left his heart and he turned his back on the maidens who had so kindly trimmed him. "It hurt most mightily awful," he said. And his remark explains how every warrior felt when his hair was plucked out. Some have said, however, that when the custom is kept up from childhood, the nerves become accustomed to the shock and little pain is experienced.

For plucking out hair the Indians had tweezers of wood or pinchers made by the shell of a fresh-water mussel, which had a natural spring hinge. This was easily held in the hand and its sharp lips would cut into the hair at its roots so that it was easily "gnawed off."

True cutting, or rather shaving, was done by means of flint or obsidian (volcanic glass) knives and razors. These were long flakes chipped from a cylindrical core. They were very sharp and cut with great efficiency. The obsidian razors of the Mexicans were particularly useful, and as many as twenty to forty might be struck from one cylinder. They had the advantage of having a rustless edge. Those that have been found cut as well to-day as when originally made. When they became dulled through use (by having the edge nicked and smoothed by the hair) they could not be resharpened, but were thrown away or reworked into small arrowheads.

Another method requiring greater skill was sometimes employed. This was burning the hair from the head by use of tapers or hot stones. The eastern woodland Indians often used this way of getting their hair "cut."

The singeing process was aided by the use of a comb, much as it is by modern barbers. The comb was shoved under the hair and the taper applied. The singeing-stones were long flat pieces of rock that would not explode when heated to a dull red. The cool end was wrapped in a piece of skin and the hot end rubbed over the hair. Where the hair was long it was grasped, held upright and the stone applied as near the roots as was comfortable.

After cutting or singeing hair, the scalp was rubbed with oils and even perfumes. Bear oil was the standard hair dressing in many localities, though buffalo fat, sunflower oil, and deer tallow were not despised.

XXIX. HOW INDIANS PAINTED THEIR FACES

Indians painted their faces, as every one knows who has read of the "wild and painted savage." Just how wild or how savage they were is a matter of debate with some authorities, but all seem to agree that Indians used considerable paint.

Painting the face with the red man was not an idle thing and done without rime or reason. The painter knew why he painted and knew just how to do it correctly. First, when he painted, he did it for one certain thing which he hoped would have four effects, the first to please the unseen spirits and secure their powerful aid; second, to frighten evil spirits and enemies; third, to make his tribe see that he was mindful of the mystic art, and fourth, to please his own sense of the fitness of things. Painting was a means of magic,—that was all, and the Indian wanted to be powerful, but if not, to look so.

Every dance and lodge among some tribes had its own style of painting the face with certain marks or symbols. Warrior associations had their symbols and so did chiefs and leaders. The face was even painted in honor of spirits to ward off sickness and in obedience to dreams.

"As I was once resting in my travels at the house of a trader who lived at some distance from an Indian town," wrote Heckewelder, the missionary, "I went in the morning to visit an Indian acquaintance and friend of mine. I found him engaged in plucking out his beard preparatory to painting himself for a dance which was to take place the ensuing evening. Having finished his headdress, about an hour before sunset, he came up, as he said, to see me, but I and my companions judged that *he came to be seen.* To my utter astonishment I saw three different paintings or figures on one and the same face. He had by his great ingenuity and judgment in laying on and shading the different colors, made his nose appear, when we stood directly in front of him, as if it were very long and narrow, with a round knob at the end, much like the upper part of a pair of tongs. On one cheek there was a red round spot about the size of an apple, and the other was done in the same manner with black. The eyelids, both the upper and lower ones, were reversed in the coloring. When we viewed him in profile on one side, his nose represented the beak of an eagle, with the bill rounded and brought to a point, precisely as those birds have it, though the mouth was somewhat open. The eye was astonishingly well done, and the head upon the whole appeared tolerably well, showing a great deal of fierceness. When we turned round to the other side, the same nose now resembled the snout of a pike, with the mouth open, that the teeth could be seen. He seemed much pleased with his execution, and, having his looking-glass with him, he contemplated his work seemingly with great pride."

In painting the face the Indians gave colors different values and meanings. *Black,* for example, usually meant death; *red,* power and success, also war; *blue,* defeat, trouble; *yellow,* joy, travel, bravery. In applying the designs color symbolism was kept in mind. Naturally there was a variation among different tribes, but it must be said that colors do have a natural suggestion as to meaning. *White* means peace, just as *red* means war, and *black* betokens death.

When candidates were initiated into the Mide Wiwin, or Great Medicine Lodge, of the Ojibwa, their faces were painted as follows: First degree, a broad band of green across the forehead and a narrow stripe of vermilion across the face just below the eyes; second degree, a narrow strip of vermilion across the temples, the eyelids and the root of the nose. Above each line thus put on a stripe of green was painted and above the green another stripe of vermilion. Third degree, red and white spots are spotted all over the face, each being as large as can be made by the finger tips in applying the colors. Fourth degree, the face was painted vermilion with a stripe of green extending diagonally across it from the upper part of the left temple to the lower part of the right cheek; or, as an alternate, the face was painted red with two short, horizontal parallel bars of green across the forehead.

Among the Iroquois those who dance in honor of the Great Sky Eagle paint each cheek with a spot of vermilion as large as an apple; those who dance the Bear Dance paint the right cheek black, while war dancers paint four red streaks on either cheek. To paint four lightning streaks upon the face, radiating from the eyes and running down the cheeks, meant that great power had been invoked from the Thunder god, and that a ceremony had given the right. This and painting lines in groups of four upon the forehead, cheeks and chin were common Iroquois designs.

Totemic animals were often painted on the face, as the Thunder-bird, otter, wolf and eagle. The North-West coast people had a whole system of totemic painting, and to make it permanent they tattooed the design into the skin.

The chest was painted with animal totems and even snakes. One striking Omaha design is a series of bars, calumets and pipe-stems. The arms were streaked with colored bands or with the jagged design of lightning. This was one of the designs of the Pueblo dancers. Sometimes each side of the body and face was painted with a different color as a background for other decorations, these, perhaps, being lines on one side and spots or circles on the other.

Since paint had a sacred or magical meaning, it was carefully kept in special bags. When needed it was put in a paint saucer and mixed with the proper grease. The face or body had been rubbed with tallow or lard before, so that when the paint was applied it lay smoothly and in well-defined lines. The Indians learned by experience that if used with grease the paint was not apt to be so irritating to the skin.

On one of our reservation rambles Jisgogo and myself were given a demonstration of how to paint our faces by our old friend Tahadondeh. He told how doomed captives had their faces painted black, how a fierce warrior painted his face both black and red on opposite sides, and how the eyes should have red circles around them when an enemy was to be detected afar. "But the best thing," said he, "is to cut four long gashes in the back of the neck and then keep them open with scalp grease. Then the scars will bulge out in white ridges."

We allowed that we did not wish to try that form of decoration.

"But it isn't decoration," he protested. "It detects the enemy when he follows behind you. When he does that the scars begin to twitch and tremble; then you know he is somewhere around and can prepare to meet him."

This brings up a totally different subject, however,—that of scarification. It is enough to speak of painting for it was less painful.

HOW INDIAN WOMEN PAINTED

Indian women painted their faces. The object was not to improve their complexions or to conceal them, but to decorate and reveal them. They even painted the part in their hair.

The art of compounding face paints was an old one with the Indian women, and they painted as often for purely ceremonial reasons as for ornament. Their idea was to have the paint seen and recognized as such for its own sake. Many of their paints were contained in neat little cases or bags, and some were put in hollowed-out bear tusks ornamented with a large pearl, as with the Hopewell people of Ohio.

The favorite paint was red iron oxide, a natural iron rust. Many times hematite was used. These red pigments were ground in small mortars and mixed with certain greases, so that they would smear easily. Black paint was made from charcoal and white paint from ground gypsum or powdered shells. Yellow paint was made from clay. Other paints were green and blue.

Women painted their faces in accordance with the rituals of their religions or their secret societies. In many instances it was applied by a second person, for mirrors were uncommon. The surface of a spring came nearest to one. There were instances where the paint was applied after singing certain songs, and in other cases before entering certain lodges or religious ceremonies.

The favorite designs were round dots, lines and large red spots on the cheeks or forehead. It was not often that the women used totemic signs like the men.

Paint was sometimes regarded as a sacred thing and kept in sacred packs or bundles so that its power would remain unspoiled. This was the case among the Iroquois, for example, who sang songs of magic over the paint, and kept it free from evil influences.

The Iroquois women also had a face powder which they regarded very highly. It was soft and fluffy and had a pleasant smell. It was used on the bodies of adults and children much as talcum powder is to-day. It was an absorbent. This powder was prepared from the red, dry-rot of the heart wood of the pine. This material comes in chunks and is easily crumbled and reduced to a powder. To make it heavy some iron oxide was put with it.

It will be observed that in the use of this powder the women wished to powder themselves a reddish hue, and not white. Their idea of a beautiful complexion was to have it red, the color which the sun gives to those whose bodies are lifted to the healing rays of the light that shines from the sky world.

The common "talcum powder" used by some of the eastern Indians was finely powdered Indian corn. Indian corn, such as was used for food, is white and soft. The meal was sometimes parched before being put on the body. This was the powder used on babies to stop chafing and to heal sore spots, due to rubbing.

Black paint was only put on to denote mourning or great distress. Sometimes after the death of their children these Indian women painted themselves black and allowed the pigment to stay on until it had worn away.

The part in the hair was painted red or yellow, and the use of paint in this way was sometimes thought a means of attracting the gaze of strange men. It was considered a vain thing to do and was condemned by Handsome Lake, the Seneca prophet.

XXX. HOW INDIANS GAVE THEIR GREETINGS

Naturally the Indians had their words of greeting for friends and strangers. They said "How do you do?" and "Halloo" in their style, just as we say it in our style.

On the great plains most of the Indians use the exclamation "How!" as a greeting. It may be a variation of the Yankee "Howdy!" or it may come from the Indian word *Hau,* meaning "good." At any rate, all the plains Indians will recognize a greeting by this word, especially if one says "How kola!" *Kola* means friend.

Up on the west coast where the Chinook winds blow and the Chinook jargon is spoken all the Indians understand *Kla-how-ya* as a greeting. Many of the tribes of Washington, Idaho and British Columbia will open up their hearts to a friendly stranger who can say, "Kla-how-ya tilli-kum!" *Tilli-kum* also means friend.

In the land of the Iroquois, and indeed in most of the eastern forest area, the Indians in calling out a general greeting said "Kou-e," a word that is pronounced something like quay. It is also a signal call used to attract attention. For instance, an Indian at a ford calls over the river to the ferryman in order to have him cross with the canoe. "Kou-ēē," calls the traveler, and the ferryman calls back "Ha-oh, I'm coming!"

The Iroquois, however, have a much better term of greeting as when they say, "Nyah-weh Ska-noh!" meaning, "I thank thee to know that thou art strong." Sometimes only the last part of the word is used. "Ska-noh," says the Indian, and it is just as if one of us to-day had said, *"More power to you."* The answer then is "Do-ges!" meaning *truly.* Then a return question is given in the expression, "Ska-noh nai?" meaning *art thou strong?*

Even these people use the word friend and to be polite one must say, "Nyah-weh ska-noh, gayah-da-sey." The last word means *friend,* but it really means new body. It is a wonderful thought, isn't it, that a friend is one who never becomes stale to one, but ever remains new, fresh, bloom-like and charming? Thus with the Iroquois, especially the Nunda Waga, a *friend* is one who is continually renewed.

The Oneida people, who are Iroquois, too, have a greeting all their own. It is "Se-go-li!"

Some years ago a well-known man, now passed away, wanted to be friendly with the Indians and so he drove very far from his home to visit the nearest reservation. Reaching it, he tied his horse and wandered through the Indian village. He had not gone far when one of the villagers approached him and shook his hand.

"Se-go-li!" exclaimed the Indian, clapping his hand on the visitor's shoulder. "I see you come visit us. Good, go round see all kinds things. You good frien', that's what I think."

The visitor was delighted at this display of friendliness and passed down the road, where he met another smiling red man. "Ah!" exclaimed the second Indian, "se-go-li, I see you come see us. Good! We frien's!"

Thus, everywhere the visitor went he received the greeting se-go-li, and it made him so happy that when he returned to his home he wrote a story saying that the Indians had named him immediately, and that all had recognized him no matter where he went and called out his name, "Se-go-li!"

When an Indian, therefore, calls out a cheery "Good morning," one must not think for a moment that this is the bestowal of a name.

XXXI. HOW INDIANS TALKED

"Soft words must come over smooth teeth, but the words of an orator must flow from the tongue of a panther who has lapped from a pot of oil." So says the red man, and in his saying is revealed some of the imagery of the Indian mind.

The Indian thinks of things in terms of pictures. He sees an image, or a similarity of what he wants to say and then he talks about the image rather than the reality. For this reason his speeches are full of metaphors and comparisons. "My heart is a frightened frog in the depths of a mud hole," he says when he is cornered unprepared. Note the subtle comparison of the fluttering heart to a cold, clammy, shivering frog in the darksome waters of a muddy pool.

Then, too, the Indian thinks of things in terms of song. He has a song about almost everything he does. He has a song of war, a song of peace, a thanksgiving song, a dance song, a planting-time song, a song that is a lullaby for babes, a song of wooing, and a chant of hate. And, in order to sing to the chug of a rattle or the tap of a drum, the song must be rhythmic. It is an innate sense of rhythm that makes many Indian speeches exceedingly smooth and expressive.

Indians ponder much upon the wonders of nature, they think of the sky with its ever-shifting, fleeting clouds, they dream over the changing lights and shades, the glow of color at dawn and at sunset, and they watch with eager eyes the twinkling of the stars. To them it is all very wonderful, and so they search the sky for some solution to its mysteries.

To them Earth is the Great Mother, the Sun is the Father of life, the Moon is Grandmother, the stars are celestial souls that shine to guide earthly wayfarers, to inspire and protect mankind. Little wonder, then, that the Indian expresses his awe of nature in everything he says.

To talk the Indian way one must think as the Indian thought,—not in words but in terms of comparison, in fitting pictures, and with a real love for the world of nature. Only one who felt the tingle of life, fresh blown from the lips of the Mighty Manitou, could sing as the red man did of the moon:

The baby moon, a canoe,—a papoose canoe, sails and sails in the Indian West.

A ring of silver foxes, a mist of silver foxes, sit and sit around the Indian moon.

One yellow star for a runner, and rows of blue stars for more runners keep a line of watchers.

O foxes, baby moon, runners,—you are the panel of memory, fire-white, writing to-night of Red Man's dreams.[1]

The Indians think much of their religious rites and ceremonies. These are chanted in rhythm or sung. Every Indian tribe has a background of numerous rituals. These affect the speech of the people in everyday life and Indians who cling to their own customs and ways of thinking retain much of their native poetry. This perhaps does not reflect itself when they speak English or another European tongue, but if their own speeches are translated we retain the original charm, though it is somewhat impaired. "I think one way,—my way," said Chief Cornplanter, "but when I talk my thoughts in English, it is like passing a flower over the fire to you. What I think wilts, and the flower has lost its perfume."

The stilted, broken English of the agency Indian is not that of his own tongue as spoken in the lodges of the warriors. Many Indians actually practiced their speeches, saying them over and over, and polishing each expression until it was well rounded, had rhythm and flowed from the tongue as the singing waters of the brook.

But added to the imagery was a cold and certain logic, and oftentimes a bitter sarcasm. Red Jacket, in answering the missionaries who came to convert his people to Christianity, thus replied:

"The Great Spirit has made us all but he has made a great difference between his white and his red children. He has

[1] "The Path on the Rainbow," by George W. Cronyn. Boni, 1918.

given us different complexions and different customs. To you he has given the arts. To these he has not opened our eyes. We know these things to be true. Since he has made so great a difference between us in other things, why may we not conclude that he has given us a different religion according to our understanding? The Great Spirit does right. He knows what is best for his children. We are satisfied."

At another time, in reply to the importunities of Rev. Alexander, he replied:

"Brother: We do not worship the Great Spirit as the white men do, but we believe that forms of worship are indifferent to the Great Spirit,—it is the offering of a sincere heart that pleases him, and we worship him in this manner."

These statements reveal the natural logic of the Indian mind in argument. In another strain is the reply of Garangula, the Onondaga chief, to De la Barre, who came to invade the Iroquois country and would have done so but for the illness of his troops. In reply to the French governor's speech, Garangula said:

"Yonondio, you must have believed when you left Quebec that the sun had burnt up all the forests which render our country inaccessible to the French, or that the lakes had so far overflown their banks, that they had surrounded our castles, and that it was impossible for us to get out of them. Yes, truly, you must have dreamed so, and the curiosity of seeing so great a wonder has brought you so far. Now you are undeceived, since I and the warriors here present are come to assure you that the Seneca, Cayuga, Onondaga, Oneida and Mohawk, are yet alive.

"Yonondio, I do not sleep. I have my eyes open, and the sun which enlightens me discovers to me a great captain at the head of a company of soldiers who speaks as if he were dreaming!"

To talk the "Indian way," one must not follow the rhythm of Longfellow's "Hiawatha," which is not exactly Indian rhythm at all, but rather one must study the texts of the Indian rituals, like that of the Pawnee *Hako,* the Navaho *Night Chant,* or the songs of the Hopi. Other examples might be the songs of the Haida, collected by Frans Boaz and John R. Swanton. The rituals of the Omaha and Osage, collated by Alice Fletcher and Francis LaFlesche, may also be studied. All these citations may be found in the numerous volumes of the Bureau of Ethnology, to be found in most libraries.

In the end it will be discovered that to talk "the Indian way" one must have an imagination clarified,—or shall we say, *mystified,* by nature, must think in terms of pictures and comparisons, must develop a terse expression of logical argument, and must know how to cover stinging words with a coat of nectar. At the same time there must be no affectation, no flowery language and nothing complex. The auditor must hear and understand and picture in his mind what you have meant that he should.

XXXII. HOW INDIANS CRACKED THEIR JOKES

Travelers and historians have written many vivid pages describing how the melancholy red man of the forest's darksome shade reflected his surroundings by expressing himself in terms of dignity or sullen taciturnity. That the Indian was solemn in mien and never saw the humorous side of life has become almost a tradition.

And yet what are the facts? Did the Indian ever joke, tell funny stories, play tricks, engage in humorous pranks, and roar himself sick over a funny situation? Who says he did not? The only writers who ever said such things are those who never knew the joy-loving red man. Indeed, the Indians did joke, and the forest more often rang with their laughter than it did with their war whoops.

Every wanderer who ever lived with the Indians for any time whatever soon saw that, far from being unmindful of humor, the first Americans reveled in jokes, and played pranks of the liveliest sort. As many a red man has explained to me, however, Indians know that it is well to conceal all emotions in the presence of strangers and to wear the face of inscrutability.

Most Indian jokes are based upon puns, upon gross exaggerations and odd comparisons, as well as humorous situations. They had a keen sense of the ludicrous. Oftentimes they cracked their jokes with straight faces, but as often they wreathed their faces in smiles and burst out into uproarious laughter. Many times I have heard an entire company of Indians laughing for hours at a time, and as I listened I found it clean, decent humor, and very contagious.

We can scarcely give many examples of Indian puns, because the Indian languages are not familiar to us, but other examples will be quickly understood, as the stories that follow will reveal.

A certain well-known ethnologist was once trying to find out what Chief Edward Cornplanter thought of his people and directed a number of difficult questions. Cornplanter at first answered truthfully, and to the best of his ability, and then he began to see that he might have some fun.

"And now tell me, Chief," inquired the ethnologist, "how it happened that the Indians became reduced in numbers. No, no, do not tell it the way the missionaries have explained to you, or as you have read. Rather tell me what you, yourself, think."

Cornplanter looked at the scientist, who mopped his

hairless head, and then without a smile began to expound. "Very long ago," began the Chief, "oh, 'bout hundred years ago, maybe more,—don't know,—anyway about the time white folks began to get thick in my country, they began to shoot us peoples. Yes, kill us, shoot us, kill womens, kill childrens, everythings kill 'em. Ho hoh! Then Frenchmens they sell scalping knives and white folks scalp Indians, all time scalp Indians. We getting killed every day. By and by we began to think maybe so we get all killed off this earth, so we went on war path and killed 'em white mans good deal of 'em, and we scalp more than Frenchmans, Englishmans, Yankees all together. By and by we get so many scalps that every time we kill 'em white mans we think got to take 'em scalp. Ho hoh, lots fighting those times! Pretty soon white mans thinks we beat unless they do somethings.

"Now white man smart, oh, ver' smart. By and by he send big army against us, every man he's wear big hat. We fight, we kill 'em, and we beat 'em. White mans soldiers he run, you bet ya'. Then we go take 'em scalp. Ho hoh! Every one of 'em white mans he's bald head. Ho hoh! Now we know white man he's sma't. So then we know we's beat,—we's licked, you bet ya! So we can't go back to tell folks we beat, because they would ask 'Where's scalps?'

"So we can't go back and we can't fight no more. What should we do? No use, we see it. So all our warriors jump in Niagara Falls,—white mans he's too sma't, Indian beat, might's well give up. Bald head he's no scalp,—we give up!"

When the first missionaries came to Onondaga they sought to instruct the Indians in the religion of Europeans. One minister thought it wise to begin at the very start of Genesis and tell the story of the "fall of man."

He explained as best he could and expanded on the story of the temptation, telling how Adam ate the forbidden apple. At this point old Chief Osahinta dropped his head on his chest and went into a reverie.

At the close of the sermon the Chief arose to reply. An ardent believer in his own religion, he sought to ridicule his friend the "black coat," as preachers were called.

"Brother Black Coat," he began, "I have heard your sermon. It is a good one and I believe it. I always did believe that it was wrong to eat apples. Hereafter I will never eat apples; I will make cider of them,—it tastes so much better!"

General R. H. Pratt, the man who built up the Carlisle Indian School, tells of a joke an Indian boy once played on him. The General was then a Captain, and as Superintendent of the school found it necessary to discipline one of the Indian printers by a sentence in the guard house. The Captain in sentencing the boy explained that men who were virtuous were rewarded in heaven as well as on earth and that evil doers must stand punishment both here and hereafter.

When the offender was out and back in his shop sticking type in the old "Red Man and Helper" office, he began a story of his incarceration. Not knowing that the Captain was hovering about the door, the Indian boy commenced.

"Last night I had a wonderful dream, a wonderful dream!"

"What did you dream?" asked the shop foreman.

"Well, I dreamed that it was the end of the world, and that the names of all the good people who were going to heaven were written in the sky in letters of gold. I wondered if mine was there so I looked up, and sure enough there were letters of gold in the sky, but there was only one name. It was Captain R. H. Pratt, and in the Captain's own handwriting!"

This is a good example of an Indian dream joke, but there are also fictitious observation jokes, these constituting the bulk of Indian humor. I once heard some of these jokes at a strike-pole dance. In this rite, clansmen on the opposite side of the fire tell jokes on one another and then give the butt of their jests small presents to heal any possible wound.

A Bear Clansman arose and, striking the pole, began his tale. "A few days ago I was out hunting," said he. "As I walked along the creek I saw a very big, brave man chasing a rabbit with a double-barreled shotgun. He was chasing the rabbit to the edge of the bank where the cliff begins, hoping to get it where he could put the end of his gun on it, because he was a good shot, under such conditions. On ran the man after the rabbit, when suddenly the rabbit spied a hole and darted into it. Then when the man came to the turn of the bank he saw a big, fierce dog standing there ready to bite him. The dog looked at him and let out a big howl. Now when this man, whom I will now reveal as my very dear friend Big Kettle,—saw the dog he thought the rabbit had suddenly grown big by magic, so he stopped breathing for a minute, and was so scared that his hair stood right up on end,—oh, about a foot. Up went his hat right on top of it. Now the rabbit found that the hole was shallow and wet, and he also feared that the dog would catch him, so he gave a great leap and landed right in Big Kettle's hair. The knock brought my dear friend back to his senses, and when he saw that the dog meant no harm, but was scared too, he breathed again and his hair came down and with it the hat,—right over the rabbit too. Big Kettle now started home, not knowing that he had any extra animals in his hair, and as he was scared a bit he went right in his house and sat down at the table. His wife had a big bowl of soup, and Big Kettle fell to eating it. It made him sweat so he took off his hat, and as he did the rabbit fell out and went right into his soup, spattering the table and his wife's face. His wife looked at him with astonishment and then exclaimed, 'My husband, why is it necessary for you to go hunting when you can just scratch your head and have rabbits fall out? I have seen things there before, but they had more than four legs!' "

At this the whole company began to roar with laughter at Big Kettle's discomfort, though he tried to smile. The dance went on and it came his turn to strike the pole. He then began his tale.

"It is true," said he, "that as my friend of the big claws (the Bear clansman) says, I am a great magician and can conjure bears and deer as well as rabbits from my head, just by thinking about them, but you have been deceived as to the manner by which I do it. I have strong thoughts in my head, it is full of great things so that it is necessary for my hair to stand up sometimes to make room for what is inside. This is not so with my Bear friend. You will notice that he has a very large head and is fond of honey. I saw him sleeping under a tree, the other day, and you know that he often sleeps under the trees. I heard a strange buzzing and at first thought that he was snoring. Looking closer, I saw that it was a swarm of bees going in and out of his mouth. Soon the bees flew away after more honey, and as I watched, a ripe walnut fell and hit my friend on the head, and *it returned a hollow sound with an echo!* Then I knew why a swarm of bees had attempted to make a hive in it."

In spite of their assumed stoicism, Indians are in reality sensitive, particularly to stinging rebukes or sarcasm. If they can return the retort, kind for kind, well and good; if not, the return may be expected later in the shape of a practical joke. This is often purely humorous though it may humiliate the first joker. It is a case of he who jokes last jokes best.

Peter Schuyler, an early mayor of Albany, once severely rebuked a Mohican Indian who was idling, naked, about the wharf. "Why don't you get to work, you lazy good-for-nothing Indian," exclaimed the mayor in disgust.

"Why don't you work, Mayor?" asked the Mohican.

"I do work, but I do it with my head," answered Schuyler.

"Huh!" replied the Indian. "Give me work; I'll do it."

The Indian was sent to kill a calf, but demanded a shilling before undertaking the task, as the mayor's barns were two miles from town. An hour later the Indian returned with the report that he had killed the calf.

"Well, where is its skin?" demanded Schuyler, knowing that it was customary to skin and dress an animal when a bargain was made to kill it.

"You said '*kill*,'" replied the Mohican. "I took you at your word. If you meant skin and dress, I would have asked two shillings."

The mayor knew that the butchered calf was not safe lying where the Indian had left it. He therefore endeavored to force him to return, but the Indian kept saying "'Nother shilling." It was therefore given, with a scowl, and off went the wily redskin.

After another hour he returned with the skin and the statement that the carcass was in great danger of being eaten by the dogs. "Give me another shilling and I will go back and hang calf in barn,—very high," demanded the Indian.

The mayor had no more shillings and so, producing a larger coin, said, "Well, here, take this but give me a shilling in change. This is a two-shilling piece." The Indian made the change and went back to his task, performing it faithfully.

Schuyler was now thoroughly angry at the Mohican's trickery and therefore when he came back he asked the redskin if he'd like to make another shilling. "I like it," answered he.

"Well, then, take this paper and give it to the Captain up at the fort, and then come back and tell me what you think of things."

The red man took the paper and the shilling but, being suspicious, took the note to one of Schuyler's negroes with the statement that the mayor wanted it taken to the fort.

The paper read, "Take this savage and give him forty lashes." The negro got the lashes, and came back, useless for the rest of the day. When Peter Schuyler saw the negro's plight he looked for the Indian, whom he soon saw idling at the wharf, unscathed.

"You dirty savage," fumed the mayor, "I thought I told *you* to take that paper to the fort."

"You did," answered the Mohican, "but I thought that if you could hire a man I could also."

"Well," reflected the mayor, "you think you've made four shillings, but I am going to tell you that one of them is lead."

"Oh, no," answered the Indian, "I gave the bad one back to you in change."

"You scoundrel!" ejaculated the mayor. "How is it that you get by with such impudence?"

The Indian now had his chance to get back to the beginning of things and immediately seized his opening.

"I do it with my head," said he.

This story is but an illustration of the extraordinary lengths to which some Indians will go to get the laugh on the other fellow. They make a studied art of it.

In an Indian tribe there are certain rules about joking. A man must never joke with his mother-in-law, for instance, and certain elderly men he is bound to respect. When jokes are cracked he must be quick to invite one upon himself, or give a present, to remove all doubts as to his hostility.

Sometimes a joke takes the form of a naive expression, as in the case of a Cattaraugus woman who came to Alleghany. "So you are down here!" exclaimed a friend. "Where are you staying?"

"My sister, she is staying with me," was the answer.

"Your sister staying with you! Why, I thought she lived here!"

"Truly, what I said, my sister she is staying with me."

"Where?"

"Over to her house!"

XXXIII. HOW INDIANS DANCED

Indians danced for the same reason that they sang: for a purpose. Sometimes a dance was of a religious nature, sometimes it was in honor of victory and occasionally it was for pure pleasure. Dancing seems to be a natural thing, and the sound of drumming or of measured song causes the feet to keep time. The native Americans were sensitive to rhythm and loved to be moved by it.

It is difficult to say where the most spectacular dances were held or by whom, but perhaps the most picturesque

FIGURE 23

War Dance from an Indian Drawing

were those of the Pueblo people of the far southwest. Here there were wonderful ceremonies in which the people dressed in strange costumes and danced in the courtyards of the Pueblos, making a stirring picture, never to be forgotten. There are those who think the dances of the Plains people the most interesting, and certain it is that the Sioux and their kinsfolk had numerous dances, some of which presented a matchless sight.

Many of the dances were owned by various societies and associations and could be performed only by them. The Crow, the Blackfeet, the Dakota and the Mandan people, the Omaha, the Osage and the Ponca, all had dances that stirred the blood and gave great delight to the dancers.

There are still others that think the dances of the forest area, including those of the Iroquois and the Algonkin people, were the most interesting. It is all in the point of view, of course.

Among the tribes of American natives the dance was considered a two-fold practice. First, it was a pleasing and even exciting exercise, and, second, it was a means of securing favor from or rendering homage to the unseen powers. In this case the dance and its song went together, and frequently the action of the dancers fitted itself to the words of the song.

If the song went, "I charge upon the enemy, I strike the foe," the dancers imitated the action by violent gestures. If the dance referred to the "sisters of the fields," the dancers swayed like the corn and then walked about each other twining their hands in imitation of the bean vine.

The rhythm of the dance was supplied by drums, rattles and the voices of singers. The time for the most part was uniform, but there were also frequent changes, either fast or slow.

The steps of the dancers varied from a shuffle or a trot to violent lifting of the knees and stamping the feet upon the ground. Not only did the feet perform in these dances but the body and arms. Some dances were so vigorous that there were pauses every two or three minutes, during which time the drum tapped briskly until the singers and rattlers again began.

One of the most common dance steps was that in which the foot was brought down with a resounding whack and then given a softer hop or shove ahead. It was a bound and rebound accompanied by gestures of the arms and twisting of the body. The DUM, *doom,* DUM, *doom* of the tom tom gave the rhythm. This step was often employed for the war dance.

When my instructor in the Great Company of Masks taught me how to do the False Face dance, he had me walk slowly, taking two steps with each foot, that is, I brought my right foot down flatly, lifted it and took another step ahead with it, at the same time bringing my left foot ahead and repeating the process. Then when the rattlers and singers began their part of the work, I was ready to do the dance properly.

The social dance or Gah-dá-shot, which was one of my favorites because of its ease, was done by trotting ahead, striking the ball of the foot first and then scuffing it ahead until the heel struck. The song that goes with this dance is lively and has melody.

I have danced the dance of the Bears, Buffalos, Wild Pigeons, False Faces and Big Feather, but I have never attempted the Seneca dance of the Eagle. It is performed by four dancers, two facing two, and in the squatting position, like the Russian dance. It is a severe test of balance and endurance.

Some tribes have certain directions in which they dance. The Iroquois dance counter-clockwise, that is, with the right hand on the outside of the circle and the left toward the inside. Other tribes dance sun-wise, that is, with the right side inside. Still others have dances in which the women dance one way and the men the other.

Indian dances are individual dances in a line. The dancers are not paired off in such a way that their arms are about each other, though there are some dances in which men and women face each other in the dance ring.

Dances were held in a council house with the benches of the singers in the middle, or they were held out of doors around a fire or a war post. The dance ring usually had a real or imaginary center.

We have stated that Indian dancers used arms and body as well as limbs, but we must not neglect to say that in war dances they used their voices as well, making the air ring with blood-curdling whoops.

XXXIV. HOW INDIANS SANG

With the Indians almost every song had a purpose,—a real purpose. It was not right to sing out a song without rime or reason, for who could tell what spirit of the unseen world might be stirred up by such singing? Careless song might even bring bad luck.

Songs were carefully thought out, they were studied and they were remembered. There were strict rules concerning songs, and a man or woman, a boy or a girl who had invented a song might forbid any one else to use it, and no one dared.

I have often gone to the council house during the New Year ceremonies and heard the old warriors and matrons of the clans sing their own private songs of thanksgiving. Some were good and some were better, but some were worse and some were beyond all powers of understanding. One old Indian whom I thought much of had a song the

SENECA (New York)

Feather Dance Song

The Bird Dance

Arranged by Frank B. Converse,
(Seneca) Chattaraugus Reservation

words of which were, "He-ga hey a heh, hey a heh, hey a heh," repeated over and over. These words simply meant, "That is it, dee dee dum, dee dee dum, dee dee dum." Still the song was thought to be a powerful charm. The tune was as simple and commenced in a high falsetto, Mi, do,—la, sol, fa,—mi, re, do,—si, la, sol. The last grunting "hey a heh" was spoken rather than sung, and ended in a weird gasp. It is said that warrior O-dan -kōt used this song as a war cry, and certainly it made me shudder as he sang it over and over.

Many of the ceremonial songs that I have heard were pleasing to the ear and had a real melody. Some Seneca and Onondaga songs have a happy cadence that is really "catching." This is especially true of some of the dancing songs that are sung to the sound of rattles and the tapping of the water drum.

There are some who say that Indian songs are not music, and some who say that the Indian scale is imperfect. There have been some, indeed, who have denied that birds sing *music* for the same reason. The white man's scale and musical tones have come very largely from his tuned instruments of strings. His voice merely follows the mechanics of a constructed scale, which we call the harmonic, or chromatic. The Indian had no stringed musical instruments, or, if any, very few. His nearest approach to a fixed scale was upon his whistle-flute. It may be that some of the quavering grace notes that he interjected came from an attempt to imitate the flute, but perhaps not. The Indian sang as naturally as a bird, though at times poor singers got very far from the bird ideal and approached that of a coyote, very ill.

In general, however, I have heard pleasant and agreeable songs in Indian homes, in camps and villages. Some of these songs gripped me as if with some mysterious spell. I was carried afar in my imagination and felt strange emotions. This was especially true when the water drum began tapping its beat and inter-beat, its heavy beat and light beat, DUM, dum, DUM, dum, DUM, dum, DUM, dum. The sound gives the very name *tom-tom*. As the ringing note sounded my heart seemed to stop beating, to choke me and then to resume its beat in strict unison with the drum. When the medicine man arose to speak, I seemed to believe every word he said and to be willing to do his bidding. I was under a spell.

It seems possible that the master minds of Indian days made their songs with the very purpose of hypnotizing those who heard them, so that some desired effect might be obtained. To this day, I like those old songs and am stirred by them to feel the presence of the Great Mystery and his invisible aides. It may be that these old Indians were pagans, whatever that word may mean, but certainly they knew how to make men feel that there was a Great Spirit in whom we lived and moved and had our being. Oddly enough, I have known white men and women who felt the same way about the songs of the red people, and they have returned again and again to the councils of the Indians to drink in this feeling of mystery, this sense of unseen powers.

Most Indians believed that songs invoked the unseen spirits of Nature, and that to sing the song pleasing to the Moon brought her help, or to sing the song of the Sun secured his aid. This is why Indians had songs for everything and why they sang to everything, even the winds, the bubbling springs and the painted clouds. Song brought them into friendly harmony with all created things.

Indians had individual songs, but the great song-cycles were sung in choruses. Everybody sang together and in that way all learned the words and music. In some cases this was a dangerous thing because there were ceremonies that required that everybody who sang, sing perfectly, both word and note. If the least mistake occurred, the leader would correct the blunder and require the whole song to be done over again.

I once sat in the circle of a mystical Night Chant. In my hand was a sacred rattle that I must shake in rhythm all the night through, never missing a beat. I knew the tunes fairly well but the words bothered me greatly. Still I sang, and when frequently my face was brushed by some bushy-headed inspector I kept right along making what I thought might be the right noise. Still I was fearful that I might be ruled out of the ceremony for spoiling it. When it was over in the morning my sponsor called me aside and told me that Mrs. Long Finger had listened to my singing, and that I did it all right as for words, but I had the tone wrong. "The tune was right," explained my friend, "but you sang bass!" As I had not had the fortune of living with the tribe all my life, but had been away at school, my shortcoming was forgiven.

XXXV. HOW INDIANS PLAYED GAMES

Indians loved excitement, they loved to laugh and play. That queer idea that Indians were sour and sad and always mooning around is as out of date as the idea that the moon is made of green cheese. Men liked games of skill like archery and lacrosse. Girls and women liked guessing games and football. Everybody liked games of chance. There was something exciting about finding out who was going to beat. Some Indians liked gaming so well that they took it too seriously, and then they gambled, often losing everything they had, even their clothes.

In my boyhood days on the reservation many games were played, such as shinny, hoop and javelin, lacrosse, whipping top and snow snake. At the tribal ceremonies there were games of platter dice, girls' contests at football played in the snow and contests of youths with the javelin and hoop. Even jack-straws were played.

Many tribes had games of shooting with bows and arrows. Every man had his arrow marked so that he could tell it. Targets were sometimes wisps of grass twisted and tied, then hung from a limb. Among the Montagnais of Laborador targets four feet square are made of sticks covered with deer skin and set up on poles eight feet high. The opposing parties back away fifty yards from their targets and each takes a turn in shooting twenty-one arrows. The one that puts the most arrows in their target wins, the aim of the whole procedure being to get the laugh on the losers. The winners make a great noise over their victory and call the other party names. Good humor prevailed and the losers kept their tempers.

The Indian game of lacrosse, now borrowed by the whites, was a general favorite among the native Americans from coast to coast. As adopted by athletes to-day its general principles remain the same as in Indian days. The object of the game was for one team to try to throw a ball into its opponent's goal, and for the other team to keep it out of its own goal and throw it in the other goal. Each team tried to get the ball as it was flung through the air or carried on a racquet by a runner.

The racquets or net-sticks used in this game differed among various tribes. The Huron and the Iroquois used a racquet much like the present one, but it did not have a flattened, scoop end. The Chippewa used a small netted ring tied or bent on the end of the handle, while the southern tribes used two racquets. Other tribes had the net in a loop, rather than a hoop.

The ball was scooped up in the net and either thrown

toward the goal or carried to it by a swift runner. Opponents could knock it out of the net or catch it as it flew through the air.

One early observer wrote, "Of all the Indian social sports the finest and grandest is ball play. I might call it a noble game, and I am surprised how these savages attained such perfection in it."

Hockey or shinny was played by both boys and girls. The game differs little from the modern one, the object being the same,—to drive the ball into the opponent's goal, and he to keep it out. With some tribes the game is played by women against men, as among the Crows, and in some tribes there are mixed teams, as among the Sauk and Assiniboin.

Another widely played game was that of javelin and net-hoop. The hoop was made as circular as possible and then divided in sections, either two or four, or completely netted like a spider web, perhaps in allusion to a mythical spider web shield. The sections of the hoop represented the four quarters of the world, and not only had each a counting value in the game, but parts of each section counted for more or less. The game was played by rolling the hoop over a level spot from one hundred to one hundred and fifty feet in length and then casting javelins or darts at it, with the object of piercing the hoop and gaining a high count. This game was played by men or boys arranged in teams, there being from two to forty on a side. Sometimes the darts were made from corncobs having a sharp awl at one end and two or three stiff feathers at the other end like a shuttlecock.

Girls were fond of a game called double-ball. This was played with a stick having a bent end. The double-ball, as its name implies, was formed by two weights held together by a thong. These weights were either balls of sand or clay covered with buckskin. The game was to lift the double-ball from the ground with the stick and throw it over a horizontal pole at the opponent's end of the field. As in lacrosse, the missile could be carried or thrown. The game had its forwards, its centers and its guards, and the teams could be of any convenient size. Only women played this game, and only women played so tame a game as football. It was a purely kicking game.

Snow snake was a man's game. It was played with long, flattened rods having the forward end rounded up like a runner, and the rear end slightly notched in order to afford a place for the finger in throwing it. The object of the game was to throw the "snake" over the snow, or through a trough made by dragging a log, for the greatest distance. A goal marker stuck a peg in the snow to indicate where each snake stopped. The game was one of skill and played for stakes. The side that won took the reward.

Guessing games were popular. One called the "four cup" game, or the "hidden ball" game, was played over the entire Southwest. To play it, four tubes or similar pieces of wood were provided, each having painted upon it the symbol of one of the four directions,—north, east, south and west. Opposing teams sat before each other, each player in turn hiding a small ball like a marble in one of the hollow tubes. The opposite player then looked at the tubes as they lay before him and guessed in which one the ball was hidden. Failing, the score went against him, and winning, the score was recorded by means of a tally stick or counter. The tubes passed down the line from player to player, and then went to the opponents, who pitted their powers against the other side. This game was sacred to the gods of war.

A bowl game with four or six dice was played by the Algonkin, Sioux and Iroquois. The Iroquois used six dice, shaped like smoothed-off hickory nuts. One side was blackened and the other was left natural. In modern times the Iroquois have used rounded and smoothed peach stones. The game was played by putting all six dice in a flat-bottomed bowl, each die showing the same color. A player now took the bowl and shook it violently, bringing it down upon a pile of skins with a whack. The counts were now looked for. All of one color up counted ten, all but one of a color up counted five, and two of a color counted two. The counters were red beans. An equal number of beans were given each side and the game was played until one side won all the beans, though sometimes the game had to be given up by agreement because it took more than four days. The game was played during certain hours of the sacred ceremonies. The winners took the stakes of their opponents.

There were so many Indian games played in so many different ways by so many different tribes that the Government, in the twenty-fourth annual report of the Bureau of Ethnology, has taken over eight hundred pages to describe them even briefly.

It may be said that games were believed to have a magical effect, and that some were played to overcome sickness. Indian doctors frequently told sick people that certain games should be played for them, or that they should take part in them. To be successful in games many charms were employed. For games of skill there were even game doctors whose business it was to tell what kind of bow-strings to use, what kind of oil or wax to use on snow snakes, what feathers to use on arrows, and many other things. Some charms, however, were merely fanciful, and of no more real value than "lucky" stones. Yet some Indians had such luck when using certain charms, such as lucky stones, that they believed in them most thoroughly. After all, who can tell what belief in a relic or charm may do to a man's mind? And there are those who say success is all in the way a man thinks. If a charm or a game makes one think right it cannot be so useless.

XXXVI. HOW BAD WERE THE INDIANS?

Many years ago I took a morning walk on an Indian reservation near my home, intending to call on an old chief. He had told me many interesting things about the old days when the red men ruled the land and knew nothing about reservations. His name was Cornplanter, but he didn't plant much corn. The name had come to him by heredity. No, he wasn't a farmer; he was the high priest of his religion.

I found Cornplanter sunning himself in his doorway and reading a book that a missionary had given him. Surprised that he should be reading instead of communing with Nature in his favorite grove by the stream, I asked him what he was thinking about.

"Missionary give me good book," he answered, "to show me how bad we are,—we Indians. I read it all about white folks fighting each other. Some burn each other, some boil, some skin alive. Ugh! Some stick in nails, some just tear off legs and arms, all just because some white folks don't believe same kind of religion."

"Oh, that was a long time ago," I replied. "Those were the days before people knew better."

"Well," he argued, "we Indians never tortured any one because they differed with us in religion. Every man could have his own totem if he wanted to, so long as he didn't bewitch the rest of us."

"But Indians did kill and scalp their enemies," I retorted.

"Yes," he admitted, "Indians a long time ago, *before they knew better,* were cruel. I read this book about martyrs and I think how bad my people were; I am ashamed and I am sorry. Indians once had wars, Indians once burned people just like white folks did down South, Indians once were bad, very bad, and I am ashamed."

He thumbed his book as he looked at the pictures of the tortures of saints and heretics. Then he went on, "Yes, Indians once bad, almost as bad as white man!"

III: DRESS AND ORNAMENT

III

DRESS AND ORNAMENT

XXXVII. HOW INDIANS DRESSED

In the mind of most Americans to-day the typical Indian,—the Indian in matters of dress,—is the Indian of the Plains. The circus and the moving picture have conspired to fix this idea and books of elementary history have made it a sacred tradition. The Plains costume is beautiful and striking at once, but our eyes should not be dazzled to other distinctive costumes used by many tens of thousands of Indians and scores of tribes.

So many types of clothing were worn and so many materials were used that an extensive book could be written upon the subject. In general, it may be said that the natives of North America, north of Mexico, had clothing for the entire body, though they did not always wear complete suits. Tribes of the more southern and warmer regions often wore little clothing.

As a general observation it may be said that, with the exception of those in the far north, the tribes of all the various geographical areas wore *breechcloths.* This was a primary garment. *Moccasins* came next, and during a portion of the warmer weather thousands of natives dressed only in these two portions of their attire. Next came *leggings,* then *shirts* or *capes,* though robes were much used. After this came the hat or bonnet, in type differing greatly even among the same people.

As might be expected the dress of the women differed from that of the men. Women wore skirts, as is proper for women, and some were long and some were short. As a rule with the tribes of the Plains the length of the women's shirt (shaped in general like a short-sleeved nightgown or a bungalow apron) combined a waist and a skirt. Dresses oftentimes had a yoke the extension of which formed the sleeves. Some forest tribes made their skirts of a single large skin which was wrapped around the thighs, secured with a belt, the flap being allowed to drop over the belt. This was the simple skirt, but when tailored, fringed and ornamented, it became a thing of beauty. The shirts worn with this type of dress were shorter than those of the men. Often they were of the poncho type.

Women of the forest and plains wore short leggings, coming only just above the knee. Women also wore moccasins, but frequently of a different cut than the men's.

Belts and sashes were worn. The belt was an important article with both men and women. When a boy was only a few weeks old some tribes placed a thong about his waist that he might become accustomed to the lacing that should support his breechcloth.

Hats of several different kinds were worn, many of them entirely without feathers. Even woven hats shaped like a big Panama with the brim turned down were worn by the Northwest coast people, while the Hupa women wore skull caps of basketry.

It may surprise many to learn that the more southern Indians wove cloth and made garments of it. Indeed, even the Plains and forest Indians did no small amount of weaving. Where buckskin could be obtained, however, it was preferred to fabrics, and thus the weaver's art was restricted to sashes, bags, garters and belts. Some of the Pueblo people dressed almost entirely in woven garments, and the Northwest coast people also used cloth of their own make.

(After Catlin)

FIGURE 24

Indian Chief in War Regalia

The robe or blanket was commonly used by most of the tribes, and this was frequently woven of bark or hemp fibers into which feathers had been twisted in such a way that they completely covered the outside, and so neatly was the weaving done that the feathers lay very

FIGURE 25
Northwest Woven Shirt

smoothly. The Lenape or Delaware people had feather robes.

Some eastern tribes cut bird skins into long strips and wove them into blankets, just as the northern Algonkian people cut rabbit skins into strips and wove capes, mantles and other garments.

Shirts were made by taking two uniform skins and putting them together. Some cutting had to be done to

(After Catlin)

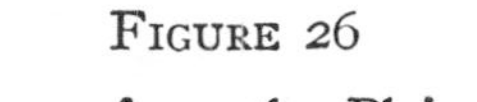

FIGURE 26

Indian Types from the Plains Country

bring about a fit at the shoulders, but the sides were left untrimmed in order to have skin to fringe. Sleeves were made from extra pieces of skin and sewed on. When decorated with porcupine quills a man's shirt was a handsome affair, especially when the sleeves were ornamented with ermine skins and scalp locks. The Plains people often did this.

Leggings were made from single skins trimmed and folded. The form of the leg was provided for and a seam run along the line. A decorated strip of quillwork or beads ornamented this flap, the outer portion of which was finely fringed.

Let it be here observed that Indian fringe is fine, neatly cut and even. Sometimes it is rolled like cords.

Leggings for men were cut with the hip portion higher, and slanting to the crotch, to allow for a better fit. The outer part was tied to the belt. Sometimes another garter tie was provided so as to hold the leggings to the front of the belt as well.

The breechcloth was a long piece of stroud cloth or skin, ten to eighteen inches wide and often as long as five feet. It was placed right side to the body, tucked through the belt, pulled down until the front part when dropped came a hand's width from the knees, thrust between the legs, drawn up through the belt and then adjusted. Properly put on, the breechcloth provided an apron of equal length before and behind the wearer. Only men wore them.

Men also wore kilts, especially among the Iroquois and among the Pueblo people. With the former the material was softly tanned doeskin and among the latter it was quite apt to be of woven fabric.

The robe or mantle was commonly used by the eastern Indians. It was made of several skins neatly sewed together and fringed. The best robes were of finely tanned

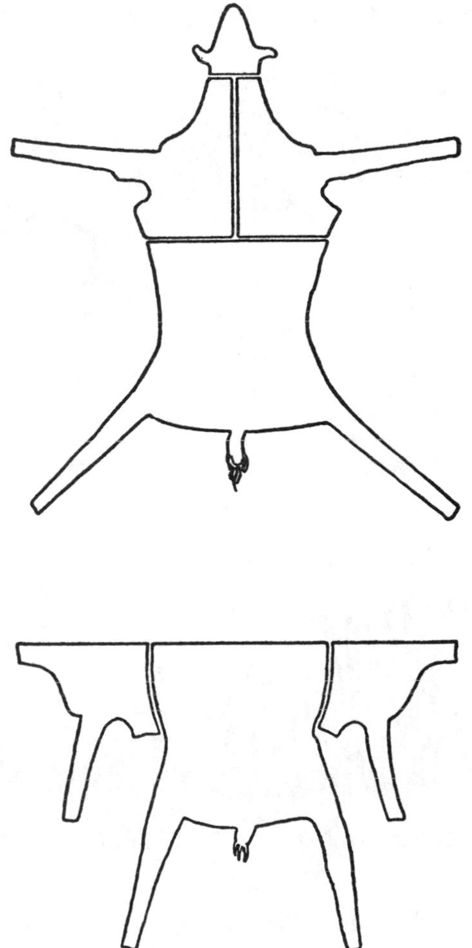

FIGURE 27

Diagrams Showing How to Make a Poncho Shirt

skins with the hair on. The pelts of black squirrels, foxes, martens, beavers, muskrat and buffalo were used. Decorations were added to give color and individuality.

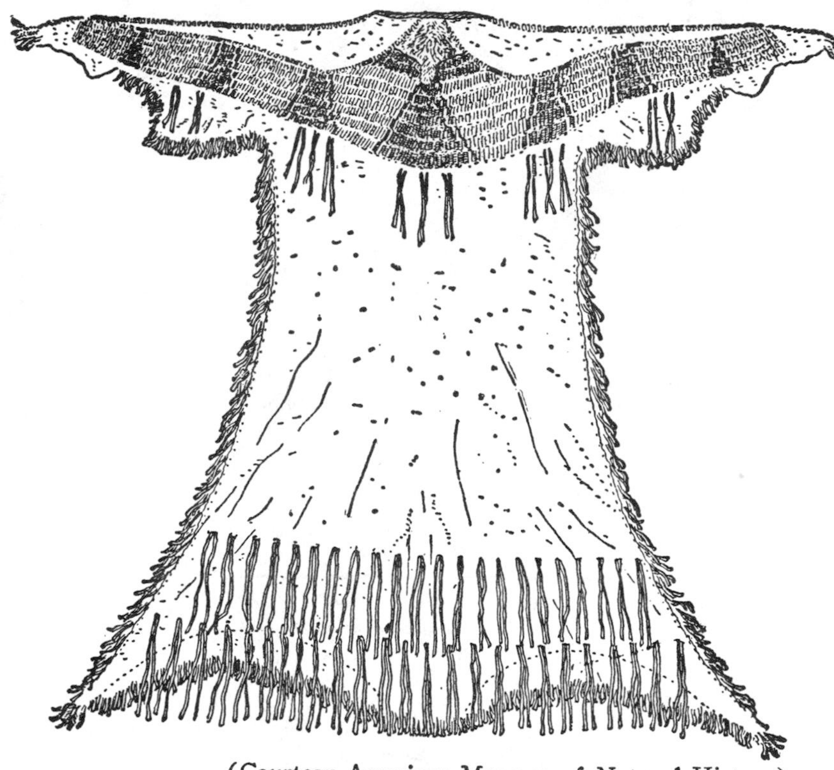

(Courtesy American Museum of Natural History)

FIGURE 28

A Woman's Dress—Plains Type

When the trader's blanket came and furs were an article of trade, these old "match coats" of native make disappeared.

In winter some tribes had undergarments of fur, but more often the winter shirt was of fur and worn without anything beneath it. To provide for warmth the match coat was drawn about the shoulders, or, as in the case of men, under one arm and over the other shoulder.

In matters of dress Indians were like other people; some were neat and some were careless. When there were ceremonies, however, most of them dressed with great care, cleaning their clothing and adding adornments.

XXXVIII. HOW INDIANS MADE THEIR HATS

Not every Indian wore a war bonnet, as most pictures would have us believe, nor, instead of a hat, did all of them stick a feather in their hair. As a matter of fact, compared with the total Indian population, only a few thousands had war bonnets. The war bonnet was unknown over vast regions. What, then, was worn?

The headgear of Indians consisted of "roaches," caps, hoods, turbans, brimless hats, woven hats with brims and basket hats. The women wore their own long hair, or, when rain and cold required, a head throw or small shawl.

Indian women did not wear feathers sticking up behind or anywhere else upon their heads. The feather was a warrior's badge and the token of a *coup*. The Hupa women of the California area wore round caps made of basketry. Nothing could be more absurd than an Indian woman in a war bonnet or exploit feather. The hair that nature gave, when neatly arranged, was sufficient.

The turban was usually of a woven fabric and was wound around the head to give it shape. It was then stitched to hold its form and then ornamented with feathers and trinkets. The Menomini as well as the Omaha wore turbans. In the Southwest some of the desert tribes, as the Navaho, wore turbans or broad head bands.

Perhaps more Indians wore round, brimless caps than any other form of headdress. They were formed of cloth or woven material and fitted the head closely. The top, however, was sometimes full and puffed. Feathers and trinkets were placed in these caps. It will be noted that in the old American days it was the man and not the woman who needed a milliner, and the Indian man was just as particular about his bonnet then as any modern woman is now.

FIGURE 29

Iroquois Feathered Hat

The feathered cap, with the Iroquois, was made upon a frame. A band of basket-splint the size of the head was sewed together and a framework of narrower splints was built over this, forming an open dome. Fastened to the top of this was a socket in which was placed a short spindle, the latter having a ball at the bottom which prevented it from falling out. The frame was covered with velvet, tanned skin or fabric and bound at the rim with a piece of ornamental quill work. On the spindle was thrust the quill of an eagle's feather, and about the socket was circle after circle of down and wing feathers. Frequently several exploit feathers trailed loosely behind.

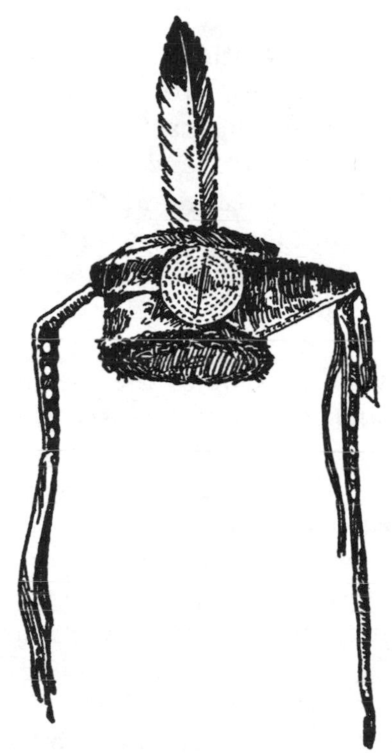

FIGURE 30
Omaha Warrior's Hat

This type of hat was called the *gus-to-weh,* meaning the real hat. When the wearer moved or the wind blew the feather at the top whirled in the socket, turning around and around. In going through the forest the twirling feather was removed.

The Omaha and Osage people wore brimless hats of fine fur, many times of otter skin. One type was shaped much like a fez but was not so high in proportion. The ornamentation in this case was around the top, where quills and beadwork supplemented by shells, large beads and jinglers found a place. The back of the hat sometimes had streamers of feathers and a short bead band.

Another fur hat of the turban shape was the otter skin headgear with a projecting tail and flap. This was ornamented in various ways and sometimes had a large rosette of beads or quillwork at the neck of the flap. Trophy feathers are often worn with this type.

In British Columbia and the adjacent region along the Pacific coast live the Salish people who wear tall woven hats looking like fancy sombreros, but with a smaller and more cylindrical peak. One of the customs of these people is to give *potlatches* or gift feasts in which they give away most of their property. For every *hyas potlatch* (heap big feast) the wearer of such a hat is entitled to have a ringed constriction upon the tube-shaped peak. The father of one of my Chilcat friends, Chief Stuiaka, had nine rings upon his hat, which made him a man of great importance, for it was a testimonial of his generosity.

Roaches of feathers placed edge to edge, the quills being fastened to a base, were worn by several western tribes. They were rather showy affairs, but were unlike the war bonnet which circled the head.

Hoods were usually of fur, draped over the head. Some of a more permanent character had buffalo horns, scraped very thin, stuck at the sides.

A number of eastern tribes, described by early travelers, notably the Erie and Susquehannock, wore the heads of animals as headgear. Panther and bear heads were chosen. Some were drawn over the face so that the lower jaw of the beast hung below the wearer's chin. Usually this type of headdress included the entire skin of the animal, which served as a shoulder robe.

These same eastern Iroquoian people also wore peaked caps of fur for protection in winter. Tradition says that some hats were made by coiling ropes of fur like an old-

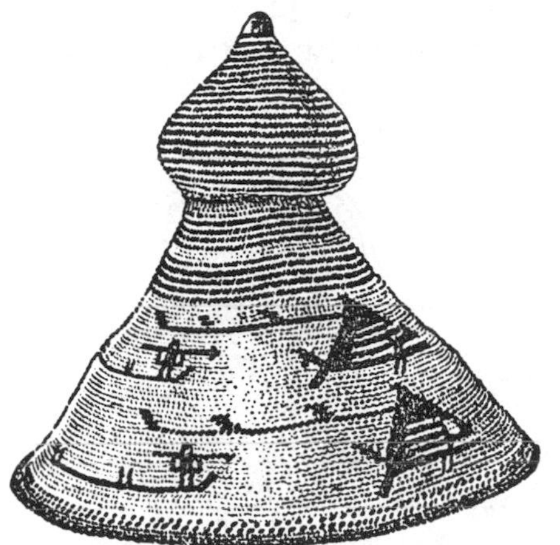

(Courtesy American Museum of Natural History)

FIGURE 31

Northwest Coast Hat

fashioned beehive, and fastening the coils by winding hempen cords over and over each two ropes. One of the thrills of my younger days was in finding in an old Indian grave a smoking pipe of clay having upon it the effigy of a human head wearing one of these coiled caps. The figure had its hands to its face and its lips puckered as if blowing something. It may have represented the face and figure of a medicine man.

In making pictures of Indians the artist must use great care in depicting the right headgear, for tribal hats varied greatly.

XXXIX. HOW INDIANS MADE THEIR MOCCASINS

Scientists have spent much time in making studies of Indian moccasins. It is something to know that the foot-gear of the American native is worthy of such attention, though moccasins are perhaps the world's most beautiful footwear, and possibly the most healthful.

Some scientists wonder just how a moccasin came to be invented and try to show that it may have started with

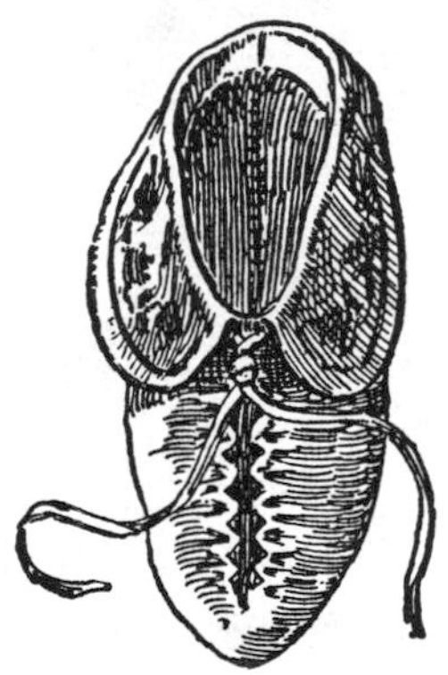

FIGURE 32
The True Moccasin

a sandal. It seems reasonable to believe, however, that moccasins originated from merely wrapping the foot in a piece of soft skin to protect the foot from both the dangers of the ground and the temperature. As a foot wrapped merely in skin presents a rather awkward appearance, the skin was cut to the shape of the foot and had its seams sewed up.

Sandals are worn by tribes that do a great deal of weaving and moccasins are worn by tribes that understand tanning best, and who weave least. Still some eastern tribes, as the Iroquois, did use sandals too. They were woven of corn husk.

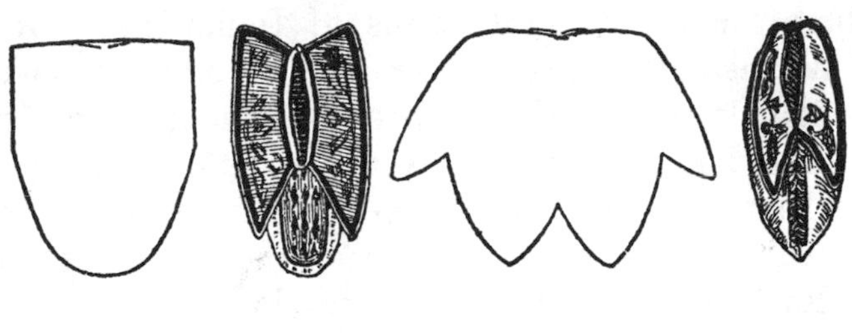

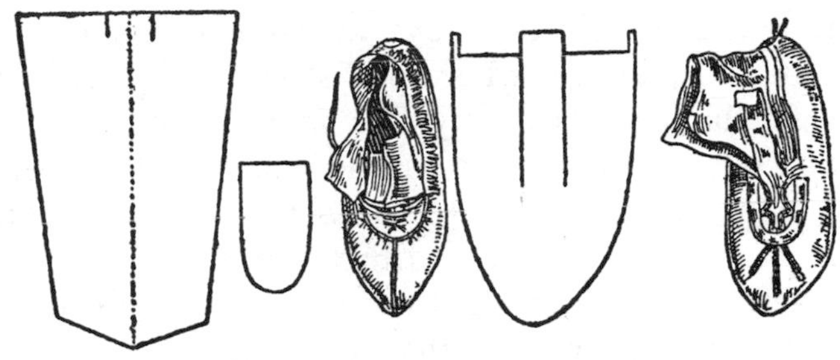

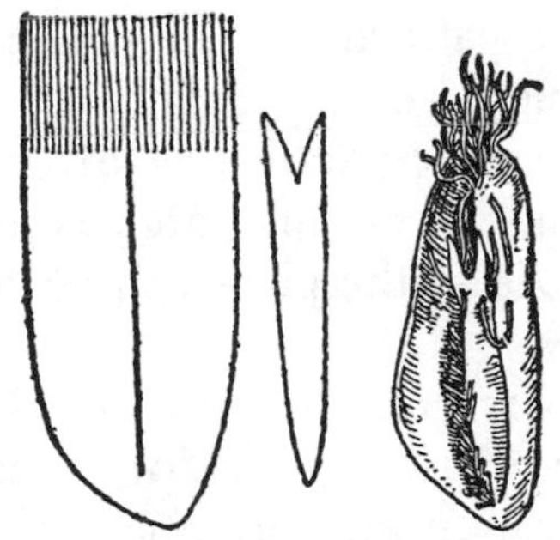

(After Wissler)

FIGURE 33

Types of Moccasins—Forest, Plains and Desert

There are two general forms of Indian footgear, the true moccasin with a soft sole and the moccasin with a rawhide sole separately attached. Even these two types have variations and at least twenty ways of making moccasins have been described. To complicate matters some moccasins have long legs that reach the knee or even the hip. Each tribe had its own moccasin pattern and form or decoration, and the moccasin became something of a tribal badge. Even the form of the sole differed many times.

The true moccasin is a low, soft-soled foot covering, made of a single piece of shaped skin. It is cut in such a manner that there are only two short seams, one at the heel and one up the middle of the instep to the opening. This puckered seam in front takes up the excess leather and is the one unsightly feature about the article. A clever needleworker can gather the puckers neatly, but wrinkles will appear over the foot notwithstanding the shaping process. Shaping consists of putting in a foot form or last, dampening the skin and then pounding it as smooth as possible.

Patterns for "one-piece" moccasins with and without flaps cut with the pattern, are shown in figure 33. To overcome the puckered appearance a U-shaped patch, decorated with beads or quills, is often placed over the seam. In some instances this patch is inserted, the moccasin being cut so that the piece can be sewed in, and not upon the foot.

The pictures of moccasins shown give an excellent idea of how to cut the various types of moccasins.

Moccasin decoration and ornamentation is an interesting study, because moccasins have upon them many symbols and decorative forms that are very old.

Moccasins were sewn with sinew thread. Holes in the skin were punched with a fine-pointed bone awl and the

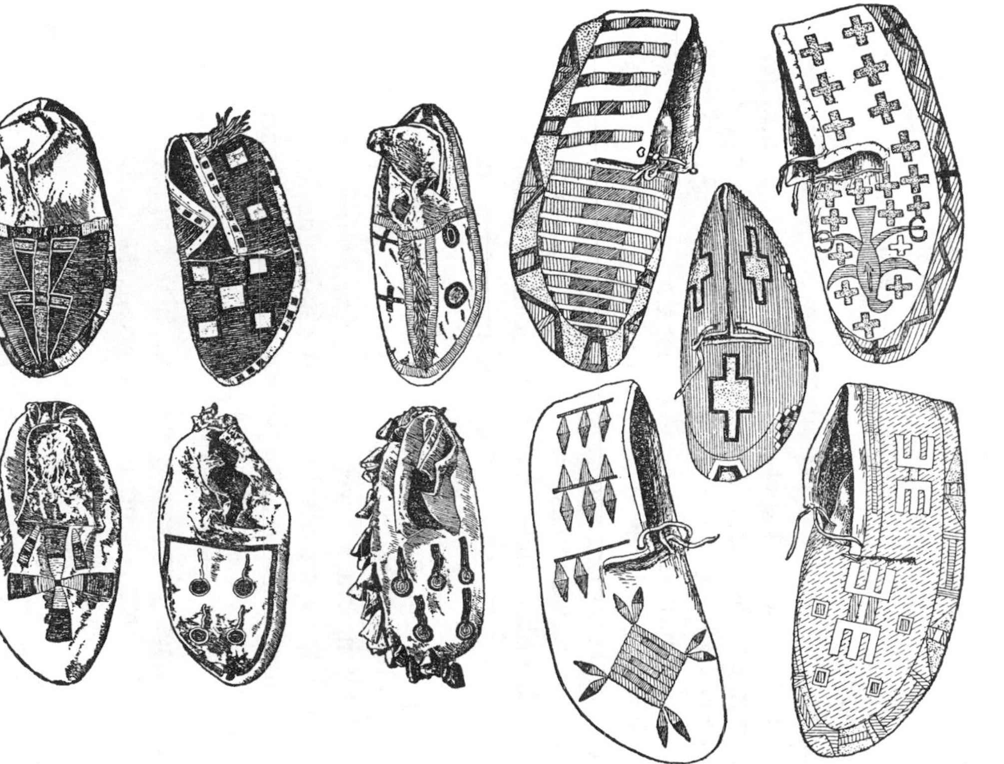

(Courtesy American Museum of Natural History)

FIGURE 34

Moccasins of the Northern Plains

sinew drawn through. Sinew is ideal for moccasins as it does not fray and rot like thread.

While moccasins are handsome things they are not durable. On long marches the soles wore through and had to be replaced. Where there were forced marches, as on long hunts or war raids, a supply of moccasins was carried. It would never do to have men walk with sore and bleeding feet.

Prisoners intended for adoption were given new moccasins to wear, that their feet might tread the right path. To put on the moccasins of another tribe was an acceptance of its laws and customs, and a giving up of one's own tribe and all its ties. At least this was the case with the Iroquois nations, who always placed new moccasins upon the feet of prisoners.

To protect moccasins there were "over-moccasins," which kept the inner moccasin clean. These overshoes were sometimes soaked in oil and filled with buffalo wool, to keep out water and keep the feet warm. As moccasins quickly took up moisture, it was necessary to wear something to protect them.

Winter moccasins were often made of bear pelts, buffalo skin or even sealskin, with the hair side in.

In warmer climes, as in the country of the Apache people, moccasins had long legs, stiff rawhide soles and turned-up toes. The shape of the toe protected the foot from being pierced with cactus thorns. The long, legging-like legs kept out the sand and protected the limb from the bite of rattlesnakes.

Among the interesting moccasins were those with ornamentation on the soles. These were worn by sick persons, in ceremonies and by lovers who liked to turn a neat foot when playing the flute for their sweethearts. Moccasins were beautiful, one Indian said, because the foot must be as beautiful as the flowers which it walks among,

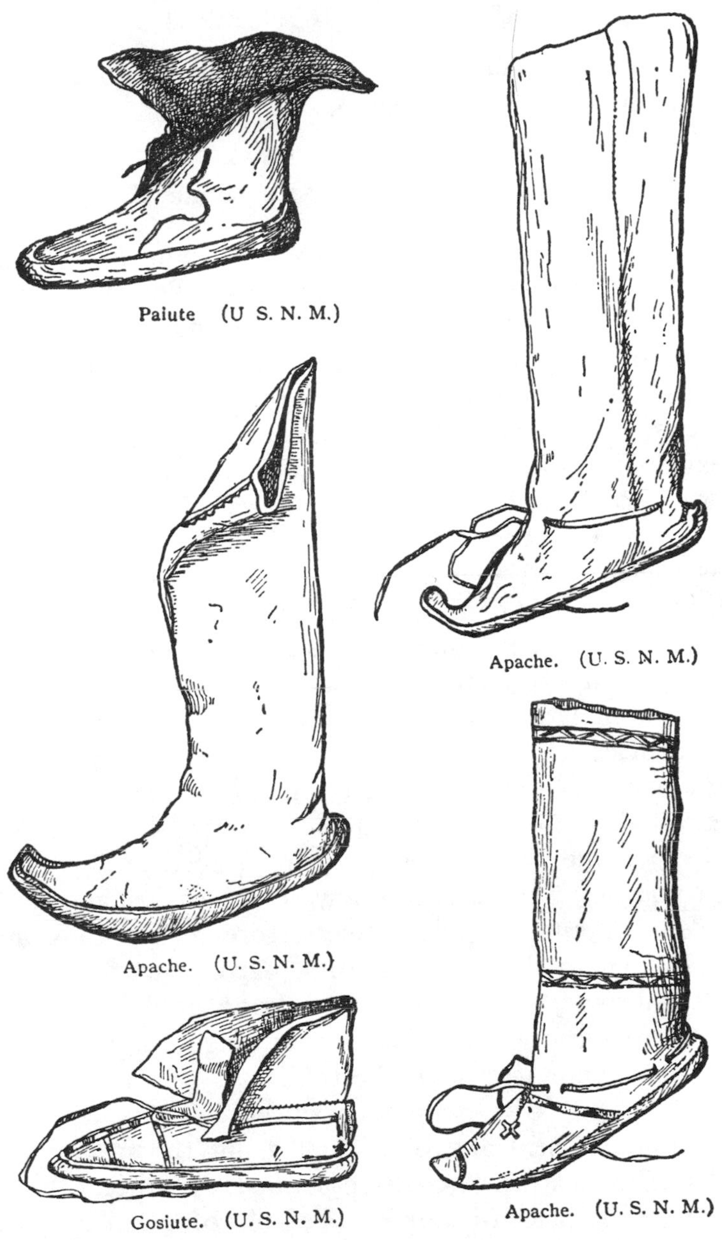

FIGURE 35

Moccasins of the Desert Region

and the earth upon which we tread must see that we are not unmindful of her presence.

XL. HOW INDIANS EMBROIDERED

Ornamentation both decorative and symbolic was an important part of American Indian art. The opportunity that a plain surface gave tempted the Indian to cover it with something that he thought beautiful or full of meaning. To this end, Indians carved the surfaces of wooden articles, they painted skins (even their own), they wove designs in baskets and blankets, and they embroidered patterns on skin, cloth and bark.

The material used for the best and most striking work was the quill of the porcupine. Some northern tribes used the bell hair of the moose. As all this material was rather short, much ingenuity was required in splicing and in concealing the matched ends.

An examination of any collection of old Indian clothing and articles of personal use at once reveals the amazing amount of quill embroidery employed for pure ornamentation. Shirts were "quilled" over the shoulders and down the front, leggings were quilled at the sides, pipe pouches were quilled as were moccasins and armbands. Porcupine quills came before glass beads and beads, even to this day, have not driven out the art of quill embroidery. It is distinctively an art of the older American and it will probably live as long as any northern Indians remain who love the traditions of their people.

The hunting of porcupines was the task of men, who also skinned them and often pulled out the treacherous quills. These are coarse, sharp-pointed, cylindrical things that take the place of hair on the body of the porcupine. The distal ends,—the ends that stick out,—are exceedingly sharp and are like barbed needles. When one punc-

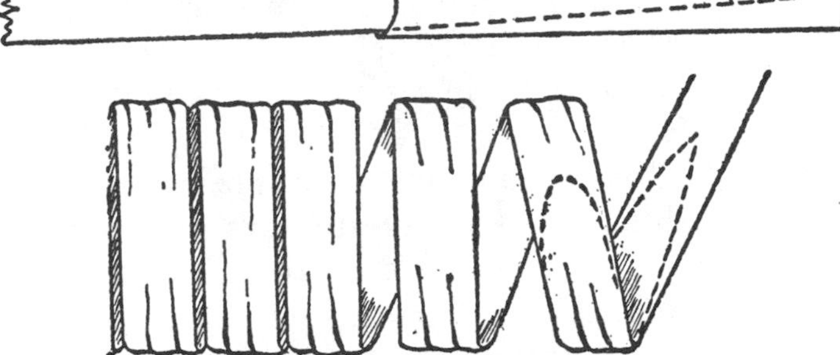

A method of splicing.

Method of fastening quills to leather.

An intricate method of crossing and folding.

FIGURE 36

Technique of Porcupine Quill Work

tures the skin it is not easy to draw it out. Quills are of various sizes and lengths, and thus are sorted, the coarser ones being the most useful if they are also long. Once sorted they were put in cases made from the bladders of elk or buffalo.

Quills were dyed various colors, these being red, yellow, blue, green and black. The purest colors were employed, and no mixed or off-shades were desired. Naturally white quills were also used.

When the worker was ready to use the quills she placed them in saucers containing a little water and soaked them for an hour or so. An elderly Indian woman who allowed me to watch her day after day, and who told me to keep still and not ask questions, drained the water and covered the quills with damp cloths or wet buckskin. Then she would take each quill, nip off the wicked point and flatten the quill with a piece of smooth, flat bone, called a quill flattener. Sometimes she would hold one end in her teeth and draw it between her thumb nail and the end of her forefinger, doing it again and again until the quill was quite flat. Then she would apply it to the skin she was decorating and sew it with a sinew thread.

The pattern employed was an older piece, or a drawing made on a piece of bark. Sometimes the pattern seemed to come out of old Gah-ah's head, for she simply worked away and produced her finery. And most Indian women did the same thing whatever may have been the time or tribe.

Holes were made in the buckskin with a fine awl and through the hole the sinew thread was drawn. As quills are rather stiff, most of the designs were geometrical in form.

Pictures and diagrams make unnecessary a detailed description of how the stitches were applied. Fortunately

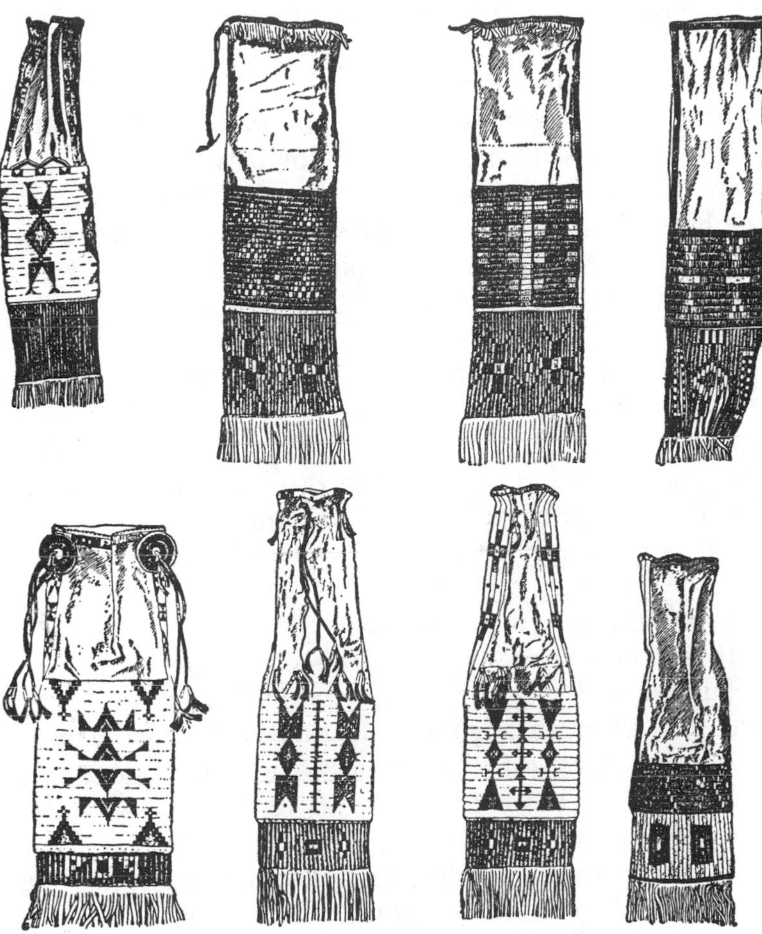

(Courtesy American Museum of Natural History)

FIGURE 37

Crow Indian Pipe Bags Showing Combination of Bead and Quill Work

Mr. William C. Orchard of the Museum of the American Indian, Heye Foundation, has made a thorough study of quillwork and his sketches are available.

Birch bark as well as skin was decorated, and in this case they dispensed with the sewing. It was only necessary to prick the design in the bark, select the colored quills and stick them through. For bark-work the quills were usually kept in the round. They were thrust through the holes, bent down and clipped. When the design was finished a piece of bark was placed against the cut ends as a lining, and to prevent the quills from being pushed out.

Moosehair was employed much as quillwork was, but as it was finer, several hairs were grouped into strands and fastened to the skin or bark by an over-and-over stitch. Moosehair was frequently thrust through from the underside of the skin or cloth and then trimmed. When floral patterns were used this trimming was done in relief, so that the flower or other form was modeled. When done in colors this was most effective.

It is interesting to note that this old Indian embroidery is durable and that the fastening threads seldom pulled out, even when, through use, the quill or hair wore away.

Another form of "embroidery" was that done with feathers. Perhaps we should call it appliqué work, for the feathers were applied one by one. Feathers were selected for size and color, and carefully graded. They were used in decorating mantles and baskets. Several eastern tribes used feathers, the Lenape and Choctaw making striking garments of them. The Pomo make wonderful baskets by weaving in the feathers of birds. To hold the feather, the quill was flattened and coiled around the warp or fastening thread.

IV: THE FOOD QUEST

IV

THE FOOD QUEST

XLI. HOW INDIANS FOUND FOOD IN THE FOREST

The forest abounds with wholesome food if one knows where to look. There are many kinds of berries, fruits, mushrooms, roots, nuts, tubers, green shoots and even bark, that may be eaten.

The thrifty dweller of the forest gathered each food in its season, and either ate it at once, or dried it, if he could, for winter. Women usually went in companies to gather wild foods, and made the occasion a holiday. Hunters on the trail, and warriors too, knew what to look for when they came to places where favorite foods grew in profusion.

In the spring of the year the tender shoots of berry bushes were gathered. Milkweed sprouts were also used. Greens were in great demand when the grass grew green after the winter's cold.

As berries ripened they were picked in baskets. Indians ate them raw and cooked. Certain berries were even cooked with meat. It was the custom of many tribes to dry berries on sheets of bark or upon great basket trays. Even strawberries could thus be dried and stored. Raspberries, blackberries, huckleberries, blueberries, june berries and cherries were favorites for this purpose.

Nuts formed one of the staple foods of the first Americans, and they prepared them in several ways. Perhaps the most widely used nut was the acorn, though its flesh is bitter and acrid. There are some acorns that have a sweeter taste but these should be treated to remove the tannin, a bitter poison. Indians did not eat acorns raw. The great Pacific coast area was one of oak trees, and the Indians who migrated down the coast settled thickly there to enjoy the abundance of acorns. It must have taken much experimentation to learn how to remove the bitter taste, but they did learn.

Acorns were collected and dried in the sun, care being taken to prevent them from molding. The shells were then cracked off and the inner kernels separated from the shucks. When this "meat" is to be used as food it is thrown in a stone mortar and ground into a flour. This is frequently sifted, and the coarser particles thrown back for repounding. A filter is now prepared and water thrown in upon the fine meal. Fine baskets were used as filters, and also finely woven cloth. Sometimes the basket was set upon a pile of gravel so that the water would drain through and trickle down into the loose stones beneath. The object of the filter was to wash out the tannic acid in the flour and make it sweet and wholesome.

When the water runs clear from the basket and the yellow stain disappears, the meal is ready. It is now saturated with water and resembles dough when handled. When stirred up in cold water to thin it, this acorn meal is cooked into a porridge, and may be either thick or thin. Acorn dough is also wrapped in corn husk and baked in the ashes. The food is wholesome, but lacks much flavor, though it is highly satisfying and is very nourishing.

Chestnuts, like the acorn, have no inner shell. Thus chestnuts were gathered with eagerness and stored for winter. They were eaten boiled, roasted or ground to a meal. They were carefully dried, much as acorns were, and when shelled they were pounded into a coarse flour and made into bread. White corn meal was often added and the combination was good. A little goes a long ways, however, and it is best to eat sparingly of nut breads, and even then to eat other things with them.

Hickory nuts, walnuts, butternuts and hazel nuts were great favorites with the eastern Indians, and to these the western people added pecans and buckeyes. Nuts were cracked and the meats taken out just as at the present day, but the first Americans also threw nuts into a wooden mortar with a deep cavity and pounded them until the shells were sufficiently broken. The mass of meats and shells was then thrown into water and the shells skimmed off. When all floating particles had been removed the liquid was boiled, there being frequent skimmings. The milky fluid was then preserved as an oily paste to eat with bread and hominy.

Nuts rich in oil, as the black walnut, butternut and beechnut, were crushed, thrown into boiling water, and the floating oil skimmed off. It was considered a valuable oil for salads and even for use in frying meats.

Nuts are seeds, but the Indians used the seeds of grasses as well. Even the tiny seed of the cat-tail was used when all else failed, the fuzz being burned off and the seed particles ground and boiled. It was a starvation ration. Much better was the seed of dropseed grass, picnic grass and floating manna grass. The seeds are gathered, freed from chaff by winnowing, parched and then ground into a flour. The seeds of wild rice were of great importance.

Root foods were perhaps the main reliance, among the wild products of nature. First came the artichoke and groundnut. The groundnut or wild bean vine has a root formed of long strings of small potatoes, numbering ten to forty. These were dug from the bottom lands and cooked as potatoes are now. They were small but of excellent taste. The women gathered them in springtime after freshets, but in the autumn it was necessary to grub with hoes for them.

The roots of a number of lilies were used as food, among them the yellow Canada lily, Turk's-cap, broad-leaved arrowhead, water arum (wild calla lily), showy orchid and yellow pond lily.

All these roots were gathered, cleaned and cooked, special treatment being given each. The yellow pond lily was dug from the pond or stream bottom and getting them was quite a task. Long poles were used, but Indian girls who were good swimmers would dive down and dig them out with their hands. Muskrats were fond of these roots and Indians availed themselves of the muskrat's work when a rat-house could be found. The root was cooked by boiling or roasting.

Perhaps the oddest bulb food is that prepared from the plant which we call Jack-in-the-pulpit, and which the Indians called "fire ball." The onion-shaped root is as fiery as concentrated pepper. When the roots are gathered in the fall and stored in damp sand they are used for winter bread. To remove the acrid taste, the roots are baked, sliced and dried. When thoroughly dry they are pounded into a meal. This is again heated and set aside to dry out. It is then free from its fire and ready to mix into a meal for cooking.

On the prairies grows the breadroot, sometimes called the prairie turnip. These roots, the size of a duck's egg, are dug by the Indian women, and often by hungry men. The tough skin is peeled off and the flesh dried, making material for an excellent flour.

Chief among the wild foods of the northern forests was wild rice. It grew in great profusion in the shallow waterways, and was gathered in canoes. The canoe was manned by a paddler and a gleaner. The gleaner bent the tall stalks over the side of the canoe and beat out the grain with two short sticks, filling the craft as the paddler sent it through the marshes. The initial gathering was the smallest part of the work, for when prepared it had to be freed of chaff by a roasting and winnowing process. The result was worth the effort, however, for wild rice is a most palatable food. The Chippewa and Menomini gathered it in abundance and used it as an article of trade. It is now considered a great delicacy in the east being sold in stores where high-grade foods are kept. If the world only knew as much about many of the old Indian foods as it does of wild rice it would demand them on its daily table.

The red man who traveled through the deep woods and hidden clearings found many seeds, nuts and roots with which he satisfied his appetite. He could eat leaves and greens, once he knew the wholesome kinds. Leaves like those of the adder tongue, wild mustard, clover, brooklime, watercress, young fern leaves before the down was appeared, corn salad, honeywort, trillium, waterleaf and wild onions when young, are all good as greens or pot herbs. Indians thought that eating greens kept fevers away and prevented rheumatism, and perhaps they were right.

When mushrooms and puffballs were in season they were gathered by Indians who understood which were good to eat and which were poisonous. Mushrooms were cooked with meat or boiled down in grease. Certain kinds like the oyster mushroom were dried for winter use, grated or milled and used in soup. Even "rock tripe" was used when nothing else could be found.

When all else failed and men were hungry the inner bark of the basswood, slippery elm, birch, striped maple and sassafras was cut up and boiled into a stringy soup. Even the inner bark of white oak has been used by starving men.

Hunters who could find a squirrel's nest robbed it of

most of its nuts, if not quite all, and failing in this they robbed the house of a muskrat for its store of roots.

The buds and leaves of trees like the sassafras, linden, and hemlock have been used. In the springtime some Indians, as the Canadian Algonkins, peeled the inner bark from the tops of pines and collected it in buckets, for it has a sweet sap that is greatly liked. Because of this habit of eating "wood," the Iroquois called these people Hadi-ron-daks, from which word we get the name Adirondacks. It means "they eat logs."

Long ago Jisgogo, my old camp mate, treated me to a taste of wilderness life in the open, in which we had to live off the land and out of the water. We lived much as the old Indians did, and with as little clothing. We found the greens, the berries, the tubers and the fruits in their season, and fish, rabbits, grouse and ducks at about all seasons, for hunger is not discriminating. We swam in the streams, we roamed the hills, far from the sight of a critical civilization and we grew hard and brown. This experience made me see the need of knowing how to find food in the forest and how to prepare it. The cooking is half the battle; knowing how to make roots and nuts fit for cooking is the other half.

Ever since those days I have brought wild foods into my camps and feasted upon them. I have even visited many Indian reservations and learned how different tribes cook wild foods from glen and glade, but nothing I ever ate tasted half so good as when hunger taught me how to relish what I could find, with my own hands and digging stick, in the woodland and in the marsh.

XLII. HOW INDIANS COOKED THEIR FOOD

Camp life makes one think of the problems of cooking that the red man must have faced. We know that he ate, but how was his food prepared? Was he finicky about it, or would he eat anything? We will answer these questions as we go along.

In the first place most of the first Americans liked their food well cooked. They wanted it *done.* At the same time they wanted it to have a good flavor, and overcooking was apt to ruin this. (I have tried to eat some game that I wished had been ruined entirely.) The Indians prized a good cook, and always praised her. Their way was not to grumble over poor cooking but to praise the good.

The Indian woman had only a few simple utensils to assist her in her art. Nevertheless she knew how to cook meat and vegetables to a turn. One favorite way was to cover game,—fish, fowl, rabbits and the like,—with clay, well worked and spread on two fingers thick, care being taken that no part of the creature, even a bit of hair, stuck out. Fish were not scaled, birds were not plucked, save for the larger feathers, but their heads and wings were removed. Sometimes the game was dressed and stuffed with pot herbs, but sometimes not. The clay-wrapped tid-bit was then placed in the embers, being covered with ashes and glowing coals.

A good fire was now built over the mound and the cooking was continued for an hour or so. When the roast was taken from the embers the clay was broken with a stick and pulled off, the fur, scales or feathers coming with it, leaving a dish fit for any epicure.

Indians, who had clay kettles, pot-roasted their meats, the pot being heaped around with embers and covered with a flat stone. Frying in deep fat was done in a clay pot. I have dug up scores of these ancient cooking vessels, and thousands of pieces of them, with the charred grease still sticking to them. The greases used were those of the deer, bear and buffalo, though there were vegetable oils made of nuts and sunflowers.

Meat could be boiled, of course, and in the form of soup it formed a common food. Cured meats, as dried venison, bear meat, buffalo, fish and even oysters and clams were pulverized and boiled with suitable vegetables.

Boiling could be done in skin or bark utensils, or even on a clay bed, by filling with cold water, dropping in the meat and then heating with hot stones taken from a near-by fire. It was safer to boil in a bark dish than in a clay pot, because of the ease with which the pot was broken. One hot stone gives off a great deal of heat, and a dozen or so used in this manner soon finishes the task of hot-stone cooking.

Meat was stuck on spits and roasted before an open fire, the spits being turned to keep the process even. In this connection it is well to note that the Indians watched their pots, and that they *did* boil. They also watched all their cooking, it being considered a sign of a poor cook to ramble away and become interested in something else. There were several amusing tales about people who forgot their meat, as the raccoon did when he went to sleep and let the fox eat his roasting geese.

A fireless cooker was commonly used for meat, beans, tubers and corn. A hole a foot and a half deep (knee deep) was dug and in it a fire was kindled. Gradually larger pieces of wood were put in until the pit was filled with glowing embers. More than this, the earth was heated a considerable distance beyond the surface. The hole was now quickly cleared, the meat or vegetables put in a pot, or suitably wrapped, and then the whole covered with ashes and hot embers. Sometimes a fire was built over the pit to keep the heat where it belonged. This fire might then die down, and the cook depart for a couple of hours. When he came back his dish was done, and done in a delicious way. It had cooked slowly and in its own juices. Indians like beans and corn on the cob cooked this way.

There is one thing about an Indian fire that must be mentioned. It is small and direct. It does not blaze away for nothing and waste heat and fuel. The fire is directly under a pot and it is easy to approach it. Such fires could be built in tipis and wigwams without danger, and when made outside they saved fuel, and the minimum of smoke did not attract enemies, nor did they set the woods ablaze.

Many times corn bread and cakes were baked in the ashes. To do this the bread was laid in a clean spot in the ash bed and then covered with white ashes and embers. Heckewelder, the missionary who lived with the Delaware people more than a century ago, says that this bread was of two kinds; one made up of green corn while still "in the milk," and the other of dry and ripened corn. This is pounded as fine as possible in a wooden mortar, sifted and then kneaded into a pasty dough. When thoroughly mixed with water it is formed into cakes about a span in diameter, round and with rounded edges, like an auto wheel.

Corn, indeed, formed the principal diet of the Indians of the eastern part of the United States and nearly all of Mexico. Its cultivation, in general, followed the drainage system of the Mississippi and Missouri rivers. There were many kinds of corn and from these varieties many different dishes were prepared. The common corn of the eastern Indians was soft white corn, sometimes called Tuscarora corn (Zea mays amylacea). Real *Indian meal* was white and floury, and not yellow and granulated as we have it now.

In order to prepare this corn for cooking it was first pulled from the husk, shelled, and then thrown in a solution of wood ashes and water. This was really a weak lye, and its strength was tested by having it just strong enough to "bite the tongue." In this the corn was boiled for twenty or thirty minutes. When the outer covering of the corn, the skin or hulls, looked swelled and loose, the first process was over. The corn was then dipped out and put in a tall washing sieve. In this it was rinsed in a brook or in a tub until the lye had been washed out and the hulls had loosened and floated away. This left the half cooked, white interior ready for grinding or smashing in a mortar. When pulverized, the soft, wet meal was sifted in a wooden basket having a fine mesh, say, one-sixteenth of an inch. This done, the meal was mixed with boiling water, just enough, and quickly molded into a flat, circular cake. The cook now dips her hands into very cold water and rubs them over the cake to give it a smooth surface,—to make it shiny. This helps keep the flavor in when cooking. Two things may now be done. The cake may be wrapped in cloth or husks and boiled, or it may be wrapped in leaves and baked in the fire, as Heckewelder described.

Sometimes red kidney beans were put in the meal, sometimes various kinds of berries or nuts. One thing is certain; this bread is fine food and once one has eaten it it remains a life-long passion. It is sliced and laid in a plate or piece of bark, and eaten with sunflower oil, nut oil or maple syrup. When cold it is excellent fried. The juice in which it is boiled,—it being done when it floats,—is saved as a gruel or thin soup.

In my boyhood days I often took my lunch to school. As our family had many things of a modern nature that other Indians lacked, I had wheat bread, roast beef, jelly cake and cookies. These I would trade with the boys from "up the hill" for their Indian corn bread and hulled corn hominy,—and I was the one who got the bargain. The hunger for these old foods still continues with the

Christian Indians, and when they hold their church socials and pink teas they have hulled corn quite as often as they have ice cream.

This hulled corn was prepared as for bread. When thoroughly freed from the hulls and outer skin it was thrown in cold water and boiled for four hours, or until the kernel burst open. Pieces of meat were added to give a good flavor.

There were many combinations of corn foods, some of which were cooked with nut meal or nut oil, some with various kinds of meat, and some with vegetables. The diet seemed to meet the taste and the needs of the Indians completely.

Sweet corn was scraped from the cob and beaten into a paste in a mortar. This paste is then placed in a large kettle lined with basswood leaves, three deep. When it is packed in, the top is smoothed off, covered with a layer of three leaves, sprinkled with white ashes, half an inch thick, and this in turn covered with glowing embers. The kettle is now placed over a small fire, which is constantly renewed, and the top embers are renewed three times. The dish is now "all set" and if the pot hangs in a sheltered place where it will not cool rapidly it may remain without fire for the night. Many times, however, the kettle is taken from its tripod and placed on the warm bed of the old fire and heaped about with ashes.

When morning comes the ashes are brushed from the top, the shriveled leaves removed, and a steaming mess of the most appetizing breakfast food ever invented is revealed. Taken from the kettle the baked corn is sliced and may be dried before a gentle fire, or if placed in trays may be dried in the sun, care being to take it in at night. The food is called Ogonsah.

Parched corn and popcorn were used by the eastern Indians. Blue soft corn was thought to be the best for parching. When well roasted it was sifted and packed in a tight receptacle. It might even be mixed with powdered meat, nuts and sugar. This formed the traveler's pemmican. To prepare it, a handful was mixed with two cups of water and then cooked for a half hour.

There were many wild foods in the forest which were gathered in season, both for ready use and for winter storage. Chief among these were berries, nuts, artichokes, mushrooms and wild fruits. Mushrooms, especially the oyster mushroom, were dried and mixed with meats. Artichokes were boiled like little potatoes, though when fresh were eaten raw. Berries were sweetened with maple sugar and eaten as we eat them now. For winter use these berries were dried on great basket trays, packed in bark containers and put away.

Nuts were pounded with their shells, flung in water and boiled until the shells had all been skimmed off. Some nuts, like the chestnut, were carefully peeled and mixed with bread and hominy.

Green foods were not lacking in the Indian's diet. He was fond of the sprouts of young plants, as wild raspberries, which he ate like asparagus.

For flavoring, sassafras, wintergreen, hemlock tips, wood ashes, bayberries, pepper root, wild ginger and the like were used. The Indians used salt sparingly, believing that an excess caused illness and an unnatural thirst. The use of white wood ashes took the place of salt when the latter was not obtainable.

Heckewelder in writing of the Lenape Indians says, "They are not only cleanly in their eating, but even delicate, and they will sometimes resist pressing calls of hunger rather than eat the flesh of those animals which they consider as not being the proper food for man."

XLIII. HOW INDIANS ATE THEIR FOOD

In the olden days the Indians rose early in the morning. The men went out into the open air and either played some athletic game or went on a hunt. The women, meanwhile, prepared the hominy and meat. An early morning meal was unusual and with some tribes there was much exercise before taking anything but copious draughts of water.

It was not uncommon for a man to hunt all day before sitting down to his single meal. A white captive named Smith complained that his host chased wild horses for exercise before breakfast and, failing to catch them, ran all day, and for a distance of one hundred miles before eating. Indeed, the record reads, "An Indian warrior can run from twelve to fourteen hours without refreshment, and after a hasty meal appears completely refreshed and ready for a second course."

The noonday meal was the first general family gathering of the day, and when all was prepared the mother of the household exclaimed, "Sed-i-kon-i, hauh, sedikoni!" which meant, "Come eat, 'tis well, come eat!" It was a welcome invitation.

Each member of the family took down his own personal dishes,—his bowl of wood or clay, his spoon or ladle, his bark plate, his awl and his knife. Food was ladled into the bowl and plate from the cooking pots. As there was no table every one sat on the ground or held his dish on his lap.

Each person was responsible for the condition of his eating utensils, and washed them or not as he desired, but it was not usual for any one else to do it. The bowls were carved from knots and knurls, and sometimes had pictures of animals or war scenes scratched upon them. The spoons were large and would hold five or six tablespoonfuls. Indeed, when the Indians first saw the small spoons of the whites, they laughed and said, "Ho hoh, white man, his arm get heap tired long before he is full!" The bowls of Indian spoons were shaped much like a clam shell and the handle rose in a graceful curve and was topped by the effigy of a duck, a dove, a squirrel or a bear. The horn spoons of the plains were made of buffalo horn and were like scoops. The handles of these were decorated with braided quills and colored feathers.

Plates were shallow bowls as large as a platter and the boiled roots and meat were put in these. They were made of bark and bound with hoops, one inside and one outside, the two holding the bark rim between them. The binding was a lace of the inner bark of the elm.

In eating, the Iroquois made every effort to show their pleasure in order to compliment the cook (whom they called Ga-kwaih). They said "Ah" as they ate their soup, and exclaimed "Oh-guh-oh," when they ate their meat. This meant "Delicious."

Men were trained not to show any dislike for ill-tasting food but to swallow it stoically. "Dainties are not for stalwart men," said their chiefs. "What one thinks poor fare in a lodge may be regarded as a dainty when on the hunt."

Hospitality was the rule of every Indian community. As each visitor came into a lodge he was offered food, and courtesy required that he take it. If he visited fifty homes in a day he had fifty meals. "The Great Spirit made food," said the wise old men. "It is for all and, like the air, what is for one is for all."

After eating a meal the Iroquois Indians said grace,—that is, they gave thanks. This was done by striking the bench or the ground with the right fist, at the same time clenching it and holding up the index finger with the exclamation, "Haih-nyah-weh!" This was to say *thank you* to the Great Spirit. The host or hostess answered, "Nyuh!" This meant, "It is well, so be it."

While visiting the Wichita Indians of Oklahoma with my friend Jisgogo we had an opportunity of eating with them. They knew that we were strangers and had taken great pains to make our banquet a memorable one. Knowing that we had visited many places and knew all the Indian agents, and even the Great Father in the White House, himself, they wanted everything right, and told us so.

We were delighted with the idea of eating a real Indian meal among these good people, and could see all the preparations from the grass lodge where we were sitting. Jisgogo talked with me of the native foods and wondered if they would be like those of the Ojibway, the Sioux and the Sauks. Soon our interpreter called us and gave us preliminary instructions.

"This feast is for you," he said. "Much food has been provided. You must eat everything placed before you, or pay the man to the right or across from you to eat it. It must be eaten. You must not insult your hosts by not eating everything."

We had taken a long ride over the prairies and were hungry. The prospect of Wichita hominy pleased us and other native dishes were subjects of great expectations.

One of the middle-aged warriors came over to act as an usher. He seated us in the very center of the "table." This table was a long strip of traders' cloth rolled out on the prairie. Our "chairs" were nothing but the ground. But, not minding this one whit, we looked at our feast.

Before each of us in resplendent glory were a loaf of National bread, a box of crackers, a tin of corned beef, steaming nicely, a can of tomatoes, a half-pound of butter, a store cake, a can of cherries and a pumpkin pie. Jisgogo looked at me with anguished eyes, and I knew that he was groaning inside. To the right of us and to the left the good people had their own native foods, such as corn tamales, done up like two balls tied together, corn hominy, squash pudding, boiled beef, rabbits and roasted game birds. These were the things that we wanted, and yet were denied. Our thoughtful hosts had driven twenty miles to get "store food" for us, fearing that the home cooking might not please us.

Let me describe the situation. We were squatted before the feast, back of us were the camp dogs, scores of them, and back of the dogs were the camp hens, all very respectful as to distance and as to activity. Still their noses and bills all pointed our way, smelling for bones and bits of corn bread. Not a dog came near, however, and not a chicken dared approach the dead line.

Jisgogo and I tried to eat. We sneaked all the crackers into our pockets, hired our neighbors to take the cherries and the cake, exchanged the bread and butter for hominy and ball bread, and then settled down to eat what we could. We did nobly and no fattened goose ever gorged so close to bursting. The pie alone remained.

Then an eager chicken, unable to restrain her appetite, flew with a simpering cackle, soaring straight for the table and directly over my shoulders. A watch-dog meanwhile gave her chase, which so excited the chicken that she landed in the middle of my pumpkin pie with a terrorized squawk. My pie was wrecked, and I hoped to be excused, but from one side the interpreter leaned over and whispered, "You must eat all that is set before you!" His tone was dismally final, and his eyes showed no relenting.

I shall never tell how I juggled that pie into my pockets

and into the husks of my ball bread, and yet appeared to eat all of it. To tell it is worth money.

We enjoyed our feast and thanked our hosts, but being full of emotion and other things, as well as gratitude, we were not very eloquent. Still we had experienced Wichita hospitality and shall never forget the food, the people, or the indiscreet hen. Nor will we forget the interpreter, who afterward told us that he had just "kidded" me about eating the pie. It was not expected, but I let him think it had been done, just the same.

Indians had certain fixed table manners and rebuked their children when they were impolite. Food first went to the old and the very young, and then the warriors took their share. It was not good form to be greedy or to snatch.

Among the Iroquois one could ask for food by saying, "Do-dus-ha," meaning *please give me,* and the host or hostess frequently asked if more was wanted.

Indians ate with their fingers, with their spoons and with their food awls. They did not put their knives in their mouths, and they had no forks. The only napkins they had were wisps of grass or corn husks. Eating was done in a natural way and it was considered as necessary to please the hostess as to satisfy the appetite.

XLIV. HOW INDIANS MADE THEIR GARDENS

How many times we have read that the "Indians are a nomadic race, living by hunting and fishing. The women do all the work while the men idle their time or engage in warfare." This is a common fable, even though it flies in the face of fact.

The truth is that there was just as much hunting and fishing as was necessary to secure food-flesh for the family and no more. Hunting was work in those days and not sport. Many tribes lived upon the products of their fields almost entirely. Indians were farmers, cultivators, plantation owners and plant breeders.

Most of the tribes of the eastern forest area, all along the Atlantic coast and extending throughout the Mississippi valley, had extensive gardens and plantations. Every discoverer and explorer mentions the Indian gardens and their products, but very few of these descriptions have reached the school textbooks.

It was Columbus who described Indian corn or maize for the first time. In the "Life of Columbus," by his son, there appears a note under date of November 5, 1492. It reads: "There was a great deal of tilled land, some sowed with those roots, a sort of beans and a sort of grain they call maize, which was well tasted, baked or dried and made into flour."

Because the Indians of the coast had their plantations of corn the Pilgrim fathers of Plymouth Rock and the settlers of Jamestown were able to live. Without it as given them by the natives they would have starved. Had it not been for the farm products of the Indians the settlers would have become discouraged and the peopling of America would have been delayed for a full century, at least so states one of the highest authorities.

The principal vegetables cultivated were corn, beans, squashes, sunflowers, tobacco and gourds. Early travelers tell of melons, and others mention sweet potatoes. The white potato in several varieties was cultivated in Peru, but for some reason it is called the "Irish potato."

Indian farms were cleared by girdling the trees, burning them down and then hoeing up the land. Brush, weeds, tall grass and all rubbish was drawn aside or burned. Fields were cleared before planting,—except in rare instances where the country was new. When the rough work had been done by the men the women began to make the corn hills. These were little mounds of soft earth into which fish or other fertilizer had been put.

From five to ten kernels were planted in a hill. These had been previously soaked in water mingled with vegetable poisons to discourage grubs, wire worms and crows. From the swelling of the grain it was possible to tell which were fertile and strong.

Fields of corn varied, just as they do now, from little patches to great plantations running for miles along the fertile river flats. With the corn, beans and pumpkins were planted and on the borders of the fields were rows upon rows of sunflowers. From the sunflower was pressed the table oil. The Indians taught the white man the whole art of cultivating corn, and civilized man has added practically nothing to the Indian method. We plant in hills and rows just as the Indian did and we have the hoeing, the hilling and the two hoeings afterward, just as taught by the first Americans. The white man has combined and improved varieties,—some of them,—and he has invented machinery, but the growing itself is now as it was before the European invader landed on these shores. It is one of the priceless gifts of the red man.

There is a pretty legend about the staple food plants. It relates, so the Iroquois say, that the Maize, the Bean and the Squash are three loving sisters who must always dwell together to be happy. The older sister is tall and graceful, the next younger loved to twine about her and lean for strength upon her. The youngest rambled at the feet of these and protected them from prowling enemies. When the moon drops low and the summer night is lit only by the mysterious light of the stars, these three sisters come forth in human form wearing their green garments and decked in blossoms. They have been seen dancing in the shadows, singing to their Mother Earth, praising their Father Sun, and whispering words of comfort to mankind. And men, to show gratitude, call the three sisters Dyoñheyko, "they sustain our lives."

Upon first thought it may seem that Indians did not need fences because there were no horses and cows, no sheep or goats to destroy the plants. The fact is, however, that the Indians did need fences and they may have erected them stockade fashion. Deer, elk and buffalos were fond of the growing corn, just as they are now. Birds, too, as crows and blackbirds, were most destructive. For this reason platforms were erected in the fields as well as on their borders, and men with arrows, fringed skins and bull roarers were stationed upon them to frighten the wild game. It was no easy task to preserve the fields from being eaten up before the harvest. Little wonder that when the precious food was gathered there was a public thanksgiving and great rejoicing.

So vast and so important were the fields of corn and other farm produce to the eastern Indians that when the French invaded the country of the Iroquois beginning about 1650 they spent most of their time in cutting down and burning them. The Governor of New France, Count Denonville, reported that in four Seneca Indian towns alone he destroyed a million bushels of their grain. This was in 1687. When Major General John Sullivan swept through the Seneca towns in 1779 to punish the Indians for helping the British, with whom they had solemn treaties from early days, he burned thousands of acres of corn, beans, squashes, tobacco, hundreds of orchards and individual fruit trees, "being resolved to leave nothing growing that might contribute to their sustenance." He was successful and drove the Indians to the protection of the British fort at Niagara, laying waste their domain and breaking the power of the Iroquois.

In the southwest certain tribes, as the Pima, grew

their corn in the desert and brought water to its thirsty roots by means of irrigation ditches fed by impounded water from the mountains. The types of corn so cultivated were planted in holes and had long roots that sought moisture far below the surface.

With the eastern Indians, particularly the Iroquois, the care of the common tribal or clan fields rested with companies of women. Each company had its chief matron and other officers. The women worked in squad formation, four abreast, in which style they walked down the rows of corn, hoeing and singing the verses of an appropriate song. As they reached the end of the row they rested while a fresh squad took up the work. Generally there was a man on guard to prevent accidents or surprise by wolves, bears or enemies. Often there was an old warrior who sat at the fire and who told joking tales and wild adventures that set the women to teasing him as a braggart. Even white women who were captives enjoyed the work in the fields. It was like a picnic and was an occasion of many festivities.

XLV. HOW INDIANS PREPARED FOR THE HUNT

To the red men of the plains the buffalo hunt was one of the principal events of the year. Next to the battlefield, it furnished the greatest excitement. The tribal buffalo hunt was not an unorganized thing but, on the contrary, a highly organized institution, and it required much ceremonial as well as practical preparation.

Among the Omaha, the Council of the Seven Great Councilors governed the tribe, but on the hunt in which the whole group of people engaged, all were under the direction of the Master of the Hunt, called the Wathon. The destiny of a nation was in his hands, and this being realized, this officer had to give evidence of high qualifications. Generally he was a voluntary aspirant to whom a dream or his own desires had urged striving for the office.

First, he had to be a buffalo hunter of seasoned experience, and, secondly, he had to have all the material for a magical staff called a *washabe*. This staff was an ash sapling bent at the upper end like a shepherd's crook. To decorate it he required the skin of a bald eagle, a golden eagle, a crow and a swan, a dressed buffalo skin, two pieces of sinew, a shell disk, a cooking pot and the stem of a calumet.

As the time approached for the hunt the candidates sent his articles to the officers of the Honga clan, which had the right to construct the sacred pole or wand of office. If the man were accepted and the staff prepared for him, the Council of the Seven sat in solemn deliberation with him and laid out the general route of the hunt. So solemn was this council that the food for the chiefs had to be specially prepared before sunrise. Dressed in buffalo robes, the councilors ate their food and then filled the two sacred pipes, meanwhile chanting the ritual of preparation.

All this was done within the sacred council tent into which nothing pertaining to war could enter. When the smoking was over, not a word being spoken, the pipes were cleaned and returned to the keeper. One of the leading chiefs then opened up the discussion and others gave their opinions and offered advice. The summing up was done by the newly-elected Wathon. There were many things to consider in this movement of hundreds of people. Suitable camping places must be thought of, wood and water must be available, and the area must be one that yielded many wild turnips, so that the women could gather them for the winter's supply.

When a decision had been reached a runner was sent out to proclaim the day fixed by the wise men. But these wise men still remained with bowed heads, their robes about them, heads on the left, tails on the right and the middle about the head like a cowl. Thus seated, a holy feast was served in seven wooden bowls which were passed four times around the council circle. As the bowls paused before each man he took a mouthful from a buffalo-horn spoon, not touching the food with his fingers. The sun sank low and was down before these men could arise from their meditations. The die had been cast; the day of the hunt had been fixed.

From now on the life of the Wathon was an austere one. He fasted and he prayed the great Wakanda for wisdom to guide his people to success and away from enemies and danger. He communed with the unseen powers and his behavior was according.

When the day of the hunt came the people were prepared. All valuable property needed was packed and ready, clothing was in its parfleche cases, food was packed upon the ponies, tent poles, covers, bedding and cooking utensils were in bundles and bags.

Dawn came and the tribe was on the way. All was bustle and movement, but there was no disorder. Every one knew exactly what was expected of him or her and the destination of the first day was known to all. Only the old men and women were left behind in the deserted village, but as they might not be able to protect the valuables that had been left behind, holes were dug in the earth and such things concealed.

Oddly enough, the Director of the Hunt remained behind to finish his fourth day of fasting. When all had gone he removed his moccasins and went on with bare feet, reaching the first camp about sundown. He went to his own tent and remained there alone to pray. Above all things this man must command respect, his mind must be clear and his judgments good. He kept the peace of the tribe, he settled quarrels and prevented jealousies and fights.

As a holy man and the Director of the Hunt, all success or failure was attributed to him. Sickness, accidents, quarrels and mistakes were charged to him. Since the people knew that no man, even one in communion with Wakanda, could overcome all obstacles, they elected an official scapegoat called a Wathon who could be blamed, thus removing from the real Wathon all stigma.

All the ceremonial articles were kept in the three sacred tents and the ceremonial staff or Washabe was carried by a virgin who kept close to the pony bearing the sacred white buffalo hide. There was also a sacred pole which was carried by its keeper. Ancient rites had prescribed these things.

As the camping spot was reached, every woman knew where to set up her tipi. There was no dispute as to this, for the organization of the camp had been completed before the start. Ponies were tethered, bundles deposited, tripods set up and travoix stowed safely. Night settled down and the people slept.

Morning came and when the Wathon let down the cover of his tipi, baring the poles, the word went out that the time had come to move on towards the haunts of the buffaloes, onward into another day. The orders of the Director were passed out to his lieutenants and these in turn passed them on to the soldiers, who kept order. Every infraction was punished. The hunt was a vast tribal game and every man and woman, every boy and girl, was compelled to abide by the rules. Life and success depended upon it.

XLVI. HOW INDIANS HUNTED THE BUFFALO

The great tribal hunt of the plains people was a mass movement in search of food and material for clothing. Added to this was the fact that it was a time of great excitement, though all undue show of this was forbidden.

As the tribe moved on through the prairie land, the leaders watched with great care for signs of the buffaloes. Scouts ran from side to side and inspected wallows, looked for trampled grass, fresh footprints and every other sign. When things looked as if the buffaloes were near, the chiefs of the Wathon and of the Washabe (the proper chiefs of the hunting council) came together and selected from the bravest and most capable men the warriors who should act as marshals of the hunt. To be selected for this position was a great honor, for it was a recognition of the rights of a warrior's crow. A *crow* is a long bustle of feathers that is tied to the waist and hangs to the ground. It is awarded when a warrior has more than once attained first honors in the first three grades of battle achievements.

Once elected, the marshals were summoned to the Sacred Tent of the White Buffalo Skin, where the leaders gave them their orders. "You are to do your full duty in preserving order and the rules of the hunt," they were told. "You are not to know the ties of relationship, neither that of father, uncle, son or brother. All must obey."

Among the rules to be enforced were those against private hunting, noise, the barking of dogs, yelling, loud calls. Barking dogs were killed and any hunter who went forward alone was put to death. The great tribal hunt was for all the people, and to avoid disappointment and danger to many, all must strictly obey.

With the detection of the presence of the big game the

Wathon, as Director of the Hunt, selected twenty young men who acted as scouts, in the language of the Omaha called *Wadonbe.* These scouts were to divide into suitable parties, or to scatter singly, as the condition of the country dictated, and to search for the herd that might be surrounded and killed. When the selection of scouts had been made, the Tribal Herald stepped in front of the Sacred Tent of the White Buffalo Skin, and chanted the order of the Wathon:

"Oh, chosen of the scouts, the land explore for me,
Go forward o'er the land, bringing knowledge to me!"

Eagerly the Wadonbe pressed forward to obey the honored command. They scanned the landscape, they followed beaten trails made by the sharp feet of traveling herds, they wriggled through the tall grass and sought lookout places on knolls. When, at length, a suitable herd had been discovered,—one large enough to be worthy of a tribal onslaught, the runners worked back toward the tribal camp, which, when they were within range, they signaled by means of the "cross-run" or *wabaha.* A single scout does this by running from side to side like a shuttle, but two scouts do it by running back and forth, crossing each other on the path. They kept up this signal until the sentinel at the Sacred Tent had been notified. Then they ran on to give a verbal report.

The signal having been seen and reported, the Sacred Pole and the White Buffalo Skin were taken from the Sacred Tent and carried to the edge of the camp, where the pole was leaned against its crotched support, and the white robe was placed over a frame, so as to resemble a buffalo lying down.

The runners now came in, singly or in pairs, each re-

(After Catlin)

FIGURE 38

The Buffalo Hunt

porting most truthfully the size of the herd. Meanwhile the tribal herald has been calling through the camp:

> "It has been told that smoke is rising from the earth,—
> Rising from the earth as far as vision reaches!"

When all was in readiness, the Director of the Hunt appointed two chiefs of the hunt whose duty it was to lead the hunters in the strategy of surrounding the buffalo herd. If the buffaloes were at some distance the camp was moved forward, this time with even more ceremony and caution. The Sacred Pole and the White Buffalo Skin were carried forward with the Seven Chiefs in the lead.

The movement upon the unsuspecting buffaloes was in four stages, at the end of each the Seven Chiefs taking seats and smoking the calumet pipe. The object of smoking was to check the excitement. There could be no grand rush at the herd when, upon pain of death, men were halted every now and then. Besides this, the pause gave the Seven Chiefs time to invoke the blessings of the great Wakanda, whose children they were. In the front among the leaders were two youths whose duty it was to cut out twenty tongues when the buffaloes were slain, and also take one heart, for sacrifice to the powers above. This would show gratitude and secure the favor of the Wakanda.

When the buffaloes were seen, the two chiefs, one with the Sacred Pole and the other with the Sacred Pipe Stem, divided and ran on either side of the herd, circling it completely and then coming together, when the pole was thrust into the ground and the stem tied to it. In their wake had followed the hunters, almost nude, save for loin cloths, moccasins, and skin blankets. On the flank were the marshals who prevented any hunter from shooting or riding into the herd. Punishment was given by striking with the rawhide quirt, a fearful lashing being given the offender.

When the order had been given to charge the herd the two youths whose duty it was to secure the heart and twenty tongues, dashed into the mêlée and slit the throat of each animal as it fell, taking out the tongue without cutting it and thrusting it upon the sharpened end of the unstrung bow which each carried. When these articles of sacrifice had been secured they were taken to the Sacred Tent.

The buffalo "surround" was an ingenious plan of attack. Hunters in two lines, armed with bows, arrows, spears or rifles, rode to the right and left of the herd, gradually closing in on it until it took alarm and began to thunder over the plains in a mad rush for safety. The swiftest horsemen dashed forward and then charged the great bulls that led the herd, turning them backward upon themselves in the opposite direction. Meanwhile missiles were flying and beasts by the score were falling.

The hunters upon their buffalo ponies in dashing against the herd plunged in their spears or shot their arrows with such effect as to go nearly through the great creatures. Frequently the bulls would lower their heads and gore a pony, or at least bowl it over. Seeing what was about to happen, a nimble rider would leap upon the back of the shaggy assailant and find safety as best he could. When excited riders were hemmed in by buffaloes which pressed against the horses, the riders would leap upon the backs of the buffaloes until a clear space was found, and then jump down, seize the skin robe about their waists, remove it and throw it skillfully into the face of the next beast that charged. This stopped the rush for a moment, and in that moment the hunter sent home a fatal dart.

The air was filled with dust, rising like an angry yellow cloud, there were snorts and bellows, yells and the thunder of trampling feet. And on the grass were great patches of blood,—the life-blood of a herd of beasts that only a few moments ago was grazing in safety. Arrows flew with an angry whizz, few missing the mark. Daring hunters, dashing against the fleeing animals, plunged their lances into their hearts, until only here and there, beyond the circle, stray buffaloes were to be seen. The ground was strewn with the big brown carcasses.

The animals that fled did not go far but turned in a dumb, hopeless way to view the slaughter of their herd. Some even trotted back into the ring of death, or were easily pursued and killed.

When the slaughter was over, and it took only about a quarter of an hour to reduce a considerable herd, the hunters rushed in and out among the beasts to identify the private marks upon their arrows, and thus learn the success of their marksmanship.

When all ceremonies had been completed and the sacrificial feast made, those whose duty it was to cut up the animals, skin them, strip the meat, and take the liver or other organs, began to get busy. Children ran about, dogs barked, there were shouts and orders, and the work of securing the gifts of the buffalo went on. The hunt was over and the securing of its benefits had begun.

From the buffalo came hair for woolen yarn and for stuffing pillows and bags, the pelt was tanned for robes, the meat was dried for winter use and the hoofs supplied glue. Almost every part of the buffalo, from horns to bones, had a use, though in most cases the material was so abundant that quantities went to waste.

In some instances buffalo herds were chased over cliffs, a man dressed in a hide being used as a decoy and placed in the distance. The buffaloes, being pursued, saw the decoy running to apparent safety. They dashed onward toward the cliff, when the man, throwing off the robe, clambered over the cliff to an overhanging shelf or cave, where he found refuge, whilst the deceived buffaloes, unable to check themselves, rushed on and plunged to destruction. Meanwhile the hunters took the trail to the base of the cliff and killed the animals who were not already dead. This method was not popular, for it had little of the sportsmanship or excitement that the plains Indians prized.

XLVII. HOW INDIANS HUNTED GAME

Hunting with the Indians was not a sport; it was the work of getting food for the family. Man's duty was to provide the meat for the house or tipi, while woman's work was to grow the vegetables, or to find them.

As every man expected to be a hunter, he began his training when a boy by learning to shoot with a bow and arrow. Boys often had shooting contests, both for accuracy and distance. Before a youth was allowed to go out on a hunt he had to satisfy his elders that he knew what to do and how to handle his weapons.

There were many things a hunter must do and almost as many he must not do. Taboos were things he must not do. Among the taboos were the laws forbidding the eating of food that smelled, like leeks or wild onions, the use of tobacco, and "thinking" songs.

Among the Iroquois the hunter had to take purges, take a cleansing bath in a sweat lodge and rub his body with certain leaves. Some Indians, as the Abenaki, rubbed their bodies with sweet ferns. The Iroquois hunter also lived alone for at least a week before going on a hunting party.

The reason for all these strange things was to have

the body clean and without any human odor. If Indians did not like to bathe for purposes of cleanliness, they had to like to do it if they wanted to go on a hunt with other men,—thus bathing became a habit from boyhood.

With their weapons in trim, with plenty of arrows, thongs, spare moccasins, dried food in the form of corn and pemmican, with knives of flint and bags of hunting charms, the party wended its way down the trail to the hunting ground.

When the region of the game was reached scouts were sent out to report what might be expected. The party then encamped and awaited the return of the scouts, who soon came back with their story. Among the Iroquois there was then a little ceremony and a dance. The pipe was passed and just one whiff taken by each man. As he blew out the smoke he thanked the Great Spirit and asked his favor. The next morning the party divided and began the hunt. The rules were to keep as quiet as possible, to avoid all talking, to eat no bark or herbs and to think no song, as the animals were supposed to love music and listen even for songs that were thought.

If deer were being hunted the men stationed themselves along the runways, keeping to windward of the game, that the scent might not reach the animals. As the creature came along it was shot. Sometimes several men shot at once, in which case the oldest man was given the kill even if his arrow had not touched it. It then became his duty to skin it. There were never any disputes among the Forest area Indians over game, because of the fixed rules. When deer were killed they were skinned when warm and their meat peeled off in sheets for drying. It was then hung up, either in sheets or stripped for the "jerking" process. This was simply drying and smoking.

Bears were hunted by brave men who walked up to

them and knocked them in the head with a war club. Of course they were sometimes shot, but the honorable way was to strike them as they stood erect. With some western tribes a hunter could count "coups" on such killings.

When the hunting party returned it brought the dried meat in great packs and in baskets. Fresh meat was brought in the green pelts, only the most choice cuts being thus saved, to reduce the weight.

When an Iroquois hunter returned to his village with game, he left it outside the limits, hidden in a secure place. He then cautiously went to his cabin and whispered to his wife where he had hidden the meat. She at once hastened to the spot and lugged it home. If it were too heavy, some clan brother helped her, or perhaps one of her sisters assisted. If the hunter had brought the meat into the village limits, the game would have been the property of his clan and his wife might be denied any right to it. This was the law.

Each tribe had its own hunting grounds, and it was an act of hostility to go over the line. If a hunter did so, and knew it, he might kill the animal, take the meat and hang up the skin. In such a case he had to paint his tribal mark and name upon it.

A man might go out hunting alone, and usually did. In summer he often went in his canoe and in winter he went on snowshoes. There were so many rattlesnakes in the East that it was deemed safer to hunt from a canoe when one was alone. Deer were shot as they came down to drink or swim a river. It was best to keep away from swimming animals in order to prevent them from climbing in the canoe, or trying to do so. There are tales of bears doing this in big dugouts, and then ambling away when the shore was reached. Deer were sometimes lured by jack lights placed along the shore. One of the best schemes, however, was to make a false salt lick, and then lure deer to it by wetting branches in salt water and waving them in the wind.

Hunting was often unsuccessful, especially when game was scarce, and often the hunter was brought to the verge of starvation, but custom required that he keep on until a kill was made. Frequently a hunter did not eat for days at a time.

XLVIII. HOW INDIANS GATHERED MEDICINE

Some Indian herb doctors knew of plants and roots that were good medicine. Oftentimes they kept the knowledge of these a deep secret, to be revealed only at the hour of death to some friend or relative. There is a common tradition that some tribes knew of a root that would cure the effects of a rattlesnake bite. Just what this root is no explorer seems to have discovered, though they will tell of having seen it used.

In the days of my youth I often went with medicine men and medicine women on their journeys for herbs. For a day or more the herb doctor would prepare his baskets, his wrappings and his bags which were to hold the medicine. These would be sprinkled with tobacco and remain so overnight. Early the next morning the medicine man would pray, looking toward the rising sun as he did. Then in the crisp air of the autumnal morning we would start for the deep woods to hunt for "nebezoon," or medicine.

Among the things carried along were little bags and bundles of sacred tobacco. In the olden days I was told that strings of wampum, arrowheads, beads, silver ornaments and quilled bands were taken along to sacrifice to the spirits of the plants.

The medicine man knew in general what he was after

and was prepared for it, but sometimes he made an unexpected discovery. As I prowled the forest and the flats with the herbalist, I noted that they collected boneset, spikenard, apple roots, hickory bark, sassafras, mandrake, prickly ash, calamus, wintergreen, lobelia, elder bark, golden seal, ginseng, cranesbill, male fern, maidenhair fern, dock, mint, sheep sorel, witch hazel, spruce and pine gum, bitney and Oswego tea. There were many other plants, as I may mention later on.

When the first of any plant was found it was spoken to as a friend but not plucked. Sometimes four plants had to be passed before one was pulled up.

The Seneca was very careful to observe the orders of the Prophet Handsome Lake, who said, "Now let this be your ceremony when you wish to employ the medicine in a plant: First offer tobacco, then tell the plant in gentle words what you desire of it, and then pluck it from the roots. It is said in the upper world that it is not right to take a plant for medicine without first talking to it."

When a plant was to be pulled the herbalist chanted a gentle song, using these words:

"You have promised that you would heal the earth,
That you were ready with your healing.
With that promise I now claim you, take you,
Take you for your healing virtues only.

"Oh, give me of your power to purge, to cleanse,
Your power to heal our people with your virtue.
I will not destroy you, but plant your seeds,
Plant them in the hole from which I take you.

"You will grow again and more than fourfold,
Oh, spirit of the herb, I'll not destroy,
Nor without purpose take you from the earth.
Accept my thanks for all your benefits."

A ceremonial fire was built and a tobacco incense offered. Then as each plant was pulled, its seeds were planted and a little offering made to it. The song was necessary only once for each class of herbs, unless another spot were gone to.

When gathered, the plants, roots and bark were dried within the lodge, great care being taken that no impure person came near them. When dried they were cut in small pieces and placed in fabric or leather bags. These were rolled in a piece of blanket or a buckskin and kept in a dry place. Bunches of herbs like boneset were kept hanging near the fireplace.

Not all Indian remedies were actually effective, because it was thought that the magic in them cured. Those whose magic always worked were thought to be especially good. For colds and fevers boneset tea mixed with prickly ash bark might be used. For stomach trouble sassafras and golden seal were effective. Mandrake was a good purge, while blackberry roots were an astringent.

Children were given the mucilage of slippery elm mingled with calamus or wintergreen for their stomach ills, but older people often took sand and white ashes, or sometimes clay with which golden seal or Solomon's seal had been pulverized.

Balms were made of bear grease and pitch, but mud was often used for stings and bruises. In the autumn the juice of the snap dragon was used for insect bites or for bruises. For mosquitoes, sassafras root was chewed up and smeared over the spots. The Seneca Indians had an oil that they used for keeping mosquitoes away. It was the crude oil from their spring.

The common medicines were gathered by housewife and hunter alike, as well as by the medicine men. The same careful ceremonies were observed by each. It will be remembered that Dr. Benjamin Rush, one of the founders of the Republic, and a noted physician of his time, studied the remedies of the Indians and wrote down many of their formulæ. Some of the most important medicines used to-day, such as mandrake, golden seal, quinine, coca (from which cocaine is derived), and bloodroot are Indian remedies.

The best of all medicines, however, were the prescriptions of pure water, plenty of air, exercise and bathing.

There were no contagious diseases in America, save one or two perhaps, before Europeans came. Smallpox, measles, scarlet fever, diphtheria, whooping cough and the like were unknown.

V: CEREMONIES AND MYSTERIES

V

CEREMONIES AND MYSTERIES

XLIX. HOW INDIANS TOOK THEIR OATHS

A fixed belief in the powers of the unseen world led the Indians to make promises of a solemn nature in their presence. This was nothing less than making a vow or taking an oath. It was believed that if the promise were violated or left undone, great harm would befall the man who made it.

"I will go alone to the village of the enemy and take the scalp of a warrior, that the death of my friend may be avenged. *They hear me!*" Thus spoke a Sioux, calling into his presence the Thunderers, to whom he referred when he said, "They hear me." Failure to do as promised or to make the effort meant that the Thunderers would seek out the man who falsely promised and kill him.

The truth of a statement or of an agreement, and its binding nature, was attested by smoking the calumet with all parties concerned. A man who smoked the calumet with the actual or implied words, "By this act of smoking I attest my word," was obliged to keep his promise and tell the truth.

When some solemn question was to be answered a dagger was sometimes heated in the fire and held up before the waist of the oath-taker. He touched the hot end with one finger, saying, "If my words be not true, may this knife pierce my vitals." This was an invitation to any who might know that his statement was untrue to stab him to death at any time. This oath with the hot dagger was a spectacular affair and regarded as one of the highest forms of swearing to the truth.

The Dakotas, in making an important statement which concerned the tribe or the honor of their social groups, often swore by Mother Earth, saying, "It is true; Earth hears me!" Should the statement be untrue, it was thought that Earth would withdraw her food, her footing and her favor, causing the false and foresworn man to perish miserably.

Among the Iroquois the testimony of truth was made by holding a wampum belt or a string of white wampum in the hand. The expression, "This belt attests my words," was common in all Iroquois councils.

When warriors were organized in associations or fraternities they had a custom of "telling the truth" on the eve of an attack. In some secret place a council was held, the war captain saying, "We may never return, therefore let us tell the truth of our actions." This was a kind of confession made under an implied oath. No matter what a man told, it must be kept a secret and no action or revenge result.

"I stole the brown horse that you missed," one warrior would say, and the victim of the theft could do nothing but keep still about it. "It was I who stole Lean Bear's wife and took her to the Cheyennes," another warrior would say, and Lean Bear could do nothing about it. "I told an untruth about Kicking Horse," confessed another, and his statement was held inviolate, though Kicking Horse blinked his eyes and yearned for vindication.

Any statement made in the presence of sacred things was an oath, the penalty being a loss of favor with the mysterious powers that were supposed to control a man's life.

Usually an Indian's word was good within his tribe and with his friends, but he thought it only right to deceive an enemy. When an Indian gave his word in the old days, he would suffer much before he would break it. A pledge upon friendship was not lightly taken.

Honor among the Indians, untouched by civilization, was highly regarded. A liar was driven away or shunned by all men. Thus when an Indian told that he would do a thing he struck his breast and cried, "I am a man!" This meant that he not only spoke the truth but felt able to do as he said.

When Alanson Skinner, the ethnologist, was among the Florida Seminole people, he so impressed them that one of the chiefs said, "Me all'e time you' fren'." The two hunted together, camped and fished for many moons in the deep everglades. On one trip Skinner was compelled to leave his money belt behind because of having to wade in deep water. He was uncertain where to hide it until his Seminole friend laughed at his perplexity and advised him.

"Leave your money on the hammock where you sleep," said his "all'e-time fren'."

"I might lose it," answered Skinner.

"Not so, my fren'," answered the Seminole. "No civilized man nearer than a hundred miles. I make you sure all'e time I keep safe what you leave here." So Skinner left his money and ten days later when he returned he found it untouched.

Later he wandered up the coast with the Seminole and discovered that he had lost his only necktie. The Indian, taking French leave, went back for it, and by the time Skinner missed him it was too late to say that ties were only worth a dollar and not to mind. Later in Jacksonville the Indian turned up with the necktie, having traveled more than a hundred miles to bring it, simply because he had promised to keep safe what had been left in his charge.

"Ingram Charlie squeezed my hand and said, 'My friend all'e time, me no forget,'" wrote Mr. Skinner in telling the incident. Not to forget was an Indian trait.

L. HOW INDIANS HELD SECRET LODGES

Very early in the period of exploration it was discovered that many Indian tribes had secret societies. Some were more mysterious than others and some were given to holding public performances, later retiring to their guarded caves, kivas or medicine lodges, to finish their ceremonies.

The Jesuits wrote about the co-fraternities of the Huron people and even described some of the weird things that they saw in those early days when missions were first established. It seems highly probable that some of these societies still continue to exist among the Iroquois, who now include many of the descendants of the Huron tribes.

More than a score of years ago my friend Chief Cornplanter, head of the non-Christian Seneca people, invited me to take his place in the Ancient Guards of the Mystic Potence (Ho-noh-chee-noh-gah). He instructed me in the legends and the songs, the rites and the customs of this strange order which still lives among the Iroquois of New York and Canada.

The ritual of this society is a dramatization in song of the story of the hero. It is performed in total darkness and is in three degrees. It takes place when no moon is shining, and is over before the first faint rays of dawn. Between each degree the fire is uncovered and the members stir themselves and smoke sacred tobacco and take of the feast,—first the juice of the strawberry, next hulled corn and lastly chunks of a bear's head torn off with the teeth.

The ritual tells of a hero, whom we may call Friendly

Hand, a kind-hearted hunter, who loved all the animals and protected them. He would feed the hungry deer in winter, scatter corn and seed for the birds and even set straight the stalks of broken corn and upturned trees. He was a loyal friend.

On a certain occasion he went to the country of the southern hills where the enemy, jealous of his power over living things, lay in wait for him. As he walked down the trail, speaking to the trees and commanding the birds to alight upon his head or hands, a rough-looking stranger approached him and asked that Friendly Hand impart his secret. He refused and, passing on, met another stranger who made a similar demand, striking him and drawing blood when he said he could not tell. The third stranger demanded the secret of his power and being told that it could not be told in words, slew him with a war-club and scalped him. The scalp he took to a distant village to hang over the poles of his wigwam to dry.

One by one the animals came, being attracted by the smell of blood. A wolf leading the others recognized Friendly Hand and proposed to the assembled creatures that an effort be made to secure the scalp. After many birds had failed, the great Dew Eagle found it and placed it back upon Friendly Hand's head, cementing it fast. Then the creatures sought to restore life, and failing, decided to sacrifice their own lives for their friend. Thereupon they took the tips of their hearts, pieces of their livers and gray spots from their brains, putting all these things in an acorn cup. The wolf gave it to the slain hero, pouring it down his throat. Then the Bear, taking him by the right hand, raised him to life, but as he was as yet in darkness the Bear instructed him to listen and follow. Friendly Hand did as told and heard many mysterious secrets. He went into a deep valley, he ascended a rushing torrent, he passed over a waterfall and then ascended a great hill upon which stood a stalk of singing corn.

Instructions continued until dawn, when light came to the eyes of Friendly Hand. With this light becoming brighter, he went back to his people and founded the Guardians of the Mystic Potence, the duty of which was to preserve the songs, the ritual, the legend, the rites and the *mystic potence* itself. This was the formula for bringing the slain to life,—the same substance that the animals, birds and plants had given to restore him. In brief, this is the outline history of the tradition. There is much which I have not related.

Societies sprang up here and there, and in 1900 there were at least six remaining. Several lodges survive and they still have the *medicine,* they still have the night song and the ceremonies. They sing to the resounding chug of gourd rattles, each member having one, and they chant, as of yore, the story of the hero.

Many of the Plains tribes have secret societies, some of which are open only to warriors. The Pueblo people have a dozen or more that are distinct and well recognized. The Zuni have thirteen, most of which are concerned with shamanism and sorcery. Perhaps the most interesting of the northern lodges is the Midē-Wiwin of the Ojibwa tribes. This society has four degrees and claims mysterious powers. Along the northwest coast the Tsimshian, the Songish and the Kwakiutl have strange societies with secret rites. Some have the Thunder Bird as a patron totem.

Ancient America was full of fraternities, secret societies, associations and clubs. They were as numerous then as now and devoted to almost as many objects. Some had ceremonies of talking with spirits, some preserved magical charms, some were devoted to the unseen powers and some were composed of warriors who had done mighty deeds. Even the Indian women had secret societies and kept the men away.

Nearly all these societies had their emblems, their regalias, their peculiar customs, their dances and songs and their special taboos. Members felt themselves bound by ties of brotherhood and observed them.

LI. HOW INDIANS DREAMED OF THEIR TOTEMS

Among many of the tribes of the east and northeast every youth was required to secure a personal totem, or dream animal. This totem was the personal protector of its "holder," and was supposed to forewarn him of danger and extricate him from difficulty.

The dream animal totem differed from the clan totem. The latter came to a man by birthright, but the dream animal came after a fast and a lonely vigil, far from human habitation. It was a personal thing, and the secret of how to invoke its aid was known only to the individual.

When a boy grew into the years of early youth, his elders, sometimes an uncle or grandfather, began to prepare his mind for his dream fast. He was instructed how to make his heart clean and how to prepare his spirit for the messages that should come from the spirit world.

As the boy approached the age of fifteen he was advised to begin the rites of purification by which he should attain the rank of a "powered" one. When the time had been set the youth bathed in cleansing waters in which herbs had been mixed, he took purges and emetics. Then he took his journey to a lonely spot, where he erected his dream bower. Chanting his songs of invocation to the unseen powers about him, he opened his heart to their whisperings. No food passed his lips as he gave himself up to prayer and meditation. He drank of the spring or brook, but only water entered his mouth. He chanted, he prayed, he sought with all his soul to know the mysteries of life and destiny, of what he should be and what he should become. He might gaze at the sun at dawn and, lifting his face to its rays, sing:

"Oh, Great Mystery, my heart is open,
I give my soul into thy keeping,
No thought is within me save of thee!
Let my manitou come to me, nor fail me,
Let him give me a promise of protection,
Let me see his visible form, his visage,
That I may know my manitou and obey him.
My heart is open, I give my soul,
I give my soul to thee, Great Manitou!
Let mine eyes see a vision of the future
That I may know myself and my destiny!"

With deep emotion the youth sang, dedicating himself to the Great Mystery and imploring his guidance. Dipping into the waters of a near-by pool he bathed and then ran back to his bower to dream,—if happily the dream might come,—to dream of his future.

Then, if the experience were normal, the youth after many days would have his prayer fulfilled. His mind would behold his totem and he would hear it speak. As the vision shifted he would see, perhaps, a fragment of his former life and glimpse of his former identity. Looking forward he would see what he was to be in this life, how he was to demean himself, and how he should meet his death. He might even catch a vision of future lives, and his final transformation from the earth to another world.

If the visions failed, the youth was considered an earthly clod, and designed for humble work about the camp. His rank was not that of a warrior but of a scullion, and even a digger of garbage holes, and lowly servant of the women. It was one of the tragedies of life to have the visions fail, and they seldom failed if the songs and prayers were followed.

Once the visions came the youth believed in them with implicit faith. He was ready to stake his life upon them and to follow their advice. Coming back from his vigil, his family and friends granted his wishes and looked upon him with awe. Warriors now took him in charge and he became a member of their associations, learning the ceremonies of their cults, and learning how to construct his mystery bundle that should protect him in battle.

Heckewelder, the missionary, says that he once took great pains to dissuade a very intelligent Indian and one who had lived for a time with the whites, from the notions of his dream fast. "All that I could say," writes the missionary, "was not able to convince him that at the time of his initiation his mind was in a state of temporary derangement. He declared that he had a clear recollection of the dreams and visions that had occurred to him at the time, and was sure that they came from the agency of celestial spirits."

Heckewelder goes on to tell that this Indian, because of his dream fast, knew of his former lives, that he had lived through two generations, had died twice and had been born a third time, and that after his next death he was nevermore to return to earth.

"It would be too long," wrote the reverend gentleman, "to relate all the wild stories of the same kind which this otherwise intelligent Indian said of himself, with a tone and manner which indicated the most intimate conviction, and left no doubt in my mind that he did not mean to deceive others, but was himself deceived."

Frequently the Indian youth received a new name after this "initiation" and bore the effigy of his totem tattooed on his breast. Oftentimes the "initiate" offended his totem, in which case he had all manner of bad luck and sickness. If he did not know how to propitiate his totem, a medicine man came to him and prescribed a sacrifice or a feast.

In many Indian tribes, the dream fast of youth was the most profound religious experience of life. As a psychological experience it seems to have been a reflection of all the religious beliefs and suggestions that had been absorbed.

The Iroquois called their dream guardian an *oki,* just as the Algonkin called it *manitou.*

LII. HOW INDIANS MADE MAGIC

Early travelers often were astonished at the magical feats of the Indians among whom they lived. They wrote of the witchcraft, the wizardry and the conjuring of the medicine men, and marveled at it. Indians as well as modern people were especially fond of sleight-of-hand tricks, but the knowledge of how they were done being less in those days, many Indians actually believed that the trick was real.

There were different kinds of magic. First there was a kind that was much like "mind reading," by which a medicine man seemed able to see at great distances and tell what was going on. He went into a trance and after a while came out of it and told what he had seen. Strangely enough, there were cases in which the medicine man told the real truth, as returning hunters would testify.

Then there was a kind of magic much like hypnotism. The conjurer would talk to a crowd of people or a single person, and then make them "see" strange things. One old Iroquois told me that the trick was easy enough. Said he, "Paint pictures on the inside of their skulls.

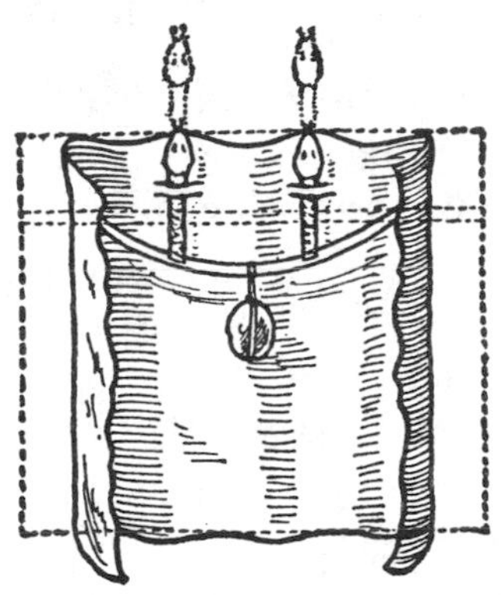

FIGURE 39
Menomini Snake-Bag Trick

Wear out their eyes, and they will turn them inward and see what you have painted there." The method was to talk in a dull monotone, repeating again and again what the conjurer wanted his victims to see or do, using in the meantime a shining object like a small mirror to flash in the "subject's" eyes.

Of course the *subject* must wish very hard to see and do as he is told. He must be interested and obey. Then the trick of hypnotism is easy. To create respect and even fear, the medicine man dressed in queer garments, and made mysterious passes. His beating of a tom-tom and flashing of a mica mirror were only to wear out the nerve centers. This done, he "turned their eyes inward, and they saw what he had painted on the inside of their skulls." Hypnotism was used in the Ghost Dance.

The magic of trickery was perhaps the commonest. It created great astonishment in crowds, especially at the medicine lodge or at councils. One of the strange tricks was to show how powerful a medicine man was, or how wonderful his medicine could be in healing wounds.

A brave soldier or a hardened hunter, who wanted to be initiated in one of the Medicine lodges, would be placed at one end of the great council house as the target. The most noted marksman would then take his bow and a "medicine arrow." He would aim and fire. The arrow would whizz through the hall, strike the victim and cause a great gush of blood. Down his half-naked body the blood would trickle while everybody wondered why he was not killed. With a whoop and a dance the medicine man would make his way to the victim, dance around him and then with a swish of his medicated moss would wipe the wound, blow upon the spot and cause it to heal completely. Only a tiny bruise or a red spot would show.

How was it done? Very simply. The arrow shaft was hollow and the arrow-point was fastened to a slender rod that pushed into the hollow reed. This pressed against the berry juice inside and caused it to gush forth and squirt over the victim. The red juice looked like blood, and everybody thought that it was. When wiped away only the bruise of the arrowhead showed, and that dangerous arrowhead had been made of a piece of soft root whittled out and colored.

Medicine men had collapsible daggers that worked the same way and would stab their victims, causing red juice to flow from the handles. They used mud bullets also, and in modern times among the Iroquois would load their guns with powder, place the bullet in the gun, ram it down and fire away. Of course the ramming would break up the mud or clay pellet and when fired only dust would come out, though a sharpshooter would pull the trigger.

Some medicine men would dance into the lodge with a bag held before them. Suddenly two snakes would stick their heads out of the open top. As suddenly the heads would disappear, and the medicine man would twist up the bag and thrust it in his pouch, or he would turn it upside down and shake it. No snakes would come out. This trick was performed by sewing parts of stuffed snakes to the inside of the bag and passing a cord beneath them. When the bag was held by each end and stretched the heads would stick out. When the bag was pressed in such a way that the ends were brought nearer together, the heads would naturally drop lower and not be seen. The bag held by the bottom when shaken did not reveal the snakes.

There are some tricks that are not easily explained, such as the binding and burial of conjurers, and their quick release. White travelers tell of a medicine man being bound tightly in a juggler's lodge and watched over by sentinels placed outside. There would be noises, songs, whoops and then silence. Then would come the juggler's voice, "Go to the Lodge of Black Beaver and get the rope with which you bound me!" Still watching the lodge, a messenger would be sent to get the rope. It would be brought back with its original knots, and one look inside the sacred tent would show the conjurer without bonds, smoking his pipe contentedly. Sometimes he would vanish and come marching back when least expected. The juggler's lodge among the Menomini Indians was called a Shi-sak-kan (tshisaqkan).

This lodge of the juggler was shaped like a cylinder, and was made of bark wound around poles. Though bound and gagged, the juggler would cause a drum to beat, rattles to sound and various voices to sound as if in earnest conversation.

Some jugglers developed the power of ventriloquism, or throwing the voice at a distance, at the same time imitating the cries of animals or other persons. One Indian who lived at the Indian "Four Corners," where my boyhood was spent, had this power, and often he amazed the school children by his powers of voice throwing. He would make us think that there was a dog fight in the bushes or some mysterious monster moaning under the ground.

Some tribes had societies of jugglers. The jugglers of the Chippewa and Menomini Indians were famous and they had a grand medicine lodge called the Midē-Wiwin. Strange things took place in the ceremonies. The Iroquois had a lodge called the Ha-dih-dos. It was supposed to be a higher degree of another secret lodge. In their ceremonies the medicine man picked up a hot stone and tossed it up and down in his hands to show that it did not burn him. He made sparks fly from a tree and caused the candidate's clothes to fall off. The conjurer also did queer things. The candidate who was being initiated was told to hide something or several things (as a ring, necklace, feather, knife or pipe) anywhere he wished in the lodge. When ready the conjurer came out of his corner wearing a mask having no eye-holes. He went directly to the spot where the object had been hidden and brought it forth. Then he walked straight to the candidate and presented it to him. By this time the man who was being initiated believed that the conjurer had a heap of power.

Another trick was to drop wampum from the mouth. In this case the conjurer walking along would greet a friend and ask him to hold out his hand. This done, the conjurer would open his mouth and expel forty or fifty wampum beads. He would do this for several people, but how he could hold so many beads or how he got them in his mouth in the first place is hard to tell.

LIII. HOW INDIAN WITCHES WORKED THEIR SPELLS

Witches and sorcerers flourished in most Indian settlements,—or at least most of the forest people thought they did. As a matter of fact, the Indians, like most other peoples of the world at one time or another, had a very positive belief in witchcraft.

They had no love for witches, however, and both sorcerers and witches were killed when discovered, or forced to give up their wicked practices.

Among some tribes, as among the Iroquois, there were secret societies of witches and the strange rites of witchcraft were taught to the unhappy initiates. Thus the methods of bewitching people were spread throughout the tribe, and many persons held the information a deep secret until an occasion arose which required it to be passed on to another.

In many instances the "witch bundle," or parcel which contained the medicines, poisons, powders, charms and tools of witchcraft, were placed in the hands of unwilling custodians, who thereafter were compelled to perform the ceremonies necessary to keep the "bundle" from harming its owner, even though they never used them for evil purposes.

I have talked to many Indians about witchcraft, and even with some who confessed to me that they were the "biggest kind of witches" and could work terrible spells. From what they said, apparently the final aim of the sorcerer is to injure some person or group that he does not like, or to obtain revenge. It seems to be a magical means of doing some great mischief or causing sickness and even death.

There are several ways of casting "spells," some of which may be briefly described. First, there is the purely mental form, which consists of strongly *wishing* pain, sickness or misfortune into the victim. The sorcerer works himself into a frenzy and then seeks to make his mind throw a spell upon the object of his wrath. Sometimes he seeks to cast actual objects, as sharp splinters or hair, into the body of his victim, solely by thought power. There are those who will testify that they have seen witches cause sharp bones or needles to fly as the witch ordered them.

The second method is to obtain the hair, nail parings, saliva or perspiration of the person to be harmed. These substances, once a part of his body, are placed in a bundle or in the body of a wooden doll, which is named after the victim. The sorcerer then seeks to work his incantations upon it and dose it with poisons with the idea of having the effect manifest itself upon the living person.

By another plan, a bark or wooden image of the victim is made and taken to a secluded spot to be tortured either by piercing, cutting or burning it. Sometimes it is scraped every day. These acts are supposed to cause the victim great pain and cause him to waste away. In other words, the victim is believed to feel the torture that the doll endures, since it is tied by the person's name which fastens his soul to it.

An Indian school girl once told me that she disliked her teacher, who she thought had been unfair. Thus, she made a "witch doll," covered its head with combings from the teacher's hair and tied a thread to the teacher's bed, and then, by aid of several spools, to the doll. Jumping out of the window, she unwound the spools until she reached a neighboring swamp, where she set up the doll and named it "Teacher." She now began her incantations, ending by scolding it and informing it that she would work great injury to "Teacher" if she was ever mean to her in class again. So saying, she stuck a thorn in the doll's neck, "just to make you believe I can hurt you." After this ceremony she wound the thread upon the body of the doll and worked her way back to the school. "Maybe you won't believe it," said the "witch" to me, "but when I got back that teacher had a big red sore on her neck, and after that she was afraid of me and treated me right."

Indian witches have bundles full of strange potions, powders, dried bugs and tiny weapons. They are reputed to be able to "shoot" these things through the air and put them into the bodies of those whom they wish to bewitch. Witches are supposed to have the power of changing into various animals, generally a big dog or a fox. They are thought to be able to fly up the smokehole and go through the air carrying with them a *ga-haih* or will-o'-the-wisp.

However foolish these ideas may seem, they have been held by many primitive races, and even by white Europeans. The story of the Salem witches is not so old, and we are told that in many out-of-the-way places there are communities where most of the people still believe in witchcraft, and take great pains to guard against it.

LIV. HOW INDIANS OVERCAME WITCHES

The belief which the Indians have in witchcraft has led to an endeavor to counteract witch influence by means of "witch doctors." Witch doctors affect to know just what magic, medicine, ceremony or measure to use when witches threaten. Through their clairvoyance they claim to be able to discover the witch who is working harm, and if not, to give a medicine that frightens away the sorcerer.

Since most witches are believed to be able to change themselves into dogs, owls, foxes, snakes, hawks, sea gulls and even moles, the witch doctor must be able to tell which animal is the witch and by killing the animal to kill the witch through it.

In the far west among the Tsimshian, the suspected witch was caught and starved into a confession, and then driven into the ocean that the water might wash away his wizardry. The Tlingit wizard was also tried by starvation, but if he finally protested innocence he was allowed to depart. With most tribes, however, especially in the eastern forest region, the witch, wizard or sorcerer, upon even the slightest proof, was killed. Indians regarded witchcraft the most heinous of crimes.

In some communities sorcerers work very quietly, and elude discovery, but if once caught at their evil incantations, they threaten that their comrades at the uncanny art will revenge their punishment,—and thus they escape injury. Thus it becomes necessary to the Indian to know how to stop a witch or wizard and cause them to abandon their ways.

Many years ago an alleged witch, who could not understand my scientific researches on a certain reservation, came to me and told me that I must throw away all my bottles and tubes, and not go in my "little room" where I had a red lamp. If I persisted, I was warned, she would work a terrible spell on me. But whatever happened I would surely die,—and she shook her crooked finger at me in truly witch style,—if I told any one she had even spoken to me.

At that I laughed in a good-natured way. "You just go ahead," I challenged, "you just start, and my greater witchcraft will make you wish you were dead!"

She eyed me and then asked, "Hoh, what would you do, —you don't know anything!"

"Do?" I echoed. "Why, I will get a crow, tear out its heart and run a skewer through it. Then I will pass it over the flame of my red lamp. As it sizzles, your heart will roast in your body and you'll die, die!"

As this was a very old way to get even with witches I thought it might frighten her, and it did. She gasped, and then said, "Oh, you won't do that, will you?"

"I certainly will if you ever disturb me," I replied, "and what's more, all the witching in the world that you do to me won't harm a hair of my head. I have the greatest witch secret in the world."

"I guess you are too much for me," she whispered, "but, please don't tell that I came. I will not try to hurt you."

She went away without asking me what my witch medicine was, and even if she had begged for it I would not have told her that it *consisted simply in not believing in witches.* It became noised about, however, that I was a great witch doctor and was in possession of big medicine.

The old Chief with whom I was staying at the time heard the rumor and then told me his experience. A certain elderly woman, he related, was reputed to be able to change herself into a large dog, and in this guise she would go to the houses of her victims and "shoot" poison through the walls at them, causing several to die.

"One night I was driving to town," said the chief, "when I saw a big dog run from the bushes and leap at my horse. It made no noise but kept leaping. The horse began to shy and then to prance. I lost control of it for a minute, but taking out my whip I lashed it steady again and then whipped the dog. It then ran alongside, making the horse nervous. I was afraid of it and took out my revolver and shot the dog. It gave a yelp and ran right for Widow Longtree's log house. There was a high fence and it tried to get over it but, being wounded, fell between some of the X bracing poles and laid there. I drove on to town and upon returning in the moonlight I looked, but saw that the dog had gone. The next day there was a great commotion and it was found that Widow Longtree was dead,—shot through the neck. I said that was funny because I killed a dog there. So the sheriff questioned me and I told him the truth, and he believed me."

"Didn't the Indians think you really knew that the dog was a witch?" I asked.

"Of course they did," he replied. "They knew it served her right for running around like a dog and frightening everybody. After that witch doctors came from four different reservations and tried to get some of my medicine, the kind I must have used to make my bullet go straight. I told them I had no witch powder and didn't believe in witches because I am a Methodist, but I couldn't make them believe I wasn't the best kind of a witch doctor myself."

Since that conversation I have often wondered just what that Methodist Indian did believe about witches, for with the Indians he had the reputation of being greatly "powered," and though constantly the object of envy, witches never seemed to get him.

One means of overcoming a witch is to undo its work bit by bit and throw back the charms. An Indian whom I knew believed himself under a spell. Calling in a doctor of wizardry, he submitted to a poultice. With magical herbs his sore hip was plastered and covered with an anti-witch napkin. Then the witch doctor sang and made passes. When the ceremony was over he drew off the poultice and searched in it for the poison. With a whoop he held up a sharp bone to which was tied a white hair. He gave it to his patient, who threw it against the wall with an imprecation, ordering it to fly to the witch and strike her fatally. The next morning, so the story goes, the witch was found dead with a splinter of bone in her breast.

I suspect that here was a bit of legerdemain and a lively imagination. The story, however, is quite characteristic.

While digging into an old Indian village site, seeking bits of ancient pottery and curious pipes of clay, I was visited by several strange Indians who warned me that as I was working on a reservation, I must expect to be "witched" unless I stopped and went away. I asserted that I would stay and that no witch who ever lived could work a spell on me. One of the Indians smiled an evil smile and then snapped, "You don't know what you are talking about. To-night, look out!"

I knew that mischief was in the air and was disturbed when some friendly Indian neighbors came over to warn me. Of course I could not admit that I had a bit of fear, except for bullets shot in the dark. I had every man in camp keep his gun hugged to his side, and then waited.

There was no moon that night and the sky was overcast. All about were dark clumps of bushes, before me was a thin bit of woodland edging a bluff which dropped twenty feet to the river. In the dimness I could see a figure moving about under a tree. I knew that there was mischief astir, but it was not the kind that I could shoot at. I had no desire to start a small war. Still I knew exactly what to do.

Taking a small pole, I placed one of the wicks from the blue-flame oil stove upon it. Then I set the wick afire and with the pole as a lever, threw the flaming wick high in the air. Each time it came down, I threw it up again. One of my comrades did the same, and we tried to throw our "fire balls" so that they would hit one another in mid-air.

Now just what were we doing? Simply imitating the greatly feared "will-o'-the-wisp," or Ga-haih, as the Indians called it. Above the fringe of trees the flames looked like dancing balls of fire, the emblems of the most malignant witches.

When we became tired of our sport we squatted in the darkness and tried to see how it affected our foes. Our lull gave them time to make a break for safety. One ran out of his hiding place and in terror dashed for the woods. With a hoot like an owl I gave chase and had the pleasure of seeing him leap over the bluff into the mire below. When some of my comrades charged the bushes by the road there was a wild sound of scampering feet, and then all was quiet. We turned in, well satisfied that we had counteracted our enemy, the wizard of High Banks.

A long time after I heard a snatch of conversation in a livery stable. Two Indians were talking. "I never travel that sand road at night," said one. "I got scared out of my wits there once. That's the place where the Ga-haih jumps up. Now I go way around on the four-mile road. You bet, I will never travel that sand road."

"How does it happen that you are so scared?" asked

the other. "Were you with the old man when he tried to witch those fellows that were digging old relics on the hill?"

"You can bet I was," he answered. "He told me a witch chased him right off the creek bank and threw him in two feet of mud."

More I did not hear, but it satisfied me that the way to cure a sorcerer is to laugh at his sorcery and then outmatch him with a few tricks. The wisest of the old chiefs and sages advise this but warn one that to outwit a witch is to get the whole company of evil doers on one's track, seeking revenge.

LV. HOW INDIANS TALKED TO ANIMALS

In my boyhood days there was an old Indian who impressed me greatly. It was rumored that he could talk to animals and that they actually understood him. This was hard to believe and I debated much about it, arguing that I couldn't see how animals could understand *his* language when they didn't talk it. At that time I did not know that language was only the effort of the mind to signal by means of *symbols,* and that the words spoken were only symbols for *thoughts.*

One day when I was walking from the farm to the neighboring village this old Indian came along in his buggy and invited me to ride with him. I accepted and did my errand in town, and then returned with my elderly friend. On the way back we met a man named Tallchief who was trying to make his balky horse move. The more he whipped it the more determined it was to stay right where it stood. Tallchief got out and was trying to pull the creature by the bit, but the balky one merely laid its ears back, rolled its eyes and showed its teeth.

At that juncture the old Indian passed the reins to me

and alighted from the buggy. Going up to the horse, he told Tallchief to get back in his rig and keep quiet. The old Indian then stroked the horse's nose, patted its flank, gave it a handful of grass and rubbed its ears. Then he took one ear and pulled it down to his mouth. I could hear him whispering something, but could not understand what was said. At that he told Tallchief to tell his horse to "jah-goh," meaning to get along. This done, the horse started off at a trot.

"What did you say?" I asked as we drove off.

"Oh, I just told him that he was acting like a bad boy and ought to know better, being a horse," said he. "Then I told him that if he would trot along nicely he would get some oats when he reached home."

Not long afterward some old hunters came back from the Allegheny mountains, where they had killed some elk. I heard them tell how one of their number had talked to the animals after they had been shot and asked their ghosts to pardon him and his companions for killing them. He had offered a little sacrifice of tobacco, some bullets and a few beads, ending by saying that the bullets that killed them were bad things and that he would never use them again.

All this mystified me, so much so, that I asked Sounding Voice, a very intelligent member of the tribe, to explain what the hunter had meant by talking to ghosts,—animal ghosts.

"Oh, that is the way," said he. "All animals have spirits and they want to know why they are killed so that they can tell the Great Spirit how they happened to come to the Sky World."

"Well, can folks talk to live animals?" I asked.

"Truly so!" he exclaimed. "I can talk to dogs and make them do what I ask,—almost any one can do that. Horses understand, too, and bears know every word.

That is the reason people must not tell animal stories except in winter. Everything understands,—bees, bugs, katydids, snakes and even coons. They are all what you might call brothers,—same Great Spirit made them all out of same thing. That's why everything understands, even dust."

Later I learned how to talk to a bear, and was instructed just how to treat one. It was Cornplanter who told me.

"Bears are next to men. They look like men when they are hurt, they stand up and they cry. That's why we must hunt bears with axes instead of guns. The way is to make a bear stand up on its hind legs and then walk right up to it and swing the axe into its foreshoulder. Brother bear will then sit down and cry."

"What does he cry for?"

"Because he isn't as brave as a man. Then I talk to him and make him understand why I am after him. I say, 'My brother, it has become necessary for me to hunt you. I need your meat and your skin for a blanket. You are good to eat and I am going to eat you. But you are weeping like some coward. If you had grabbed me and eaten me up, I would not have said a word, because I would know that that's the way you do things. Now be ashamed of yourself before I knock you on the head.' "

With this warning the hunter knocked the bear on the forehead and then skinned it. Heckewelder writes of a similar address made to a wounded bear and chided the Indian for talking to a mere animal.

"Do you suppose that bears can understand you,—can even know what you said?" asked the missionary.

"Certainly," replied the Indian, "did you not notice how ashamed that bear looked when I accused him of being a coward?"

Thus, the Indians talked to animals, fully believing that they understood them. "It is not the word so much," said Cornplanter, "not the word so much, as what we *think* when we say the words. The animals catch what we think, and sometimes no words need be spoken."

And, who knows but that animals can understand men when those men tune their minds to the key of the common brotherhood?

LVI. HOW INDIANS VENERATED THE EAGLE

Most mysterious and most majestic of all winged creatures is the eagle. No other bird so stirred the imagination of the first Americans. They watched it soar into the heights of the great blue (as they called the sky), and they saw it communing with the clouds. It feared nothing and even braved the face of the sun with open eyes. The eagle was manitou, it was wakon, it was orenda, it was mighty medicine.

There were orders of eagles, to the Indian mind, and some were more highly regarded than others, the golden eagle taking high rank. Most potent, however, was the magical sky eagle which the Iroquois called Shadahgeyah (S'ha-dah-gey-ah). This noble bird seldom came below the clouds, according to native myths, but stared in the very face of heaven. Only the most holy of the high priests ever saw it or obtained its feathers.

Nearly every tribe had an Eagle clan and there were songs to the eagle, eagle dances, eagle ceremonies and even secret societies called the Order of the Eagle, or some similar term.

The eagle was used in the heraldry of most of the Indian tribes, and if it were dreamed about in an initiation ceremony, or in a holy vigil, many privileges were given the novice. Among these was the right to paint the eagle crest upon a medicine shield. In ordinary decorative symbolism eagles appeared on baskets, pottery, quill work, textiles, house posts, pipes and rattles.

The eagle god of the Hopi was Kwahu and there were elaborate ceremonies of invocation and propitiation among them. The Thunder Bird, among many of the central tribes, seems to have been an eagle and the same mythical creature that the Iroquois called the sky eagle. In some instances there was a belief that the great sky eagle was both bird and human, and might on occasion lay aside its feathered form and come among men. This thought seems to be expressed by many of the mound builder carvings representing men or gods with wings. Some of these effigies of the mound building tribes are done in repoussé copper.

The eagle as a bird of power was sought by nearly all tribes. In many instances only special warriors or priests could shoot an eagle. There were elaborate ceremonies of preparation, and the rites that secured fitness to hunt the sacred bird were strict.

Eagles were difficult to shoot with arrows, and it was not until Europeans brought guns that there was any considerable success in shooting them at any distance. The ancient practice was to approach a nest when the birds were away and to conceal oneself until they returned, when an arrow was let fly.

Another method was to dig a pit and to cover it with boughs. The eagle hunter then placed a slain deer over the pit and concealed himself below. The smell of blood attracted the great bird who was allowed to eat and fly away. The hunter remained at his vigil awaiting a second coming. Then as the bird began its task of tearing at the flesh he thrust up his arm and grabbed it by the tail. As the eagle flew away it left many of its prized feathers in the hunter's tightly clasped hand. Some tribes used this strategy as a means to secure the bird itself. Its legs were grabbed and tied very quickly with a noose. This was secured and drawn tightly down to an anchor pole below. The hunter then emerged, explained the situation to the frightened creature, and then using great caution, covered its head, bound its wings, secured its talons and bore it off in triumph. If the victim was to be killed it was strangled by pressure on the thorax, great care being taken not to spill a drop of blood.

Some tribes as those of the Pueblo region, kept captive birds for their feathers. The shamans of the Iroquois may have done the same, if their legends are to be believed. They tied the creature to a cross piece of a tall pole, covered the eagle with wampum and other sacred articles. The pole was then erected. From a safe distance candidates for the hand of a chief's daughter shot their arrows at the bird, the successful suitor being the one who killed it. The wampum strings and the ceremonial prizes shaken off fell to the ground and became the property of the bride.

LVII. HOW INDIANS TAMED ANIMALS

Hunters who went into the depths of the forest often found the young of various animals. These were playful and funny balls of fur, and excited admiration. It was quite natural that the Indian hunter should bring them back and try to rear them in captivity.

Wolf cubs were sportive little villains and looked like good pets, but only a few were ever really tamed. These few, however, who during the ages stayed about camp and mingled with the cub coyotes and the cub foxes, in time grew into dogs, and so provided the red man with canine friends.

The taming of these wild creatures was a matter of

feeding when young, and a gradual acquaintance with human creatures. In this way they were kept in camp, and especially in the larger villages of the eastern Indians.

Some tribes tried to catch turkeys, hawks, owls and eagles and tie them to perches or keep them in cages. The Pueblo people kept many eagles tied to their houses in order to get the feathers as they were shed. It cannot be said, however, that these birds were ever tamed. They were treated well and given food and water.

Indian boys are said to have made friends with many birds and to have coaxed them to alight on their heads and fingers. This was done by keeping still, watching the bird and showing it that it might have food if it would alight in the hand. The boy would then talk to the bird and tell it to fly away to the good spirits and tell them what the boy wanted. Sometimes boys and girls had pet squirrels and chipmunks who would approach them and eat from their hands.

In some places and at certain seasons of the year the deer were tame and could be touched with the hand. As an old Indian friend said to me, "The animals are not wild; it's men who are wild and frighten them. Animals know what men think and know when the hunter wants to kill them and so they run." The deer must have learned this now for when seen in the woods they bound away as if in fear of their lives.

The same old Indian told me that in ancient times, hunters would bring bear cubs to the village and make log pens for them. As they grew tame they would let them out to play with the boys and dogs.

"Boys had to be careful when wrestling with bears," said my old friend, "because bears would scratch and where they scratched hair would grow out." I can readily believe that bears will scratch but the superstition about the hair is a myth.

The old Chief told me that as the bear cubs grew older they became cross, in which case they were kept in a cage and fed until killed for food. This is as near as the Indians went toward growing "domestic" meat. If the buffaloes had been tameable their calves might have formed tame herds, but apparently they could not be domesticated. It is said by old hunters that when a buffalo cow is killed, her calf will follow the hunter and suck on his finger all the way home. Thus they were easy to catch and keep about camp for a few days, but the chances are they did not stay long.

Often the tamed or partly tamed cubs of bears, wolves and other animals were treated kindly and then let go in order that they might return and tell the other animals that men were friendly. A legend is told that a hunter was once pounced upon by a bear that was about to kill him, when it fell back and grinned. The hunter recognized it as one of his old pets and grinned back. Whether they shook hands or not my informant did not say.

Some tribes have stories about boys who lived with mother bears. The tale is told that a little orphan who was driven from home by a cruel uncle found his way to a clearing where he saw a bear picking berries. The boy knew the bear because it had been one of those kept in the village only a year before. He played with the bear and trotted after her when she went to her den. All the autumn through he stayed in her company and the two grew to be fast friends. Nights began to get cold and the boy slept close to the bear who began to get cross and crosser, but did not hurt him. After a while some hunters came and found the bear's hiding place but the boy rushed out and saved her. Then were the hunters glad that they had found the boy for they had been looking for him many weeks.

In some stories the bear has cubs with whom the boy

played, and in these tales the boy is afraid to rush out from the tree and allows the bear to do so. She is killed, and the hunters are sorry when they see that she has taken care of the boy. It is from tales like these that the Indians thought it a good thing to be kind to animals.

Indians had pet woodchucks and raccoons. The coons were perhaps the favorites for they were full of antics. It was not easy to keep them because they chewed up the thongs with which they were tied.

Once in a while a wounded crow, if young, was tamed and even in those olden days it is said that a crow talked, and thus was regarded as one of the wisest of birds. The sacred bird of the ghost dance was the crow.

Indians thought that the animals and birds were brother creatures and that they had just as much a right to live as men. They even thought that animals had souls and went to heaven just as human souls do. This is why they talked to an animal when they had killed it and told it why they had slain it for necessity and not for sport.

LVIII. HOW INDIANS USED THE CALUMET

Although the native American had many types of smoking pipes many of which were highly ornate, none was regarded as sacred as the *calumet,* or peace pipe.

The calumet was indeed more than a mere pipe; it was the sacred instrument in which was smoked the consecrated incense so pleasing to the unseen powers of the universe. Originally the stem was a wand through which the breath of the petitioner was drawn in order that he might have power within him from "on high." Because of this, the stem or wand was decorated with objects that were believed helpful in attracting power. Symbolic paint was applied to the wood that it might resemble the sky and thereby please the Great Mystery, while, if there was a second pipe, its stem was painted green to represent the growing things of earth. Two calumets were used in one of the more sacred rites. The Omaha people, a Siouan tribe, call them *weawan.*

In the calumet dance ceremony of "making a sacred kinship," the two *niniba weawan* are held upright by crotched sticks driven into the soil at the rear of the dancing lodge. No pipe bowl is used in this ceremony, there being the preserved head and neck of "the green-necked duck" instead. From this point, extending for about six inches the yellowish feathers of the great horned owl are attached to the stem. Then come the long wing feathers of the bald eagle, split and attached lengthwise in three places. Next in order is a wisp of horse hair dyed red, wound around the stem and secured with a tie of sinew thread. Over this is a strip of white rabbit fur, with fringed ends that hang down. Hair is wrapped around the stem in two other places, about six inches apart. Near the mouthpiece and close to the last tuft of hair is the split head of a woodcock, with the lower bill removed, facing the tip. Two eagle plumes hang from this point, and then a number of other feathers secured to the shaft by antelope skin string. To contrast the stems, one having the wood painted blue has the female feathers, and the stem painted green has the male feathers.

The dance in which the calumets are used is an adoption ceremony among the Omaha, and the child who is taken into the family must be less than ten years of age.

The pipe calumet was used in councils, and all who smoked it gave their pledge of honor. It was thought that smoke drawn into the mouth through the consecrated stem made one think clearly. For this reason, when a treaty was made each party took a draught of smoke, and blew it out slowly and with sober thoughts.

One tradition, that of the Pawnee, relates that the calumet was given to men by the Sun. When smoking, therefore, the pipe is lifted upward that the sun may see it.

During a battle, when one party feels that the bloodshed should stop, it may lift high a calumet, that the enemy may see it. If so, and the calumet is accepted, peace is declared, and the warring tribes come together in a council of peace, whereby they decide to settle their differences by treaty rather than war. The calumet was, therefore, something to swear by, something to make a contract sacred and the means through which the smoker might draw inspiration from the unseen powers.

Having these beliefs, it is little wonder that many Indians lavished the stem with symbolic decorations, and guarded them from ever touching the ground, or from otherwise being profaned.

VI: STRANGE DANCES

VI

STRANGE DANCES

LIX. HOW THE SUN DANCE WAS PERFORMED

Most spectacular of all the ancient rites of the plains Indians was the great Sun Dance. It was the one great drama that drew the tribe together and gripped it with religious emotion.

It was a time of great excitement and there was something in it for every one, even to the children who had their ears pierced. It was a time when blood flowed as a sacrifice to the sun god.

Strangely enough, though the sun gives life and warmth, brings color to the sky and tints the flowers, all races who worship the sun have associated that worship with great cruelty. Somehow or other the sun god was a cruel god who loved to see human suffering.

The sun dance of the plains Indians was a dance of suffering, and yet, it had a highly religious purpose. General Hugh L. Scott, who saw the Kiowa dance, wrote, "Every step of this ceremony he regarded as pure and holy, and in following it out the Indian was as sincere and reverent in his worship as any churchman of our time."

Like all the ceremonies of the Indians, this dance was not a simple thing, but organized and held to fixed rules. Its purposes were fourfold, though in general the aim was to secure power or celestial aid. One man who went through the ceremonies said that it is to fulfill a vow, to secure divine aid for another, for self or to gain supernatural power for one's self. This power was thought to make a man a great Shaman or medicine man. The dance and ceremony were in honor of the sun, who, because it was pleased, would grant the prayers of those who submitted to the rites. The very fact that a warrior endured the tortures of the dance gave him rank among his fellows as having the four virtues, Bravery, Generosity, Fortitude and Integrity,—and his whole life thereafter was to be devoted to demonstrating them in all that he did.

A man who wished to be a candidate for the dance selected a teacher who should instruct him in all the religious myths of the tribe, and who told him how to live and get power from the unseen spirits. After that came the ceremony of the sweat lodge by which the candidate was prepared and purified for his initiation. After that he may seek a vision from the other world, and learn from his teacher the names of all the spirits that go to make up the Great Wakanda.

Thus instructed the candidate is provided with his dancing regalia which consists of a red skirt made of soft deerskin, a cape of otter fur, two arm bands made of buffalo hair, two ankle bands made of rabbit fur, a whistle made from an eagle's wing bone, and a hoop made from a willow wand. He may have any insignia that belongs to him and also a pipe and enough tobacco to last for the four days' ceremony.

It is important to build the sun dance circle according to ancient rules, and for this purpose the sun dance camp circle is set up in horse-shoe shape, with an opening to the east. A sacred lodge is erected for the candidates. The sacred tree is then searched for, and, when discovered, it is marked with circles of red paint on four sides. It is later cut down to form the sacred sun pole, from which are suspended long thongs of buffalo hide which are to be tied to holes in the dancers' backs or chests.

(After Catlin)

FIGURE 40

The Sun Dance

The raising of the sun pole is a ceremony in itself, and it is decorated in a suitable way with pelts and streamers. The thongs are tied to it that the dancers may be hung upon them. All about the circle are strange things connected with sun worship. The Kiowa had earthen incense burners, rattles, a fan and the effigy of a head called a Taimay. At the entrance of the sacred circle was a stone. All these things were sacred and gave authority to the ceremony.

When the candidates were ready they were announced. They were placed on a robe or blanket, face down, and then a Shaman came forward. An earnest speech was made extolling the bravery of the young man and recounting his noble deeds. After thanking the Shaman, the young man lay down while four men held him rigidly, and a fifth raised the muscles of his back and pierced them with a knife, running wooden skewers through the incisions. The breasts might also be pierced.

When the candidate was in readiness he was led to the sacred pole about which he threw his arms and prayed, while the officers of the rite fastened the thongs in the holes through his flesh. He now placed the bone whistle in his mouth, moved back violently and danced for many exhausting hours until the flesh gave way and he fell. Throughout the horrible ordeal he kept gazing upward at the sun, though his eyes must have been soon blinded.

Maidens who witnessed the scene often wiped the blood from the streaming wounds upon wisps of sweet grass which they afterward burned as prayers that they might gain and hold the love of some noble warrior.

Oddly enough, most scientific men who have seen the sun dance defend it as a religious custom worthy of respect. They speak of its symbolism and describe the important place that it had in tribal life. Its bloody features have shocked the missionaries who conceive of religion as requiring other beliefs in order to secure the favor of the powers above. The Government stopped the sun dance in 1883, but in some form it has survived into recent years.

Perhaps, after all, it is a dim recognition of the world-wide belief that there must be some one who must suffer for the sins of others and through that suffering upon the tree purchase the favor of the Great Spirit.

LX. HOW THE GHOST DANCE WAS DONE

The Ghost Dance of the plains Indians as it was performed between 1888 and 1895 was a new thing. Its principles are old, as old as the hopes of mankind, but the ceremonies of the so-called "ghost dance outbreak" were an invention of the early '90's, having started with a delirious dream of a Paiute Indian named Wovoka.

As the western country was settled by ranchers and cattle men, the roving life of the red men was at an end. The Government believed it best to establish reservations, but the Indians did not like this. They wanted to be free, and Sitting Bull, a famous Sioux leader in speaking to his tribesmen stated, "God made me a free man and not a reservation Indian."

The whites became more numerous and as the buffaloes grew less and less the Indians were forced to take up a different form of life, and being deprived of their hunting ranges, they had to live on rations issued by Government agencies. They became greatly dissatisfied. They longed for a deliverer. They prayed that the old days might be restored. The mind of the plains people was ripened for the idea of a messiah. Then came the dream of the Paiute; like a prairie fire his vision was whispered through the tribes.

The teaching of the vision was that the white man should go, that the buffaloes would come again, that the earth would tremble and the Indians rule supreme again.

A special dance was ordered and even special shirts made, having upon them "magical" painting. They were supposed to protect their wearers from the bullets of the white man. All who were faithful and who followed the teachings of the prophets were told that they should have visions, should fall as dead and visit the heaven world, and then come back to life with great power.

To perform the dance properly many songs and ceremonies were invented. All these had to be rehearsed in a medicine tipi. These rehearsals were in charge of men who acted as masters of ceremony. In the government report, James Mooney gives us a glimpse of the strange things that went on inside the tipi of Black Coyote, who taught the Sioux how to do the ghost dance.

Black Coyote began the meeting by filling the red stone pipe and lighting it. He then offered it to the sun above, taking a whiff and blowing it upward; next he smoked toward the earth, then to the lodge fire. After that he smoked to the east, the south, the west and the north. This done, he offered a prayer for the welfare of the tribe, for help and for the coming of the messiah. Praying was done by standing and extending the hands, palms down. When the prayer was over, the people practiced the songs and had their meaning explained. Oddly, the crow was the sacred bird of the ghost dance, and all ceremonies ended with the "Crow signal" song.

In preparing the dance ground, the leaders sprinkled it with a sacred powder, praying as they scattered the consecrated dust. During this process one of the leaders who was a hypnotist would beat the ground with the palm of his hand.

The sacred number in this dance was seven, and the

FIGURE 41

Indian Buckskin Record of the Ghost Dance

dancers formed in groups of seven or fourteen. There were seven leaders of the ceremony.

All persons connected with the dance were given a sacred crow feather, each of which was specially painted and ornamented. The painting of these feathers was a matter of great concern, and stated days were set aside to make them in accordance with the visions of those who had been in the mystical trance.

As if this were not preparation enough, each dancer had to have his body painted after a pattern that some one had seen in a vision. The designs were in many colors. Blue was daubed on the face, with a red and yellow line at the part of the hair. The symbols for suns, moons, stars, crosses and crows were the most common decorations used.

When the dancers had been prepared by painting, by wearing their ghost shirts and other requirements, they could enter a dance circle. The leaders, who had great powers of hypnotism, caused criers to go about the camp, announcing the start of the dance. When all is ready, the leaders enter the dance ground and form their rings of dancers. All join hands by intertwining their fingers, and face inward.

The first song is sung in a soft tone, the performers remaining standing. This done, they sing in a full tone and move about the circle from east to west. The dance step is slow and is done by slowly dragging one foot after the other, scarcely lifting them from the ground.

The singing attracts the people from their tipis and they come flocking to the circles, forming groups of from fifty to five hundred. All wear blankets and hold them on in some artful way.

The singing goes on as if it were a prayer, "Father, I come," they sing. "Father, I come, Mother, I come, Brother, I come, Father, give us back our arrows!" goes one song. Over and over they repeat it while the leaders wave their wands and cloths. The earth becomes worn and dusty, excitement runs high. The wands and feathers still wave before the fascinated eyes of the dancers. When a dancer seems to be tired or in ecstasy, the medicine man goes to him and waves his feather or handkerchief up and down, or whirls it, chanting "Hu! Hu! Hu!" He fixes his gaze upon the subject, waves his sacred feather. If possible the medicine man tries to turn the subject so the sunlight falls directly in his face. It is an ancient hypnotic process.

Soon the subject falls to the dusty earth, eyes fixed and in a twitching trance. Others stand rigidly with their arms extended before they fall, and still others rush madly into the open and run in circles. Observers have seen "hypnotized" dancers spin on their feet like whirling dervishes. They whirl until they fall in uncomfortable heaps, apparently entirely unconscious.

The Governmental authorities felt that the ghost dance excitement was an evil influence and sought to prevent it. Orders were issued against it but the Sioux resisted. While the warriors were away from Wounded Knee, a Sioux village, the troops came and a battle ensued. There were a few men in the group, one of whom fired at the soldiers. The troops turned their machine guns on the women and children and massacred hundreds of them, even firing into the groups of fleeing women. Their bullet-riddled bodies lay upon the snow for several days, and at length they were buried in great trenches, the bodies being pitched in.

This was the end of the ghost dance, so far as its grip upon the people of the plains went. The bullets of the white man were stronger than all the magic of the medicine men, stronger than the ghost shirts and stronger than prayers for a messiah.

The terrible massacre of women and children by Government troops has never been forgotten by the Sioux, and many Americans to-day in reading the official accounts of the so-called battle of Dec. 29, 1890, feel that this official deed reflects no glory upon American arms.

The U. S. Bureau of Ethnology report reads: "The first volley of the Hotchkiss guns trained on the camp opened fire and sent a storm of shells and bullets among the women and children who gathered in front of the tipis to watch the unusual spectacle of military display. The guns poured in 2-pound explosive shells at the rate of nearly fifty per minute, mowing down everything alive. . . . There can be no question that the pursuit was simply a massacre where fleeing women with infants in their arms were shot down after resistance had ceased. . . ."

The ghost dance was nothing but religious ferver gone wrong, but its chief teaching was simply this: "You must not fight. Do no harm to any one. Do right always." Thus spake Woroka. The lesson of the dance was that the dream of the white man fading out and the red man coming back to power was an impossible dream. Eventually the Indians came to see that it was work and not magic that would bring them new power.

LXI. HOW INDIANS DANCED WITH SNAKES

Dancing with snakes is not a pleasant form of amusement. I never did it but once, and, as the dance was not in a regular ceremony, the snake seemed to know that I was not a medicine man and therefore bit me, whereupon I wrung the neck of the ungrateful creature. The snake was a harmless one, but for an hour or two I was a frightened boy. My fright no doubt caused my hand to puff up, for a blacksnake has no means of injecting venom.

My first interest in the snake dance came from hearing

FIGURE 42

Dress and Ornaments Worn by Snake Dancers

No. 1. Rattle made of a turtle's shell and sheep's toe nails. No. 2. Bandelier worn over the right shoulder. No. 3. Fox skin which is attached to top of Kilt at small of the back. No. 4. Rattlesnake used in the dance. No. 5. Kilt made of buckskin, colored a dull pink, with stripe of black and white zigzag in shape. No. 6. Fringed moccasins, of buckskin. No. 7. Snake dancer, showing head dress. No. 8. Amulets and bracelets. No. 9. Snake "Bosky, Boskay, Bosque." No. 10. Snake Estufa or Keva at Walpi. No. 11. Ba-hoo placed at the Springs. No. 12. Ba-hoo used in Snake Dance.

from a traveler, who had been with a Government survey, that the Hopi Indians of the deserts of the strange South-West had a weird dance in which they used snakes. In recent years much has been written about the Hopi snake dance, and one with steady nerves and a stout stomach will find it a thrilling adventure, though not one calculated to bring happy dreams.

Every two years, two fraternities among the Hopi pueblos of Arizona conduct their ceremonies. At that time the Antelope fraternity and the Snake fraternity hold a joint session, which is a prayer for rain. Among the Sia Indians who live nearby, the snake ceremony is a part of the initiation into the Third Degree of the order, and the candidate is literally "snaked" into the creepy brotherhood.

Somehow or other, the Hopi have an idea that the snakes have some secret power which may be invoked for the purpose of making the clouds gather and the rain to fall. According to a legend, a certain Great Plumed Serpent has control of the waters of the underworld. Its home is supposed to be in the Red Land of the South. This may refer to the land of the Mayas or Aztecs, whose plumed serpent is seen on many stone carvings. Another legend asserts that the Hopi snake clansmen are the direct descendents of snakes.

Among the Pueblo people, the men are organized into many societies and "cults," each of which has its *Kiva* or under-ground lodge room. In these, mysterious rites are performed. All have altars and during the ceremonies the floors are decorated with strange designs, "painted" on with colored sands.

During the middle of August, the members of the Snake fraternity hold meetings and then prepare to catch the snakes. The members paint and decorate themselves, arrange their costumes and take up their rattles, snake whips and wands. It would be interesting to know just what goes on within the circular well that forms the secret chamber beneath the mesa's floor, when for eight days the Snake men prepare their ceremony.

For four days the snake hunt proceeds, the first day being to the north, the next to the east, the next to the south and last day to the west. Every rock crevice, every hole, every chink in a cliff and every refuge in a clump of sage brush is examined. Hands are thrust into such places without fear, and as each soft-skinned serpent is found it is thrust into a snake pouch. Indians do not put salt on the tails of the snakes in order to catch them, but they do sprinkle them with sacred meal. It is then supposed to understand what is wanted, is seized a few inches back of the head and captured.

When sunset tells that the day's work is done, the hunters return to the Kiva, where they empty their pouches into the snake jars. There are two kinds of rattlesnakes, the bull and the whip snake, making four species, two poisonous and two harmless. The results of the four days in the four directions with the four kinds of snakes, furnish the reptiles for the spectacular dance. The jars are secure and filled with strange quarry. The time has come for the spectacular ceremony of snake washing.

Deep down in the Kiva are the Priests of the Snake cult seated upon the stone benches around the wall. Here they wait with their snake wands made by tying two eagle feathers to a short stick. The altar is erected and decorated, the sand floor is painted with symbolic designs, and the washing bowl stands in readiness. The snakes are herded in bags which priests guard, while the snake washer arrayed as a warrior, and attended by two assistants waving feathered wands, steps to a position near the bowl within which is a consecrated water.

A ceremonial song now commences, this being the signal for the washer to begin his part in the rite. Into a bag he thrusts his hand, grasping a squirming handful of snakes, and plunging them into the consecrated water. This done he drops the reptiles upon the sand, some coiling in a threatening way. Immediately they are straightened out by a priest with a snake whip.

When all are washed in the strange liquid and cast upon the sand for drying, they are left in charge of a group of boys, naked and barefoot, who herd them, poke them about, allow them to crawl over their feet, and who even pick them up and play with them. Rattlesnakes as well as the non-poisonous whip snakes are handled with impunity by these boy snake herders. The watching and the sport of handling and tossing the creatures goes on for about two hours. All the snakes must be dry before the ceremony of the dance can begin.

One part of the ceremony is a great race of the members of the society, starting at the spring and ending at the distant mesa where the Kiva forms the goal. The speed and endurance of the runners is amazing, and it will be remembered that Tewanima, one of the great long distance runners of modern times, was a Hopi Indian, and that when he returned to his people, an older man beat him in a desert race. To run well and speedily is a part of a Hopi's training.

While the Antelope fraternity is performing on the plaza, marching about it four times and stamping upon a small board, the rattle of which is a sort of door-knocker to the under-world monsters, the Snake fraternity has been enacting the strange rites of their cult in the depths of their Kiva. The snakes, meanwhile, have been placed in a bower of cottonwood boughs called a Kisi,—the word sounding like the *hiss* of its occupants.

The sun is sinking now and the chant of the Antelope priests blends weirdly with the crisp, raspy chugging of

FIGURE 43

Snake Dance at Mishonganovi

their rattles. A new song is started, commencing in low tones and then increasing in volume. The lines of dancers sway back and forth, and the Snake dancers begin to appear, bursting into a dance as the song reaches a certain point. Forming in groups of three, the Snake men dance in a peculiar way like a half-stopped jump. On they go in a line toward the snake house or Kisi, each carrier dropping to his knees before the Kisi hut.

Once down before this covering of serpents, he thrusts in his arm, grasps a snake, draws it forth, takes it by the middle in his mouth (the snake's head being to the left), and then holds the dangling body in his hands, one above the other. In a moment he is on his feet again and dances four times around the plaza of the pueblo. When the four circuits have been made, the snake is dropped to the ground, but is picked up instantly by a member of the dancing trio, for returning to the Kisi.

Meanwhile the Hopi women have been gathering about the dancers to sprinkle them with sacred corn meal. This they carry in trays of woven basketry. Whatever the women may think of snakes, they get very close to them on such occasions.

The dancers return to the Kisi until all the snakes have been carried according to ceremony and returned to their temporary quarters.

When all the snakes have been carried, the dancers pause until a priest of the cult draws a sacred cloud and six direction picture on the ground, using a trickle of corn meal to form his outlines. At a given signal the "collectors" throw all the snakes on the sacred picture.

Then comes a wild scramble to pick up the snakes and rush them away to the "four quarters of the earth," which means that the dancers rush down the rocky trail and deposit the reptiles at north, east, south and west points below the pueblo. The priests then return and take a violet emetic.

Some authorities say that the snakes never bite a dancer or participant in the rites. This may be due to the method of handling the fearful creatures, though one cannot see that rattlesnakes are handled any more cautiously than the more harmless kind. Apparently the snakes are not stupefied and certainly their fangs are not pulled out or blunted. Other authorities say that bites do occur once in a while and that the Indians have a medicine for it in the form of a plant known to scientists as *Aplopapus spinulosus*. The Indians of the pueblo at Sia, not knowing Latin, call it *hatini.*

Not all Indians danced with snakes, though most of the tribes had ceremonies that had something to do with superstitions about reptiles. Some of the so-called snake dances were merely serpentine marchs in which the dancers imitiated the motions of snakes.

Many of the tribes venerated serpents, particularly the ratttlesnake and it may be that these beliefs are a reflection of the great religion of the red plumed serpent of ancient Mexico. The civilized Mayas of Yucatan and the later Aztecs must have had a great influence over the wilder tribes to the north.

VII: WAR AND STRATEGY

VII

WAR AND STRATEGY

LXII. HOW INDIAN TRAILS WERE MADE

It is said by some who watch the fowls of the air that they seem to have familiar trails over which they go when they flock north or south. Those who know the scaly folk of lake and stream think that even fishes have definite trails through the water which they follow, generation after generation, when they school to their spawning beds.

We cannot see the trails of the creatures of sky and sea, but all who have watched in the open have seen paths made by the fur folk. The muskrat, the woodchuck, the deer and the buffalo all have their roadways.

This is important for mankind to know,—to know that animals made the first paths. We cannot scoff at this, for animal paths were the paths followed by mankind when the early tribes wandered afar from the great homelands.

In America, the buffaloes made deep and indelible trails from one feeding ground to another, and from their feeding places to far-away salt licks. The same is true of the deer and the elk. These great ruminants were the makers of the first trails over the continent. Any farmer boy who has followed cattle over pasture, over hill, down dale and across streams knows that even a cow will pick out the best route possible. It can graze a hill on a contour line, or discover the shallow places in streams where there are good fords. Every pasture with a rugged terrane proves that the beast with the cloven foot is a natural engineer.

There was a time when there were no men. There was

a time when the only men in America were a few on the west coast. There was a time when all eastern America was without a human population. Gradually, from the

(After Maximilian)

FIGURE 44

Assiniboine Warrior with Bow

west, tribes began to wend their way across the mountains, along the waterways, across the plains and into the eastern forests. Nor was it a trackless wilderness that they found, but a wilderness cut in every direction by the trails of the elk and buffalo.

Over paths trodden deep by the big game animals came man. He found the grassy clearings, the refreshing springs, the pools where salt might be found; he found meat and drink and a pleasant abiding place. And, as the red man found his way into a continent, so did the white man roam from the fastness of Asia and into Europe, where the musk ox, the auroch, the reindeer and the antelope had paved the way.

Thus the first roadways of man were those of the animals. The Indians knew that the animal trail went to a point where food might be found, and so he carefully observed every natural trail. When he came to lay out his own paths, many were laid directly over those made by the beasts. Others were blazed through the woods and wound through the trees, avoiding marshes, turning aside for rocks, seeking good stream crossings, finding lookouts where the country might be swept for fires, enemies, game and even fine scenery.

Often trails became "blind" for a distance, in order to deceive the enemy. This meant that the trail would run to a great flat rock or along a stream, or perhaps up a stony hill, in such a manner that it was not easily picked up again when these obstructions were passed. In other instances when the traveler came to a portion of the trail that was to be concealed, he carefully obliterated his tracks, straightened up the grass, replaced twigs, concealed broken sticks and avoided making any litter of leaves or leaving traces of food or clothing.

Sometimes new trails through the woods were secretly marked by sticks placed in a certain way, by stones arranged as pointers or by a twig placed so as to indicate direction. Indian boys were carefully trained to observe small things, for often life itself depended upon them.

I can vividly remember getting lost by following a trail that became blind. It was moonlight and together, Sekosa, my friend, and myself, wended our way through the low underbrush, following a trail over the sandy hills. The moon then went down and we could just see the trail by the light of a few dim stars. We went down a sandy hill, went on for a few hundred feet and then the trail stopped. We could tell exactly where it stopped, not only by the feeling of the ground, but because when the lightning flashed,—a storm was coming up,—we could see the worn trail with sand in it, and then ahead nothing but grass. There was just an abrupt little bank, the width of my hand, and then no trail. It had vanished. We recalled all the old legends of how trails by magic went down into the earth or up into the sky, and we wondered which one we were upon. The storm rumbled and there were terrifying flashes of Heno's ragged darts, and there we stood, not frightened at the storm, but terrified by the fact that the trail ended, when manifestly a trail so well beaten should go on and on.

Luckily we found an abandoned cabin near by and, casting out all fear of ghosts and darkness monsters, we crept in, just in time, too, for the storm broke, sending down great torrents of rain.

The next morning we awoke, stiff and confused by our dilemma. We ran to the trail, now wet and soggy. We observed its "end," and to our surprise and delight found that it had only apparently ended. It was where the sand ended and the firmer clay began. The clay had not powdered away, making a deep trough, as the sand had, but had retained its grass and showed little trace of travel.

LXIII. HOW INDIANS SENT SIGNALS

When the sturdy pioneer trekked his way across the Great Plains in his covered wagon, his restless eye swept the landscape in every direction. Not a movement in the prairie grass escaped him, not a distant whoop or a cloud of smoke. To him these things were signals that bade him be wary. He knew that the Indians could send messages for many miles and in a few minutes.

If he saw puffs of smoke like little clouds ascending in regular order, he knew that hostile Indians had discovered him and were sending signals to their comrades. On clear days these puffs of smoke could be seen at great distances, and by means of relays, the messages could be sent great distances, across the plains, over rivers and over mountains.

Signal fires were made by building a small fire and as soon as it became brisk, smothering it with damp grass and then throwing a blanket over it. By quickly removing the blanket a balloon-shaped cloud of smoke would ascend, driven upward by the hot air. By replacing the blanket and then withdrawing it more smoke could be produced and then released. Two or more persons holding the pelt or blanket were best. By a dot and dash system, much like telegraphy, numerous messages could be sent.

Signal fires were built on mountain ledges overlooking wide valleys or plains, or they were built on points of greatest elevation. This was not only to cause the smoke to rise rapidly, but to afford a vantage point from which the signal could be seen.

Frémont, the explorer, who in 1842 to 1844 explored the Rockies, wrote, "Columns of smoke rose over the country at scattered intervals—by which means the Indians here, as elsewhere, communicate to each other that enemies are in the country."

Frequently several fires were built a few yards apart in order to send up parallel columns of smoke. Such multiple fires were used by the Pima, Papago and other south-west Indians to designate the number of scalps taken.

The Apache used three columns of smoke to signal an alarm, and, if the danger was near, more fires were built. The density of the smoke was produced by using scrub cedar, pine or other desert evergreens. With these were mixed leaves and grass. When these Indians established camp they sent up a signal of two columns of smoke.

Night signals were produced by means of fire. By making a brisk flame and then smothering it for a moment, a series of dots and dashes could be produced. Torches were also waved in accord with a given code.

The American natives had no skyrockets, but they did use fire arrows. These were long arrows, the ends of which were wrapped in loose tow dipped in oil. After the white man came, the arrows were gummed with pitch and smeared with gunpowder. Once lighted, these signals blazed across the sky like meteors, and watching sentinels knew what they meant.

Belden, the White Chief, describes the fire arrow as being prepared by using chewed bark mixed with gunpowder glued to the arrow shaft. He says that when such an arrow is to be shot, one warrior fixes it to his bow, draws it, and then another warrior applies a taper to the inflammable end. The arrow is then shot, and when it has gone upward a short distance the bark fuse ignites the powder, which flashes until the arrow falls.

Among the Santee, he tells us, one arrow means, "The enemy is about." Two arrows from the same point mean "danger"; three, "great danger." Several arrows mean "The enemy is too strong; we are falling back." Two fire arrows shot at the same moment mean "We will attack." After this three fire arrows mean *soon,* four *now.*

Belden writes, "The Indians send their signals very intelligently and seldom make mistakes in telegraphing each other by these silent monitors. The amount of information they can communicate by fires and burning arrows is perfectly wonderful. Every war party carries with it bundles of signal arrows."

Many of the western tribes had blanket signals. To signal *halt,* the end of the blanket is waved downward several times. To say, "How will we treat the enemy or game just discovered?" the blanket is folded and waved to the right and left in front of the body. To say that "there are *many animals or men ahead,*" the blanket is waved before the body upward and downward. The sign for *"discovery"* is made by running or riding in a circle, holding the blanket by two corners and waving it over the head. When a sign of *"peace"* is to be conveyed the blanket is grasped by two corners and waved over the head, thrown upward and allowed to spread itself upon the ground.

When strangers are met and discover each other at a distance, one party signals the question, "Who are you?" by pointing his folded blanket at arm's length toward the person and then waving it right and left in front of the face.

During a battle if a chief takes a blanket, opens it and hangs it in front of his body, then waves it in a circle, it means, "We are surrounded." If the folded blanket is held still high above the head it signifies *"surrender,"* though its meaning is "I want to die right now." In other words, it says to the enemy, "Do what you will, I'm through."

General Dodge, in his "Plains of the Great West," says that he was once standing on a knoll overlooking the valley of the South Platte when he witnessed an Indian military drill below him. There were fully one hundred warriors on horses moving with exact rhythm, though their chief stood at a distance of two hundred yards from them on a knoll opposite the General. Wrote the observer, "For more than half an hour he commanded a drill which for variety and promptness of action could not be equalled by any civilized cavalry in the world. All I could see was an occasional movement of the right arm. He afterward told me that he used a looking glass."

By means of reflecting surfaces afforded by sheets of mica or polished quartz, and even plates of native copper, the prehistoric Indian could send his heliograms to considerable distances and have them relayed to any given point agreed upon.

Marvelous as these methods of signaling may seem, there were medicine men who claimed that they could send their thoughts through the air and make things come to pass afar. Others could send their mind's eyes to distant places and discover what was happening. White explorers have written of these things, but to say just *how* it was done must remain for modern medicine men to tell us.

LXIV. HOW INDIANS TRACKED AND ELUDED THEIR ENEMIES

Early in life Indian boys were taught to observe the tracks of birds and animals and to recognize their calls. They were taught that each bird and animal had a seasonal call or cry, and that it differed in spring and autumn. They were shown the moccasins of different tribes and told how to recognize the footmarks of these moccasins. They were even instructed in the minute differences in clothing, painting, smells, food, customs and habits of the various tribes around them, and how to recognize a tribe by a snatch of conversation.

The older men in taking a company of boys on a hike would make a contest in observing things, and often award a small prize to the most proficient. Then they would sit around a camp fire and tell how they had tracked their foes or had eluded them. Boys soon understood that it was quite necessary to know the "secret language of the trail," a language written in signs and sounds that the ordinary eye and ear know nothing about. When white men and boys were captured and adopted, they were instructed how to know the woods and what was in them. Thus, some have written of their experiences so that we have a way of knowing how true it was that the Indians knew the ways of the forest.

In John Heckewelder's interesting old account of the Pennsylvania Indians he mentions the Indian raid upon the settlers on the Big Mahanoy, whereby fourteen whites were killed.

The survivors were shocked and enraged. They determined that if the Indians had fallen upon them they would kill the first Indian they could find. It so happened that Luke Holland, an affable Indian of the Lenape tribe, was among them, and had long been known as a friendly and inoffensive fellow. Even his name was one that the whites had given him, in respect for his friendliness (though it sounds queer to name an Indian thus). The esteem of the whites was turned to hatred, however, when they beheld their friends and relatives dead, and knew that others had been carried off into captivity. Poor Luke tried to explain that his people were peaceful and that the deed must have been committed by a party of Mingoes. The whites would not listen, but determined to have their revenge. In desperation Luke begged that if a party of men would go with him he would surely find the raiders and prove that they were not of his nation.

The whites at length consented, but threatened his life if he showed the least treachery. Luke led them to a secluded spot on a rocky part of the mountain, tracking the unseen enemy over ground where the whites could see no marks whatever. This excited great suspicion, and they thought that the Indian had led them away from the trail that the enemy might escape.

With great pains Luke showed his party that there were bits of moss that had been loosened, sticks that had been moved, small pebbles that had been rolled aside, moss on the rocks that had been pressed with the human foot and other evidences that a number of men had passed by. He could see all these things as he hurried along, but the white men with him had to stoop over and look at the ground to see what he pointed out. Finally Luke told them that he would soon show them the footprints of the enemy. Shortly they came out on softer ground and there, sure enough, were the prints of moccasined feet. The Indian explained that there were eight men in the enemy's party and that the camp was not far off. The pursuers crossed the valley and climbed a neighboring height from which they plainly saw the enemy making their evening camp. Some were asleep and others were drawing off their leggings. Swinging on the scalp poles were the scalps they had taken.

"See, there is the enemy!" whispered the Lenape. "They are not of my nation, but Mingoes, as I truly told you. They are in our power. Come on, we are nearly two to one. Come on and you will have your revenge!"

The settlers, as Heckewelder says, were overcome with fear and would not take up the fight. They urged Luke to lead them home by the nearest route, which he did, whereupon they told a lively story about discovering the enemy in numbers so great that they did not dare attack.

Not all settlers were afraid, however, and some learned to track as ably as the most subtle redskin. It is the art of tracking that makes a real woodsman and frontiersman. There is nothing mysterious about it, for it is all a matter of *practiced observation.*

When the enemy pursues, safety demands a quick and

skillful retreat. This is sometimes difficult when the enemy is also quick and skillful, but old warriors have told me how they escaped when death seemed upon their very heads.

Of course much of the success in escaping depends upon how many enemies there are that pursue. If they spread out in a long thin line the difficulty is increased. If there is only one man chasing a victim, there is a much better chance of getting away.

Many of the old legends tell of boys who escaped monsters by crawling into hollow logs, feet first, of course, and then piling up rotten wood before their faces. In one tale a youth found a good log and crawled in just as a spider let itself down and spun a web over the opening. The pursuers suspected the log but were deceived by the web. With many tribes the spider is a sacred creature and never killed, but whether the belief springs from such a legend or not is not easy to tell.

In the woods it is sometimes easy to get out of sight quickly by climbing into the branches of a thick-leaved tree, or into a pine or hemlock. By clinging to the trunk and keeping very quiet, this is sometimes a good plan, but if once discovered, it is a shining mark for arrows.

An old Indian named Dondey once told me that he escaped pursuit by crawling into a hollow tree, but found it an uncomfortable place. He also told a story of how a man in such a place was discovered because he looked through a knothole.

There are tales of youths who escaped by quickly diving and then swimming under water to a convenient spot along the bank where they could let their heads up under the "curling bank."

There are stories of maidens and boys without weapons who were chased through the tall grass of the plains, and yet who escaped when the foe seemed directly upon them. The trick was turned by crawling into the carcass of a frozen buffalo that had been eaten out by wolves. It must have been an unsavory refuge, but it was better than torture.

Two old scouts once told me how they had escaped by burrowing under the leaves of the forest mold and by piling branches over themselves. One described how he had disappeared in the desert by having a blanket smeared with pitch and covered with sand. He simply dug a little hollow the size of his body and then lay down in it and covered himself with his blanket. When his pursuer came in sight there was nothing to see but sand everywhere.

In all these tricks, the utmost care must be taken not to leave telltale tracks. Tracks or other signs are sure to be seen right around the hiding place, and caution must be displayed in attracting the enemy from the scent. This is often done by false leads, as by running in the soft soil of a river bank, as if one had jumped in, and then back-tracking to harder ground.

Back-tracking is a real art because a skilled woodsman can tell whether the tracks show walking backward or not. In snow this is especially true. Care must be taken not to drag the foot so as to give away the whole deception.

There were some Indians who were trained as spies and who could disappear right under the noses of their pursuers. Some of these spies carried "false feet" with them, by which they led their pursuers to believe only animals had gone over the trail. The feet of bears, wolves, horses, cows and even deer were used to make tracks in the mud. The Catawba Indians were reputed to be clever at this type of deception and were greatly feared.

The best plan for getting away when hunted down by the enemy is to create a false trail and then run quietly to a refuge, taking care to cover up any marks, broken twigs or trampled grass. Where there is danger of being seen, one must run in such a way that a large rock or tree is kept between the pursuer and the pursued. When the enemy does come into sight, it pays to keep very still. Indians crouched down so as to look like the rocks or clumps of tangled underbrush. It is not easy to see an object that is still, but once it moves the eye immediately is attracted.

Most of the forest Indians were cautious about covering up their trails. It took time but it meant safety. When walking through tall grass they slid their feet through it rather than trampling it by stepping, but if a bunch became bent over they straightened it and moved on. In this manner when they heard the enemy they kept quiet and, as their tracks were covered, it was not easy to trace them.

To escape, therefore, lie low, keep out of the line of vision, make no noise, cover up your tracks, make a false trail to a jumping-off place, back-track to safety, and if possible lead the enemy into a trap where he will become the victim and not you. But it takes a real woodsman, an experienced scout and a clever red man to know exactly what to do in all cases. Escape all depends upon circumstances.

LXV. HOW INDIANS SWAM UNDER WATER

There is an ancient tale that tells of war. It was the war of the Cherokee against the Seneca bands on the Ohio,—a war that raged for centuries, because of an old-time feud, the origin of which was long forgotten.

Up came a great horde of the Cherokee, armed and ready to glut their revenge upon the Seneca villages. Cherokee spies soon discovered a Seneca hunting camp at the bend of the river, and planned battle. One spy, however, climbed a tall tree and saw that the Seneca had at least fifty canoes fastened together on the river bank. The chiefs then held a conference and decided that all escape must be cut off, so that the Seneca hunters should

FIGURE 45

How Indians Swam Under Water

be compelled to fight and that none be permitted to rush ahead and tell the warriors in the neighboring village.

It was therefore planned to cut the canoes loose and let them float down stream. How to send a spy ahead and over a trail that was well guarded was a problem. Then one Cherokee warrior told how he would do it. He would swim under water for a mile or two and land at the "canoe place," where he would cut the moorings and set the canoes adrift. His whoop would call his tribesmen to the fray and an answering whoop of the raiders would attract the attention of the Seneca and bring on the battle. All was prepared. The swimmer made ready for his long under-water journey.

His plan was to set adrift some logs and an uprooted tree, which should float down stream. Then he pushed another tree into the water and prepared to float down under it. This tree was a stub, that is, a trunk which had been "topped" of branches. It was really a log with a few stubby roots. Once in the water the spy fastened himself under the log and then took a hollow reed, placed it in his mouth and let the free end stick up among the roots, where it could not be noticed. Thus prepared, he began his long float under the log and under the water, where the watchful Seneca could not see him.

The journey was not an easy one, but by aid of the tube he breathed freely, and in due time floated past the encampment and came near the landing-place. He now freed himself of the log and swam cautiously to the canoes. Here he cut the cables and pushed the canoes into the river, where the swift current caught them and bore them onward. He then plunged into the river, crossed it and gave a loud whoop. In another moment he heard the answering whoop of his tribesmen. All now seemed well, and he expected to witness a mighty battle in which the Seneca hunters would be exterminated.

He crouched in a tall clump of bushes and awaited the clash. But just as he settled in fancied security he heard the footfall of some one behind him and, turning, he saw a husky Seneca with a tomahawk. He leaped up to give battle, but before he could draw his own blade the Seneca struck him a glancing blow upon the head.

When he regained consciousness he was at another spot on the river, and what he saw caused him much astonishment. Another band of Seneca had caught the canoes down stream and were transporting them overland across the bend of the river, above the Cherokee camp. Then they would float by in a continual stream, going down the river to the bend, transport their canoes as before, launch and sail down again.

"Our plan is to deceive your tribesmen," said his captor. "They came to give us battle, and as we were few in

FIGURE 46

Seneca Strategy

number we told them that it was a poor time to fight because one of our greatest bands of warriors was about to paddle down stream to the fortified town. Your people are watching. You will never see them again."

And so, until sunset, the same fifty canoes paddled down the stream, rounded the horseshoe bend, crossed the narrow neck and sailed down again, completely deceiving the Cherokee raiders. The heavy undergrowth and tall grass at the portage hid all chance of seeing the strategy.

Night came and the tired Seneca, never good canoemen, took their prisoner back to camp. An advance guard simulating great friendliness visited the Cherokee camp and advised it to break and depart while safety could be assured. The Cherokee took the hint and silently stole away, wondering where so many Seneca warriors ever originated.

In the flicker of the evening fire the Seneca chiefs told the prisoner to muster his courage. They did not hint of his fate, but fed him, gave him clothing and a comfortable bed. This he felt was but the lull before the torture.

The next day he was taken to the village, where he ran the gauntlet and, coming out safely, was adopted. It was then that the chiefs asked him how he had passed their camp and cut the canoe moorings. He told his secret and showed the kind of reed to use for breathing under water. It became a Seneca secret.

Years later a Seneca Indian who was a veteran of the Civil War told me this tale and then related how he, himself, had tried the same trick in a river of the South, swimming past the boats of the Confederate army and carrying an important dispatch to Yankee headquarters. Thus did an old-time legend assist a modern army and show that an old trick is still worth the turning.

LXVI. HOW INDIANS RAN THE GAUNTLET

Running the gauntlet was one of the most spectacular things that occurred in an Indian village or camp of warriors. Prisoners and captives were required to run the gauntlet upon entering an Indian settlement, that the villagers might see of what texture the prisoner was made.

The gauntlet was an ordeal, or test of nerve and courage. It was formed by placing two lines of men (and sometimes women) about four paces apart, and facing inward. Each person in line had a switch, a spear, club, tomahawk or knife. At the far end of the gauntlet lines was a striped pole having upon it a bunch of waving feathers or other decoration. Near by was a wigwam where refuge might be taken if the captive successfully ran the gauntlet.

The captive was given courteous treatment as he was brought to the gauntlet line and by motions and even by an actual demonstration he was shown that he must run through the lines and reach the goal post, then make with all possible haste for the wigwam of refuge. His safety was then assured.

Courage and skill in dodging missiles was at once seen by the victim to be primary requirements. He dashed into the opening between the lines (which rule required must not crowd in on him), and dodged the thrusts of spears, dodged the tomahawks, ducked the clubs, endured the lash of whips, avoided tripping over sticks thrust at his legs, knocked aside the knives that were stuck out at him, and did his best to get to the safety goal, even though seriously hurt. Here he clung, sometimes dizzy and fainting, but no hand was laid against him. Each warrior in the gauntlet line was required to keep his place and not chase the victim unless he left the lines and ran outside of them. Sometimes the prisoner did break through the line and run with speed inspired by grim terror, but if he reached the goal he was not struck. His next move was to get to his wigwam and sit down at the fire. Here his wounds, if any, were dressed and both clothing and food given him by the lodge matron.

There are many accounts of gauntlets in the annals of the border, and some prisoners ran from two to eight.

Oddly enough, with so many of the enemy against one man, only a few were seriously hurt. The artful dodger who was swift of foot could escape.

During the Revolutionary War, a boy named Horatio Jones was captured by the Senecas and taken to the Genesee Country, where there were many Seneca towns. Though a mere lad, he was a soldier in the army of the Patriots and his fate as a prisoner of war was a matter of council. It was decided that he should run the gauntlet. He entered the line with a spirit of bravado and escaped the shower of stones, javelins, arrows and clubs, and was just about to reach his goal when Sharp Shins, a young brave, struck at him with a tomahawk. Young Horatio wrenched the weapon from Sharp Shins and brought the blade down upon his assailant's shoulder, wounding him severely. Then he scampered on and reached the safety post with a laugh. An opponent, angry at his quick success, dashed at him, but Jones dipped into a big kettle near by and, lifting out a boiling squash, thrust it under the shirt of the young Indian, who dashed off howling with pain, to the great amusement of all the Indians, who shouted in their way, "Served you right!"

Indian boys were trained to run the gauntlet in order that they might acquire skill. In my own boyhood days on the reservation the boys from the Pine Woods district would pit themselves against the Four Corners' boys and have a gauntlet back in the bushes. They used switches and cornstalk clubs. The only boy who ever got hurt was one who bumped against a tree. Of course, some had smarting shins from the lashing of stout willow whips, but that didn't count.

In gauntlet running the rules are strict and the warriors of the lines kept their places, otherwise the run would have been a grand mêlée in which the opposite sides would injure one another.

LXVII. HOW INDIANS WENT TO WAR

The early Indians were not warlike. The principal implements that any archeologist finds in ancient Indian village sites are those of peaceful pursuits. War came when there were sudden invasions by which one tribe was displaced and thrown upon the other. The coming of the white man and the loss of old homelands caused Indians to look for other places in which to dwell. They had to steal them from other tribes. Wars followed.

"The Fighting Cheyennes" have a reputation of being great fighters, and they were. Yet these people have a tradition, says George Bird Grinnell, who has written their history, that there was a time when war was unknown and peace prevailed. Mr. Grinnell believes that the introduction of the horse roused the fighting spirit and caused one tribe to covet the other's horses. The lust for property and booty grew as there were successful raids. The Cheyennes think that their first battles were with a people whom they call the Hohe, probably some of the northern Algonkian tribes.

In ancient times each tribe had its own boundaries, and as these were ample there was no need for trespassing. Nevertheless there appears to have been a great disturbance among the tribes at a time when the great Maya empire of Mexico broke up. There may have been a northern sweep of southern tribes, and a time of warfare. It was at this time that the Iroquois, another people who have been thought warlike, marched up the Ohio to the position where they were found at the time of European exploration. For some time the effort of the Iroquoian people to make a homeland caused friction and even a long series of wars that were still in process when the French and English first knew them. Nevertheless the Five Nations of the Iroquois organized their famous

League of Peace, protesting against war and declaring that the very name of their government was the Great Peace. To make that peace an assured fact they had to

(After Maximilian)

FIGURE 47

Assiniboine Warrior with Shield and Spear

resist the onslaughts of all surrounding tribes and nations. Thus to gain peace they became the fiercest of warriors.

It is not an easy matter to generalize about Indian

warfare. Each tribe had its own customs, but it may be said that the act of actual warfare was the result of many councils and much ceremony. Let us take a typical Plains tribe, the Omaha, and trace their customs of war.

With the Omaha there was a theory that the Thunder god ruled the battlefield and that he either preserved life or caused it to be lost. He alone might be blamed for death; it was his will.

There were three kinds of warfare: defensive (or *tiadi*), aggressive warfare (or *nuatathishon*), and unauthorized war.

When the tribe had suffered some wrong and found that it could not obtain satisfaction, an able leader went to the Keeper of the Sacred Pack and asked for a feast to the War Bundle. If the priest of the pack consented there was a ceremony and the war captain was told what he must do to be successful in battle. He was also given some of the tribal charms and stuffed birds from the war bundles to secure magical aid. An authorized war party had to declare its intention to the religious leaders of the tribe and have their help.

Omaha war parties often took only eight men or they might include a hundred warriors. All were volunteers and went in order to unburden their hearts of some sorrow, real or fancied. Once a man declared that he would join the party, he lived a careful life and made sure that his family would not be distressed by his absence.

The title of the war captain was Nudonhonga. It was his duty to direct the movements of his troops, to drill them, give them the necessary instructions and to look after the success of the party.

Once the warriors were together the Nudonhonga divided them into four sections, though if the scouts were counted it made five. These sections were, (1) hunters who secured game for the party as it moved forward,

(2) moccasin carriers whose duty it was to secure and carry the necessary footwear and to give the men new moccasins as their old ones wore out, (3) kettle carriers whose duty it was to carry the pots, look after the utensils and to cook the food, (4) provision carriers whose duty it was to carry the food supply, get water and make the fires.

Scouts were men of high rank and the most trustworthy that could be found. It was their privilege to smoke the Sacred War Pipes in testimony of their honor and then to scour the country in advance of their troops in search of the enemy. A scout must ever be truthful in his reports and do his duty at the risk of his life. His honor must never be sullied by cowardice and he must show by every act that his life belonged to his people. Scouts had many ways of concealing themselves, and knew how to climb hills unseen in order to observe the enemy.

The war captain was also a man of tested honor and it was his duty to use the best of judgment in exposing his men to risk. He, too, must be ready to sacrifice his life for the benefit of his party. To seek safety when his warriors were exposed meant a lifetime disgrace.

The military costumes of Omaha warriors were simple. They wore no war bonnets and no shirts. When the battle was ordered they took off their leggings and dressed only in breechcloth and moccasins. They were literally stripped for the fray. Sometimes they wore a wolf skin slit across the back. They thrust their heads through this and let the head of the wolf hang down on their chests. The robe might also be ornamented with feathers.

Just before departure to the field of battle, the war party engaged in a ceremonial dance called the Mikaci, or wolf dance, that they might take on the cunning of wolves and roam with the same freedom. This dance was a dramatic imitation of the movements of the wolf. There was a rapid trot and then an alert stop, as if to observe the approach of danger.

Contrary to common opinion, the Indians had very strict military rules of their own, and their fighting was under as much control as any military body to-day. There were subordinate officers and signals of command. Fighting was an art and not a wild assault of a mob. When noncombatants and women went along, these assisted in throwing up breastworks with their hoes in order to afford a refuge when their troops were hard pressed. Indian fighting, while under direction, was not done in squad or platoon formation. The position of the men was irregular and each sought to carry out the intent of the expedition as best he could.

The duty of a warrior was to kill or capture the enemy. Capture was considered a higher war honor than killing, and to walk up to the enemy, denounce him and slap his face, then turn away in disdain, was considered the highest coup.

The Omaha people marched into battle singing. As the party spread out each warrior shouted his own charm song, invoking the aid of the powers that had appeared to him in his mystery dreams.

The gun and the horse gave the Indians the tools of war. They could strike afar with these. How well they did, the tales of old plainsmen testify. Warfare is a cruel thing but it has been the pursuit of mankind for many centuries. Somehow, even civilized people to-day count the honors of war above the honors of peace.

LXVIII. HOW INDIANS SCALPED THEIR FOES

How the thought of an Indian's scalping knife once caused us to shudder! Indeed, the idea of scalping is closely associated with Indian warfare, and there is scarcely a fanciful picture of the "horrors of bloody massacres" that does not show a grinning savage bearing aloft the bleeding trophy, fresh from some settler's head.

According to the records of our Government, preserved in the Bureau of Ethnology, the custom and practice of scalping was originally confined to the eastern portion of the continent about the St. Lawrence valley and the country south to the tribes of the Muskhoge. It was not a general custom on the Great Plains, the Canadian Northwest, the Pacific region, the Pueblo country or even New England. It was absent for the most part along the Atlantic coast, and the only place in South America where it prevailed was in the Gran Chaco country. The amazing conclusion, therefore, is that the Indians before contact with white men did not scalp, save for the Iroquois and the Muskhogean Choctaws, Chickasaws and Creeks. How then did the practice spread?

"The spread of the scalping practice over a great part of central and western United States," says the Government report, "was the direct result of the encouragement in the shape of scalp bounties offered by the Colonial and more recent governments, even down to within the last fifty years—"

Scalping, it will be seen, was spread by white men and the Indians took up the bloody work in order to hold the support of their white allies. The British as well as the American colonies offered bounties for Indian scalps and paid as high as $50.00 for them. In some instances the dead body of an Indian child brought this amount, its mother brought $130.00 and a warrior $150.00.

Indians had never had the cunning to conceive of a traffic in scalps or bodies, but our own historical records prove how well a civilized people stimulated the gruesome trade.

The scalp proper is a circular patch of skin and hair at the crown of the head. In many cases Indians allowed this lock to grow long and abundant. The rest of the hair was either trimmed off or cut short in order to allow the scalp lock to flow as a conspicuous ornament to the head. In it were put the trophy feathers, the magical charms and other things believed to have mysterious power.

As the custom of scalping was spread over the plains, urged on by bounties and by the thousands of "scalping knives" which were given, sold and traded by the traders and governmental agents, Indians sought to take scalps from their enemies without thought of any bounty. The scalp then took on a new significance. It became an emblem of defiance to the enemy, as if to say, "Come on, my enemy, take me if you can!" A belief grew up that a man's life was somehow mysteriously bound up in his scalp lock. It became the seat of his destiny,—where the scalp was, there was the life. To take a scalp, therefore, put the soul-destiny in the hands of the warrior who took it.

Scalping was usually a painful process, but not always a fatal one. Many victims, both white and red, lived to tell of their experiences. Often an Indian enemy once overcome was scalped and sent back to his tribe as an insult.

In taking the scalp, a circular incision was made about the coveted lock, which was then pulled off from the fleshy layer of the skull. It was sometimes necessary to kneel upon the victim's back and alternately pull and peel the scalp from the head.

Scalps, whatever may have been their value, were not considered the first honors of war, and the man who killed his enemy in battle did not always scalp him, but might leave the task to another. The first honor was the "coup" (coo). This was the first strike when the victim was attacked. As many as five strikes by as many warriors were allowed, the honors being graded accordingly, and a feather with an appropriate symbol awarded.

Scalps when taken were disposed of in different ways. One method was to sacrifice them to the sun, to the water or to the earth. In such cases the scalp was held up to the sun and offered with a song and a prayer, or placed in the water with a similar invocation, or it was put upon the bosom of Mother Earth, and consigned to her keeping. If taken back to the tribe as a trophy, it was cleaned and sometimes painted on the under side, half black and half red.

Scalps designed for dance trophies were taken in the large, that is, nearly the whole scalp was peeled off, stretched on a hoop, cleaned and dried, painted on the under side, decorated with trinkets, and then fastened to a short pole. This pole and hoop were carried by the women in the dance of triumph.

Scalps of this kind were often cut into strips to furnish fringe for the war shirt or horse bridle, or they were thrown aside where they might crumble away and free the spirit believed to be held in them. Some were kept in "medicine" bundles to give the tribe greater power over its enemies.

LXIX. HOW INDIANS CONDUCTED ADOPTIONS

In the neighborhood of Indian reservations one often hears of the "adoption" of white people. Sometimes there is an elaborate ceremony, sometimes Indians are brought to a town or city and "caused" to initiate and adopt the mayor or other prominent citizen. To be adopted by Indians by some is considered a novelty, and by others a real honor. A *genuine* adoption, however, is a great rarity. Frequently the mere bestowal of a name is thought to be an adoption. Real adoptions are the concern of the nation and its clans.

With many tribes there were numerous *clans;* the Seneca, for example, had eight clans, or tribal divisions, each with a totemic sign, as the bear, turtle or wolf. Each clan had a fixed list of names which might be bestowed upon its members. There were as many as three sets of names in each clan, one for children, one for grown persons, and one for civil chiefs. The power of a clan and its influence with the tribal "guardian spirits" depended upon having each name occupied. Each name was a *power* and by a certain combination of *powers* the tribe was made successful.

When warriors with mighty names were killed in battle, therefore, the tribe not only suffered the loss of the man himself, but lost the "power of his name." The Huron and the Iroquois, as well as many other tribes, overcame this difficulty by adopting captives taken in battle, or kidnaped on the trail.

The captive who surrendered and was brought back to the Indian village was welcomed with songs and regaled with feasts. Only a few,—a very few,—were ever tortured and killed. The missionary Heckewelder in writing on this subject says, "But I may be permitted to say that those dreadful executions are by no means so frequent as is commonly imagined. The prisoners are generally adopted by the families of their conquerors in place of lost or deceased relations or friends, where they soon become domesticated, and are so kindly treated that they never wish themselves away again. I have even seen white men who, after such adoption, were given up by the Indians in compliance with the stipulations of treaties, take the first opportunity to escape from their own country and return with all possible speed to their Indian homes; I have seen the Indians, while about delivering them up, put them at night in the stocks to prevent their escaping and running back to them. It is seldom that prisoners are put to death by burning and torturing."

The prisoner, after preliminary ceremonies,—one of which might be the ordeal of the gauntlet, to symbolize a new birth,—was stripped of his clothing, washed in water that had been charged with transformation magic, was slashed to let out (in a ceremonial way) the blood of his birth-nation, taken by the women and given new clothing and then seated where he might be seen by all, as the adoption songs were sung by the clan and the woman that took him.

In some cases the captive was taken on a ceremonial walk or made to dance a number of times about a council fire, to represent the passage of years, and then given a man's name and clothing. He was then taken by the hand and led to the wigwam of the family that had chosen him in place of a slain relative. His was an honored position now, and rendered doubly secure by the fact that he had restored the name that was lost, and stood as a memorial to the one who had gone to the world of souls. Thus, the lot of an adopted member of the tribe was a happy one, unless by odd chance he had been taken in to replace some person whose name and office had been an humble one, but this was rarely.

By the law of the forest, a captive who surrendered to the foe gave himself to it. He virtually said, "Do what thou wilt, and I shall be satisfied." By his very act of surrender he died unto his own tribe, and adoption was a ceremonial rebirth. Thus, a man with a wife and family, who became adopted, might remarry in the new tribe. He was compelled by the belief of the times to give up all allegiance to his own tribe, to forget his wife and children and to pledge his unswerving loyalty to the people who had honored him with life and a new home.

He was expected to live up to the new name that had been given him and to go to war against his own people if necessary.

The rite of adoption was considered a most sacred thing and there are few records of any man or woman who thus became a member of a tribe ever proving a traitor. The fiction of the rebirth was so complete that the adopted person often became the leading member of the tribe and its most stalwart warrior. On the other hand, the family and tribe that gave the adoption looked upon their new recruit with great favor, bestowing gifts, seeking to educate him in their ways, avoiding offense or other rebuffs that would make him wish to return to the tribe of his birth, and placing responsibility upon him that would enlist his loyalty.

The Iroquois adopted many thousands of captives, often taking whole villages, and even tribes, of their foes. By the close of the seventeenth century more than half the members of the Iroquois tribes were captives or the descendants of captives. Thus were the losses in war overcome and the "power of names" kept potent. Many tribes that history says were "exterminated" by the Iroquois were in reality only wiped out as political units through a general adoption of the survivors of a conflict.

In the wonderful description of the Omaha tribe by Frank LaFlesche and Alice Fletcher, is an account of an adoption ceremony among these plains people. The Omaha took captives to replace the loss of a child, or to supply a "son" to a family that was without one.

When an adoption was to take place, the captor sent invitations to the wise men and peacemakers of the Tsi-zhu division and also to the masters of the rites of war of the Ingronga subdivision. A feast was prepared and set before these notables, and then the host in a solemn speech detailed his wish to adopt the captive.

When the *desire* had been made known, the tribal leaders sent for the masters of the rituals, consisting of the Nu-xe people, supposed to have descended from the upper world, and said, "I am Nu-xe, ice," and the Opxon people, called the Elks, and the Ibatse, or Wind People, and the Watsetsi or Water people, and the Honga, or leaders of the tribal hunt.

When all were assembled in the great tipi, the captive was placed in the rear of the lodge opposite the entrance upon the seat of the stranger. The rites of "introducing the child" were then performed, new moccasins given and the captive's feet placed upon a stone, in token of stability and strength. In the ceremony, one of the priests chanted the introduction song. Taking his place at the door, the priest raised his right hand toward heaven, palm upward, and chanted in a clear, ringing voice:

"Ho! Ye Sun, Moon, Stars, all ye that move in the heavens,
I bid you hear me!
Into your midst has come a new life.
Consent, I implore you!
Make its path smooth that it may reach the brow of the first hill."

In a similar strain the priest invoked "Ye Winds, Clouds, Rain, and Mist, that the second hill of life might be reached"; again he sank to "Ye Hills, Valleys, Rivers, Lakes, Trees, and Grasses, that the third hill of life might be reached"; continuing in another stanza to invoke, "Ye Birds, Animals, Insects, that the fourth hill might be reached," and finally, the priest sang:

"Ho! All ye of the Heavens, all ye of the Air, all ye of Earth:
I bid you all to hear me!

Into your midst has come a new life,
Consent ye, consent ye all, I implore!
Make its path smooth—then it shall travel beyond the four hills!"

The four hills are the hills of infancy, youth, manhood and old age, and the appeal to the powers of the earth and the air is a recognition of man's dependence upon other created things.

The story of the tribe and its principal myths were now recited, together with an account of the four stages of man's existence. At the close of this recital the captive was conducted by Chief of the Household peacemakers to the leaders of the War ceremonies on the south side of the council circle. Thus the captive symbolically passed from north to south, from peace to war, from household responsibilities to those of warfare. The meaning was that he was to share all that concerned the tribe.

The war chief then drew forth a sharp flint with which he made a quick slash at the captive's nose, causing blood to flow, that all might see that his original blood had gone from him. The peace chief now took a bandage or bit of moss and wiped away the blood. The Water chief then brought a bowl of water, and the Food chief brought a bowl of corn or meat, which the captive took.

The sacred pipe was then smoked by the captive, filled with cedar incense provided by the Chief of the Wind people. The Nu-xe chief now brought buffalo fat with which the candidate's body was anointed, after which the Opxo chief (the Elks) painted two black stripes across the face, diagonally from the left eyebrow to the lower part of the right cheek. When this was done the Household chief announced the new name, "No-wathe," meaning "made to live," and the captive became the child of the adopting family. This new name was soon dropped and without further ceremony the "father" gave a warrior's name in recognition of his satisfaction.

Indian adoptions were serious things, and a genuine adoption meant that the person "consenting" gave up the nation of his birth and transferred his allegiance to the people who gave him "new life." Henceforth he became a member of the tribe, and abandoned contact with all others.

In modern times, Indians who control the real rituals of adoption do not use them in the entertaining shows that are sometimes put on to deceive people into believing that an adoption has been performed. Certain "show Indians" have derived a good income by faking up "adoptions," which at best can only be called honorary namings.

A wealthy merchant once challenged me to prove that he had not been adopted by a tribe. I asked him if he had foresworn allegiance to the United States and had been placed upon the tribal rolls, and drew the per-capita money that the Government owed the tribe. He replied that he was a full American citizen, was not on a tribal roll, and drew no income from the tribe. All this went to prove that he had not been adopted by the tribe but *named* in a complimentary way by a certain family who wished to honor him in its humble way. To receive a name in these modern times is not necessarily to receive an adoption.

LXX. HOW INDIANS USED EAGLE FEATHERS

The eagle feather was a symbol of power or of attainment. It was used by the men only, and was not worn by the women. Indian women did not put them in their hair or head bands.

Perhaps the most striking article of Indian clothing was the eagle feather head-dress or so-called "war-bonnet." Indeed, many moderns think it the most majestic head gear ever worn by men anywhere. It is the one characteristic article which the Indian wore, but not all tribes used it by any means.

The most prized feathers were tail plumes of the war eagle,—that is, the long, finely-formed feathers with black tips. One perfect tail was worth one pony with some plains tribes. Some groups, however, preferred the feathers of the golden eagle.

Smaller feathers were used as decorations for clothing, and the down was prized as a sacred article in the ceremonies of the Pueblo people. The down of eaglets was especially valued, its light, airy appearance being a symbol of the intermediate between things of the earth and things of the spirit. Hopi prayer sticks are adorned with eagle feathers and crested with down.

As symbols of the honors of war, the eagle feather held first place. Among the Omaha these honor symbols were as follows:

For the first grade of honors the warriors were entitled to wear erectly held, white-tipped feathers from the tail of the golden eagle, a single feather being employed.

The honor of the second grade was a white-tipped tail feather of the golden eagle fastened to the scalp lock in such a manner that it projected horizontally from the side of the head.

The third grade honor symbol was an eagle feather fastened to the scalp lock so as to hang tip downward.

The fourth grade honor sign was an arrow thrust through the scalp lock, or a bow carried in the hand in the ceremonial dance.

The fifth honor was similar to the third, and was a suspended eagle feather.

The sixth honor was simply the privilege of acting as

master of ceremonies at the feast attendant to the meeting of the Company of Warriors, or Hethshka society.

In addition to the honor symbols, the first, second and

FIGURE 48

Head Decoration of a Warrior

third honor men were entitled to wear the deer tail roacl This was made from deer tails fastened together so : to form a roach and dyed red, and having with it tl black neck-bristles of a wild turkey. In this decoratic one partly stripped feather was placed so as to lean forward, another stood upright and the third, just over the base of the scalp lock, leaned backward slightly. (See Fig. 48.) A most interesting account of these trophy feathers is found in LaFlesche's work on the Omaha, published by the United States Bureau of Ethnology.

Eagle feathers were worn by the Dakota and the Hidatsa as trophies of courage and acts of war. Some of these feathers are shown in Figure 49.

An eagle feather to the tip of which is fastened a tuft of eagle down or red horse hair, denotes that the wearer has killed an enemy and was the first to strike him with a "coup stick." This stick or wand was used by warriors on the battlefield to touch the slain enemy, and to do so in the face of flying arrows or bullets was thought to denote courage.

A feather with one red bar, with the Hidatsa, denoted that the wearer had been the second to touch the slain enemy.

A feather with two red bars near the base meant that the wearer had been the third to count the "coup."

A feather with three vermilion bars meant that the wearer had been the fourth to "strike the enemy," as coup counting was called.

Beyond the fourth coup there was no credit given. Other feathers, however, told of the exploits of battle.

An eagle feather dyed red indicated that its wearer had been wounded in an encounter. When a woman had been killed by accident or intention during a battle, the fact was shown by wearing a feather having attached to it a narrow strip of rawhide wrapped from end to end with red and white porcupine quills, in such a manner that it appears banded. Some fine specimens have the quills neatly wound directly about the quill.

Among the Dakotas the sign for having killed an enemy is made by painting a red spot upon the larger web of a feather, about a third of the distance from the tip.

A feather notched just below the black tip, on the larger web, denotes that its wearer has cut the throat of an enemy and scalped him.

A feather with the tip cut completely off and edged with red denotes that an enemy's throat has been cut.

Dakota coup counts are: third to strike, a feather notched at one side at the base of the black tip; fourth to strike, a feather with the tip cut off, and the edges saw-toothed all the way down; fifth to strike, a plume with the tip cut off, two serrations at one side, and all the webbing stripped from both sides of the middle.

A warrior who has suffered many wounds in battle wears a plume split from tip to a point just above the base quill.

A plain plume denotes a war exploit in which an enemy was slain.

LXXI. HOW THE WAR BONNET WAS MADE AN HONOR SIGN

In ancient Indian days, before a man could wear a war bonnet, it was necessary that he should have proved himself a man and warrior. More than this, he was required to have many war-credits and battle honors. Not every Indian could legally wear the regal crown of plumes, and to wear one without the sanction of the company of warriors was regarded as great a breach of military etiquette as for a modern soldier to wear officer's symbols above his rank.

When a warrior desired to possess and wear a war bonnet he secured the consent of the company of fighting men with which he was associated. If this permission were given it meant that the applicant was highly regarded and had sufficient honors of war to be entitled to the necessary feathers. The warrior then gathered the plumes, selecting them with care, secured the skin for the cap and tail-piece and asked some woman friend to make the beaded bands. If the bonnet were to be more ornate, he brought together white weasel skins, a crown decoration and the temple buttons or "moon shells." When all the material was at hand the warrior proclaimed a feast, to which he invited his warrior friends and such women as might assist in the construction, help with the cooking, or who were otherwise entitled and desired to come.

Fellow warriors handled the feathers and "spoke into them" brief accounts of their own exploits, as a means of honoring the plumes. Then the warrior took the feathers one by one and related his own war-credits, looking his fellows in the eyes that all might see that he spoke the truth. Holding up the feather, he would look at it and say, "This plume testifies" that in such-and-such a battle I did such-and-such a thing. Then he handed the warrior who was making the bonnet the feather, which was put in the place selected for it. If a scalp had been taken a fringe of red horse hair was glued to the tip of the feather, and the feather itself must be the record of a first, second or third class honor. These fringed tips were placed in front.

Only a noted warrior might wear the long-tailed bonnet, for in its construction more than fifty feathers were often required. In such a case, as each feather had to be "justified" by a recital, two to four days were sometimes consumed.

The ermine skins were hung at the sides of the bonnet in order that the wearer might have the qualities of the weasel, that is, be quick and skillful in attack, and especially apt in eluding capture by foes. The crown of the cap, inside the feathered circle, was covered with the

FIGURE 49

Exploit Feathers

1. First to strike an enemy.
2. Second to strike an enemy.
3. Third to strike.
4. Fourth to strike.
5. Wounded by an enemy.
6. Killed a woman by accident.
7. Killed an enemy.
8. Cut throat and scalped enemy.
9. Cut enemy's throat.
10. Third to strike an enemy. (Hidatsa Tribe)
11. Fourth to strike.
12. Fifth to strike.
13. Received many wounds.
14. Scalp feather.
15. Bonnet feather.

shorter feathers of the eagle and in the center was fastened a bone tablet upon which was sewed a bone socket into which was inserted a great exploit feather. If such were not authorized, then a magical bird skin (stuffed or otherwise) was placed in a nest of down, and, lacking this, some totemic object was placed there,—an object of which the warrior had dreamed in one of his dream rites.

While the feathered crown was being made there were many songs of war, of magic and of invocation. There were also dances and addresses by older and more experienced warriors, and the "candidate" was urged to wear his symbol with honor and distinction that his countrymen might never suffer through his lack of military ardor.

The women, who made the decorations of porcupine quills or beads, and who cooked the feasts, were rewarded with presents, and likewise the friend who made it.

Once a warrior attained rank, experience and great respect, he acquired the right to make a bonnet of the second class for the son of another warrior, especially if that warrior had risen to great esteem. Thus he would gather the bonnet-makers together and have the bonnet made, honoring each feather by speaking his own deeds into it.

This done, the warrior announced the gift, and with a ceremony to which many were bidden, the emblem was presented. This was the "challenge bonnet," and was not regarded as a genuine war bonnet. It meant that its donor held the youthful warrior as a worthy son who should now emulate his father by deeds of valor.

When the gift was accepted, speeches were made by the older friends and relatives of the youth. The ceremony was solemn and considered a signal honor. Because of its import, however, the women of the family set up a wail when the bonnet was brought into the house, weeping and cutting their hair as an expression of grief, since the youth must now justify the faith placed in him by exposing his life to danger,—and youth was reckless.

With the breakdown of ancient customs the sacred war bonnet, because of its striking appearance, fell from its once high meaning. It was regarded as the prime decoration of an Indian, and it was difficult to think of the lordly red man without thinking of his feathered crown. Because of this, artists and showmen insisted that the Indians they employed wear war bonnets. Nowadays, therefore, every circus Indian, every artist's model and every railroad station advertising Indian is expected to wear his headdress. Thus has the symbol of attainment become a mere decoration, and one now worn by tribes of Indians that originally never used it. The white man's fancy has become the Indian's fashion.

VIII: FACTS ABOUT INDIANS

VIII

FACTS ABOUT INDIANS

LXXII. HOW INDIANS CAME TO AMERICA

For many thousands of years America was without human inhabitants. The animals ruled supreme, never dreaming of the two-legged creatures who were to come. Then, without warning, men and women were seen wandering over the land, making that strange thing called fire and sending darts through the air. These were things that no animal could do. The beast world was destined to have a new ruler.

Mankind at first was not numerous. From some primal homeland in Asia, possibly in the now sunken regions between Siam and Java, small groups of strange-looking men began to push their way northward until they had penetrated the plains of Asia. For reasons which any scientist will explain, men began to increase in numbers. They found places of refuge and secured themselves from attack by the flesh-eating animals. After many thousands of years they discovered how to make knives of flint. After much experience they learned to put a sharp flint on the end of a pole, and thus a spear was invented. By throwing chunks of flint against certain rocks they found out how to make fire. They also discovered how to produce fire by friction, that is, by rubbing or twirling two sticks together. By this time the skins of beasts were used as clothing.

Century after century passed and early man kept up his war with the animals, killing tigers, lions, poisonous serpents and monster bears. Mankind fought his way to supremacy by aid of his simple inventions and discoveries. He was the softest and most defenseless animal by nature, but within his body were wonderful talents. More than this, man was "upright," he stood on his hind feet, and thus his fore-feet became hands which he could use freely for grasping.

Man was curious, he wanted to know things, to make things, to find a way to use power and to project that power at a distance from his body. Mankind was endowed with a marvelous brain, with a keen memory and with speech. With this equipment he increased in numbers, spread out in numerous groups and began to dominate other created things.

In time, the bow was discovered and also the art of making boats. These inventions helped in the securing of food and in traveling great distances. The tribes of men increased. There was trouble between them, due very largely to trespassing upon each other's hunting grounds. Some tribes wandered west, some southwest, some north and some northeast. These tribes were pushed up into the cold regions of northeastern Asia, where they hugged the seacoast and hunted the back country for game.

Possessed of clothing, the knowledge of how to build huts, how to make bows and arrows, how to make seaworthy boats, how to make fire and how to tan pelts, these tribes were able to dwell along the coast and secure a good livelihood. But who were these people, and when did they live along the ice-bound coast of Siberia?

Without doubt, the dwellers of the coastlands of Siberia's eastern projection were members of the proto-Mongoloid stock that afterward populated eastern and central Asia. They were not Chinese and not Japanese. They belonged, however, to the same early stock that thousands of years afterward grew into the Mongolian race. Just as two kinds of apples may grow from seeds from the same tree, so the wanderers of the north grew more and more different from the tribes that lived to the south.

In time some bold hunters, possibly chasing polar bears or flocks of birds over the ice, crossed the frozen seas of Bering Strait. They found the food supply far better on the new coast that was discovered. Returning, they spread the news of their findings. Food in plenty and a world for new adventures was ahead.

It must not be thought that the journey to the north was a rapid one; on the contrary, it occupied many hundreds of generations, and came about through pressure from other tribes, rather than as a deliberate measure. The world had seen many changes in climate and in geographical conditions. The glaciers had come for the last time and had melted away, making possible the occupation of the coasts of Siberia.

The Behring Strait country was still cold, however, and only a very hardy people could live there. The rigorous north made them strong and capable. Such were the men and the women who crossed the cold seas either over the ice or in frail boats.

Before them was a world without other human beings. There were few fierce animals there save the great white bears. The seas along the coast teemed with fishes of many kinds, and in summer the land was pleasant. These first bold sojourners went back to the homeland and told of their discoveries, and in time it was noised about that stirring adventures awaited those who would seek the further east.

Tribes came and they pressed onward down the coast. The further south they went the more salubrious the climate and the more abundant the food supply became.

Thus the Pacific coast, between the sea and Cascade range, became the pathway of innumerable tribes, all flowing southward toward pleasant climate and an abundant food supply.

Many tribes went southward into Mexico, journeyed far into the wilderness of Central America and Panama, eventually reaching South America to its uttermost tip at Terra del Fuego. The great mountain ranges west of the coast were formidable barriers, and it was many centuries before any considerable number of tribes passed over the Rocky Mountains into the Great Plains.

It is quite possible that the great migrations commenced as long ago as twenty thousand years. Lesser migrations may have been even earlier, and the duration of the migration period may have continued for ten thousand years.

Thus the tribes that came over differed greatly from each other, and the newcomers looked unlike the seasoned groups that had lived upon the soil of the new world. A long period of time elapsed and as the tribes began to mingle and establish themselves they began to take on certain common characteristics.

Soil, climate, food, weather, sunshine and rain, and that indefinite thing called "the continental influence" all began to mold the wanderers from Asia into a new race. No longer were they Asiatics, but Americans,—children of the soil.

Time went on and the rage for migration ceased, largely, perhaps, because the tribes of the New World grew in numbers and power sufficiently to resist further invasion. Thus, each great group of natives found a territory where it worked out a plan of living. The languages of each became different and customs grew up to make each group unlike the other.

Thus did the primitive American, like the early European, come out of Asia, out of the Asia that is the motherland of all mankind.

LXXIII. HOW INDIANS MADE THE UNITED STATES

There were many factors entering into the establishment of the United States of America, and with some we are quite familiar. With others we have no acquaintance, but perhaps these obscure factors are of as great importance as any. Let us see.

America is a mighty expanse, stretching from the Atlantic to the Pacific, skirting the northlands as the Great Lakes and the St. Lawrence direct, and pressing southward to the Rio Grande, another natural boundary. Within this continental belt are many naturally bounded sections. New England is one, the Middle Atlantic States another, the Gulf States another. In the old Northwest is another section, as is the present Pacific Northwest. The Desert region of the Southwest constitutes a special area. All these areas are natural domains and suited to special nationalities. They are regions where independent nations might rise and expand with the same facility as they have in Europe.

Indeed, when the European invasion of America started there were hopes of a New France, a New Netherlands, a New England, a New Sweden, a New Granada, and as time went on there might have been a project for a New Prussia, a New Belgium, a New Italy, a New Poland, and a New Russia. Surely there was room for all early immigrants and a special corner for each. But it was willed otherwise.

In the eastern forests were men, nations of men, nations of native Americans who loved their homelands, and were willing to die in defending them against invasion. America already had a population, and one ready to dispute with all comers who were unfair in their demands.

When the European settler, eager for a new farm, a new mill or grazing ground, pressed too far, native Americans appeared and asked that the settler move back into an area set aside by treaty. The settler may have moved or he may not have done so. Soon trouble started. Indians were cheated, they were besotted with rum, they were robbed and many murdered. Their anger was aroused, but they held their tempers until their patience was exhausted. Then they became the terror of the border, killing, burning, fighting in any way possible, to drive back the uninvited settler who threatened to take their homelands.

The settler was in general a good man, though rugged in his mind as in body. He saw no reason why "savages" should bar his way. The savage did not need the land. The settler consulted his preachers and found that the pulpit pronounced the natives "cumberers of the ground," Philistines, Canaanites, and as such doomed to die before the onward march of "God's chosen people."

Now the first Americans had no desire to die and they did not know what Canaanites were. So they fought back with all their awakened ferocity. All settlers, all colonists, whether British, Dutch, French, Swedish, Spanish or German, were held back against the Atlantic seaboard. The Indians prevented any effective penetration of the country. So far they interfered with any hope of establishing in the new world new dominions of the old. The Frenchman, the Dutchman, the Englishman and the German all mingled in a limited strip not far back from the east coast.

There was grumbling, there was anger, there were wars against the bloodthirsty red men who barred the way, and yet did not use the land as a white man would. Why should savages bar the paths to new empires?

The region of the east coast began to fill with energetic people. They developed trade and manufacture. They tilled vast fields and they built up institutions. The very air of the new world was filled with the tonic of liberty. The thrill of liberty stirred the souls of the immigrants from across the sunrise sea. It grew as a seed that was destined to bear a new fruit.

Trouble with the mother country came. England had used the Iroquois as allies in the defeat of the hopes of France; England had taken over the holdings of the Dutch, England was the mistress of the east coast, and within her colonies other nationalities dwelt, now thinking not so much of the old world as of the new, and all thinking not so much of England as of something vague called America.

Trouble became intensified,—the dispute became a war. The Revolution broke out and in the end those matchless heroes who loved liberty most and who served country best, overthrew the hold of the king and his cohorts. America was free. America was filled with the spirit of victorious men.

The continent lay before them, and theirs was the will to own it. On they went for a half century, plunging over the Alleghenies, crossing the plains, colonizing the Gulf shores, buying out Spain, laying hold of Louisiana, crossing the Rockies, and by 1850, lured by gold, taking the Pacific coast from the feeble fingers of Spanish control.

What a pageant of the Will to Conquer was this onward march! Across the land moved German, Englishman, Dutchman, Swede,—on they trekked, founding territories and states, building up great centers of wealth, and establishing governments.

But how did these resolute souls move onward? Did they move westward to found dominions, principalities, sub-kingdoms, republics or old world nationalities? To the everlasting benefit of mankind, no!

When the Revolution was over, these colonists from the thirteen states had born within them a new consciousness of nationality. No longer were they Dutchmen, Englishmen, Swedes,—they were Americans!

On they went, sweeping aside all barriers, plowing through tribes of natives, marching onward with resistless force,—carrying with them one dominant thought, speaking one language, bearing aloft one starry banner, and loyal to one common national ideal.

The resistance of the first Americans to those who would become the new Americans had made a republic possible. Why, then, should we revile those who, more than any other material force, brought coherence out of racial diversity? May it not be that the hand that rules the destiny of mankind willed that the first Americans should hold back the separate racial desires of the throngs from Europe? May it not be that the Indians in their struggle to preserve their own homeland were only holding shut the flood-gates of colonization, which were destined to break in time and sweep the land from ocean to ocean? Consider the subject as you will, and it must be admitted that the first American played a providential part in the destiny of America. He furnished the resistance so necessary to test the quality of a race; he gave Americans a foil worthy of their steel, and held them back until there had dawned the greatest nationalistic idea that the world has ever known. Is America forgetting her debt to those first Americans who molded her destiny?

LXXIV. HOW CIVILIZED ARE THE INDIANS TO-DAY?

It was once thought that Indians could not be civilized and that all efforts in that direction were a waste of time and money. For that reason, and because of the fact that the Indians owned much land and resources, the early settlers thought it right to kill them or drive them further back. As time went on this work grew harder and more costly. Besides, there had been established by the missionary bodies of the churches several mission schools, and it had been shown that some Indians could be educated in the white man's civilization.

At the time of our Civil War the Indians of the West had traded furs and other valuables for guns and had learned how to use them with success. This made it so hard to hunt down and kill Indians that the Government found the cost reached the enormous sum of two million dollars per Indian. It was then that two new ideas were launched. The first was to drive the Indians upon reservations, and the second was to send them to school.

Though the Indians did not wish to take reservations, at length they were placed upon them both by warfare and by peaceful treaties. It was then possible to establish schools. While there has never been a sufficient number, nevertheless, many thousands of children were taught the elements of a white man's education, and were thus able to live with the whites on better terms. Some even went away from the reservations and lived with the whites. Many educated Indian women went with their white husbands to towns and to regions where there were only white people.

Thus the knowledge of the white man's civilization gradually spread throughout the Indian country. There were many things that Indians did not understand about that civilization, as it seemed to say one thing and do another. Indians who did not trouble themselves too much because of this began to succeed.

The great school founded by Richard H. Pratt, an army captain, did much to prove that Indians not only could be educated, but liked to be, and profited by it. They came to Carlisle (Pa.) in their buckskins and feathers, and departed as business men and women. Other schools sprang up, and Indians even sought training in boarding schools among the whites and at the various colleges. They entered into the spirit of our civilization and showed that they were capable of becoming anything that any other American was. Of course, many lagged behind on the reservations and made slow progress.

Indians quickly became ranchers, blacksmiths, surveyors, lumbermen, clergymen, toolmakers, lawyers, newspaper men, doctors, teachers, nurses and even watchmakers.

There is Sherman Coolidge, a full-blood Arapahoe from Wyoming. His family was massacred by the soldiers in a mistaken raid. The boy was taken to the fort, adopted by the Captain and sent to school in New York. He went to military school, to college and then to divinity school. He is now Canon of the Cathedral of Denver. Carlos Montezuma, an Apache, was a prominent Chicago citizen. He was born on the desert and lived the roving life of his tribe. As a boy he, too, was taken away. He was graduated from the University of Illinois and became a great stomach specialist in Chicago. Many Indians have become physicians, being graduated from medical schools and hospitals.

Indians take to law, and in the Dakotas and Oklahoma are numerous Indian lawyers. Indeed, South Dakota and Oklahoma to-day are largely controlled by its Indian voters. In Wisconsin is a well-known band master who became a lawyer. This is Dennison Wheelock, the Oneida, who is a corporation lawyer.

Among the well-known scientists is Dr. Frank LaFlesche of the Smithsonian Institution. He is an Omaha, and his sister, Dr. Susan Picotte, was one of the first Indian women to be graduated from a medical school.

Indians of mixed white and Indian blood, instead of being degenerates, as dime novels say, have risen to high places in society. Charles Curtis, whose mother was a Kaw Indian, is one of the most prominent members of the United States Senate, and Senator Robert L. Owen has about the same ancestry. There have been several tribal Indians, like Charles D. Carter, in Congress.

There are three hundred Indians in New York City. Many of these Indians are ironworkers and bridge builders. Some have worked on the newspapers, some run garages, and one Apache, Vincent Natalish, was a division engineer on the Elevated railroad.

Indian women are found throughout the country as nurses, stenographers, physicians, teachers and milliners. Some, like Angel Decora, a Winnebago, have been artists of note.

The facts show that Indians can not only be civilized but are capable of promoting human welfare. Men like Howard E. Gansworth, the Tuscarora, of Buffalo, N. Y., are business men with a leaning for social service. Mr. Gansworth is a Princeton graduate and is now a successful business manager. His brother was once president of the Printers' Union of Iowa, and delegate to the International Typographic Congress. An Indian girl in Buffalo is a teacher of Americanization classes there, and so the story goes.

The following information is compiled from the latest statistics at the Bureau of Indian Affairs:

The Indian population of the United States, exclusive of Alaska, is 349,876. Of this number 101,506 belong to the Five Civilized Tribes, including freedmen and intermarried whites. All Indians are now citizens of the United States.

Of 54,729 families reported to the Indian Office, 44,-239 live in permanent homes, 26,617 of these houses having wooden floors, and 9,485 live in tipis, tents and temporary structures.

Including the Five Civilized Tribes, 298,341 wear modern apparel.

Among the Indians there are 991 churches, 630 working missionaries and 93,388 church attendants.

Of 1,601 marriages, 348 were by tribal custom and 1,253 by legal procedure.

The property (tribal and individual) belonging to the Indians is valued at $1,693,844,806.

Estimated value of oil and gas and other mineral resources, is $1,033,947,224.

There were 32,234 Indians farming for themselves, a total of 644,873 acres, which yielded products valued at $7,798,778.

There were 44,847 Indians engaged in stock raising upon 29,098,459 acres of grazing land. The value of their stock is $28,777,866.

During 1926 approximately 10,000 Indians received rations at a total cost of $137,000, and farming implements, tools, etc., were gratuitously issued to about 3,000 Indians to the value of $26,300. These do not include Indians who received miscellaneous supplies for which they performed labor in payment.

There were 8,018,216 acres of tribal land leased for grazing and farming purposes.

To June 30, 1926, there had been approved 231,611 allotments covering 37,960,716 acres.

There are 84,553 Indian children of school age, 7,417 of whom are ineligible for attendance by reason of physical or mental defects, ill health, absence from the reservation, or other reasons, leaving 77,136 eligible for school attendance, of whom 69,892 are in school.

There are 37,730 Indian children attending public schools.

THE END

A CATALOG OF SELECTED

DOVER BOOKS

IN ALL FIELDS OF INTEREST

A CATALOG OF SELECTED DOVER BOOKS IN ALL FIELDS OF INTEREST

CONCERNING THE SPIRITUAL IN ART, Wassily Kandinsky. Pioneering work by father of abstract art. Thoughts on color theory, nature of art. Analysis of earlier masters. 12 illustrations. 80pp. of text. 5⅜ × 8½. 23411-8 Pa. $3.95

ANIMALS: 1,419 Copyright-Free Illustrations of Mammals, Birds, Fish, Insects, etc., Jim Harter (ed.). Clear wood engravings present, in extremely lifelike poses, over 1,000 species of animals. One of the most extensive pictorial sourcebooks of its kind. Captions. Index. 284pp. 9 × 12. 23766-4 Pa. $12.95

CELTIC ART: The Methods of Construction, George Bain. Simple geometric techniques for making Celtic interlacements, spirals, Kells-type initials, animals, humans, etc. Over 500 illustrations. 160pp. 9 × 12. (USO) 22923-8 Pa. $9.95

AN ATLAS OF ANATOMY FOR ARTISTS, Fritz Schider. Most thorough reference work on art anatomy in the world. Hundreds of illustrations, including selections from works by Vesalius, Leonardo, Goya, Ingres, Michelangelo, others. 593 illustrations. 192pp. 7⅛ × 10¼. 20241-0 Pa. $9.95

CELTIC HAND STROKE-BY-STROKE (Irish Half-Uncial from "The Book of Kells"): An Arthur Baker Calligraphy Manual, Arthur Baker. Complete guide to creating each letter of the alphabet in distinctive Celtic manner. Covers hand position, strokes, pens, inks, paper, more. Illustrated. 48pp. 8¼ × 11. 24336-2 Pa. $3.95

EASY ORIGAMI, John Montroll. Charming collection of 32 projects (hat, cup, pelican, piano, swan, many more) specially designed for the novice origami hobbyist. Clearly illustrated easy-to-follow instructions insure that even beginning papercrafters will achieve successful results. 48pp. 8¼ × 11. 27298-2 Pa. $2.95

THE COMPLETE BOOK OF BIRDHOUSE CONSTRUCTION FOR WOODWORKERS, Scott D. Campbell. Detailed instructions, illustrations, tables. Also data on bird habitat and instinct patterns. Bibliography. 3 tables. 63 illustrations in 15 figures. 48pp. 5¼ × 8½. 24407-5 Pa. $1.95

BLOOMINGDALE'S ILLUSTRATED 1886 CATALOG: Fashions, Dry Goods and Housewares, Bloomingdale Brothers. Famed merchants' extremely rare catalog depicting about 1,700 products: clothing, housewares, firearms, dry goods, jewelry, more. Invaluable for dating, identifying vintage items. Also, copyright-free graphics for artists, designers. Co-published with Henry Ford Museum & Greenfield Village. 160pp. 8¼ × 11. 25780-0 Pa. $9.95

HISTORIC COSTUME IN PICTURES, Braun & Schneider. Over 1,450 costumed figures in clearly detailed engravings—from dawn of civilization to end of 19th century. Captions. Many folk costumes. 256pp. 8⅜ × 11¾. 23150-X Pa. $11.95

STICKLEY CRAFTSMAN FURNITURE CATALOGS, Gustav Stickley and L. & J. G. Stickley. Beautiful, functional furniture in two authentic catalogs from 1910. 594 illustrations, including 277 photos, show settles, rockers, armchairs, reclining chairs, bookcases, desks, tables. 183pp. 6½ × 9¼. 23838-5 Pa. $9.95

AMERICAN LOCOMOTIVES IN HISTORIC PHOTOGRAPHS: 1858 to 1949, Ron Ziel (ed.). A rare collection of 126 meticulously detailed official photographs, called "builder portraits," of American locomotives that majestically chronicle the rise of steam locomotive power in America. Introduction. Detailed captions. xi + 129pp. 9 × 12. 27393-8 Pa. $12.95

AMERICA'S LIGHTHOUSES: An Illustrated History, Francis Ross Holland, Jr. Delightfully written, profusely illustrated fact-filled survey of over 200 American lighthouses since 1716. History, anecdotes, technological advances, more. 240pp. 8 × 10¾. 25576-X Pa. $11.95

TOWARDS A NEW ARCHITECTURE, Le Corbusier. Pioneering manifesto by founder of "International School." Technical and aesthetic theories, views of industry, economics, relation of form to function, "mass-production split" and much more. Profusely illustrated. 320pp. 6⅛ × 9¼. (USO) 25023-7 Pa. $9.95

HOW THE OTHER HALF LIVES, Jacob Riis. Famous journalistic record, exposing poverty and degradation of New York slums around 1900, by major social reformer. 100 striking and influential photographs. 233pp. 10 × 7⅞. 22012-5 Pa $10.95

FRUIT KEY AND TWIG KEY TO TREES AND SHRUBS, William M. Harlow. One of the handiest and most widely used identification aids. Fruit key covers 120 deciduous and evergreen species; twig key 160 deciduous species. Easily used. Over 300 photographs. 126pp. 5⅜ × 8½. 20511-8 Pa. $3.95

COMMON BIRD SONGS, Dr. Donald J. Borror. Songs of 60 most common U.S. birds: robins, sparrows, cardinals, bluejays, finches, more—arranged in order of increasing complexity. Up to 9 variations of songs of each species. Cassette and manual 99911-4 $8.95

ORCHIDS AS HOUSE PLANTS, Rebecca Tyson Northen. Grow cattleyas and many other kinds of orchids—in a window, in a case, or under artificial light. 63 illustrations. 148pp. 5⅜ × 8½. 23261-1 Pa. $4.95

MONSTER MAZES, Dave Phillips. Masterful mazes at four levels of difficulty. Avoid deadly perils and evil creatures to find magical treasures. Solutions for all 32 exciting illustrated puzzles. 48pp. 8¼ × 11. 26005-4 Pa. $2.95

MOZART'S DON GIOVANNI (DOVER OPERA LIBRETTO SERIES), Wolfgang Amadeus Mozart. Introduced and translated by Ellen H. Bleiler. Standard Italian libretto, with complete English translation. Convenient and thoroughly portable—an ideal companion for reading along with a recording or the performance itself. Introduction. List of characters. Plot summary. 121pp. 5¼ × 8½. 24944-1 Pa. $2.95

TECHNICAL MANUAL AND DICTIONARY OF CLASSICAL BALLET, Gail Grant. Defines, explains, comments on steps, movements, poses and concepts. 15-page pictorial section. Basic book for student, viewer. 127pp. 5⅜ × 8½. 21843-0 Pa. $4.95

BRASS INSTRUMENTS: Their History and Development, Anthony Baines. Authoritative, updated survey of the evolution of trumpets, trombones, bugles, cornets, French horns, tubas and other brass wind instruments. Over 140 illustrations and 48 music examples. Corrected and updated by author. New preface. Bibliography. 320pp. 5⅜ × 8½. 27574-4 Pa. $9.95

HOLLYWOOD GLAMOR PORTRAITS, John Kobal (ed.). 145 photos from 1926–49. Harlow, Gable, Bogart, Bacall; 94 stars in all. Full background on photographers, technical aspects. 160pp. 8⅜ × 11¼. 23352-9 Pa. $11.95

MAX AND MORITZ, Wilhelm Busch. Great humor classic in both German and English. Also 10 other works: "Cat and Mouse," "Plisch and Plumm," etc. 216pp. 5⅜ × 8½. 20181-3 Pa. $5.95

THE RAVEN AND OTHER FAVORITE POEMS, Edgar Allan Poe. Over 40 of the author's most memorable poems: "The Bells," "Ulalume," "Israfel," "To Helen," "The Conqueror Worm," "Eldorado," "Annabel Lee," many more. Alphabetic lists of titles and first lines. 64pp. 5³⁄₁₆ × 8¼. 26685-0 Pa. $1.00

SEVEN SCIENCE FICTION NOVELS, H. G. Wells. The standard collection of the great novels. Complete, unabridged. First Men in the Moon, Island of Dr. Moreau, War of the Worlds, Food of the Gods, Invisible Man, Time Machine, In the Days of the Comet. Total of 1,015pp. 5⅜ × 8½. (USO) 20264-X Clothbd. $29.95

AMULETS AND SUPERSTITIONS, E. A. Wallis Budge. Comprehensive discourse on origin, powers of amulets in many ancient cultures: Arab, Persian, Babylonian, Assyrian, Egyptian, Gnostic, Hebrew, Phoenician, Syriac, etc. Covers cross, swastika, crucifix, seals, rings, stones, etc. 584pp. 5⅜ × 8½. 23573-4 Pa. $12.95

RUSSIAN STORIES/PYCCKNE PACCKA3bl: A Dual-Language Book, edited by Gleb Struve. Twelve tales by such masters as Chekhov, Tolstoy, Dostoevsky, Pushkin, others. Excellent word-for-word English translations on facing pages, plus teaching and study aids, Russian/English vocabulary, biographical/critical introductions, more. 416pp. 5⅜ × 8½. 26244-8 Pa. $8.95

PHILADELPHIA THEN AND NOW: 60 Sites Photographed in the Past and Present, Kenneth Finkel and Susan Oyama. Rare photographs of City Hall, Logan Square, Independence Hall, Betsy Ross House, other landmarks juxtaposed with contemporary views. Captures changing face of historic city. Introduction. Captions. 128pp. 8¼ × 11. 25790-8 Pa. $9.95

AIA ARCHITECTURAL GUIDE TO NASSAU AND SUFFOLK COUNTIES, LONG ISLAND, The American Institute of Architects, Long Island Chapter, and the Society for the Preservation of Long Island Antiquities. Comprehensive, well-researched and generously illustrated volume brings to life over three centuries of Long Island's great architectural heritage. More than 240 photographs with authoritative, extensively detailed captions. 176pp. 8¼ × 11. 26946-9 Pa. $14.95

NORTH AMERICAN INDIAN LIFE: Customs and Traditions of 23 Tribes, Elsie Clews Parsons (ed.). 27 fictionalized essays by noted anthropologists examine religion, customs, government, additional facets of life among the Winnebago, Crow, Zuni, Eskimo, other tribes. 480pp. 6⅛ × 9¼. 27377-6 Pa. $10.95

FRANK LLOYD WRIGHT'S HOLLYHOCK HOUSE, Donald Hoffmann. Lavishly illustrated, carefully documented study of one of Wright's most controversial residential designs. Over 120 photographs, floor plans, elevations, etc. Detailed perceptive text by noted Wright scholar. Index. 128pp. 9¼ × 10¾. 27133-1 Pa. $11.95

THE MALE AND FEMALE FIGURE IN MOTION: 60 Classic Photographic Sequences, Eadweard Muybridge. 60 true-action photographs of men and women walking, running, climbing, bending, turning, etc., reproduced from rare 19th-century masterpiece. vi + 121pp. 9 × 12. 24745-7 Pa. $10.95

1001 QUESTIONS ANSWERED ABOUT THE SEASHORE, N. J. Berrill and Jacquelyn Berrill. Queries answered about dolphins, sea snails, sponges, starfish, fishes, shore birds, many others. Covers appearance, breeding, growth, feeding, much more. 305pp. 5¼ × 8¼. 23366-9 Pa. $7.95

GUIDE TO OWL WATCHING IN NORTH AMERICA, Donald S. Heintzelman. Superb guide offers complete data and descriptions of 19 species: barn owl, screech owl, snowy owl, many more. Expert coverage of owl-watching equipment, conservation, migrations and invasions, etc. Guide to observing sites. 84 illustrations. xiii + 193pp. 5⅜ × 8½. 27344-X Pa. $8.95

MEDICINAL AND OTHER USES OF NORTH AMERICAN PLANTS: A Historical Survey with Special Reference to the Eastern Indian Tribes, Charlotte Erichsen-Brown. Chronological historical citations document 500 years of usage of plants, trees, shrubs native to eastern Canada, northeastern U.S. Also complete identifying information. 343 illustrations. 544pp. 6½ × 9¼. 25951-X Pa. $12.95

STORYBOOK MAZES, Dave Phillips. 23 stories and mazes on two-page spreads: Wizard of Oz, Treasure Island, Robin Hood, etc. Solutions. 64pp. 8¼ × 11. 23628-5 Pa. $2.95

NEGRO FOLK MUSIC, U.S.A., Harold Courlander. Noted folklorist's scholarly yet readable analysis of rich and varied musical tradition. Includes authentic versions of over 40 folk songs. Valuable bibliography and discography. xi + 324pp. 5⅜ × 8½. 27350-4 Pa. $7.95

MOVIE-STAR PORTRAITS OF THE FORTIES, John Kobal (ed.). 163 glamor, studio photos of 106 stars of the 1940s: Rita Hayworth, Ava Gardner, Marlon Brando, Clark Gable, many more. 176pp. 8⅜ × 11¼. 23546-7 Pa. $11.95

BENCHLEY LOST AND FOUND, Robert Benchley. Finest humor from early 30s, about pet peeves, child psychologists, post office and others. Mostly unavailable elsewhere. 73 illustrations by Peter Arno and others. 183pp. 5⅜ × 8½. 22410-4 Pa. $5.95

YEKL and THE IMPORTED BRIDEGROOM AND OTHER STORIES OF YIDDISH NEW YORK, Abraham Cahan. Film Hester Street based on Yekl (1896). Novel, other stories among first about Jewish immigrants on N.Y.'s East Side. 240pp. 5⅜ × 8½. 22427-9 Pa. $6.95

SELECTED POEMS, Walt Whitman. Generous sampling from *Leaves of Grass*. Twenty-four poems include "I Hear America Singing," "Song of the Open Road," "I Sing the Body Electric," "When Lilacs Last in the Dooryard Bloom'd," "O Captain! My Captain!"—all reprinted from an authoritative edition. Lists of titles and first lines. 128pp. 5³⁄₁₆ × 8¼. 26878-0 Pa. $1.00

MY BONDAGE AND MY FREEDOM, Frederick Douglass. Born a slave, Douglass became outspoken force in antislavery movement. The best of Douglass' autobiographies. Graphic description of slave life. 464pp. 5⅜ × 8½. 22457-0 Pa. $8.95

FOLLOWING THE EQUATOR: A Journey Around the World, Mark Twain. Fascinating humorous account of 1897 voyage to Hawaii, Australia, India, New Zealand, etc. Ironic, bemused reports on peoples, customs, climate, flora and fauna, politics, much more. 197 illustrations. 720pp. 5⅜ × 8½. 26113-1 Pa. $15.95

THE PEOPLE CALLED SHAKERS, Edward D. Andrews. Definitive study of Shakers: origins, beliefs, practices, dances, social organization, furniture and crafts, etc. 33 illustrations. 351pp. 5⅜ × 8½. 21081-2 Pa. $8.95

THE MYTHS OF GREECE AND ROME, H. A. Guerber. A classic of mythology, generously illustrated, long prized for its simple, graphic, accurate retelling of the principal myths of Greece and Rome, and for its commentary on their origins and significance. With 64 illustrations by Michelangelo, Raphael, Titian, Rubens, Canova, Bernini and others. 480pp. 5⅜ × 8½. 27584-1 Pa. $9.95

PSYCHOLOGY OF MUSIC, Carl E. Seashore. Classic work discusses music as a medium from psychological viewpoint. Clear treatment of physical acoustics, auditory apparatus, sound perception, development of musical skills, nature of musical feeling, host of other topics. 88 figures. 408pp. 5⅜ × 8½. 21851-1 Pa. $9.95

THE PHILOSOPHY OF HISTORY, Georg W. Hegel. Great classic of Western thought develops concept that history is not chance but rational process, the evolution of freedom. 457pp. 5⅜ × 8½. 20112-0 Pa. $9.95

THE BOOK OF TEA, Kakuzo Okakura. Minor classic of the Orient: entertaining, charming explanation, interpretation of traditional Japanese culture in terms of tea ceremony. 94pp. 5⅜ × 8½. 20070-1 Pa. $3.95

LIFE IN ANCIENT EGYPT, Adolf Erman. Fullest, most thorough, detailed older account with much not in more recent books, domestic life, religion, magic, medicine, commerce, much more. Many illustrations reproduce tomb paintings, carvings, hieroglyphs, etc. 597pp. 5⅜ × 8½. 22632-8 Pa. $10.95

SUNDIALS, Their Theory and Construction, Albert Waugh. Far and away the best, most thorough coverage of ideas, mathematics concerned, types, construction, adjusting anywhere. Simple, nontechnical treatment allows even children to build several of these dials. Over 100 illustrations. 230pp. 5⅜ × 8½. 22947-5 Pa. $7.95

DYNAMICS OF FLUIDS IN POROUS MEDIA, Jacob Bear. For advanced students of ground water hydrology, soil mechanics and physics, drainage and irrigation engineering, and more. 335 illustrations. Exercises, with answers. 784pp. 6⅛ × 9¼. 65675-6 Pa. $19.95

SONGS OF EXPERIENCE: Facsimile Reproduction with 26 Plates in Full Color, William Blake. 26 full-color plates from a rare 1826 edition. Includes "The Tyger," "London," "Holy Thursday," and other poems. Printed text of poems. 48pp. 5¼ × 7. 24636-1 Pa. $4.95

OLD-TIME VIGNETTES IN FULL COLOR, Carol Belanger Grafton (ed.). Over 390 charming, often sentimental illustrations, selected from archives of Victorian graphics—pretty women posing, children playing, food, flowers, kittens and puppies, smiling cherubs, birds and butterflies, much more. All copyright-free. 48pp. 9¼ × 12¼. 27269-9 Pa. $5.95

PERSPECTIVE FOR ARTISTS, Rex Vicat Cole. Depth, perspective of sky and sea, shadows, much more, not usually covered. 391 diagrams, 81 reproductions of drawings and paintings. 279pp. 5⅜ × 8½. 22487-2 Pa. $6.95

DRAWING THE LIVING FIGURE, Joseph Sheppard. Innovative approach to artistic anatomy focuses on specifics of surface anatomy, rather than muscles and bones. Over 170 drawings of live models in front, back and side views, and in widely varying poses. Accompanying diagrams. 177 illustrations. Introduction. Index. 144pp. 8⅜ × 11¼. 26723-7 Pa. $8.95

GOTHIC AND OLD ENGLISH ALPHABETS: 100 Complete Fonts, Dan X. Solo. Add power, elegance to posters, signs, other graphics with 100 stunning copyright-free alphabets: Blackstone, Dolbey, Germania, 97 more—including many lower-case, numerals, punctuation marks. 104pp. 8⅛ × 11. 24695-7 Pa. $8.95

HOW TO DO BEADWORK, Mary White. Fundamental book on craft from simple projects to five-bead chains and woven works. 106 illustrations. 142pp. 5⅜ × 8. 20697-1 Pa. $4.95

THE BOOK OF WOOD CARVING, Charles Marshall Sayers. Finest book for beginners discusses fundamentals and offers 34 designs. "Absolutely first rate . . . well thought out and well executed."—E. J. Tangerman. 118pp. 7¾ × 10⅝. 23654-4 Pa. $5.95

ILLUSTRATED CATALOG OF CIVIL WAR MILITARY GOODS: Union Army Weapons, Insignia, Uniform Accessories, and Other Equipment, Schuyler, Hartley, and Graham. Rare, profusely illustrated 1846 catalog includes Union Army uniform and dress regulations, arms and ammunition, coats, insignia, flags, swords, rifles, etc. 226 illustrations. 160pp. 9 × 12. 24939-5 Pa. $10.95

WOMEN'S FASHIONS OF THE EARLY 1900s: An Unabridged Republication of "New York Fashions, 1909," National Cloak & Suit Co. Rare catalog of mail-order fashions documents women's and children's clothing styles shortly after the turn of the century. Captions offer full descriptions, prices. Invaluable resource for fashion, costume historians. Approximately 725 illustrations. 128pp. 8⅜ × 11¼. 27276-1 Pa. $11.95

THE 1912 AND 1915 GUSTAV STICKLEY FURNITURE CATALOGS, Gustav Stickley. With over 200 detailed illustrations and descriptions, these two catalogs are essential reading and reference materials and identification guides for Stickley furniture. Captions cite materials, dimensions and prices. 112pp. 6½ × 9¼. 26676-1 Pa. $9.95

EARLY AMERICAN LOCOMOTIVES, John H. White, Jr. Finest locomotive engravings from early 19th century: historical (1804–74), main-line (after 1870), special, foreign, etc. 147 plates. 142pp. 11⅜ × 8¼. 22772-3 Pa. $10.95

THE TALL SHIPS OF TODAY IN PHOTOGRAPHS, Frank O. Braynard. Lavishly illustrated tribute to nearly 100 majestic contemporary sailing vessels: Amerigo Vespucci, Clearwater, Constitution, Eagle, Mayflower, Sea Cloud, Victory, many more. Authoritative captions provide statistics, background on each ship. 190 black-and-white photographs and illustrations. Introduction. 128pp. 8⅞ × 11¾. 27163-3 Pa. $13.95

EARLY NINETEENTH-CENTURY CRAFTS AND TRADES, Peter Stockham (ed.). Extremely rare 1807 volume describes to youngsters the crafts and trades of the day: brickmaker, weaver, dressmaker, bookbinder, ropemaker, saddler, many more. Quaint prose, charming illustrations for each craft. 20 black-and-white line illustrations. 192pp. 4⅜ × 6. 27293-1 Pa. $4.95

VICTORIAN FASHIONS AND COSTUMES FROM HARPER'S BAZAR, 1867–1898, Stella Blum (ed.). Day costumes, evening wear, sports clothes, shoes, hats, other accessories in over 1,000 detailed engravings. 320pp. 9⅜ × 12¼. 22990-4 Pa. $13.95

GUSTAV STICKLEY, THE CRAFTSMAN, Mary Ann Smith. Superb study surveys broad scope of Stickley's achievement, especially in architecture. Design philosophy, rise and fall of the Craftsman empire, descriptions and floor plans for many Craftsman houses, more. 86 black-and-white halftones. 31 line illustrations. Introduction. 208pp. 6½ × 9¼. 27210-9 Pa. $9.95

THE LONG ISLAND RAIL ROAD IN EARLY PHOTOGRAPHS, Ron Ziel. Over 220 rare photos, informative text document origin (1844) and development of rail service on Long Island. Vintage views of early trains, locomotives, stations, passengers, crews, much more. Captions. 8⅞ × 11¾. 26301-0 Pa. $13.95

THE BOOK OF OLD SHIPS: From Egyptian Galleys to Clipper Ships, Henry B. Culver. Superb, authoritative history of sailing vessels, with 80 magnificent line illustrations. Galley, bark, caravel, longship, whaler, many more. Detailed, informative text on each vessel by noted naval historian. Introduction. 256pp. 5⅜ × 8½. 27332-6 Pa. $6.95

TEN BOOKS ON ARCHITECTURE, Vitruvius. The most important book ever written on architecture. Early Roman aesthetics, technology, classical orders, site selection, all other aspects. Morgan translation. 331pp. 5⅜ × 8½. 20645-9 Pa. $8.95

THE HUMAN FIGURE IN MOTION, Eadweard Muybridge. More than 4,500 stopped-action photos, in action series, showing undraped men, women, children jumping, lying down, throwing, sitting, wrestling, carrying, etc. 390pp. 7⅞ × 10⅝. 20204-6 Clothbd. $24.95

TREES OF THE EASTERN AND CENTRAL UNITED STATES AND CANADA, William M. Harlow. Best one-volume guide to 140 trees. Full descriptions, woodlore, range, etc. Over 600 illustrations. Handy size. 288pp. 4½ × 6⅜. 20395-6 Pa. $5.95

SONGS OF WESTERN BIRDS, Dr. Donald J. Borror. Complete song and call repertoire of 60 western species, including flycatchers, juncoes, cactus wrens, many more—includes fully illustrated booklet. Cassette and manual 99913-0 $8.95

GROWING AND USING HERBS AND SPICES, Milo Miloradovich. Versatile handbook provides all the information needed for cultivation and use of all the herbs and spices available in North America. 4 illustrations. Index. Glossary. 236pp. 5⅜ × 8½. 25058-X Pa. $6.95

BIG BOOK OF MAZES AND LABYRINTHS, Walter Shepherd. 50 mazes and labyrinths in all—classical, solid, ripple, and more—in one great volume. Perfect inexpensive puzzler for clever youngsters. Full solutions. 112pp. 8⅛ × 11. 22951-3 Pa. $4.95

PIANO TUNING, J. Cree Fischer. Clearest, best book for beginner, amateur. Simple repairs, raising dropped notes, tuning by easy method of flattened fifths. No previous skills needed. 4 illustrations. 201pp. 5⅜ × 8½. 23267-0 Pa. $5.95

A SOURCE BOOK IN THEATRICAL HISTORY, A. M. Nagler. Contemporary observers on acting, directing, make-up, costuming, stage props, machinery, scene design, from Ancient Greece to Chekhov. 611pp. 5⅜ × 8½. 20515-0 Pa. $11.95

THE COMPLETE NONSENSE OF EDWARD LEAR, Edward Lear. All nonsense limericks, zany alphabets, Owl and Pussycat, songs, nonsense botany, etc., illustrated by Lear. Total of 320pp. 5⅜ × 8½. (USO) 20167-8 Pa. $6.95

VICTORIAN PARLOUR POETRY: An Annotated Anthology, Michael R. Turner. 117 gems by Longfellow, Tennyson, Browning, many lesser-known poets. "The Village Blacksmith," "Curfew Must Not Ring Tonight," "Only a Baby Small," dozens more, often difficult to find elsewhere. Index of poets, titles, first lines. xxiii + 325pp. 5⅜ × 8¼. 27044-0 Pa. $8.95

DUBLINERS, James Joyce. Fifteen stories offer vivid, tightly focused observations of the lives of Dublin's poorer classes. At least one, "The Dead," is considered a masterpiece. Reprinted complete and unabridged from standard edition. 160pp. 5³⁄₁₆ × 8¼. 26870-5 Pa. $1.00

THE HAUNTED MONASTERY and THE CHINESE MAZE MURDERS, Robert van Gulik. Two full novels by van Gulik, set in 7th-century China, continue adventures of Judge Dee and his companions. An evil Taoist monastery, seemingly supernatural events; overgrown topiary maze hides strange crimes. 27 illustrations. 328pp. 5⅜ × 8½. 23502-5 Pa. $7.95

THE BOOK OF THE SACRED MAGIC OF ABRAMELIN THE MAGE, translated by S. MacGregor Mathers. Medieval manuscript of ceremonial magic. Basic document in Aleister Crowley, Golden Dawn groups. 268pp. 5⅜ × 8½. 23211-5 Pa. $8.95

NEW RUSSIAN-ENGLISH AND ENGLISH-RUSSIAN DICTIONARY, M. A. O'Brien. This is a remarkably handy Russian dictionary, containing a surprising amount of information, including over 70,000 entries. 366pp. 4½ × 6⅛. 20208-9 Pa. $9.95

HISTORIC HOMES OF THE AMERICAN PRESIDENTS, Second, Revised Edition, Irvin Haas. A traveler's guide to American Presidential homes, most open to the public, depicting and describing homes occupied by every American President from George Washington to George Bush. With visiting hours, admission charges, travel routes. 175 photographs. Index. 160pp. 8¼ × 11. 26751-2 Pa. $10.95

NEW YORK IN THE FORTIES, Andreas Feininger. 162 brilliant photographs by the well-known photographer, formerly with *Life* magazine. Commuters, shoppers, Times Square at night, much else from city at its peak. Captions by John von Hartz. 181pp. 9¼ × 10¾. 23585-8 Pa. $12.95

INDIAN SIGN LANGUAGE, William Tomkins. Over 525 signs developed by Sioux and other tribes. Written instructions and diagrams. Also 290 pictographs. 111pp. 6⅛ × 9¼. 22029-X Pa. $3.50

ANATOMY: A Complete Guide for Artists, Joseph Sheppard. A master of figure drawing shows artists how to render human anatomy convincingly. Over 460 illustrations. 224pp. 8⅜ × 11¼. 27279-6 Pa. $10.95

MEDIEVAL CALLIGRAPHY: Its History and Technique, Marc Drogin. Spirited history, comprehensive instruction manual covers 13 styles (ca. 4th century thru 15th). Excellent photographs; directions for duplicating medieval techniques with modern tools. 224pp. 8⅜ × 11¼. 26142-5 Pa. $11.95

DRIED FLOWERS: How to Prepare Them, Sarah Whitlock and Martha Rankin. Complete instructions on how to use silica gel, meal and borax, perlite aggregate, sand and borax, glycerine and water to create attractive permanent flower arrangements. 12 illustrations. 32pp. 5⅜ × 8½. 21802-3 Pa. $1.00

EASY-TO-MAKE BIRD FEEDERS FOR WOODWORKERS, Scott D. Campbell. Detailed, simple-to-use guide for designing, constructing, caring for and using feeders. Text, illustrations for 12 classic and contemporary designs. 96pp. 5⅜ × 8½. 25847-5 Pa. $2.95

OLD-TIME CRAFTS AND TRADES, Peter Stockham. An 1807 book created to teach children about crafts and trades open to them as future careers. It describes in detailed, nontechnical terms 24 different occupations, among them coachmaker, gardener, hairdresser, lacemaker, shoemaker, wheelwright, copper-plate printer, milliner, trunkmaker, merchant and brewer. Finely detailed engravings illustrate each occupation. 192pp. 4⅝ × 6. 27398-9 Pa. $4.95

THE HISTORY OF UNDERCLOTHES, C. Willett Cunnington and Phyllis Cunnington. Fascinating, well-documented survey covering six centuries of English undergarments, enhanced with over 100 illustrations: 12th-century laced-up bodice, footed long drawers (1795), 19th-century bustles, 19th-century corsets for men, Victorian "bust improvers," much more. 272pp. 5⅜ × 8¼. 27124-2 Pa. $9.95

ARTS AND CRAFTS FURNITURE: The Complete Brooks Catalog of 1912, Brooks Manufacturing Co. Photos and detailed descriptions of more than 150 now very collectible furniture designs from the Arts and Crafts movement depict davenports, settees, buffets, desks, tables, chairs, bedsteads, dressers and more, all built of solid, quarter-sawed oak. Invaluable for students and enthusiasts of antiques, Americana and the decorative arts. 80pp. 6½ × 9¼. 27471-3 Pa. $7.95

HOW WE INVENTED THE AIRPLANE: An Illustrated History, Orville Wright. Fascinating firsthand account covers early experiments, construction of planes and motors, first flights, much more. Introduction and commentary by Fred C. Kelly. 76 photographs. 96pp. 8¼ × 11. 25662-6 Pa. $8.95

THE ARTS OF THE SAILOR: Knotting, Splicing and Ropework, Hervey Garrett Smith. Indispensable shipboard reference covers tools, basic knots and useful hitches; handsewing and canvas work, more. Over 100 illustrations. Delightful reading for sea lovers. 256pp. 5⅜ × 8½. 26440-8 Pa. $7.95

FRANK LLOYD WRIGHT'S FALLINGWATER: The House and Its History, Second, Revised Edition, Donald Hoffmann. A total revision—both in text and illustrations—of the standard document on Fallingwater, the boldest, most personal architectural statement of Wright's mature years, updated with valuable new material from the recently opened Frank Lloyd Wright Archives. "Fascinating"—*The New York Times*. 116 illustrations. 128pp. 9¼ × 10¾. 27430-6 Pa. $10.95

PHOTOGRAPHIC SKETCHBOOK OF THE CIVIL WAR, Alexander Gardner. 100 photos taken on field during the Civil War. Famous shots of Manassas, Harper's Ferry, Lincoln, Richmond, slave pens, etc. 244pp. 10⅝ × 8¼.
22731-6 Pa. $9.95

FIVE ACRES AND INDEPENDENCE, Maurice G. Kains. Great back-to-the-land classic explains basics of self-sufficient farming. The one book to get. 95 illustrations. 397pp. 5⅜ × 8½. 20974-1 Pa. $7.95

SONGS OF EASTERN BIRDS, Dr. Donald J. Borror. Songs and calls of 60 species most common to eastern U.S.: warblers, woodpeckers, flycatchers, thrushes, larks, many more in high-quality recording. Cassette and manual 99912-2 $8.95

A MODERN HERBAL, Margaret Grieve. Much the fullest, most exact, most useful compilation of herbal material. Gigantic alphabetical encyclopedia, from aconite to zedoary, gives botanical information, medical properties, folklore, economic uses, much else. Indispensable to serious reader. 161 illustrations. 888pp. 6½ × 9¼. 2-vol. set. (USO) Vol. I: 22798-7 Pa. $9.95
Vol. II: 22799-5 Pa. $9.95

HIDDEN TREASURE MAZE BOOK, Dave Phillips. Solve 34 challenging mazes accompanied by heroic tales of adventure. Evil dragons, people-eating plants, bloodthirsty giants, many more dangerous adversaries lurk at every twist and turn. 34 mazes, stories, solutions. 48pp. 8¼ × 11. 24566-7 Pa. $2.95

LETTERS OF W. A. MOZART, Wolfgang A. Mozart. Remarkable letters show bawdy wit, humor, imagination, musical insights, contemporary musical world; includes some letters from Leopold Mozart. 276pp. 5⅜ × 8½. 22859-2 Pa. $7.95

BASIC PRINCIPLES OF CLASSICAL BALLET, Agrippina Vaganova. Great Russian theoretician, teacher explains methods for teaching classical ballet. 118 illustrations. 175pp. 5⅜ × 8½. 22036-2 Pa. $4.95

THE JUMPING FROG, Mark Twain. Revenge edition. The original story of The Celebrated Jumping Frog of Calaveras County, a hapless French translation, and Twain's hilarious "retranslation" from the French. 12 illustrations. 66pp. 5⅜ × 8½.
22686-7 Pa. $3.95

BEST REMEMBERED POEMS, Martin Gardner (ed.). The 126 poems in this superb collection of 19th- and 20th-century British and American verse range from Shelley's "To a Skylark" to the impassioned "Renascence" of Edna St. Vincent Millay and to Edward Lear's whimsical "The Owl and the Pussycat." 224pp. 5⅜ × 8½.
27165-X Pa. $4.95

COMPLETE SONNETS, William Shakespeare. Over 150 exquisite poems deal with love, friendship, the tyranny of time, beauty's evanescence, death and other themes in language of remarkable power, precision and beauty. Glossary of archaic terms. 80pp. 5³⁄₁₆ × 8¼. 26686-9 Pa. $1.00

BODIES IN A BOOKSHOP, R. T. Campbell. Challenging mystery of blackmail and murder with ingenious plot and superbly drawn characters. In the best tradition of British suspense fiction. 192pp. 5⅜ × 8½. 24720-1 Pa. $5.95

THE WIT AND HUMOR OF OSCAR WILDE, Alvin Redman (ed.). More than 1,000 ripostes, paradoxes, wisecracks: Work is the curse of the drinking classes; I can resist everything except temptation; etc. 258pp. 5⅜ × 8½. 20602-5 Pa. $5.95

SHAKESPEARE LEXICON AND QUOTATION DICTIONARY, Alexander Schmidt. Full definitions, locations, shades of meaning in every word in plays and poems. More than 50,000 exact quotations. 1,485pp. 6½ × 9¼. 2-vol. set.
Vol. I: 22726-X Pa. $16.95
Vol. 2: 22727-8 Pa. $15.95

SELECTED POEMS, Emily Dickinson. Over 100 best-known, best-loved poems by one of America's foremost poets, reprinted from authoritative early editions. No comparable edition at this price. Index of first lines. 64pp. 5³⁄₁₆ × 8¼.
26466-1 Pa. $1.00

CELEBRATED CASES OF JUDGE DEE (DEE GOONG AN), translated by Robert van Gulik. Authentic 18th-century Chinese detective novel; Dee and associates solve three interlocked cases. Led to van Gulik's own stories with same characters. Extensive introduction. 9 illustrations. 237pp. 5⅜ × 8½.
23337-5 Pa. $6.95

THE MALLEUS MALEFICARUM OF KRAMER AND SPRENGER, translated by Montague Summers. Full text of most important witchhunter's "bible," used by both Catholics and Protestants. 278pp. 6⅝ × 10. 22802-9 Pa. $11.95

SPANISH STORIES/CUENTOS ESPAÑOLES: A Dual-Language Book, Angel Flores (ed.). Unique format offers 13 great stories in Spanish by Cervantes, Borges, others. Faithful English translations on facing pages. 352pp. 5⅜ × 8½.
25399-6 Pa. $8.95

THE CHICAGO WORLD'S FAIR OF 1893: A Photographic Record, Stanley Appelbaum (ed.). 128 rare photos show 200 buildings, Beaux-Arts architecture, Midway, original Ferris Wheel, Edison's kinetoscope, more. Architectural emphasis; full text. 116pp. 8¼ × 11. 23990-X Pa. $9.95

OLD QUEENS, N.Y., IN EARLY PHOTOGRAPHS, Vincent F. Seyfried and William Asadorian. Over 160 rare photographs of Maspeth, Jamaica, Jackson Heights, and other areas. Vintage views of DeWitt Clinton mansion, 1939 World's Fair and more. Captions. 192pp. 8⅞ × 11. 26358-4 Pa. $12.95

CAPTURED BY THE INDIANS: 15 Firsthand Accounts, 1750–1870, Frederick Drimmer. Astounding true historical accounts of grisly torture, bloody conflicts, relentless pursuits, miraculous escapes and more, by people who lived to tell the tale. 384pp. 5⅜ × 8½. 24901-8 Pa. $8.95

THE WORLD'S GREAT SPEECHES, Lewis Copeland and Lawrence W. Lamm (eds.). Vast collection of 278 speeches of Greeks to 1970. Powerful and effective models; unique look at history. 842pp. 5⅜ × 8½. 20468-5 Pa. $14.95

THE BOOK OF THE SWORD, Sir Richard F. Burton. Great Victorian scholar/adventurer's eloquent, erudite history of the "queen of weapons"—from prehistory to early Roman Empire. Evolution and development of early swords, variations (sabre, broadsword, cutlass, scimitar, etc.), much more. 336pp. 6⅛ × 9¼. 25434-8 Pa. $8.95